ALL
THINGS
NEW

Books by
Lynn Austin

All She Ever Wanted
All Things New
Eve's Daughters
Hidden Places
Pilgrimage
A Proper Pursuit
Though Waters Roar
Until We Reach Home
While We're Far Apart
Wings of Refuge
A Woman's Place
Wonderland Creek

REFINER'S FIRE

Candle in the Darkness
Fire by Night
A Light to My Path

CHRONICLES OF THE KINGS

Gods & Kings
Song of Redemption
The Strength of His Hand
Faith of My Fathers
Among the Gods

THE RESTORATION CHRONICLES

Return to Me
Keepers of the Covenant

ALL THINGS NEW

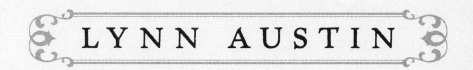

LYNN AUSTIN

BETHANYHOUSE
a division of Baker Publishing Group
Minneapolis, Minnesota

© 2012 by Lynn Austin

Published by Bethany House Publishers
11400 Hampshire Avenue South
Bloomington, Minnesota 55438
www.bethanyhouse.com

Bethany House Publishers is a division of
Baker Publishing Group, Grand Rapids, Michigan

Printed in the United States of America

Library of Congress Cataloging-in-Publication Data
Austin, Lynn N.
    All things new / Lynn Austin.
        p.   cm.
    ISBN 978-0-7642-1055-6 (hardcover : alk. paper) —
    ISBN 978-0-7642-0897-3 (pbk)
    1. Plantations—Virginia—Fiction. 2. Reconstruction (U.S. history, 1865-1877)—Fiction. 3. Mothers and daughters—Fiction. 4. Freedmen—Virginia—Fiction. I. Title.
    PS3551.U839A795 2015
    813'.54—dc23   2012028883

Scripture quotations are from the King James Version of the Bible.

This is a work of historical reconstruction; the appearances of certain historical figures are therefore inevitable. All other characters, however, are products of the author's imagination, and any resemblance to actual persons, living or dead, is coincidental.

Cover design by Kirk DouPonce, DogEared Design

14   15   16   17   18   19   20   11   10   9   8   7   6   5

To my husband, Ken
and to my children:
Joshua, Vanessa, Benjamin, Maya, and Snir

And God shall wipe away all tears from their eyes;
And there shall be no more death, neither sorrow,
   nor crying,
·Neither shall there be any more pain: for the former
   things are passed away.
And He that sat upon the throne said,
"Behold, I make all things new."

Revelation 21:4–5

1

APRIL 3, 1865

Josephine Weatherly thought she'd already lived through the darkest hour of this endless war, but she had been wrong. Now all hope was truly gone. She huddled with her sister by the upstairs window in her aunt's home, watching smoke churn into the sky above Richmond, Virginia, like thunderheads. How could the city where she and her family had taken refuge descend into such terror and anarchy? President Davis and the Confederate government were fleeing. Hungry mobs were looting downtown. The enemy invasion everyone had long feared was about to begin.

"Shouldn't we leave, too?" her sister, Mary, asked. "Everyone else is." All day they'd watched streams of refugees fleeing Richmond, along with the Confederate government officials, their wagons and carts and wheelbarrows piled high with household goods.

"Where would we go?" Josephine said with a shrug. Hunger made her listless. She couldn't tear her gaze from the view of the city, barely visible beyond the distant treetops.

"I-I don't know," Mary stammered, "but . . . I mean . . . shouldn't we follow all the others? The Yankees are coming! Someone must know a safe place where we can hide."

No place is safe, Josephine wanted to say, but she held her tongue when she saw the fear in her sister's eyes. Sixteen-year-old Mary had gnawed her fingernails and the flesh around them until her fingertips were raw. "Stop doing that," Josephine said, pulling Mary's hand away from her mouth.

"I'm sorry . . . I can't help it! I'm so scared!" Mary laid her head on Jo's shoulder and wept.

"I know, I know. But we'll be all right. We're safe here." Josephine was lying, and God hated liars, but what difference did it make?

For all of her twenty-two years, Jo had tried to be good and to do what the Bible said, but God hadn't paid her any notice. Nor had He answered a single one of her prayers during these unending years of war. She had asked Him to protect her two brothers as they'd marched off to battle, but Samuel had been killed, and no one had heard from Daniel in weeks. She had begged God to watch over Daddy after the Home Guard drafted him for duty, but he'd died of pneumonia last winter. Josephine had pleaded with the Almighty to watch over her and Mary and their mother, three women left all alone on their sprawling plantation, outnumbered by slaves. In reply, He'd sent a flood of Yankees into the countryside, forcing her family to flee here to Richmond for safety. She didn't know if she would ever see White Oak Plantation again.

In the months since they'd lived here with Aunt Olivia, crowded in with other refugee relatives, Josephine had fervently prayed for their daily bread and deliverance from evil, but famine and fear had moved into this house on Church Hill along with them. Dawn never arrived; the long nightmare refused to end. And so Josephine had decided in church yesterday morning that prayer was a waste of time. The Almighty would do whatever He wanted, heedless of her pleas. She wouldn't ask for protection from the fire or the spreading chaos or the Yankee invasion. A person who had the chair yanked out from beneath her countless times no longer tried to sit down.

"Aren't you afraid, Jo?" Mary asked.

"No." She felt wrung of all emotion, including fear. One way or another, by death or deliverance, the uncertainty and sorrow would finally end. Jo no longer cared about the outcome. She simply wished it would come soon.

She heard footsteps and turned to see her mother, Eugenia, standing in the bedroom doorway. Mary saw her, too, and ran into her arms. "Is there any more news?" Mary asked. Josephine dreaded her mother's answer.

"The colonel was kind enough to stop by before leaving to tell us what's going on. He said not to worry, that the smoke is from bonfires outside the capitol building. The government is packing their most important documents and burning the rest. They'll probably burn the tobacco and cotton that's stored in the city warehouses, too, rather than let the Yankees profit from them."

Jo studied her mother's beautiful face, usually so calm and serene, and knew by the crease between her dark brows that there was more bad news. "What else did the colonel say? Are the mobs still looting all the businesses?"

Mother hesitated, then said, "Yes. He warned us to stay away from the commercial district, and so . . . I don't want to alarm you, girls, but I think we'd better pack, just in case."

"Are we leaving with everyone else?" Mary asked.

"Not yet," Mother said, stroking Mary's dark hair. Josephine remembered the soothing gesture from when she was a child, sitting on her mother's lap, secure in the comfort of her arms. But she was too old to run to Mother now, and her grief was beyond soothing. Besides, Mother had a wellspring of grief all her own. "We'll wait here a little longer," Mother said, "but I think we should be ready to leave if we have to."

"Are we taking everything?" Jo asked. She surveyed the trunks and crates of belongings stacked in their tiny bedroom. War had stripped their lives bare the way wind and frost strips leaves from a tree, until their once-flourishing life had been whittled down to a single room.

"We'll pack only what we truly need, this time," Mother said. "And only what we can carry. We'll leave the rest to God's will."

Jo wondered if these last few possessions would survive or if

God would take them, too. She and Mother had clung to these reminders of their old life ever since the day a Confederate captain and his handful of men had ridden to their plantation, fifteen miles from Richmond, to warn of the advancing enemy.

"It isn't safe to stay here any longer, ma'am," he'd told them. He'd removed his hat out of respect, but he hadn't dismounted. The horse snorted impatiently, fogging the chilly air with its breath.

To Jo, another loss had seemed unimaginable, coming a mere month after Daddy's death. "But we can't leave our home!" Jo had blurted out. "It's all we have!"

Mother had stood proud and strong as she'd absorbed the news. Her inner strength seemed to be made from the same glue that held the universe together and kept the stars in place. She reached for Jo's hand and squeezed it. "What will happen if we decide to stay here?" Mother had asked the captain.

"The enemy could be here within a day, ma'am, so I strongly advise you to leave. The Yankees are savages with no code of decency or chivalry." He glanced around at the family's slaves who had stopped work to listen and added, "Besides, there's no telling what your Negroes will do once the Yankees get them all stirred up, promising freedom and all."

Jo's breath seemed to freeze in her lungs as she waited in the icy air to hear what Mother would do. The captain's horse fidgeted and pulled at the reins as if eager to gallop. "We'll have soldiers patrolling the roads into Richmond for as long as possible, ma'am. They'll watch over you all the way. But we can't guarantee your safety once we pull back."

"Thank you, Captain." Mother smiled, still the poised and lovely matron of White Oak Plantation. "Good day and good luck to you and your men." She then went inside and closed the door. For the rest of the morning she had calmly issued orders as Ida May and Lizzie and the other house slaves had packed up the household, loading bedding and clothing, a few pieces of furniture, and trunkfuls of valuables into the carriage. Otis harnessed their only horse to the overburdened carriage and drove them to Aunt

Olivia's house in Richmond, leaving the remaining slaves alone on the plantation.

The city had been swollen with refugees and pulsing with fear. It bore little resemblance to the Richmond Josephine had visited before the war, but it had provided safety and shelter for the past few months. But no longer.

She turned away from the window and looked around the jumbled room. What should she pack? The things that once seemed so important to her—her brush and mirror set with the ivory handles, her diary, her grandmother's opal necklace—hardly mattered anymore. These were treasures for another time and place, unnecessary weights in a struggle for survival. She had brought several dresses with her to Richmond, but the only one she needed now was the green muslin one with their gold coins sewed into its seams. She unbuttoned her bodice and changed into that dress. Her mother and sister were changing, as well.

Josephine packed some essential toiletries in a canvas bag, then decided to add the photograph of her father, Philip Weatherly. It seemed like the very last token of the life she'd once known, and she feared losing the memory of his handsome face just as she'd lost everything else. When she finished, Josephine carried her bag downstairs and sat down in the parlor with the rest of her family to wait. Aunt Olivia and her three daughters had also packed their bags, but Great-Aunt Hattie refused to pack a single thing. "I came into this world with nothing," she insisted, "and I expect that I'll leave it the same way."

The sun had set, shrouded behind the smoke-filled sky by the time they were all ready. The parlor grew dark and cold. Aunt Olivia made sure everyone had a quilt to huddle beneath. Fuel had become very scarce, and they needed to conserve every stick of firewood for cooking. They had long since run out of lamp oil, but Aunt Hattie produced a tallow candle she had been saving "for such a time as this," and opened her Bible to read aloud to all of them: "'God is our refuge and strength, a very present help in trouble. Therefore will not we fear . . .'"

Josephine stopped listening. The others may find the Scriptures soothing—and Aunt Hattie certainly had enough faith to move a mountain all by herself—but Jo didn't. She considered the Bible nothing but fairy tales. She closed her eyes, wishing that God would end their lives quickly, if that's what He had determined to do. As the evening dragged on and on, she began to doze.

A loud banging on the front door awakened her. Aunt Olivia went to answer the door herself, having sent all of her slaves to their own quarters behind the house for the night. Without a word, Josephine rose and followed her aunt. Their next-door neighbor stood on the front step, nervously twirling his hat in his hand.

"Won't you come in?" Aunt Olivia asked, as if she was having a dinner party and he'd arrived a few minutes late. He shook his head.

"I saw the candle through your window and wanted to make sure everyone was all right. I see you decided to stay?"

"Yes. My sister Eugenia and I decided that we were better off here at home than out on the road somewhere in the middle of the night. Besides, we have no place to go. This is my home. I'll stay here and defend it the best I can and take my chances with the Yankees, if they come."

"Oh, they're surely coming," he said. "But they're not our biggest problem. I just walked down to the center of Richmond and . . ." He glanced at Josephine with a worried look before continuing in a softer voice, as if hoping she wouldn't hear him. "You need to stay inside with your doors locked. There's no law and order in Richmond tonight, and the looting is out of control. These aren't the Yankees, mind you, but our own citizens."

"Do you think the violence will spread up here to Church Hill?"

"No one knows what might happen, Mrs. Greeley. And that's not all . . ." He glanced at Josephine again, and she knew he didn't want to say more in front of her.

"Go ahead," Josephine said. "You won't frighten me." But when he spoke, his voice was softer still.

"The guards at the state penitentiary have abandoned their posts. All the prisoners are on the loose."

"Oh, Lord, help us," Aunt Olivia breathed.

"I'm going to let all of our slaves sleep inside our house tonight. Strength in numbers, you see."

"Thank you for telling me. I believe I'll do the same." Aunt Olivia closed and locked the door again, then went out to the slave yard to order them inside. Jo heard the slaves stirring in the basement kitchen below her a few minutes later.

"You're not letting the slaves come into the parlor with us, are you?" Aunt Hattie asked when Olivia returned with the news.

"Certainly not. I told them to stay down in the kitchen and to make sure they bolted the back door."

Mother reached into the satchel she had packed and retrieved a small leather-covered box Josephine had seen in her father's desk drawer. Aunt Olivia looked horrified when Mother opened the box and pulled out a pistol.

"Eugenia! Is that thing loaded?"

"Yes, it is," Mother replied, calmly inspecting it.

"Do you know how to use it?"

"Of course. And I will, if I have to. I suggest you get the pistol your husband left you, as well."

"But I . . . I really don't think I could . . ."

"You don't need to shoot it, Olivia. Merely pointing it at someone acts as a deterrent."

Olivia went into her husband's study and fetched the pistol and ammunition. "Here, Eugenia. You'll have to load it for me." Mother's hands were steady as she loaded it. The two women sat with the pistols in their laps as Aunt Hattie resumed her Scripture reading in the flickering candlelight.

"'Let not your heart be troubled, neither let it be afraid . . .'"

"We're going to lose the war, aren't we?" Josephine said as Hattie paused between verses. Everyone stared at her in the darkness. "General Lee's army is leaving, and the Yankees are going to conquer Richmond. The war is over, and we've lost."

"We've had setbacks before," Mother replied. "But our cause is just. Virginia joined the Union voluntarily, and we have every right to leave it. Right is on our side."

"But can't we be right and still lose?" Josephine asked. No one replied. "Do you think God is punishing us?"

"No! What for?" Mother said. "All we asked for was to live in peace the way we always have. The enemy is trying to conquer us and force us to change, but I've been to Philadelphia and I've seen the way they live up north—and believe me, it is very much inferior to our way of life."

"How are they different?" Josephine asked. "I know they don't own slaves but—"

"All they think about is money. They may criticize us for the way we treat our slaves, but they treat immigrants much worse. At least we provide food and shelter for our workers. No one up north cares if those poor foreigners starve to death in the streets. The North has none of the graciousness of our way of life and they worship the almighty dollar. The most important things to us are our families and our land and our traditions."

"But if we lose the war—" Josephine began.

"Win or lose," Aunt Hattie interrupted, "we must learn to pray as Jesus did in His darkest hour: 'Nevertheless not as I will, but as thou wilt.'"

"If the war does end, at least the killing will end," Aunt Olivia murmured. "We've lost so many loved ones already." Her pistol lay limp in her lap; Mother gripped the handle of hers in her fist.

"If General Lee is forced to surrender," Mother said, "it will only be because they outnumbered us, not because they outfought us."

"I just wish we knew what was going to happen next," Aunt Olivia said, "and when all this will end."

"I wish we didn't have to be afraid all the time," Mary added. She was chewing her fingernails again. Josephine reached to take her sister's hand and hold it in hers. A moment later, Aunt Hattie snuffed out the candle, plunging the room into darkness. One of Josephine's cousins began to cry.

"Think of how dark it must have seemed to Jesus's disciples after Calvary," Hattie said. "Their Messiah was dead. All hope was gone. But then resurrection came on Easter Sunday, not just for

Christ but for all of us. The Almighty has kept us safe throughout this day, and we can trust Him for tomorrow."

What if tomorrow is even worse? Josephine wanted to ask, but she kept her thoughts to herself. Aunt Hattie began singing hymns, but Jo didn't join in. This seemed like the longest night of her life as she sat waiting for the dawn. Exhausted, Josephine finally leaned against her sister and began to doze.

An enormous explosion jolted her awake. The blast shook the entire house and rattled the windowpanes. Mary leaped from the sofa and into Mother's arms, Josephine's cousins sobbed and wailed, and slaves screamed in the kitchen below.

"The Yankees are shelling us!" Aunt Olivia said. "Their gunboats must have made it up the James River."

Another explosion followed, louder than the first. Josephine ran to the window and parted the curtains. The sun hadn't risen yet, but the entire sky glowed with an eerie, unnatural light.

More blasts followed, one after the other like a hundred cannons firing, until the whole earth seemed to reverberate. Josephine raced upstairs to peer out the window that had the best view of the city and saw molten flames leaping into the sky beneath clouds of thick, dark smoke. This wasn't a bonfire like yesterday. The city was burning. She stumbled downstairs again to tell the others. "It-it looks like the whole city is on fire." Everyone stared at her, mute with shock.

Aunt Hattie spoke first. "It says in Scripture that at the end of the age 'the heavens shall pass away with a great noise, and all the elements shall melt with fervent heat.'"

Stop it! Jo wanted to scream. *Just stop it! You said that tomorrow would be better, but it isn't!* Her sister and cousins couldn't stop crying, and it seemed to Jo that the end of the world had truly come. There was nothing to do but wait for it. Aunt Hattie tried to gather everyone together to pray, but Jo wanted no part in it. "I'll go watch in case the fire spreads this way," she said. She climbed the stairs again, alone.

Josephine had no idea how much time passed, but eventually

the sun rose and the sky began to grow lighter. She could glimpse a small stretch of Franklin Street between the houses and trees and saw a moving wall of dark blue marching down the hill toward the center of town, toward the flames. Wagon wheels and marching feet rumbled like distant thunder. The enemy had arrived.

If God was good, and if He loved Josephine and her family, how could this have happened? She had prayed! They all had. She covered her face and wept, not for her lost nation but for her lost faith.

Another hour or more passed, and the view grew dim behind a haze of smoke. Josephine dried her tears and went downstairs to rejoin the others just as their neighbor arrived at the door again. This time Aunt Olivia led him inside so everyone could hear his news.

"The Yankees are here," he said quietly. "Richmond has surrendered. The explosions we heard before dawn were our own gunboats, the *Virginia*, the *Beaufort*, and the *Richmond*. We blew them to smithereens in the harbor so the Yankees wouldn't get them."

"It looks like the city is on fire," Josephine said.

"Yes, the commercial district is ablaze, and our fire and police forces are nowhere to be seen. But the Yankees are working hard to quench the flames. Church Hill should be safe."

"How could this happen?" Aunt Olivia asked. No one replied.

"Well, at least the worst is over," Aunt Hattie said. She was the only one who hadn't been weeping. "From now on, we'll face whatever we must with faith in God."

Jo didn't want to hear it. She returned to her bedroom, her faith in God as shattered as the Confederate gunboats. Why pray when God wasn't listening? Besides, her only prayer would be that the Confederate Army would surrender and the war would end—and her family would call her a traitor if she said that out loud. But why keep fighting? Why prolong this nightmare?

Josephine opened her diary, then closed it again. It recorded her past, but there was nothing left of her old life. Everything she'd learned during the past twenty-two years would have to be revised. Not simply cleaned up and pruned the way the slaves back home trimmed the bushes and cut the weeds, but dug up and yanked out by the roots so that something altogether new could be planted in its place.

Jo still believed in God; only a fool could deny the existence of a Creator. But she no longer believed in prayer or in a God who cared about her suffering. It was time to bury her childish faith in a God who was her loving Father, watching over her, doing what was best for her.

As far as she was concerned, He was as distant and unreachable as her own beloved father.

2

Eugenia Weatherly couldn't bear to watch her daughters go hungry another day. A week had passed since the war ended and the South had surrendered, and Eugenia's household was starving. She was the strongest one. She had to find food. She wrapped a shawl around her shoulders against the morning chill and strode toward the door to the slave yard, determined to find her manservant and enlist his help. But just as she reached the door, her sister Olivia called to her, "Eugenia, wait!"

Eugenia paused with her hand on the knob, impatient to be on her way. Her mind was made up and she wouldn't let her sister talk her out of it. "What now, Olivia? Your neighbor said to get there early, before the line gets too long."

Tears brimmed in Olivia's eyes and soaked her wadded hanky. "I can't bear the thought of you begging. Father must be turning in his grave. Isn't there any other way to get food?"

"No. There isn't. The larder, the root cellar, and all of our stomachs are empty. The market is a charred ruin, our children are hungry, you can't stop crying—"

"Only because of the news. I can't believe that General Lee has truly surrendered."

"Well, he has. The war ended a week ago, and we're at the mercy of our enemies. If the United States Christian Commission is distributing free rations downtown, then I believe we're entitled to some."

"Who would have ever thought we'd have to accept charity?" Olivia wept.

Eugenia kept her chin raised with pride. "I refuse to think of it as charity. The Yankees stole everything we had, so it's high time they gave some of it back." She opened the door again, bringing a gust of cool air and the stench of the stables and slave yard into the tiny hallway. "I'll be back as soon as I can."

"Wait. You shouldn't go alone. Let one of us go with you."

Eugenia shook her head. "I'd rather go by myself. You're still unwell and I won't allow my daughters out in the streets with Yankee soldiers everywhere." Nor did Eugenia want her girls to witness her disgrace as she begged for food. "I'll take my manservant with me—Amos or Otis or whatever his name is."

"Are you certain he's still here? It seems like more and more of my slaves are slipping away every day. The Yankees are telling them they're free to go."

"I think it's cruel to grant freedom to people who don't know what it means or what to do with it. It's like giving a lit torch to a baby. If my slave isn't here, I'll see if one of your people will accompany me."

"Be careful, Eugenia. Everyone says it's dangerous downtown."

"I know . . . And, Olivia, please don't tell the others where I went." She hurried through the back door, eager to get this distasteful errand over with as quickly as possible. She was unaccustomed to using the slaves' door and nearly tripped over a young black boy sitting on the stoop, whittling a scrap of wood. He jumped to his feet when he saw Eugenia and stood with his arms stiff at his sides like a soldier at attention. "Yes, ma'am?"

"Do you know where I might find the slave who drove me here from White Oak Plantation?"

"Otis? Yes, ma'am. He's probably in the stable, taking care of that horse of yours and shining up your carriage."

Eugenia felt a wave of relief that Otis hadn't run off like so many of the others had—or that he hadn't stolen her horse. "Tell him I would like a word with him." The boy raced across the barren yard to the stable and returned a minute later with Otis. The big Negro halted ten feet from Eugenia and removed his straw hat. He was a tall, well-muscled field hand, and although Eugenia always found it difficult to determine a slave's age, she guessed him to be around thirty. He was a docile slave and kept his eyes lowered, as well he should.

"Yes, ma'am?"

Eugenia was suddenly aware that she no longer owned him and had no right to order him to do anything. She would have to *ask* him to go with her—and Eugenia had never asked a Negro for a favor in her life. She steeled herself for his refusal.

"I have an errand to run downtown near St. Paul's Church, and I don't think it's safe for me to go alone. I wondered if you would accompany me?"

"I been down there and seen the mess for myself, ma'am. I'm willing to go with you but . . ."

"But what?" Was he going to ask to be paid?

"Well, I hope you ain't planning on taking that carriage of yours. People see you got a horse, they be stealing him away quick as lightning. The carriage, too."

Eugenia hadn't considered that possibility. The commissary where the food was being dispensed was at least a dozen blocks away, and she was unaccustomed to walking. But how would she get home to her plantation if someone stole her horse? "I suppose we'll have to walk then," she finally said. "Find an empty burlap bag to bring with us."

They walked two blocks to Franklin Street, then headed down the hill toward the capitol building, its white roof and the spire of St. Paul's visible in the distance. The closer Eugenia got to the center of Richmond, the more the landscape degenerated into a nightmare. She had tried to prepare herself for the devastation, but it shocked her just the same. Mere skeletons of buildings stood in the deserted commercial district with blackened holes like vacant eye sockets for windows. Rubble lay knee-deep in the streets. Lovely homes had been reduced to piles of charred bricks and beams and tottering chimneys. The heart of Richmond—lovely Richmond—was in ruins.

Otis tried to avoid the worst areas, leading Eugenia around mounds of debris and past crumbling walls that threatened to topple in the wind. The breeze blew grit and cinders into Eugenia's eyes and left the taste of destruction in her mouth. Her shoes weren't made for such rugged walking. They turned black with soot, and if she hadn't been dressed in mourning, the soot would have stained the hem of her skirt, as well.

"Wait. I need to rest a moment." Eugenia paused, feeling lightheaded. The burned-out hulk in front of her was the bank where her husband, Philip, had done business. What had become of all the money? The bank records?

At least St. Paul's Church still stood intact and the capitol building across the square. The sight cheered her until she saw the hated Union flag flying from the capitol's rooftop. The grassy square in front of the building was a sea of indigo uniforms. Eugenia looked away, pressing her fist to her chest as her heart squeezed painfully. Had the war been for nothing? Had Philip and their son Samuel died in vain? She recalled the words of one of Aunt Hattie's psalms, mourning Israel's defeat by her enemies, and never had the words seemed so bitterly appropriate: *"By the rivers of Babylon, there we sat down, yea, we wept, when we remembered Zion."*

She drew a breath and started forward again, bypassing Capitol Square as she made her way toward Broad Street and the commissary. A line of people stretched away from it for nearly two blocks. Eugenia steeled herself as she took her place at the end of the line, distressed to see that all manner of unsavory people had lined up with her—trashy whites and saloon girls, worthless beggars and Negroes—people that Eugenia had never associated with in her life. She swallowed a knot of anger at being forced to stand in line with them, forced to seek charity. The jostling crowd nudged her forward each time the line moved and she lost her balance for a moment and fell against her manservant. He gripped her arms to steady her, then quickly recoiled.

"Sorry, ma'am! Sorry! You all right?"

"I'm fine." But tears of rage and humiliation stung her eyes. Eugenia had never dreamed she would stoop this low. She turned her gaze away from the filthy people crowding around her and silently vowed that she would never, ever, stoop this low again. Her dignity would be the very last thing that the Yankees would ever take from her.

"I need rations for my entire household," she told the clerk when she finally reached the distribution counter, "as well as food for the . . . servants." She had nearly called them slaves.

"How many people?"

"Eight. My servant can tell you how many Negroes we have left." She gestured to Otis.

"A handful," he said with a shrug. "Plus some little ones." Too late, Eugenia realized that he probably couldn't count.

The clerk reached behind him and lifted a sack of cornmeal onto the table. He added sacks of flour, dried beans, and rice, a ration of salt pork, and a greasy package of lard, grimacing while he worked. Otis placed everything in the burlap bag and swung it over his shoulder. Eugenia's task was done. She walked away, refusing to thank the Yankee for giving back what was rightfully hers.

She had to stop and rest several times as they plodded up Church Hill again. The sun had become too warm for the shawl, and Eugenia felt weary with hunger. When they finally reached home, Otis stopped her outside the back door. "Can I ask you something, ma'am?" He stared down at his worn shoes, not at her.

"Yes? What is it?"

"Everyone's saying we're free now, and some of the others are saying they ain't working for Miz Olivia no more."

"And I suppose you want to leave, too?"

"Well . . . I promised Massa Philip that I'd watch over you and

Missy Josephine and Missy Mary while he's away. He said if I did, he would give my two boys their freedom when he got back— though I guess they're free now anyway. I kept my promise and helped y'all come to Richmond, but now I'm missing my wife and family something terrible. I'd like to head on back to White Oak and see if they're okay."

"How will you get there?"

"Guess I'll be walking home, ma'am."

Home. It called to Eugenia, bringing tears to her eyes. She lifted her chin, determined to remain strong. "You don't need to walk, Otis. If you can wait a few more days, we will all go back. You can drive the carriage for us."

He broke into a wide grin. "Yes, ma'am. I'd be happy to do that."

Eugenia was going home. She wanted to tell her sister of her decision right away and found Olivia sitting at her writing desk in the morning room, alone. "You're back!" Olivia said, springing from her chair. "I've been so worried about you. Did everything go well?"

Eugenia nodded. "We have enough food for a couple of weeks. But listen. I've decided to go home to White Oak."

"Oh, Eugenia, you can't leave! It's much too dangerous! The Yankee soldiers are everywhere, along with all sorts of vagabonds wandering the countryside. Refugees and Negroes and—"

"White Oak is my home. It's where the girls and I belong." She crossed the room to take her sister's hands in hers, pleading with her. "You should understand how I feel, Olivia. You didn't want to leave your home and so you stayed here through the very worst of it, when everyone else said it was too dangerous to stay. Now I intend to go home, too, no matter what anyone says. I'll trust the Almighty to keep us safe."

"But think this through, Eugenia. How many slaves did you own? Dozens? Suppose they turn against you?"

"Philip always treated them well. I doubt that they're dangerous. My manservant told me just now that he's been watching over the girls and me because of a promise he made to Philip."

Olivia pulled her hands free. "Don't be naïve. Who knows what your other Negroes have been up to while you've been away."

"Nevertheless, I'm leaving, Olivia. The girls and I are going—"

"Where, Mother? Where are we going?"

Eugenia turned to see her daughter Josephine standing in the doorway. "Home, dear. We're going back to White Oak."

A faint smile lit up Josephine's face, the first that Eugenia had seen in weeks. "When?" she asked.

"In a couple of days. Next week at the latest. I've only just decided this morning."

"I don't think you're considering your daughters' welfare, Eugenia. Or their safety."

"I'm not afraid. Are you, Josephine? Because if you are, I won't make you leave Richmond against your will. Mary either."

Josephine crossed the room to stand beside her. "I'm not afraid. I want to go home, too."

Eugenia caressed her daughter's cheek, then turned to Olivia again. "There, you see?"

"I think you're being very foolish."

Eugenia exhaled. She recognized the stubborn look in her sister's eyes, but she could be just as stubborn. She had won the argument this morning and had brought food supplies home. She would win this battle, as well.

"Josephine, would you please give your aunt and me a moment to talk in private? Thank you." Eugenia waited until she and Olivia were alone, then said, "I need to think of my daughters' futures. They deserve more than this cowering fear, this day-to-day existence, wondering what tomorrow will bring or if there will even be a tomorrow. They've become so quiet and withdrawn, and it makes me furious to think they've lost their girlhood to this war, the best years of their lives." She reached for her sister's hand again. "Remember when we were their age, how we would lie in the poster bed, giggling with secrets? Remember the dances we went to and the gowns we wore? And that delicious game of courtship? How we loved to tease and flirt! Those years were filled with laughter and joy, but my girls don't know any of that happiness."

"I understand, but those things are going to take time—"

"All the more reason to get started right away. We've lost five years of our lives, Olivia—five years that we'll never get back."

"At least wait until Daniel returns. He'll probably be home from the army soon. Why not wait until he's there to protect you?"

"Because Daniel and the other boys have fought so hard, for so long. Even when they were outnumbered they kept on fighting for their homes and their country. I want to make sure my son has a comfortable home to return to."

Olivia's eyes filled with tears. "I-I don't know how to say this but . . . but what if White Oak is gone? What if the Yankees destroyed it?"

Eugenia released Olivia's hand and turned to gaze through the window. The sun that had shone so warmly on the way home from town had disappeared behind a dark cloud. "I've lost my husband, my firstborn son, and the life I once knew," she finally said. "If I find that my home is also gone, I don't know how I'll go on—but I will. The enemy can defeat us, but they can't break our spirits unless we let them. With God's help, I'm going to win back everything the Yankees have stolen from me."

3

April 21, 1865

Lizzie was out in the kitchen behind the Big House, scrubbing an iron kettle when she heard one of the other house slaves calling to her. "Lizzie! Lizzie, come quick! There's a carriage coming up the lane."

Lizzie dropped her scrub rag and ran outside, praying beneath her breath. *Oh, Lord, please! Please let it be my Otis coming home.* From the moment Miz Eugenia had made Otis load up her belongings last winter and drive her and the two missies to Richmond, Lizzie had been wondering if she'd ever see her husband again. She'd heard Miz Eugenia talking about needing money real bad after Massa Philip died. Suppose she decided to sell Otis? Suppose Lizzie never saw him again? *Please bring him home, Lord Jesus!*

Winter had turned into spring and there had been no news from the white folks in Richmond. Neither Lizzie nor any of the other slaves who'd been left behind knew a thing about what was happening. Every day Lizzie's boys were asking her, "Where's Papa? When's he coming home again?" What could she say? Life on Slave Row was filled with uncertainty and suffering, and that's all they'd ever known. Loved ones got snatched away sometimes and were never seen again.

Lizzie's mama had warned her not to fall in love and get married. "Just get your heart broken when he's torn away from you," she'd said. "Hard work and suffering's bad enough, but losing people you love is the heaviest load you'll ever carry."

"But I want to get married and have babies someday," Lizzie had tried to argue. Her mother's voice had grown sharp.

"You listen now. If you have babies, you gonna love them. Then you have to watch them grow up and be slaves just like you, living this miserable life. And nothing you can do about it. You wish they could be running around all happy like the white babies, but as much as it hurts, you got to teach your children to obey, no matter what. They belong to the white folks, not to you. Listen to me now, Lizzie. Don't ever fall in love. Just makes this life harder than it already is."

Lizzie had thought about her mother's warning all winter after Otis left, unable to shake it out of her head. But it was too late. She loved Otis more than anything in the world, and nothing could change that. His children loved him, too. But each time they pestered her she'd scold them and say, "Stop thinking about him. Stop asking about him. Maybe we never see him until we get to heaven someday, so quit asking and hoping."

Impossible to do. That burden of love was such a heavy load that sometimes Lizzie sank to her knees beneath the weight of it. She would never stop hoping or praying, asking Jesus to please bring Otis home.

She was still drying her hands on her apron as she ran to the side yard for a view of the long tree-shaded lane. Something was kicking up a big cloud of dust, so for sure there was a carriage coming. She could hear the horse's hooves thumping in the soft dirt, the carriage springs squeaking and creaking. But she could only catch glimpses of movement between the trees.

There'd been other visitors to the plantation in the past few weeks, and each time Lizzie called herself a fool when her hopes were raised, then dashed. All kinds of strangers had wandered up the road from the village, some saying the war had ended, others saying all the slaves were free. A bunch of Massa's field hands had left the plantation for good, but Lizzie and the others who worked in the Big House had stayed, scared to death of leaving for fear of being hunted down and whipped half to death if it turned out it ain't true. No, Lizzie and her kids would wait right here for Otis. And now, *Please, Lord, please*, maybe he was coming.

Lizzie halted beside Dolly, the cook, watching to see who was going to appear out of the dust ball boiling up the lane. "If this is Miz Eugenia," Dolly said, "just wait till she sees what them Yankees done to her house."

"I hope she don't blame us."

"Of course she's gonna blame us. You know she is."

Lizzie held her breath as the coach rounded the gentle curve in the lane. *Please, Lord!* Then—was she seeing things? No, that really was her Otis sitting tall and handsome in the driver's seat! Her knees went weak, and she sank down on the grass. She pulled her apron over her face and wept with relief. *Thank you, Lord! Thank you!*

"You okay, honey?" Dolly asked, rubbing her back.

"It's Otis! My Otis is back!" Her apron muffled her voice as she tried to contain her joy.

"He sure is, honey. And that means Miz Eugenia and her girls are probably back, too."

"Mama! Mama!" Lizzie heard her sons calling from behind her as they raced up from Slave Row. "Is he here, Mama? Is Papa here?"

She struggled to her feet, grabbing their skinny arms just in time to stop six-year-old Jack and eight-year-old Rufus from running to their papa. "Hold on. Just wait, Rufus, honey. You just wait now." Lizzie longed to run straight into Otis's arms herself and hold him tight, but he would have to help unload everything first. Miz Eugenia had carted a whole pile of things with her to Richmond in that carriage. Lizzie knew because she'd helped pack everything up, wrapping fancy dishes in towels and newspapers to keep them from breaking.

Miz Eugenia's old carriage driver, Willy, limped up from the stable to help Otis as Lizzie watched from a distance, still gripping

Rufus and Jack. They were as eager to run as hounds on the scent. It seemed to take forever for the men to bring in all the trunks and boxes and pictures and whatnot that Miz Eugenia had taken with her.

"We probably have to help unpack everything now," Dolly mumbled.

"She gonna be glad she didn't leave it here for the Yankees to take."

"Glad? Honey, she always finds something to complain about. Won't be any different this time, either."

At last, the white folks and all their belongings were back in the Big House. Otis could drive the empty carriage down to the stables, where Lizzie and the boys were waiting for him. Finally, after all these months apart, after all the waiting and worrying and praying, Lizzie was in his arms again. Otis held her for a long, long time. Then he turned to their boys, who were tugging on his raggedy pants and clamoring for his attention. He lifted Rufus in one arm and Jack in the other as if they weighed nothing at all.

"You're crying, Papa!" Rufus wiped his father's tears with his dirty hand, leaving a smudge on Otis's cheek. "Why you so sad?"

"I'm crying because I'm happy, not sad. Look at your mama. She's crying, too. Sometimes folks cry when they're happy, don't you know that?"

No, Lizzie's boys probably didn't know that. Not much to be happy about in the life they lived, always working, always hungry. This was probably the happiest day of their lives. It sure was one of Lizzie's.

"Where's Roselle?" Otis asked, looking around. He set the boys down and turned to unhitch the horse from the carriage.

"She was working with Cissy up in the Big House before you came. Miz Eugenia's probably giving her a hundred things to do by now." But Lizzie knew that her daughter wasn't here to welcome Otis home because she didn't feel the same way about him that Rufus and Jack did. Otis was their real daddy, but he wasn't fifteen-year-old Roselle's father.

Lizzie watched her man fussing over the horse, removing the bridle and brushing him down real good before putting him in the stall. He was being so careful to finish the job while Lizzie's iron pot sat waiting in the kitchen and she didn't care one bit.

"You boys grab some rags and help me clean the dust off this carriage," Otis said. "I been worrying over this rig since the day I drove away from here. Lord knows how much trouble I had in Richmond, keeping Massa Philip's horse and carriage from getting stolen." Otis was working as if Massa might come out and holler if he didn't. Lizzie wondered why Otis bothered. Massa and all his sons were gone, and Miz Eugenia never would set foot in this old stable.

"Everyone's saying the war is over and we ain't slaves no more," Lizzie said as she watched him work. "Is that true?"

"Yep, it's true, Lizzie-girl. I heard lots of folks talking about it in Richmond. The Yankees won and the white folks have to let all us slaves go free."

"Me too, Papa?"

"All of us, Jack."

"We heard the same thing," Lizzie said, "but nobody around here knows what it means. Saul and some of the others think we get to live in the Big House now, and the missus has to move out. He says we get to take over everything." Lizzie would never dare to dream of living in the Big House even though she knew every inch of it, upstairs and down. Her cabin on Slave Row was the only home she'd known since the day she was born. Otis laughed out loud at Saul's silly notion.

"That sure ain't true! Everything still belongs to the white folks, except us. They don't own us no more. We're free to leave White Oak and go anywhere we want."

"Anywhere? How can that be?" Lizzie sat down on an overturned barrel as she tried to take it all in. "We can leave . . . anytime we want?"

"Yes, Lizzie-girl! The door is wide open for all of us now."

"But where would we go? We'll be needing food and a place to sleep at night. And what would we do all day?"

"Well, first we'll have to change the way we think about things and start thinking like free people, I guess. Start deciding for ourselves."

"But we ain't supposed to decide things. Never in our life, Otis. They do all the thinking for us up there." Lizzie tilted her head in the direction of the Big House. "Every day of our lives someone tells us what to do and how to do it, and we ain't allowed to want anything for ourselves. They treat us like we're no better or smarter than that horse." And in the lowest times of her life, Lizzie feared they might be right.

"Do we have to move out of our cabin, Papa?" Jack asked. It was the only home he'd known, pitiful as it was. Neither him, his brother, nor his father had ever been inside the Big House, even when the white folks were away. Lizzie didn't ever want her boys to know what they were missing. But Roselle worked up there. She knew. Maybe that's why she always had her head in the clouds, dreaming up something new.

"Don't worry. We can probably keep on living here for now," Otis said.

"Some folks already run off," she told him. "Rest of us been too scared to leave. We been taking care of things because that's all we know how to do. But if what you say is true, what are we supposed to do now?"

Otis didn't answer right away. "Well . . . I been giving it a lot of thought. The war's been hard on the white folks, and they're as bad off as we are. People in Richmond are starving, Lizzie. I saw Miz Eugenia standing in line for her food just like we used to do with the overseer every month because she and the missies didn't have anything left to eat. All the plantations around here are trampled and run-down, the slaves gone who knows where. This is the only home we got, and we have three children to feed. I know we have to work hard here, but Massa ain't never been mean to us."

"Massa's dead."

"I know, I know . . ."

"Are you saying we should stay? Keep working here when we could walk away and never look back?"

"Well . . . I think—"

The clanging dinner bell outside the kitchen interrupted him, and it wasn't even close to dinnertime. Lizzie leaped up. "What should I do? Do I have to go see what she wants?"

"You better go, Lizzie. For now." But Lizzie wrapped her arms around her husband one more time and gave him another big hug before she did.

Cissy was ringing the life out of that bell, and Lizzie had to cover her ears when she got close to it. "What're you making all that racket for? There a fire or something?"

"Miz Eugenia's calling all the house slaves inside. Wants to talk to us."

Dolly emerged from the kitchen, which was a separate building behind the Big House, joined by a wooden walkway. The white folks wanted hot meals, but they didn't want their rooms getting hot in the summertime, so they built the kitchen outside.

"Otis says it's true—we're free," Lizzie whispered to the other two women as they went inside, "and we don't have to do a thing she says no more."

"Better see what she wants, though," Cissy said, shaking her head.

Miz Eugenia was waiting for them in the dining room, her chin high in the air as usual. The other house slaves were all lined up in a row, waiting like soldiers, but Lizzie's daughter, Roselle, was looking out the dining room window as if she didn't care a thing about what Miz Eugenia was going to say. That gal was probably dreaming of fairy tales and happy endings again. Lizzie walked over to her and nudged her with her elbow. "How many times do I have to tell you to look down at the floor when the missus is talking?" she whispered. "Pay attention now." They had better behave the way they always had until they knew for sure that they didn't have to.

"We're home from Richmond to stay," Miz Eugenia began. "We

brought some food supplies back with us, but they were very hard to come by, so please try to make them last."

Lizzie remembered what Otis had said about Missus having to stand in line to get that food. Could it really be true? Miz Eugenia gestured to the dining room table. The fine, polished tabletop was scarred and pitted with cigar burns. It sure hadn't looked like that when she left.

"What happened here? Can you tell me, Lizzie?"

"After you left, a bunch of Yankee soldiers moved in for a while. They went all through the house and the barn and the root cellar, looking for any bite of food they could find. Good thing you told us to hide all the food or they would of cleaned us out."

"That doesn't answer my question. What happened to my table?"

"Them Yankees moved into this room, ma'am," Lizzie said. "They set in here with all their papers and maps and cigars and muddy boots and they used this dining room like it was their own. They were none too careful, either. They took over the whole house, in fact, and they even slept in—"

"Stop!" Miz Eugenia held up both hands. "I don't want to know where they slept. I don't need to have that image in my mind every time I lay in bed. Did you wash everything thoroughly after they left?"

"Yes, ma'am."

"Why are so many things missing around here, like my beautiful rugs?"

"Them Yankees stole your rugs and your paintings and a lot of other things, too."

"Did they now?"

Lizzie knew from her tone of voice and raised eyebrows that Miz Eugenia was really asking if maybe the slaves had stolen all those things instead. It made Lizzie hopping mad. Didn't Otis say they were free now? Lizzie found a tiny seed of courage deep down inside, planted there by the good news about being free, and said, "You can go on down to our cabins and search them for yourself, ma'am, if you're thinking we stole your things. But all we cared about after you went away was getting the kitchen garden planted so we'd have enough food to eat."

"How long were the Yankees here?"

"Couple of days. Maybe a week or two."

"Well, which was it?"

Lizzie's nugget of courage grew a little larger. "Slaves don't keep track of time, ma'am, because every day's exactly the same." She dared to glance up at Miz Eugenia, and she knew by the stiff way she stood and how her skinny lips were pinched together that she was losing patience. Then there'd be trouble.

"We need to come to an agreement about work," the missus finally said. "I suppose you know that you're all free to go. We're not allowed to *own* you anymore. But if you decide to continue living here and eating my food, then I expect you to work for me just like you did before the war. The same goes for all of my field hands, and you can tell them that for me."

"Most of them are gone already, ma'am," Lizzie said. Miz Eugenia ignored her.

"If you decide *not* to work for me, then you'll need to move off my land. I'll give you a week to move out—but I expect you to keep working as usual until then."

So much for freedom. Miz Eugenia still ruled the roost and bossed everyone around, just like always. But at least the door was open now, and they could walk on out if they wanted to.

"Ida May, I could use your help unpacking my clothes," Miz Eugenia continued. "Roselle, see if Josephine and Mary need your help upstairs. Cissy, you may start unpacking some of these boxes. Put the books back on the shelves in Master Philip's study, and *please* be careful with the dishes and breakables. Dolly and Lizzy, I'm sure there's plenty to do in the kitchen to get dinner on the table on time."

"Yes, ma'am." Lizzie went back out to the kitchen to finish scrubbing the pot. She still didn't feel free, but thank the good Lord at least Otis was back. And if what he said was true, then nothing and nobody could ever tear them apart again.

4

April 25, 1865

Josephine looked out her bedroom window and wondered how long it would be until she felt safe from calamity, until she really believed that more bad things weren't going to happen. Her family had returned home from Richmond four days ago, and she was glad to be back. But life at White Oak Plantation was still chaotic, with very little food to eat. Her stomach hadn't felt full in a long time.

Jo didn't know what to do with herself all day in this strangely altered world the war had created. It was dangerous to go outside with refugees and Negroes and soldiers from both sides wandering the roads, trying to get home. She hardly dared to leave the house. But she had grown bored with reading, bored with talking to Mary—and her sister was likely bored with her. It seemed a waste of time to embroider things for her hope chest. She had no talent for drawing or watercolors, and besides, there was no money to buy more paint once she used up her colors. Jo had attempted to practice the piano, but without a teacher it was difficult to make progress. All told, there was very little to do all day except wander around the echoing house—and even that disheartened her.

Everywhere Josephine looked she saw gaping holes. The Yankees had stolen their beautiful Turkish carpets, leaving behind ghostly images on the floors where the sun had faded the wood. But the biggest hole was the one left by her daddy. Jo still hadn't gotten used to the fact that he was gone forever. Whenever she walked past his study and saw his favorite chair, it seemed wrong that he wasn't sitting there writing in his ledger book or playing chess, filling the room with fragrant cigar smoke.

Her brother Samuel was gone, too. He'd been a constant fixture at Daddy's side and would have taken over the plantation one day, just as Daddy had taken Granddaddy's place. Proud mothers used to come calling with their daughters, hoping the handsome Samuel Weatherly would show an interest in them. Where would all those girls find husbands now that Sam and so many of his friends were dead?

Josephine kept watch from her bedroom window, hoping her brother Daniel would return home soon and get the plantation going again. Before the war, he had been away at college for so much of the school year that Jo was used to the hole he'd left behind. Still, the mothers used to come calling when Daniel was home, hoping to make a match with him, too. No one had made social calls since Jo and her family had returned from Richmond, which was fine with her. There was no tea or coffee to serve them and no slaves to wait on them. All but a few of White Oak's slaves were gone.

The plantation seemed unnaturally quiet. No bell clanging in the morning to wake the slaves, no haunting songs as the workers made their way to and from the cotton fields. The fields were empty of everything but weeds, the barn empty of animals. Fragrant aromas from the kitchen were things of the past. Everywhere Jo looked she saw emptiness, and silence followed her everywhere she went. She missed music most of all, the laughter and gaiety of the parties Mother used to hold. Would there ever be music and laughter in their lives again?

Josephine moved to a different bedroom window for a different view and saw Lizzie, one of the house slaves, shuffle out of the kitchen and pick up a hoe to work in the vegetable garden. The slaves had planted it before they'd been set free, and Lizzie was the only one left to tend it. The day looked so fresh and hopeful that Jo's longing to escape this stuffy, claustrophobic house suddenly overwhelmed her. She tied a straw bonnet on her head and hurried downstairs and out through the front door.

She drew a deep breath, then sighed. The air smelled of spring and woodsmoke from the kitchen. She took her time walking around the house to the back, noticing the overgrown bushes and weed-filled flower beds. The grounds around the house had fallen into ruin now that the slaves who did all the gardening had left. It hadn't rained in days and the ground was rock hard and dusty beneath her feet.

When she reached the kitchen garden, Josephine opened the gate to the enclosed plot of land and went inside, shutting it behind her again. Lizzie seemed to snap to attention. "You needing something, Missy Josephine?"

"No . . . well, yes. I need to get out of the house for a while, and it looks like such a beautiful morning."

"Yes, ma'am." Lizzie bent to her task again, the hoe rasping against the hard earth.

"Are you going to leave White Oak, too, Lizzie? Like all the others?"

"No, ma'am. We decided to stay for now. But Lord knows I can't do all this work by myself. Neither can Otis."

Otis. That was the name of the field slave who had driven their carriage to Richmond and back. Jo had grown up with these slaves, yet she knew very little about them. "Is Otis your husband?"

"Yes, ma'am."

Jo watched her work for a few minutes, inhaling the fresh spring air. "Do you enjoy working in the garden?"

"Like it or not, it's got to be done, Missy Jo, or nobody's gonna eat around here."

Josephine wondered if she should help. Of course it was a scandalous idea. But everything else in Jo's life had changed, and if she wanted to eat, as Lizzie said, then someone had to help her.

Besides, Jo had nothing else to fill the long, empty hours. "Would you like my help?" she asked.

Lizzie stared at her before catching herself and looking away. "Miz Eugenia's never gonna let her daughter do slave work. No, ma'am." Jo heard the outrage in her voice.

"Everything is different now, Lizzie. I think I should learn how to grow our own food in case you decide to leave us, too." As the idea took shape, Josephine realized how much she liked the thought of making something happen for once, instead of waiting for things to happen to her. She could decide her own fate and work to grow food herself instead of slowly starving. "Will you show me what to do, Lizzie?"

"No, ma'am. You gonna get me in a mess of trouble, Missy Jo."

"I promise you won't get into trouble." She took the hoe from Lizzie's hand. It was heavier than she'd imagined, the wooden handle rough and splintery. "Show me what to do."

Lizzie looked frightened as she took a step back. It occurred to Josephine that all these changes must be hard for her, too. Their circumstances had reversed: Lizzie had been set free, and now Josephine was the one enslaved in a world of poverty and uncertainty. Since neither God nor her daddy was taking care of her anymore, Jo would have to take care of herself—beginning with growing her own food. She turned her back on Lizzie and started chopping at the dirt so Lizzie wouldn't see her sudden tears. "Like this?" she asked, trying to mimic Lizzie's actions.

"Wait! Let me get another hoe, Missy Jo, and I'll show you the right way." Lizzie fetched the hoe leaning against the garden fence, then bent to ruffle her fingers through a row of tiny plants, like delicate green lace. "These here are carrot plants, Missy Jo. The rest—like this here—are weeds. I'm chopping out the weeds so the plants have a chance to grow. But I need to be careful not to be chopping the plants or there'll be nothing to eat. I use the pointy part of the hoe, see? Like this."

"Is this right?" Jo asked, trying to imitate her.

"Yes, ma'am." They continued down the rows, working side

by side. It felt wonderful to Josephine to be doing something useful. But she could tell that Lizzie was nervous, glancing up at the house as if to see if Mother was watching them. Jo decided to make small-talk—one of the feminine arts that Mother had tried to instill in her daughters and something that Josephine had never been good at doing, especially with young men. Of course, she was never supposed to talk to the slaves at all except to issue orders.

"Why is there a fence all around the garden, Lizzie?"

"You don't want rabbits getting in here, Missy Jo."

"We have rabbits around here? So close to the house?"

"Yes, ma'am. More than ever. Massa Philip's hound dogs liked to chase them off in the old days, but . . ." She paused, glancing up at Josephine as if she might have said the wrong thing. "Otis sets snares around the fence and sometimes catches us a rabbit for dinner," Lizzie said.

The thought of eating rabbit meat repulsed Jo, but Lizzie was finally relaxing a bit, so Jo kept quiet about that. "What's that wooden cross for?" she asked instead, pointing to a pair of branches tied together. Rags fluttered from it in the breeze. Was it part of a slave superstition?

"You mean that?" Lizzie smiled. "It's a scarecrow, Missy Jo. Or at least it's supposed to be. It needs fixing up just like everything else around here, or it won't scare nothing away. Them crows are supposed to think it's a person so they'll stay away from our garden."

"What about those bunches of sticks that look like Indian teepees?"

"Them are for the pole beans to climb on when the plants get a little bigger."

"There's so much I don't know," Jo said with a sigh. "I've lived here at White Oak all my life and the food simply arrived at my table. I'm sorry to say I never thought much about where it came from or about the whole process of guarding it from birds and rabbits and weeds while it was growing."

Maybe there had been holes and empty places in her old life, too, and she had just never noticed. Holes in her practical knowledge of how her food was grown and gaps in her usefulness, as well. How had knowing how to play the piano or paint with watercolors or engage in polite conversation helped her or her family through the bitter years of war? And how would those skills help anyone now?

Josephine reached the end of the row and looked back at her work. It didn't look nearly as straight and neat as Lizzie's row, and Lizzie had reached the end much faster and had started down the next row. Jo gripped the hoe with renewed determination. "When will these carrots be ready to pick?"

"Not for a long, long time, Missy Jo." She managed a brief smile. "In another week or so we'll have to thin them out so the carrots can get nice and fat."

"How do you do that?"

"Pull out some of the plants and leave the rest."

"That seems a shame. Especially if the plants take so long to grow." And yet the changes in Jo's life had seemed to come just as mercilessly, with people she loved snatched away from her. Samuel and Daddy had been alive and running the plantation one day, and quicker than carrots or beans could sprout, they were gone. Last fall, dozens of slaves had worked in the fields, but now both the cotton and the slaves were gone. "What made you decide to stay, Lizzie?"

She paused, leaning against her hoe. "Me and Otis got three kids to think about. Can't let them go hungry."

Lizzie was a mother? That was something else Josephine hadn't known. "What are your children's names?"

"Roselle, Rufus, and Jack."

"Wait. Roselle is your daughter? But you don't look nearly old enough to be her mother!"

Lizzie looked away, lowering her head as if embarrassed. Jo was sorry for speaking without thinking—something Mother would chide her for doing. But Lizzie looked so young, certainly no more than thirty. Which meant that she must have been fifteen or sixteen—the same age as Mary—when Roselle had been born. Why had Lizzie chosen to marry and have children at such a young age?

Before the war, finding a suitable husband had occupied most of Josephine's life, dictating her activities and social engagements. She'd had to learn to make herself attractive and poised so her charms would outshine the other girls' and catch a man's interest. Marriage had been the prize at the end of the contest. Jo thought of the long lists of names that the minister had read in his solemn voice every Sunday throughout the war, men fallen in battle like her brother Samuel, young men she had once socialized with. Gone—all of them. How could any of their lives ever be the same?

"I'm glad you decided to stay and work for us," Jo finally said to break the long silence. "And I'm grateful that you're teaching me to—"

"Josephine!"

She looked up, startled. Mother stood by the back door with her hands on her hips. "I've been looking everywhere for you. What in heaven's name are you doing?"

"Working in the garden."

"Come inside this instant!" The door slammed shut behind her as she returned inside.

Josephine saw the look of fear on Lizzie's face and smiled to reassure her. "Don't worry. I'm the one who's in trouble, not you." She removed her straw hat as she slowly walked up to the house, wiping the sweat off her forehead with her sleeve. Mother was waiting inside the door, arms crossed.

"What in the world were you doing? We have not yet sunk so low that you are forced to work outside in the hot sun like a field hand. What will people think of us? Do you want your skin to turn brown and your hands to get all blistered like a slave's?"

"I'm bored, Mother. There's nothing else to do and I thought I should learn how to put food on our table in case Lizzie decides to leave, too. Besides, it felt good to work outside. And the work isn't hard. . . ." Jo could tell that Mother wasn't listening.

"There has never been a Weatherly who had to work like a Negro, and so help me God, there never will be."

But that's just it, Jo wanted to say. *God isn't helping us.*

41

"Did you know that Otis is Lizzie's husband?" Jo asked. Mother looked at her as if she had lost her mind. "And Roselle is Lizzie's daughter. They have two other children, too."

"What in the world is wrong with you? As if it isn't bad enough that you're working with slaves, now you've decided to converse with them, too? Really, Josephine!"

"They aren't our slaves anymore. They're people. We shouldn't treat them like slaves."

"I believe the hot sun has addled your brain. Go splash some cold water on your face and tidy your hair." Mother turned and strode away. Jo followed her down the hall and into the foyer.

"But we have to change the way we do things, Mother. Nothing is the same as it used to be."

"Well, so help me God, I'm going to change everything back."

Josephine let her mother walk away this time while she remained in the front foyer alone, gazing at the empty holes again—the dusty space where the hall clock had stood, the darker patch of wood on the floor where the rug had been. And if she looked to her right into Daddy's study, she knew she would see his empty chair.

No, God wasn't going to help any of them. And it would be impossible to change anything back to the way it had been.

5

April 28, 1865

Eugenia didn't recognize her son at first. The stranger walking up the lane toward her house looked like a beggar, his mismatched clothing no longer resembling a Confederate uniform, his shoes something only a slave would wear. She saw him approaching and guessed him to be a refugee or a vagabond coming to beg or to steal from her. Eugenia groped in her skirt pocket for the pistol she carried everywhere, then went out to the porch to order the man off her property. But the stranger was Daniel.

Before Eugenia could move or speak, he saw her in the doorway and ran the rest of the way up the road toward her, bounding up the front steps to pull Eugenia into his arms. Daniel! Daniel was home! She tried to say his name but couldn't speak, her throat choked with tears. Daniel's entire body trembled, and she realized he was sobbing. He had been barely twenty years old when he'd gone off to war, filled with swagger and bravado. "We'll lick the Yanks in no time, and I'll be home in time to return to college in the fall." Instead, five years had passed.

Daniel was Eugenia's golden boy, blond and handsome and full of life, the jokester in the family, able to make everyone laugh. Now joy and sorrow overwhelmed her as she held him in her arms. He was so thin, so ragged, so timeworn. But then all of them were.

"Oh, Daniel!" she murmured. "You're home at last." He couldn't stop sobbing, a broken man. She pulled away and reached up to brush his sandy hair off his forehead. "No more tears now," she said. "No tears. You're home."

He seemed taller than before but so much thinner. He had grown a beard and mustache, and they made him look shaggy and unkempt. But the biggest difference was his eyes. Eugenia saw so much sadness there, as if they had seen things he wished he could forget. Daniel had aged much more than five years.

"I'm so proud of you," she said. "You fought so hard."

"The Yanks might have outnumbered us," he said, drying his eyes on his sleeve, "but they didn't outfight us."

"I know. I know." Eugenia caressed her son's shoulder as she watched him survey the yard and the fields from the porch steps. "I'm sorry everything is so run-down. We only returned home from Richmond a week ago." Surely he could see how much had changed since he'd been away, how their lovely plantation had fallen into disrepair, how empty the cotton fields were.

"Did all our slaves run off?" he asked. "We saw hundreds of Negroes wandering on the roads."

"All but three are gone, I'm afraid. We have one field hand and two house slaves left."

"That's not enough to run a plantation."

"I know. I'm told that some Negroes are living out in the woods between here and the village, though I'm not certain if any of them are ours. Good thing you arrived in daylight. No one feels safe here after dark anymore."

She heard footsteps thundering down the stairs inside the house, and a moment later Mary and Josephine ran out to greet their brother. Eugenia felt a stab of sorrow as she watched her children embrace one another. Their father and older brother deserved a hero's homecoming, too, but they would never get it.

"Grab your bag and come inside, Daniel," Eugenia said, leading the way. "What you need is a nice long rest and some good hot food to get your strength back." Although how he could regain his strength on the meager diet they were forced to eat, Eugenia didn't know. "We've been expecting you ever since we heard all of our soldiers had been paroled. I told Lizzie to make sure your room was ready."

"It's been a while since I slept in a bed. My friends used to joke that the best thing about getting wounded was having a clean bed to sleep in and a pretty nurse to feed you dinner." Mary smiled at her brother's humor, but neither Josephine nor Eugenia did.

"You heard that Harrison Blake lost his leg, didn't you?" Eugenia asked.

Daniel looked away. "Yeah . . . How is Captain Blake doing?"

"We haven't been to see him yet, but he's finally home from the hospital in Richmond. We should pay him a visit and cheer him up." They were all standing in the foyer at the foot of the stairs, and Eugenia didn't know what else to say. She wasn't ready to talk about Philip or Samuel. "Well," she said, exhaling. "You go on up and make yourself at home. And if there's anything you'd like—anything at all—you just ask."

"How about a hot bath?" He grinned, and for a moment he was her young, carefree son again. But his smile quickly faded.

"Of course, darling. Would you like to shave, too? I can have Lizzie look for some soap and a razor."

"Maybe," he said, stroking his chin, "I don't know. I've worn a beard for so long I might feel naked without it. But tell the slaves to throw these clothes away. They're probably infested with lice and fleas."

Eugenia shuddered. She couldn't imagine all that he had suffered. Daniel gripped the banister to go upstairs, then changed his mind and walked into his father's study. He let his bag drop to the floor as he gazed all around. "It's hard to believe Daddy's really gone," he said.

Eugenia didn't reply. She didn't follow Daniel into the room but stood in the doorway, watching as he took in the details.

"Are you all right, Mother?" he asked after turning to her. Eugenia nodded. "He would expect us to keep going."

Daniel crossed the room to open the cabinet where Philip kept his liquor. He wouldn't find any. "The Yankees took it all," she said before he could ask. "They took nearly all our rugs, too—or at least that's what the slaves would have me believe."

"We have to call them servants now, Mother," Josephine said from behind her.

Eugenia waved her words away. "I know, I know . . . How can I possibly forget when you keep reminding me all the time?"

Daniel went to his father's desk. He looked exhausted, but he hesitated, as if reluctant to sit in Philip's chair. He looked up at Eugenia, his expression that of a small boy who had lost his way. Then, to her horror, he covered his face with his hands and wept. Eugenia turned to shoo her daughters away.

"Josephine. Mary. Go find the slaves and tell them to start heating water for Daniel's bath. Go! Quickly!" When the girls were gone, Eugenia went to comfort her son. Lord knows how many tears she had shed in this room after hearing the terrible news. But Daniel was a man, and men didn't cry. "I can't even imagine what you've had to endure," she soothed as she held him close. "My poor Daniel . . ."

How hard it was to watch her children suffer! Soon, very soon, she would start making everything right for them again, making up for all they had lost. Daniel's weeping gradually tapered off. Eugenia gently guided her son up the stairs to his room. "You'll feel better after you've rested and bathed and changed into clean clothes," she told him. "I'm certain of it."

For the next few days, Daniel slept a great deal. Once or twice Eugenia thought she heard him weeping in the night, but she didn't go to him or acknowledge that she'd heard. When Daniel was awake, Eugenia watched from a distance as he wandered the house or the plantation grounds, often stopping to stare into space or wipe tears from his eyes. She made up her mind that the best way to help him get back on his feet was to encourage him to be with his friends. The other planters and their sons were in the same situation that she and Daniel were in, so perhaps he would draw comfort and courage from them.

"You must miss the camaraderie you experienced during the war," she said one morning at breakfast. "You fought every battle with your friends, and you must have grown very close after so much time."

"We were together from the very beginning—those of us who are left."

"Why don't I tell Otis to harness the carriage for us? I think we should visit Harrison Blake and his mother this morning. Mary and Josephine, you need to come, too."

"I would prefer to stay home," Josephine said.

Eugenia's temper flared before she could stop it. "Why? So you can work in the garden in the hot sun and talk to that wretched slave again?" She paused to regain control. "You need to converse with people who are our social equals, Josephine. Harrison's mother is one of my dearest friends, and it has been much too long since we've visited with her."

"I was there when Captain Blake lost his leg," Daniel said, his tone somber. "He and Samuel were right beside each other when the bombs started falling. If I had been twenty feet closer . . ." His voice trailed off, shaky with unshed tears.

Eugenia drew a breath to steady her own voice, aware that her son Samuel had died at his friend Harrison's side. "You mustn't think of all the 'what ifs,' darling. You're home now, and that's all that matters. I'm sure Captain Blake would enjoy visitors. He was in Chimborazo Hospital for such a long time. His mother and fiancée spent months there, taking care of him. I'm certain he'll be happy to see you." And maybe Daniel would finally climb out of the doldrums when he realized how much he had to be thankful for—including his life and all of his limbs.

An hour later they were finally on their way, although Eugenia felt as though she was dragging all three of her children there against their wills. When they arrived, a smaller carriage was already hitched to the rail in front of the house. "They have company," Josephine said. "We should leave."

"Nonsense. We can at least say hello." Eugenia's driver helped her climb from the carriage, and she was relieved when a Negro servant came to the door to greet them. At least her friend Priscilla still had domestic help. "Are we intruding?" Eugenia asked the servant. "I see the Blakes already have company."

"It's just Miz Emma, ma'am. She and Miz Priscilla will be happy to see you."

Eugenia motioned to her children, who were lagging behind. "Come on now. The carriage belongs to Harrison's fiancée."

The servant herded them into the former study, now converted into a main-floor bedroom. Harrison's father had died a few years before the war, leaving the plantation to his only surviving child. The draperies in the study were drawn shut, making the room seem dreary. Eugenia waited for her eyes to adjust to the darkness, then tried not to reveal her shock when she saw Harrison lying in bed, propped up with pillows. He resembled a corpse, his face as white as the bed sheets he lay on. She couldn't help noticing the outline of his legs beneath the covers, one stretching full length, the other stopping above his knee.

She moved aside as her children entered the room and was embarrassed to see tears in Daniel's eyes. Mary and Josephine had quickly looked away from Harrison, unable to disguise their horror. Maybe this visit had been a mistake.

Or maybe Daniel would finally find his strength by helping his former captain. Maybe her daughters would stop behaving like timid mice and learn how to handle themselves with poise and grace. Bashful girls seldom attracted the best husbands, nor did gloomy ones.

"Hello, Harrison," Eugenia began. "We were so happy to hear that you were home and so we decided to pay you a visit." She turned to his mother and fiancée. "Priscilla, Emma . . . you must be thrilled to have him home. We know how glad we are to have our Daniel back." She continued the conversation for several minutes, doing most of the talking and getting mere grunts from Harrison in return. His mother and fiancée seemed unusually subdued, as well. Eugenia had the feeling that her visit had interrupted something dramatic or emotional.

"Well, come on, ladies," Eugenia finally said. "Why don't we go into the parlor to chat and let our two men catch up, shall we?"

When they were all seated in the front room, Eugenia noticed that Harrison's fiancée was close to tears. "It must be very difficult to see the man you love so ill," Eugenia said, resting her hand on Emma's in sympathy. "We must pray that he'll regain his full strength."

"It's not his health that worries me, Mrs. Weatherly. Harrison is in such low spirits and I . . . I don't know how to cheer him." She retrieved a handkerchief from her sleeve and dabbed her eyes.

"Daniel is dispirited, too. It's only natural, considering everything they've seen and suffered. Imagine losing the war after fighting so hard and paying such an enormous price."

"Harrison says terrible things to me, hurtful things. It's as if he's deliberately trying to drive me away," Emma said.

"I don't know what has gotten into my son to talk the way he does," Priscilla added. She looked fragile and faded, like a flower that has been dried and pressed flat between the pages of a heavy book. Her eyes were as pain-filled as her son's.

"It's his illness speaking," Eugenia said. "People can't be held accountable for what they say when they aren't well." Her own son barely spoke at all, and she wondered which was worse, to have a child who was sullen and withdrawn like Daniel, or one who spewed wounding words like Harrison.

"Listen, Emma," Priscilla said. "I meant what I said earlier. If you're having second thoughts about the engagement, no one in the world would blame you for breaking it. Least of all me."

"But I love him, Mrs. Blake. He wrote such beautiful letters to me, saying how much he loved me and that he looked forward to starting our new life together after the war. I saved all of them, and I read them over and over again. I was so afraid I'd never see him again, and now . . ."

"War changes people," Priscilla said. "None of us are the same people we were. And Harrison has changed most of all."

"We must not give up," Eugenia said. "We've all had our share of grief and sorrow, Lord knows. But we can't give in to it. Our men need us to be strong now more than ever. I honestly believe we've finally touched the bottom of this deep well, and we can begin to climb out. We *must* climb out."

"How?" Priscilla asked. "I don't think I have the strength."

"Then we'll help each other. And maybe that's what our men need, too. Daniel misses talking with the other men around the campfire at night. After all, they traveled and fought alongside each other for five years. I told him to invite everyone over to White Oak some evening. I have nothing at all to serve them, mind you, but it will do them good to be together again. Harrison should come, too."

"He won't go," Emma said. "He'll hate the idea. Harrison hates having everyone see him this way, lying in bed, helpless. He said he doesn't feel like a man anymore."

"That's just the illness talking. He'll cheer up now that he's home."

"I pray you're right, Mrs. Weatherly."

"We so enjoyed making social calls before the war, didn't we, ladies? And now we simply must see one another more often. It will lift our spirits if we do." And Eugenia was reminded that she must work hard at finding husbands for Mary and Josephine. So many young men had died that competition for husbands would be fierce. Josephine was a plain girl, truth be told, but charm and personality could make up for a lot of faults. She simply must make more of an effort.

They chatted for a while longer until Eugenia began to feel the strain of carrying the conversation. Daniel's visit with Harrison was lasting much longer than a usual social call, and she was running out of small-talk. She rose to her feet, smoothing her skirt. "We mustn't keep you, Priscilla. I'm sure you have so much to do. Emma, would you mind telling Daniel we're ready to leave?"

Emma left the room but was back again almost immediately

with a strange look on her face. "Daniel is gone, Mrs. Weatherly. Harrison said he left a long time ago to walk home."

How odd. And how rude. But Eugenia didn't voice her thoughts. "Of course, Harrison needs to rest. And Daniel probably didn't want to make us feel rushed. I promise we'll come back another day, Priscilla dear. And it was so nice to see you again, Emma."

Eugenia thought they might catch up with Daniel on the way home and give him a ride, but there was no one on the road at all. How long ago had he left? Where had he gone?

"You girls were certainly quiet today," Eugenia said as they removed their hats and gloves in the foyer. "I fear you have forgotten how to engage in polite conversation."

"I didn't know what to say," Josephine said.

"Me either," Mary added. "Harrison looks like he's dying, and everyone seemed so sad. I wouldn't blame Emma if . . ." She didn't finish.

"It's wrong to desert the people you love in difficult times. Things will get better, eventually. Do you girls remember the thunderstorms we used to have during the summer months, and how the wind would blow all the leaves and branches down in our yard? Sometimes the lane would flood, too, remember? But in time, everything would get cleaned up and the water would disappear, and we could forget all about the storm."

"Harrison Blake isn't going to grow a new leg."

"Josephine! What a thing to say! What has gotten into you lately?"

"Well, it's true, isn't it?"

Eugenia exhaled. "What am I going to do with you?" She felt as though she had lost touch with her daughter during the long years of war, the way they had lost touch with Daniel when Petersburg had been under siege. Yes, the war had been long and terrible, and sadness still lingered over the South like fog. But Eugenia made up her mind to bring in fresh air and sunlight to drive it away. She would help Daniel find a wife and see that her daughters were settled in their own homes with husbands to watch over them. And in time, White Oak Plantation would be restored to the way it once was.

6

May 3, 1865

It wasn't just the inky-dark night that frightened Lizzie. Truth was, she had never left White Oak Plantation in her life, and the thought of leaving it now terrified her. But Otis had kinfolk among White Oak's former field hands and Lizzie knew he longed to see them. The only family Lizzie ever had was her mama, and she had died long before the war. Lizzie never had known her father.

"Why do we have to go at night?" she asked him, stalling a moment longer.

"It's the only time we have off. I want to see my brother and find out how he and the others are all doing," he said. "I ain't seen Saul since I came back from Richmond."

"Can I come with you?" Roselle asked.

"No," Lizzie said quickly. "You stay here with Jack and Rufus." Roselle might sweet-talk Otis into letting them come along, but Lizzie wanted them home where it was safe. She couldn't shake the idea from the old days that Negroes who left the plantation got hunted down with dogs and punished with whippings.

"I haven't seen my friends in a long time, either," Roselle said, sulking.

"They'll all be asleep by now—like you should be."

"But it isn't fair—"

"Come here, Roselle." Lizzie pulled her daughter real close, speaking quietly so the boys wouldn't overhear. "Listen to me. This is only our first time out at night since . . . well, since they're saying we're all free. Wait and see what happens and maybe you can come next time. Now, be a good girl and mind what I say."

Lizzie grabbed Otis's hand and hurried out of the cabin before Roselle could argue—and before Lizzie could be tempted to change her mind and tell Otis to go by himself. She had to get used to being free, and this was a good first step, small as it was. The crickets were making a big racket as she and Otis walked up the small rise from Slave Row and crossed the backyard by the chicken coop. Lizzie wasn't expecting to see a dark shape hunched on the back step of the Big House, and she gasped in fear.

"Who's there?" a voice called out. Missy Jo's voice. It took a moment before Lizzie's heart slid back down out of her throat so she could speak.

"It's Lizzie. Me and Otis was just taking a little walk. You needing something, Missy Jo?" Lizzie held her breath, half wishing that Missy Jo did need her so she would have an excuse to stay home.

"No . . . I'm just admiring the pretty evening. You all have a nice walk."

"Thank you, Missy. I-I will."

"See?" Otis whispered. "I told you everything would be fine."

"You don't think she'll tell on us, do you?"

"Ain't nothing to tell. We can take a walk if we want to." He gave Lizzie's hand a gentle tug, and they started forward again, passing the stables and continuing down the lane away from the house. "I know a shortcut through the cotton fields, but it might be too hard to cross that rough ground at night."

"Sure is dark out here," Lizzie said, clutching his arm.

"Why're you so nervous, Lizzie-girl?"

"Can I tell you something?"

"You know you can."

"This . . . this here is the first time I ever been off the plantation."

"That can't be." He looked down at her, frowning. "You ain't gone on errands with Miz Eugenia sometimes?"

"No sir. She's always saying I'm nothing but a field hand like my mama, and she always took Ida May or Cissy with her."

"I never knew that. Next time we'll have to go in daylight so you can see the world better." They kept on walking, their shoes scuffling in the dirt, kicking up little clouds of dust.

"Ain't it strange," Lizzie asked, "that something we get punished for all our life, like walking off the plantation after dark, is fine all of a sudden? I can't get used to it."

"Things always seem scary the first time."

"Well, how long will it be until I feel free? Until I know we can walk away from here whenever we want to without somebody chasing us down, making us come back?"

"Gonna take some time, Lizzie-girl. That's for sure."

They reached the end of the tree-lined lane and turned down the wider road that led into the village of Fairmont. A carpet of stars filled the sky, shining clear down to the horizon above the barren cotton fields. The moon was behind Lizzie's back, and she and Otis cast long shadows on the dirt road in front of them as they walked. Before long, they reached the end of the cotton field and the beginning of the woods. Lizzie halted.

"I seen the forest from a distance when I worked in the fields, but I never walked this close to it before." The tree branches were all tangled together, and the ground beneath them was overgrown with bushes and weeds and fallen logs. She didn't see how they'd find their way.

"Here's the trail." Otis pointed to a narrow path leading into the woods. "Saul and me used to explore these woods when we were kids—when we could get away with it, that is." He chuckled softly. How could Otis have happy memories of growing up in this place, when all of hers were filled with fear?

They walked single file, with Lizzie clinging to the back of Otis's shirt. Before long she heard voices and saw the faint orange light of a campfire flickering in the woods. Lizzie sighed with relief when they reached the makeshift campground and saw Otis's brother,

Saul, and a bunch of other slaves from the old days sitting around the fire. Beyond them was a cluster of shacks and lean-tos made from old boards and burlap sacks. She heard a stream trickling nearby and a baby crying in one of the huts. The clearing smelled of woodsmoke and roasting meat.

"Hey, Otis! Lizzie! Good to see you!" Saul welcomed them with hugs and slaps on the back. "I heard you came back from Richmond with Miz Eugenia."

"That's right, nearly two weeks ago. Massa Daniel is home from the war, too, and they have me driving the carriage for them. Nobody's saying a word about planting cotton, though. I been wondering how you been getting on and decided to come see for myself." Someone rolled a dead log into the circle of firelight, and Lizzie sat down on it close to Otis, listening to the sound of the creek and the crackling fire, swatting mosquitoes as they landed on her bare arms and legs.

"You here to stay with us?" Saul's wife asked Lizzie. "Where's your boys and Roselle?"

"They're back at the cabin. We ain't decided to leave White Oak just yet." Lizzie didn't say so, but living in the woods like wild animals didn't seem like any kind of a life for her kids. "Why'd you move out here?" she asked Saul.

"Well, I decided that since I was a free man, I wasn't going to live like a slave no more or listen to somebody telling me what to do all day."

"What happens when it rains or when the weather turns cold?" Lizzie asked.

"Or when the owner of this property comes and chases you off?" Otis added.

"We'll have our own land to live on by then."

"Your own land?" Lizzie asked. "Where you gonna get your own land?"

"There's a new white fellow come to Fairmont, sent by the government up in Washington. He's helping all us Negroes. Said we're entitled to farms of our own."

"You sure it ain't a trick?" Lizzie asked. She liked the idea of living out from under Miz Eugenia, and she'd like to see Otis plowing land for himself. But her fear of the unknown ran too deep.

"No, it ain't a trick," Saul said. "They call it the Freedmen's Bureau, and the fella who runs it is a Yankee—the same Yankees that won the war. He's passing out food and clothes and things over in the village, and saying we're gonna get our own land."

"He's a white man?" Lizzie asked.

"Yeah, but he says it's his job to help us get settled and get enough to eat. Talk to him, Otis. Hear what he has to say. He claims we can move out West where there's lots of land and farm it ourselves."

Lizzie knew by the quiet way Otis was staring into the fire that he was pondering Saul's words. "Next time you go see this man, maybe Lizzie and me can come with you and hear what he has to say."

"It don't work that way. We have to go into Fairmont one at a time. The white folks around here don't like to see a whole gang of us Negroes all together."

"Maybe we can go right after supper some evening when the chores are done," Otis said. "Think the man will be there after supper?"

"He lives upstairs above his office. It's in that little brick building that used to belong to the railroad. Know which one I mean? Right behind the train station?"

"I think so."

"You can't miss it. And the man should be there most all of the time."

They talked for a while longer, catching up on the news and telling stories from the old days. It was good to see Otis laughing with his brother again. The night didn't seem quite as dark on the way home, but Lizzie still didn't like the idea of walking all the way into Fairmont. "Can't you go talk to this Yankee man by yourself, Otis?"

"I could, but I want you to hear what he has to say, too. Anything we decide, we need to decide together, you and me."

"Saul says he's a white man. You trust white men?"

"I don't exactly trust them . . . but I do trust Jesus."

"Dolly says that Jesus was a white man, too."

"Dolly's wrong. He's the Son of God, and He ain't no color at all. He was born a poor slave, just like us. He knows just how we feel."

"That don't make sense to me. Doesn't God own the whole world, Otis? Why would He let His Son grow up poor?"

"I can't explain it exactly. Besides, we better hush up the rest of the way home. Voices travel a long way at night, and if Massa Daniel wakes up, he might think we're thieves and get out his shotgun."

Two days later, Otis told Lizzie to be ready to walk to the village as soon as she finished feeding the white folks their supper. She had all day to think about it and didn't know if she was scared or excited. Probably both. All her life, people would come and go from White Oak to Fairmont and back again, but Lizzie had never once stepped foot off the plantation or seen a town for herself.

She was still fretting about it late that afternoon when Roselle came running into the kitchen, shouting, "Mama, come quick! I want to show you something."

"Not now," Lizzie sighed. "I got too much to do, and I need your help with it." Roselle was such a fanciful girl that if it poured down rain she'd want to go look for a rainbow and the pot of gold at the end of it. "Just tell me what it is, honey. I got work to do."

"Well, Rufus and Jack and me were taking a shortcut past the stables and all of a sudden this great big bird flies up right in front of us, flapping its wings and making an awful racket. It liked to scare me half to death! I started to run, but then I realized it was a duck. A duck, Mama! I looked a little closer and saw it had a nest full of eggs. Eight of them."

"Did you get them for me? They'll taste real good for our breakfast tomorrow."

"Mama, no! There might be baby ducks inside those eggs."

"Well, there might be baby chickens inside hens' eggs, too, and we eat those every morning. Duck eggs taste real good."

"Mama! Now I'm glad I didn't show you!" Roselle was outraged, standing with her fists clenched as if ready to defend her nest. "I'm not letting anybody eat those eggs, Mama. I hid behind the bushes and watched for a while, and there's a mama and a papa duck guarding the eggs, keeping them warm and safe until they hatch."

Her daughter's soft heart amused Lizzie. "Do whatever you want. But don't be surprised if a raccoon or a fox gets them first. Now wash your hands and help me fix dinner."

Lizzie and Otis left for the village right after supper. "How far is it?" she asked as they reached the main road at the end of the lane.

"Only a few minutes by carriage," Otis said. "It'll probably take us close to an hour to walk there." Before long they passed the woods where the Negro shantytown was, then came to a white plantation house that looked a lot like White Oak—only smaller, with tall pillars and a wide front porch.

"That's where Miz Eugenia goes visiting with her friend, Miz Blake," Otis said. "When we start seeing houses that are real close together, you'll know we're in the village." And sure enough, pretty soon there were houses on both sides of the road, and they were nearly as close to each other as the cabins on Slave Row. Otis pointed to a pretty white building with a tall, pointy tower on top. "That there is the church where the Weatherlys go on Sunday."

Lizzie saw more and more houses, and then a long row of shops with big windows out front. White people and Negroes were walking around or riding in carriages, but she drew to a halt when she saw a group of Yankee soldiers gathered on one of the corners. "They look just like the soldiers who lived in the Big House after you and Miz Eugenia left."

"We don't have to be afraid of them, Lizzie. The Yankees in Richmond treated us real good. And if they hadn't put out the fires, the whole city would have burned to the ground. They gave us food, too. I think we can trust them."

They eventually came to a dirtier part of town with run-down shacks and warehouses and the railroad station. "I believe that little brick building is the one Saul was talking about," Otis said. "Come on."

The front door stood open, and a young Yankee soldier sat be-hind a desk inside. Lizzie and Otis knew better than to go through the front door, so they walked around the building and knocked on the back door. A moment later, the same young man opened it.

"May I help you?"

Otis removed his hat and gave a little bow. "Good evening, sir. We're looking for the Yankee who's helping all the slaves. Is this the Freedmen's Bureau?" He spoke the title clumsily, as if unused to the strange words.

"Yes. You've come to the right place. I'm Alexander Chandler."

Lizzie stared as the man extended his hand for them to shake. When neither of them took it, he lowered it again. Mr. Chandler looked much too young to work at such an important government job. He was tall and skinny, and instead of a beard he had a lot of bushy whiskers on both sides of his face but not on his chin or below his nose.

He smiled, and his light blue eyes looked kind. "What can I do for you?"

"Well, sir. I'm Otis and this here is my wife, Lizzie, sir." She could tell that Otis was nervous. She was, too.

"Pleased to meet you both. Come on in. And listen, you don't need to use the back door. Come in the front way next time." He led them through an unlit room crowded with boxes and into the office in the front of the building. A big desk, piled with papers, filled most of the space. "You know, this is really *your* office, " he told them.

"*My* office?" Lizzie echoed. What in the world did she need with an office?

"Yes. It was set up to help freedmen, like you. Have a seat." There were two chairs right in front of his desk, but neither Lizzie nor Otis dared to sit in them.

"Excuse me, sir," Otis said, "but I never have sat down with a white man in my whole life. It ain't allowed."

"I understand." Mr. Chandler nodded and remained standing, as well. "Where are you folks staying?"

"We belong to one of the plantations just outside of town called White Oak."

"You mean you *used* to belong to them," Mr. Chandler said with a smile.

"Yes, sir. Well, we're still working and living there, even though everyone else is gone. My brother, Saul, said we should come talk to you. He says we need to hear what you have to say."

"I'm glad you did. We know there are a lot of freedmen like you who are wondering what to do and where to go, so this agency was set up by the government to help you get a new start. And since food is scarce down here, we're trying to make sure you're all fed, too."

"Thank you, sir," Otis said. "Miz Eugenia says she'll feed us if we keep on working for her, but the white folks don't have much to eat, either."

"You can take some supplies home with you tonight. Do you have children?"

"Yes, sir," Lizzie said. "Three of them." Mr. Chandler smiled again, and she thought he must be a contented person, deep inside. She couldn't get over the fact that he was talking to them as if they were as white as he was and they were all sitting around his parlor having a chat. Couldn't he see they were Negroes?

"How old are your children? School age?"

Lizzie had to think for a minute. She kept track of their ages by counting how many planting seasons had passed since they were born. "Jack is six, Rufus is eight, and my daughter, Roselle, is fifteen."

"The reason I ask is because we're opening a school here in the village next week for all the Negro children. The American Missionary Association sent us a teacher, and we're going to use the empty storage room in back as a classroom. Your children can start attending school on Monday. You may attend, too, if you'd like."

The news stunned Lizzie. "You mean . . . learn to read and write?"

"Yes," he said, laughing. "And all the other school subjects, too."

Lizzie covered her mouth, afraid she might burst into tears.

"I want my children to go to your school," Otis said. "It's the only way they'll ever have a better life than we do. Lizzie and I will gladly stay and work at our old plantation if it means my kids can go to your school."

"Wonderful. They will be welcome here. What is the current working arrangement where you're living? Are you tenant farmers? Sharecroppers?"

"I don't know what any of that means, sir. Massa Daniel only got back from the war a little while ago, and nothing's been planted yet except the kitchen garden. I'm the only field hand left, and besides, we don't have any mules for plowing."

"Miz Eugenia says we can keep on living in our cabin," Lizzie added, "if I keep on working for her up at the Big House."

"I see. Well, if you'd like, I can help you draw up a working contract with the plantation owners. You'll work the land for yourself, and when the crops are harvested, you'll give a portion of the profits to the owners. The rest will be yours. You earned it. Each individual case is different, but the contract also spells out the arrangements for food and lodging."

"Like I said, Massa Daniel just got back from the war," Otis said. "He ain't got hisself together yet."

"I understand. You can let me know whenever you think he's ready. And of course your children may start attending school right away."

Lizzie felt like she was in a dream, afraid she might wake up any minute. She wanted to sit down but didn't dare. "Can I ask you something?" she said.

"Sure, anything."

"Does being free mean that nobody can ever take Otis or my children away from me again?"

"That's right. Only the good Lord has a right to separate you from each other."

Lizzie covered her mouth again to hold back her tears. It was too much for her to take in. By the time they said good-bye and left for home with a sack of provisions, she felt dizzy. "Am I dreaming, Otis?" she asked.

"If you are, then I'm dreaming, too. Wait till I tell Roselle and the boys that they can learn to read and write! . . . But that means staying on with Miz Eugenia, you know."

"I know. I guess I can stand it there a while longer."

She trusted Otis. He was the only sure thing in her life, and the only source of love she'd ever known. With him, she felt like somebody. She slipped her hand into his, determined to do whatever he thought was best.

7

MAY 10, 1865

Josephine sat at the breakfast table listening to her family's litany of grievances. Their endless complaints were wearing holes in her threadbare soul like a constant scrubbing. Mother complained the most of all. "If only we had bacon to go with these eggs," she said with a sigh. "I can't even remember the last time we ate bacon, can you? It's bad enough the chickens barely squeeze out enough eggs for breakfast every morning, but it's hardly a proper meal without bacon or ham."

"I would dearly love some of Dolly's strawberry jam to go with these biscuits," Mary said. "They're so dry."

Josephine tried not to think about such luxuries as bacon and jam.

"I would like a cup of real coffee for a change," Daniel said before disappearing behind his week-old newspaper again. More than a week had passed since he'd returned home, and Josephine kept hoping that he would climb out of the doldrums and get the plantation running again. He could never take Daddy's place, of course, but it seemed to her that Daniel wasn't even trying.

"I can remember when our smokehouse was filled to the rafters," Mother continued. "And oh my, the hams! Remember how Dolly used to baste them with molasses and stud them with cloves? The fragrance was just heavenly."

Yes, Josephine remembered. But she didn't want to be reminded of how happy their life used to be before the Yankee invasion. They might never have bacon or strawberry jam again, so why not fold up those memories and store them away for good?

"Listen, Mama—" she began, but Mother interrupted.

"Remember all the guests we used to entertain at our dinner table? Your father knew such interesting people. They used to rave on and on about our smoked hams."

Josephine wanted to beg her to stop. God had told the survivors of Sodom and Gomorrah not to look back after they'd been rescued from death and destruction, and if Jo's family continued to gaze into the past, they were going to become stuck in place like pillars of salt, too. In order to get them to move forward with her, Josephine feared she would have to chip away at their rock-hard stubbornness one bucketful at a time and haul them toward a new future against their will.

"Those disgusting Yankees not only cleaned out our smokehouse," Mother continued, "but they ruined our dining room table. I cannot sit in this room without becoming furious at their boorishness."

"Then why eat in here at all?" Josephine asked. "Why can't we eat in the morning room like we did after Daddy died?"

"Because we must reclaim our home from our enemies," she insisted. "We will eat our meals in here the way every generation of Weatherlys have since Granddaddy built the house."

Daniel looked up from his paper again. "Father would have fought to the death before allowing a single one of those savages into our home."

"I know. But what could we do?" Mother asked. "We were three women, here all alone. We had to flee to Richmond."

Mother picked up the little silver servants' bell and gave it an impatient ring, as if expecting a host of slave girls to pour into the dining room to wait on them. But all the house slaves had quit except Lizzie and Roselle, and they not only had to serve the food but cook it, too. A minute passed, and when no one responded, Mother rang the bell a second time. Lizzie finally shuffled in, drying her hands on her apron. Mother gave an aggrieved sigh.

"Did you not hear me ringing? Shall I buy a louder bell?"

"I heard it, ma'am. But I was busy putting wood on the fire. Next time I'll be sure and drop what I'm doing right away."

Josephine held her breath. She saw the fury in her mother's lovely face—her pinched lips and arched brows, her glittering eyes. Slaves were supposed to reply, "Yes, ma'am" or "No, ma'am" or "I'm sorry, ma'am." They certainly weren't supposed to offer excuses for their failings. But Lizzie wasn't a slave anymore. It must have galled Mother to hold back the angry response she would have given in the past. "Where is Roselle?" she asked. "Is she too busy to wait on us, as well?" Each word pricked the quiet room, as sharp and pointed as a tack, but Lizzie seemed immune to the prodding.

"She's in school today, ma'am. My Roselle's going to that new school for colored children now. Both my boys are going there, too." Lizzie's gaze should have reached no higher than the floor when speaking to a white woman, but her chin lifted with pride.

A sliver of tension as thin as a knife blade slit the room. Mother made Lizzie wait before making her next move, the way Daddy sometimes paused to study each piece on the chessboard when playing the game. In a battle of wills, no one could beat Eugenia Weatherly. Yet if Lizzie quit like all the others had, the family would be helpless—and everyone in the dining room knew it. The balance of power had shifted ever so slightly from master to servant since the war ended, but to a proud woman like Josephine's mother, the world must have shifted on its axis.

"We're finished eating," Mother said at last. "You may clear the table now."

"Yes, ma'am."

Josephine found the interchange embarrassing. She was sick of all the pointless maneuvering as Mother tried in vain to run their household by the old rules. The war had changed all the rules. Life would never be the same, and the sooner Mother stopped looking back and got used to the way things were now, the better off they all would be. But as Lizzie silently made her way around the table gathering dishes, Mother tried to reassert her authority by daring to do what she had done all her life, speaking in front of Lizzie as if she were stone deaf or didn't understand English. "What in the world do Negro children need with a school?" she asked.

"It's a lot of foolishness, if you ask me," Daniel replied. "Someone needs to put a stop to it."

Josephine was desperate to cut the tightening strands of tension. "Do you have plans for today, Mother?" she asked.

"Yes, dear. We're going to go calling."

Josephine stifled a groan. Social calls were another useless relic of the antebellum years. There was so much work to be done if their household hoped to survive, work that Lizzie and her husband, Otis, couldn't possibly accomplish by themselves. But Mother refused to accept the truth, much less go out to the kitchen or the garden and tackle some of the work. "I would like both of you girls to get dressed and accompany me," she said.

Mary made a face. "I don't have anything to wear. It's embarrassing to be seen in the same old dress all the time."

"What difference does it make?" Josephine asked. "No one else has new clothes to wear, either."

"Besides, all of my gowns hang on me like old rags, without petticoats," Mary continued. "We're no better dressed than Lizzie and Roselle. Can't we please coax Ida May to come back and sew for us again?"

"We'll see," Mother murmured.

Josephine rolled her eyes at such an impossibility. When Ida May had been their slave, Mother used to find fault with the smallest things and make poor Ida May tear out all her tiny stitches and sew them over again. No, she could never be coaxed back. As a free seamstress, she could choose her own customers now.

"We used to have wardrobes full of clothes before the war,"

Mary said, gesturing as if the dining room had been filled with them, too. "Now we have nothing!"

"You're hardly naked," Josephine mumbled, but no one seemed to hear her. Jo had been seventeen before the war began, and Mary eleven, but now they had both outgrown their clothes. Ida May had done her best to remake their dresses to fit, but the worn fabric had been turned and resewn so many times during the past five years that the cloth was nearly threadbare.

"How will Jo and I ever find respectable husbands dressed in these rags?"

Josephine shook her head, holding back her thoughts. At least her sister would have a husband one day, since the boys Mary's age had been too young to fight in the war. Josephine was likely to die an old maid now that so many of the partners she waltzed with before the war had perished. With such a shortage, the men who had returned home could choose a bride who was much prettier than her.

"Now, remember," Mother said, "the quality of the lace on your gowns isn't what makes you beautiful. Beauty and charm come from within. A pretty smile and kind words can make up for a dozen petticoats and yards and yards of frills. A sweet demeanor and good manners are much more important than the clothes you're wearing."

Daniel lowered his newspaper again. "Did Lizzie say her boys weren't here?"

"They went to *school!*" Mary said. She rolled her eyes as if the idea were as absurd as teaching a hound dog to read. Josephine winced, watching Lizzie's reaction as she continued to make trips back and forth to clear the dishes. But the servant's face might have been carved from the same mahogany as the table.

"I suppose that means they'll be gone all day," Daniel said. The paper rustled as he folded it angrily and set it down in front of him. "What's the use of paying for our Negroes' upkeep if they aren't here to help when we need them?"

"We simply must find more workers," Mother said. "I saw Willy, our old carriage driver, the other day—just standing on the street corner in the village, watching the people go by, lazy as can be."

"That's why we need to pass a vagrancy law," Daniel said. "Negroes will have to prove they are gainfully employed or go to jail."

"But Willy has rheumatism," Josephine said. "You wouldn't send a crippled man to jail, would you? Why not ask him to come back and work for us?"

"Because it's not worth the bother of feeding him until we get more horses," Daniel replied. "I don't know how we're supposed to get anywhere without decent carriage horses. And how do they expect us to plow our fields without mules?"

Josephine listened to her brother's complaints and knew that what he missed the most was his leisurely life. Since Samuel had been destined to inherit the plantation, Daniel never had to worry about planting crops or overseeing slaves or mending the roof when it leaked. He had attended college in Williamsburg, free of responsibility as he'd sported with his friends. But Daniel would have responsibilities now—not the least of which was taking care of his mother and two sisters, making sure they had necessities like food and clothing and a roof that didn't leak. It seemed to Josephine that the war had changed him into an altogether different person. His lazy grin had disappeared behind the sandy mustache and beard he'd grown while he was away, and his eyes had changed from the color of sunny skies to a shade of gray that reminded her of thunderclouds.

Josephine wanted to stomp her foot and say, *Stop it, all of you! I am so tired of your complaints!* How did it help to look back at what they'd lost? Life wasn't easy for any of them, but the incessant whining made it worse.

But of course she didn't say anything. She had learned to remain silent during those terrible years, holding her thoughts and feelings and fears inside, never voicing them out loud. Mother had spoken for all of them during the war, standing up to anyone who threatened them in her lovely, imperious, self-assured way as if she were a commanding general. Josephine had tried so hard not to be seen or heard that now she could scarcely remember how to express herself. She was twenty-two years old, but one scolding look from Mother or a single warning glance from Daniel would make the words tangle together in her mind like a fine silver chain.

"Must I go calling with you today, Mother?" she asked.

"Of course, Josephine. You know Priscilla Blake is expecting us."

"But we just visited her last week," Mary said.

"I know. But Harrison is doing so poorly. I promised Priscilla we would stop by as often as we could and help lift his spirits."

"He barely spoke a word to us the last time," Mary said, "and he seemed just as miserable when we left as when we arrived."

Harrison Blake had turned out to be the bitterest complainer of all, a man whose anger over the Confederacy's losses knew no bounds. He was eight years older than Josephine and had been wounded in battle near Petersburg. The last time they visited him, he cursed the surgeons who had saved his life but not his leg, and let everyone know he wished he had died. Listening to him, Jo had longed to say, *Oh, go ahead and die, then, and put all of us out of your misery!* Nobody had been surprised when his fiancée finally broke their engagement. And nobody blamed her.

"Captain Blake is a war hero," Mother said, "and we will treat him with the respect he deserves. His mother is my dearest friend. You girls are coming with me and that's that."

"May I be excused, please?" Josephine asked. She was already on her feet before Mother replied, and quietly left the house through the back door before anyone seemed to notice. She had no idea where she was going at first, but as she hurried past the vegetable garden and the stables, she remembered the huge live oak tree where she used to find refuge as a girl. Her brothers had built a tree house in its branches, and Josephine had often climbed up the crude board ladder in a very unladylike way when she wanted to hide from everyone.

She hurried to the graceful old tree now, planning to climb up to her old refuge. But she was disappointed to find that most of the ladder boards had rotted away, leaving her no choice but to remain on the ground. She paced beneath the branches until her anger finally boiled over and everything she had longed to say came spewing out.

"I'm so sick of this!" she yelled at the top of her voice, causing a flock of birds to take flight. "Everyone is so angry and bitter all the time! When do we get to be happy again? Why can't we forget the past and start new lives? If I have to listen to one more complaint about what we've lost, I'll scream!"

Her face became flushed from the effort, but it felt so good to finally speak up that she drew a deep breath and continued. "They gripe about stupid things like bacon and petticoats and carriage drivers, and meanwhile the weeds are growing in the cotton fields, and there's nothing left to eat in the root cellar, and no work is getting done anywhere! But what does Mother want to do? Go visiting. Visiting! Harrison Blake is a bitter, crippled old grouch and I can't be nice to him for one more minute! I can't and I won't!"

Josephine finally ran out of steam. She sank down at the base of the tree, covered her face, and sobbed. During the war, she had been forced to be brave and courageous, even when she was terrified, and she had learned never to show fear or sorrow. "That's our way of fighting back," Mother had insisted. "We must never let the enemy think that we're weak." But Josephine was tired of pretending. She was tired of it all. And so she wept.

Suddenly a chunk of rotted board fell from above, barely missing her head, landing beside her. She looked up to see where the board had come from and saw a man's boot. Someone was up in the tree house!

Josephine leaped up to run home, but after only a few steps one of her worn-out shoes finally ripped apart and she tripped on the flapping sole. She stumbled and fell, landing painfully on her hands and knees.

"Are you hurt, miss?" She looked up at the man peering over the side of the tree house. He was young, about Daniel's age, with a narrow face and straight brown hair. He was clean-shaven except for the fuzzy whiskers he wore on the sides of his face like bushy sideburns. "You don't need to run away, miss. I don't mean you any harm, I assure you." He was a Yankee. She could tell by his accent. "I would gladly come down and help you," he continued, "but I think you'd feel safer if I stayed up here. Am I right?"

"Stay away from me!" she said in her fiercest voice. She struggled to her feet, brushing dirt from her palms and her skirt while keeping an eye on him. The man held up his hands in surrender.

"Yes, ma'am. I will, I will."

Had he been up there all this time, listening to her angry rant? The thought turned her fear into anger, and she planted her hands on her hips, glaring up at him. "Who are you, and what are you doing on our property?"

"My name is Alexander Chandler . . . and I'm very sorry if I've frightened you."

"It takes more than a treed Yankee to frighten me. Why were you eavesdropping on me?"

"I never intended to eavesdrop, miss . . . but I was here first, if you see what I mean. When you came along, I didn't want to startle you by calling out or suddenly climbing down. I figured you would leave eventually. But I sat still for such a long time that my foot fell asleep, and when I tried to move it . . . well, that's when that board fell off and startled you."

"You have no right to be up there in the first place!"

"I know, I know . . . and I'm sorry. I was out for an early morning walk, you see, and when I happened upon your tree house it reminded me so much of the one I had back home in Pennsylvania that I simply had to climb up. Then you came along and—"

"Don't you know that Yankees aren't welcome here? Go back to Pennsylvania! Haven't you done enough damage already?"

"Now, miss, I just heard you saying how tired you were of angry, bitter people and how you wanted to forget the past and be happy again. . . . Well, excuse me for saying so, but you sound pretty angry and bitter yourself right now."

"How dare you!"

"I'm only trying to help. That's the reason I came down here to work at the bureau in the first place—"

"What bureau?"

"I'm an agent with the Bureau of Refugees, Freedmen, and Abandoned Lands. I've been assigned to set up an office in Fairmont to help people rebuild their lives now that the war is over. Isn't that what you just said you wanted to do? Start over?"

"Are you the one who started the school for the Negro children?"

"Well, yes, but not all by myself." He had the nerve to grin, as if he was proud of his accomplishment. "I contacted the American Missionary Association and they sent us a teacher."

"You must know that you and all your Yankee friends aren't welcome here, and neither is your school."

"Oh yes, miss, I do know it. I've been running into a lot of brick walls, built out of the same things you're talking about—resentment and bitterness. The government started the Freedmen's Bureau to help sew up all the wounds so planters and former slaves can get on with their lives like you're wanting to do, but—"

"You Yankees have a lot of nerve! First you destroy everything and now you come back claiming you want to help us rebuild? The best way to help us is to go home and leave us alone."

"See? I hear bitterness again, and I was sure I just heard you say you were sick of it. How can you expect everyone else to change their ways and be happy again if you're not willing to change?"

"How dare you!"

He hung his head for a moment before looking at her again. "I do apologize. I've been told that I have a very bad habit of speaking my mind when I should keep quiet. I'm sorry. I didn't mean to offend you."

"I'm leaving now. Kindly get out of our tree and off our property."

"I will, I will. But if I may be so bold . . . I would like to offer a word of advice, if I may, for your situation."

"My situation?"

"Yes. You mentioned that you wanted to be happy again, and I have found that one of the keys to lasting happiness is gratitude. When I take the time to be grateful for all the little things around me like blue skies and green grass and . . . and this fine tree house, then pretty soon all those little joys add up and I'm happy."

Josephine was about to say, *How dare you!* but then realized she had said it twice before. The best way to end this unwelcome conversation was to walk away. "Good-bye, Mr. . . ." She had already forgotten his name.

"Chandler. Alexander Chandler. And good day to you, too, miss. I hope the next time we meet, it will be under happier circumstances."

"I hope I never see you again."

She turned toward the house, wishing she could stride away with her head held high and her pride intact, but she had to pick her way carefully, watching her footing because of her ruined shoe. The sound of his Yankee accent, the fact of him here on her family's land, infuriated her. But what angered Josephine the most was that he was right. She was as bitter and angry as everyone else.

8

Eugenia had finished eating her insubstantial breakfast half an hour ago, but she sat alone at the dining room table, gazing into space, trying to summon the energy to move. She shouldn't feel this weary so early in the day, but lately she felt tired all the time. In the old days before the war, Ida May or Cissy or one of Eugenia's other house slaves would have followed her upstairs to her bedroom to help her lace up her corset and slip her petticoats and hoop skirts over her head, and pin up her hair. But Ida May and Cissy were gone now, and so were the petticoats. All of the servants were gone except for Lizzie, and she was nothing but a field hand who had somehow connived her way up from the cotton fields and into the manor house. Until the other slaves returned and things could get back to normal, Eugenia had to do everything herself. Surely the Negroes would come to their senses soon, wouldn't they? Philip had always treated them fairly. Couldn't they see they'd had a decent life here as part of her household?

Daniel said that dozens of slaves were camped out in the woods, doing nothing at all. The thought made her shudder. That's why she kept her pistol close at all times. If only Daniel would round them up and convince them to go back to work. There was so much work to be done. Eugenia had seen the destruction on the way home from Richmond—bridges and rail lines destroyed, fences gone, buildings burned. But even more damage was now being done through neglect; all of that once-beautiful plantation land, including her own, was falling into weedy ruin. No one seemed to know where to begin, but Eugenia was determined to try.

She sighed and went upstairs to change out of her dressing gown into a proper dress. It would be black, of course. She still wore mourning for Philip and Samuel. Even when her official days of mourning came to an end, she would have nothing else to wear except black, nor could she purchase fabric for new dresses with Richmond in ruins and her money nearly gone. Besides, wearing black gave Eugenia a sense of sisterhood with all the other black-garbed women. They understood how it felt to wake up to grief day after day or to walk into a room expecting to see their loved one dozing in his favorite chair beside the hearth and feel the jolt, like a missed heartbeat, when they remembered he was gone.

She finished buttoning her bodice and skirt, then sat down at her dressing table to fix her hair. Her reflection in the mirror spoke the unwelcome truth that at age fifty her beauty was fading. Her face was much too thin, her cheeks colorless, and the silver strands in her coal black hair were becoming more and more noticeable. When Eugenia had been Mary's age, she'd been so beautiful that suitors from all over the county had fought for her hand. And before she'd been Josephine's age, she'd already married the handsomest one with the most prosperous plantation, the loveliest home. She had chosen well.

Dear, dear Philip. Eugenia had seen his love for her every time he gazed at her. He had worshiped her, indulged her. They'd had a good marriage, blessed with two sons and two daughters. How she missed him. She picked up her handkerchief and quickly blotted her tears. It was too early in the day to give in to grief. She had too much to do. Tears would have to wait until nighttime.

Eugenia forced herself to keep rolling forward like a carriage on a muddy road, knowing that if she stopped being in charge and issuing orders and commanding her household for even a moment, she would sink into hopeless muck. She let anger propel her like a coachman's whip, providing a reason to get up in the morning, to get dressed, to keep moving. She would not let the Yankees defeat her. She would win back everything they had taken from her. Except for Philip and Samuel, of course. God knew she could never have them back.

But someday, if she remained strong enough and worked hard enough, life would return to normal. Her daughters would be taken care of, with fine homes and good husbands of their own. And Daniel would figure out how to make their land prosper again. He might be young and spoiled, but he had inherited many of his father's fine qualities such as tenacity and courage. He would get their work force of slaves back—although the Negroes would have to be *hired* now. No one was allowed to *own* them anymore. Josephine continually nagged her, reminding her that she must speak to Negroes differently now, and treat them differently, too. But how could she be expected to change a lifetime of habits overnight? Eugenia had been commanding slaves since she was a young girl with her mammy, Ruby.

Eugenia thought of Lizzie, wishing Ida May had decided to stay instead of her. Eugenia didn't like the way that girl talked to her or looked at her with bold eyes. But for now, she had no choice. Lizzie was the only slave left. The others had all refused to return to work. Refused! Who could imagine such a thing? After everything Eugenia had done for them over the years.

But she didn't have time to indulge in self-pity this morning. Eugenia pulled her hair back to showcase her dramatic widow's peak and pinned it up in a graceful twist at the nape of her neck. She was ready. Now she must make sure her girls were getting ready. She strode down the hall to their bedroom and found Mary all alone, sitting at her vanity table, brushing her hair. She looked exactly like Eugenia had at age sixteen, with her lustrous black hair and delicate heart-shaped face. And though Mary had changed into her best frock, it broke Eugenia's heart to see her dressed so shabbily. She was such a beautiful girl. She should be wearing taffeta and silk, stiff with petticoats and trimmed with ribbons and lace.

Eugenia forced a smile. "Are you almost ready?"

"Yes, Mama."

"Where is Josephine?" Mary lifted her shoulders in a careless shrug. "Please do not use that gesture, Mary Louise Weatherly. Shrugging your shoulders is a sign of laziness that I will not tolerate in a young lady of your stature. It's something a common person would do in place of a proper reply."

"I'm sorry, Mama. But I don't know where Jo is. She left the house right after breakfast and hasn't returned."

Eugenia went to the window and parted the curtain to peer out, hoping Jo hadn't gone outside to work in the kitchen garden again. But the only figure on the scarred patch of earth was the raggedy scarecrow Lizzie had made to frighten away the crows. Eugenia let the curtain fall closed and turned back to the room. "She should be getting ready. She knows we need to leave soon. Here, let me help you with your hair." Her daughter's wavy black hair, the same color and texture as her own, moved like silk beneath Eugenia's fingers as she brushed it. She was fastening Mary's hairnet in place when Josephine burst into the room, sweaty and red-faced.

"Josephine! What in the world . . . ? Look at you! You're perspiring like a field slave."

"I went for a walk. It's quite warm outside." She sounded breathless, as if she had run all the way home instead of walking demurely.

"You went out *alone*? You know better than that. Kindly get ready. It's late. I thought I heard Otis bringing the carriage around."

"I can't go with you. My shoe has torn apart beyond repair. Look." She held it up for Eugenia to see. The sole dangled from the shoe like an open mouth.

"You shouldn't have been running. Haven't I taught you to walk with grace and poise, Josephine?"

"Yes . . . but I've been wearing these shoes for more than five years. Today they simply gave out."

"I'll lend you a pair of mine until they can be mended. But you are still coming with us." Josephine's shoulders sagged forward as if she carried a bale of hay on her back. "Stand up straight, please," Eugenia said. "You'll have to dress quickly. Mary can help you with your hair."

Eugenia returned to her bedroom to fetch a pair of shoes, wondering where she had gone wrong with Josephine. She would always be a plain girl, to be sure, even dressed in silk and lace. She had limp brown hair and a broad face, both characteristic of Philip's side of the family. Josephine had grown from a child to a woman during the war, at a time when day-to-day survival had been more urgent than developing womanly charms. Along the way, she had acquired several bad habits that needed to be changed, such as slouching instead of standing tall, and wearing a frown instead of a smile. She was also much too timid, hesitant to take part in the simplest of conversations. And she liked to wander off alone, as she had this morning. Worst of all, Josephine had no idea at all how to behave around young men, even though the competition for husbands would be fierce. She could practice with Harrison Blake today.

"Here. Try on these shoes, Josephine," she said as she swept back into the girls' room with a pair of her own. Jo grimaced as she tried to force one of the shoes onto her foot.

"They're too small."

"Well, I'm sorry but they will have to do. And please do not make that face, dear. It is most unbecoming."

They were ready at last, but Eugenia's weariness seemed to have settled deeper into her bones. She led the way down the sweeping staircase and found Daniel waiting for them out front with the carriage. He looked tired and defeated, as if he had arrived home from the war only a moment ago. Eugenia wished she knew how to change him back into the happy, carefree young man he once had been. It would take time, she told herself. Give him time.

"I'm sorry, but I can't come with you today," he said as he helped Eugenia into the carriage. "There is too much work to be done."

Eugenia caressed his shoulder. "I understand, dear." But she wondered what, exactly, Daniel planned to do. He spent hours in Philip's office or out in the stables but nothing ever changed. They still had no bacon for breakfast, and her stomach continued to rumble in hunger.

"Listen, Daniel. Please talk to the other planters when you get a chance and find out where we can purchase some hogs. Aren't they born this time of the year, during the spring?"

"I suppose so. What will I use for money?"

"Leave that to me, dear." There must be something left among her hidden valuables, something she could trade. "I intend to have bacon in our smokehouse again," she said. "We may have to wait for the animals to fatten up, but by this time next year we'll be eating ham for Easter dinner like always."

"I'll see what I can do, Mother." Daniel trudged up the steps into the house as Otis flicked the reins. They were finally on their way.

Eugenia paid calls to two neighboring plantations first, saving her visit with Priscilla Blake for last. She was surprised when neither Priscilla nor her servant came out to greet them. Eugenia knocked, then opened the door to her friend's house and sailed inside with her daughters trailing behind her like ducklings. Priscilla must be home. With no transportation she couldn't have gone anywhere.

"Priscilla?" she called. "It's me, Eugenia." The front parlor looked dingy with the curtains drawn closed. The dining room table and sideboard were dusty and unpolished. Eugenia continued down the hall and finally found her friend in the basement kitchen, of all places, washing her own dishes.

"Priscilla? For goodness' sake, what are you doing? Where is your servant girl?"

"She quit several days ago. Harrison threw a plate at her and . . . and she quit like all the others."

Eugenia folded her friend in an embrace. "You poor dear. I'll talk to our Lizzie. Maybe she knows someone who can help you."

Priscilla pulled away, shaking her head. "No, don't." She glanced at Eugenia's daughters and dropped her voice to a whisper. "We . . . we can no longer afford to pay anyone." She leaned against Eugenia as her tears flowed.

Eugenia motioned for her girls to leave the kitchen. "Go read to Harrison now," she told them, shielding her friend from further shame. How horrible it must be to suffer such distress, much less have others witness your breakdown. She held Priscilla tightly, rocking her in her arms. "Shh . . . shh . . . Everything will work out. You'll see."

"No, it won't. I can't go on any longer, Eugenia. I'm not as strong as you are. I don't know what to do anymore."

Eugenia pulled a handkerchief from her sleeve and handed it to her. "First of all, let's leave this mess and go sit in your parlor." She wrapped her arm around Priscilla and guided her upstairs to the front room, feeling a shiver of dread when she noticed how frail Priscilla's body felt beneath her well-worn dress.

"There, isn't this much better?" Eugenia asked after opening the drapes and sitting down beside her on the sofa. Priscilla dried her eyes with the handkerchief.

"I think Harrison is dying."

"Dying? Did Dr. Hunter tell you that? What's wrong with him?"

"I don't know . . . nothing that anyone can see. But he's lost his will to live and I don't know how to help him."

"Daniel seems very discouraged, too. It's only natural after everything they've been through. But our boys are young. They'll—"

"I can't go on, Eugenia. If Harrison dies, I'll have to sell this place."

"Don't talk that way," she said, gripping Priscilla's hands in her own. "He isn't going to die, and you cannot sell your land. It's all we have. Besides, Daniel says the Yankees are the only ones who can afford to purchase property these days, and they'll take advantage of you, cheating you out of what your land is really worth."

Priscilla sat with her head lowered, gazing down at their clasped hands. "What good is land?" she asked. "Harrison will never be able to oversee the planting himself. And all our slaves are gone. How will we live if we don't plant crops? I don't know what else to do except sell everything and move to Baltimore to live with my sister." She finally looked up at Eugenia. "She offered to help

80

me take care of Harrison. I just can't do it by myself now that the engagement has been called off and Emma Welch has left."

Eugenia felt a stab of anger, not toward Priscilla or Emma but at the prospect of yet another defeat. Priscilla Blake was her dearest friend, and if she gave up and moved away it would be another loss in Eugenia's life, another victory for the Yankees. She would not let them take her friend. Or her land. Or Harrison.

"Listen now. You need help, Priscilla. Will you accept help from me until Harrison is back on his feet and—" She stopped, appalled by her poor choice of words. Harrison would never be back on his feet. "Forgive me, dear. I meant to say, until things can return to normal." But Priscilla seemed too distraught to notice the error.

"I don't believe things ever will be normal. Not after all we've lost."

"Nonsense. Of course they will. It's only a matter of time. When the slaves get hungry enough, they'll come to their senses and go back to work. Daniel says they might pass a law that Negroes must prove they are gainfully employed or be arrested as vagrants. The Yankee soldiers will soon be gone. I understand that many of them have left already. We *will* recover what we've lost, Priscilla."

"Except for our loved ones. Nothing will ever bring them back."

"I know," Eugenia murmured. "I know." She pulled Priscilla into her arms again to hide her own tears, not daring to cry.

"I wish this war had never happened," Priscilla wept. "I wish we could have our life back the same as it was."

"We will. But you must stay strong and not give up."

They were still clinging tightly to each other when Eugenia heard a carriage pull to a stop out front. "Are you expecting someone?" she asked.

"It's probably Dr. Hunter. He stops by to see Harrison when he is out this way."

"Dry your eyes, dear, and be strong. I'll let him in." Eugenia composed herself as she made her way to the door, smoothing her skirt and tucking her hair into place. She raised her chin and smiled pleasantly as she opened the door to greet the doctor. "Good afternoon, Dr. Hunter. How are you?"

"Mrs. Weatherly!" He snatched off his hat and gave a respectful bow. "How nice to see you."

"Haven't I scolded you before for not calling me Eugenia?" she said with a flirtatious smile.

"Yes . . . thank you. You look wonderful, Eugenia." He couldn't seem to move from the doorstep, gazing at her with admiration in his eyes—and perhaps longing. The doctor had been a friend of Philip's before the war, stopping by occasionally to play chess with him and sip bourbon. *"I believe David Hunter comes here to see you, not me,"* Philip used to tease her. *"He never fails to tell me how beautiful you are, and what a lucky man I am."*

The doctor cleared his throat. He seemed embarrassed, as if he'd read Eugenia's thoughts. "I . . . um, I haven't had a chance to talk to you since the war ended, but I wanted to tell you how sorry I was to hear about Philip and Samuel."

"Thank you. And I understand that you lost your wife, as well?"

He nodded solemnly. "I sent her to stay with her mother while I was away, thinking she would be better off in Savannah, but she and her mother both died of a fever."

"I'm so sorry. Please come in, David. I know Priscilla is eager to talk with you about Harrison."

"Yes, of course. I'll go see my patient first, if you don't mind." He disappeared into Harrison's bedroom on the first floor, and a moment later Josephine and Mary filed out to give him privacy. The girls looked as relieved as escaped prisoners.

"I'm being a terrible hostess, aren't I?" Priscilla said. "Would you ladies like some tea?"

"No, don't fuss," Eugenia said. "We're fine, aren't we girls?" Mary nodded and sat down with them in the parlor to chat, and it did seem to buoy Priscilla's spirits to engage in pleasant conversation for a while. Josephine disappeared as usual. Eugenia heard the soft clatter of plates and cups down in the kitchen and guessed that her daughter was washing the dishes. Why in the world did that girl insist on playing the role of a servant?

Fifteen minutes later, the doctor emerged from Harrison's bedroom with a worried expression. "May I have a word with you, Mrs. Blake?"

Eugenia stood. "We should be on our way," she said, but Priscilla gripped her hand.

"No, wait! Please! I don't want you to leave. If it's bad news, I-I need you . . ."

"Of course, dear. Mary, kindly wait outside by our carriage. I'll be along in just a moment."

"How is he?" Priscilla asked when Mary was gone. Tears filled her eyes before Dr. Hunter even had a chance to reply.

"There is nothing physically wrong with him, Mrs. Blake. His wound has fully healed. I know that he's been complaining of phantom pain in his missing leg, but that's very common."

"He barely eats, and he's growing weaker every day. He ended his engagement with Emma Welch and now he has driven all our servants away."

"Yes, he told me about Miss Welch."

"He keeps saying that he wants to die, and I'm so afraid he will do something . . . that I'll find him . . ."

The doctor rested his hand on her shoulder. "I don't know of any cure for despair. I'm so sorry. But I promise to stop in to visit him more often, if you'd like. And I'll see about getting some government rations for both of you. They are distributing them in the village at the Freedmen's Bureau. Maybe a change of diet will help."

"I would appreciate that very much. Thank you for coming, Doctor."

Eugenia walked with him to the front door. He paused on the doorstep and said, "It was wonderful to see you again, Eugenia. You look as lovely as always."

"Thank you, David." His admiration lifted her spirits, even if he wasn't a member of her social class. She had been relieved to see that his house in town had survived the war, but she didn't want to imagine what it must look like on the inside with no wife to attend to it. Dr. Hunter and his wife had never owned slaves.

When he was gone, Eugenia went back inside and found Josephine downstairs in the kitchen, which now looked clean and tidy. Her feet were bare, the ill-fitting shoes cast aside. Eugenia shook her head, holding back a rebuke. "We're leaving in a few minutes, Josephine. Go out and wait in the carriage with your sister."

"Won't you stay and visit a little longer?" Priscilla begged as Eugenia prepared to leave. "You can't imagine how lonely it is here all day. At least you have your daughters for company."

"We'll come again soon, I promise." But as Eugenia hugged her friend good-bye, an idea began to take shape in her mind. She released Priscilla, taking her hands in her own. "Listen, dear. How would it be if Josephine moved in with you for a while? She could help you with Harrison, and she would be good company for you, too. What do you say?"

"Oh, but I couldn't—"

"Nonsense. Of course you can. We'll let Jo come home with me today and pack a few things, and then we'll drive her back here on Sunday after church. No, don't argue with me, dear. My mind is made up. We'll see you Sunday." She strode out to the waiting carriage before Priscilla could protest.

Eugenia waited until the horse was plodding down the long lane to their house before telling her daughter about her decision. "Listen, Josephine. Priscilla confessed to me today, in strictest confidence, that if she doesn't get help soon, she will have to sell her plantation and move away. Coping with Harrison's illness has been extremely difficult for her, and I've come to realize that she isn't as strong as we are. She needs our help, so I have offered her your assistance."

"What! My assistance? Why me?"

Eugenia gazed into the woods on the edge of their property, not meeting her daughter's gaze. "Because you are a very kind, capable young woman."

"But I don't want to take care of Harrison! He's so bitter and hateful! Mary can tell you if you don't believe me, but every minute in that room with him is horrible! I don't mind helping Mrs. Blake, but please don't make me take care of him. Please, Mother."

"I've already promised Priscilla that you would. It'll only be for a short time, until their situation improves. I told her you'll move there on Sunday, right after church."

Josephine sagged forward in despair. Eugenia resisted the urge to remind her about her posture and instead laid her hand over her daughter's. "Harrison and his mother have no one else, Josephine. I know they would gladly help us if the tables were turned and our Daniel was the one who'd lost his leg."

Josephine didn't reply, but a tear rolled off her chin and dropped onto Eugenia's hand. "No tears, darling," she said. "Be strong now. We must be strong."

9

As soon as the white folks left to go calling, Lizzie untied her apron and went outside to sit in the sun on the back stoop. She wasn't nobody's slave, and she didn't have to work like one. Besides, she couldn't do the work of five house slaves all by herself, no matter what Miz Eugenia thought.

The moment she sat her weary body down, the raggedy clump of backyard chickens came running to see if she was tossing them some crumbs, poking and jostling each other like naughty boys. The hens were so scraggly-looking that Lizzie wouldn't have much plucking to do when it came time to cook one of them. But as long as they gave up an egg or two every day, they were safe from the stewpot. They must have known the truth because they kept on scratching and laying, bartering eggs for their lives.

Miz Eugenia was always whining for more eggs. Lizzie couldn't make her understand that she needed to let the hens roost a while. Once the baby chicks hatched out and grew up, there'd be plenty more eggs to eat. "You gotta do without for now," she'd told Miz Eugenia, "so it'll be better later on." But the missus wasn't listening.

Lizzie flapped her apron to shoo the little flock away. "Go on. Quit pestering me. I ain't got nothing for you." They fluttered off, ruffled and clucking, then went back to pecking for insects in the dirt. Lizzie closed her eyes, letting the sun warm her face. The chickens' mindless murmuring sounded just like Miz Eugenia and her friends when they used to sit in the front parlor talking about the weather and whatnot. Every now and then one of them ladies would let out a cackle or a squawk and get all the others doing it, too, just like them chickens. The thought made her smile.

When she opened her eyes again, she saw Otis striding toward her from the stables. He waved at her and broke into a grin. "Look at you—sitting in the sun like a free woman."

Lizzie couldn't help smiling back. "That's because I am a free woman."

He came to a halt in front of her, standing so tall and strong-shouldered that he blocked out the sun. "Them women gone for now?"

"Yes, but you better watch out because Massa Daniel ain't with them. He's sure to come looking for you before long."

"I know exactly where he is," Otis said, laughing. "He sent me up here to fetch him a drink of water."

"Now why's that so funny? How can being his errand boy make you laugh?"

"Because the joke's on him. He thinks I'm his errand boy, toting his water, but he's still down there working in the stables, and I'm taking a break." Otis sat down on the stoop beside her. "And I'm stealing a kiss from the prettiest gal in the county, too." He tipped her face toward his and kissed her. Lizzie loved his familiar scent of earth and sweat. She would like nothing better than to sit here and kiss him all day, but she pulled away.

"You better stop that now," she said, swatting him with her apron strings. "Massa Daniel might be watching, you know. I'll go get you something to carry that water." She stood and went into the kitchen to look for two jugs. Massa Daniel would no sooner share a jug of water with a Negro than he would drink from the pig trough. Otis followed her inside and watched as she looked around the disheveled kitchen.

"See this mess I gotta clean up?" she said. "I thought being free was supposed to be better, but it ain't. Now I'm the cook and the scrub maid and the chambermaid and the housekeeper all rolled into one. Miz Eugenia acts like there's still five of us—telling me to do one thing, then before I get a chance to do it, she's hollering for me to do something else. I can't do it all."

"I know, Lizzie-girl. I know. You'd think all the troubles those white folks had would've made their hearts softer, not harder."

Lizzie turned to look at her Otis, standing there so patiently, not a line of worry on his face. She moved into his arms, resting her head on his shoulder. His shirt was damp with sweat. "Listen to me, complaining all the time. I'm as bad as the missus. How come you ain't never complaining, Otis? They're trying to make you do the work of fifty slaves."

"It won't be for much longer. Massa Daniel's gonna choke on that pride of his one of these days, and he'll have to start hiring more help."

"Some days I'd like to walk on out of here and never come back. There must be a better place for us than here."

"Now, you know we can't quit. As long as our kids have a chance to go to school, we gotta stay here. We'll get our own place someday, I promise you, Lizzie-girl. Then nobody's gonna tell us what to do."

Lizzie gave him a squeeze, then released him. She carried the two jugs she'd found out to the pump, primed it using water from the bucket, then pumped the handle until both containers and the bucket were full. "Sometimes, working here for Missy and her girls, it's like the war never happened and nothing's changed. I feel like I'm still a slave and always will be one."

"It's in here," Otis said, pointing to his heart. "Here's where we know we're free. Don't matter what nobody says. When the white folks start nagging at you, remember they're just words, Lizzie. Don't hang on to them. Throw them out the back door like a bucket of slops."

"Is that what you do when Massa Daniel starts treating you bad?"

"Yes, ma'am, that's exactly what I do." He bent to pick up the jugs and kissed her neck. "See you tonight, Lizzie-girl."

She watched him walk away, wondering why such a gentle, easygoing man would pick a fearful, worrying gal like her for his wife. He turned around just before he reached the stables and smiled at her as if he knew she would be watching him. She lifted her hand and waved, her love for him swelling inside her until she thought she just might burst from it. She hated to see him treated like a slave every day, overworked and looked down on by Massa Daniel. Otis was just as good as any white man—better, even. But he was right. If they stayed a little while longer and kept their kids in school, and if they worked hard and saved their money, they could have their own place someday, just like the Yankee man in town said.

Lizzie thought of the chickens again and how Miz Eugenia would be better off if she didn't gobble down all the eggs every morning. That's what Otis was trying to tell Lizzie: *You gotta do without for now so it'll be better later on.* She sighed and went back into the house to work.

It was nice to have the house all to herself while Miz Eugenia went calling. But the missus wasn't home half an hour before she started ringing her little bell to call for Lizzie. Why couldn't that woman walk on down the hall and see for herself how busy she was instead of interrupting her all the time? Lizzie dried her hands on her apron and followed the jangling noise to the front hall.

"Yes, Miz Eugenia?"

"Look here," she said, pointing to the hall table. "My daughters and I went calling today, and our hats and gloves still haven't been carried upstairs and put away."

"I ain't had time, ma'am." If she were a little braver, she would ask why Miz Eugenia and those two girls couldn't carry them upstairs themselves.

"As I've explained before, you need to wrap the hats in tissue paper and put them in their proper hatboxes—and be careful not to crush any of the flowers or feathers. Then check the gloves to see if they need to be washed and dried and mended."

And if there was one tiny little spot on one of the gloves or a single loose feather on her ridiculous hat, Lizzie would hear about it. She waited, wondering if there was more.

"A friend of mine seems to be without a servant at the moment," the missus finally said. "Surely you must know of someone who could work for her, don't you?"

Lizzie bit her lip pretending she was thinking things over, but she was really stomping down on an angry reply. Did Miz Eugenia think slaves had a whole flock of friends they ran around visiting all the time? Did she think colored folks had time to waste making social calls the way white folks did? Lizzie fought to keep her face expressionless, to answer quietly.

"No, ma'am. I don't know of nobody."

"Would you ask around for me, please? When you see the others?"

"What *others*?" The words spurted out before Lizzie could stop them. "I never see anybody, Miz Eugenia, because I'm working here for you all day." She was sorry the moment she'd spoken, but the missus knew exactly how to yank her handle, just like the pump outside, until all of Lizzie's anger came gushing to the surface.

Miz Eugenia remained calm, as if it was beneath her to argue back. She would probably make Lizzie pay for her outburst some other way. "Well, kindly keep my friend in mind if you do hear of someone who's looking for work. My daughter Josephine will be moving there at the end of the week to help out."

Lizzie didn't reply. Instead, she turned to leave without waiting to be excused. She knew better. And she also knew it would make Miz Eugenia real mad—maybe even as mad as Lizzie felt right now.

"Lizzie."

She halted, then slowly turned to face her without speaking. They were like two riled dogs, circling each other, hackles raised, neither one daring to pounce first or back down.

"Did you make our beds and tidy the bedrooms?" Miz Eugenia asked.

"I ain't had a chance, ma'am." If she was going to ask what Lizzie had been doing all morning, she was ready with a list—and everything on it was more important than making beds for two spoiled young gals who could do it themselves, for once.

"Well, did you at least empty the upstairs chamber pots? Don't let them wait too late in the day, please. The weather is getting warm, you know."

"Yes, ma'am." It didn't matter how hot the weather got, emptying those pots was a job Lizzie hated. A slave's job.

"You need to develop a routine, Lizzie, and do the most important tasks first."

"Yes, ma'am." She backed out of the room, ready to explode. *The most important tasks first?* Would Missus rather have the beds made or food on the table?

Lizzie returned to the kitchen to mix up a batch of bread, knowing she was only punishing herself if she didn't put the hats away or if she allowed the chamber pots to fester. But punching and kneading the dough helped use up her anger. After putting it near the fire to rise, she finally went upstairs to do her chores.

Later that afternoon, Lizzie went outside to hoe weeds in the kitchen garden, using it as an excuse to keep an eye out for her kids who would be walking home from school soon. She worried half to death over them, knowing what a long walk it was into the village and how dangerous it was for them to be coming down that long road all alone. There were plenty of white folks who didn't like to see little Negro boys anywhere but on Slave Row. And it was even more dangerous for her daughter, Roselle, who was fifteen and as pretty as a peach tree in bloom.

Lizzie halted in surprise when she reached the garden. There was Missy Josephine already at work with a big straw hat on her head to keep her white skin from turning pink. They both knew how mad it would make Miz Eugenia when she caught her doing slaves' work, but Missy Jo didn't seem to care. "Can I ask you something, Missy Josephine?" Lizzie asked.

"Of course."

"Why do you want to work out here in the garden like a slave? You know it's only gonna upset Miz Eugenia."

"Because I like working in the garden. I feel like I'm accomplishing something useful. Besides, Mother is taking a nap."

Lizzie set to work alongside her, glancing up every minute or two, watching for her children—and the missus. She attacked the weeds with the same fury she'd used on the bread dough that morning, using up all her worry and fear, until she finally saw Jack and Rufus plodding up the lane, pitching stones into the weeds and stirring up the dust with their bare feet.

The boys were alone.

Lizzie felt the wind rush out of her as if someone had kicked her in the stomach when she saw that Roselle wasn't with them. She dropped the hoe and hurried out to the road to meet them, leaving the garden gate swinging and Missy Jo looking puzzled.

"Where's your sister?"

Young Rufus looked up at her with the same calm expression his daddy always wore. "Roselle left school at lunchtime, Mama, and never did come back." The boot landed in Lizzie's stomach a second time.

"What? Where'd she go? She with anyone?"

"I don't know where she went, but Lula and Corabelle never did come back, neither."

There was nothing Lizzie could do but wait. And worry. She'd been counting on Roselle to help her fix supper, and now she'd have to cook and serve it all by herself. Where could Roselle be? What if something terrible happened to her? Should Otis go look for her?

By the time Roselle finally wandered home, supper was boiling and so was Lizzie's temper. "Where you been? Why ain't you in school this afternoon like you're supposed to be?"

Roselle glanced at her brothers, who were busy filling the woodbox. "Me and my friends just started walking around Fairmont for a while, and it felt so nice to be free, with no one telling us what to do . . . I guess we just forgot to go back to school."

"It ain't safe to walk all around on your own!" Lizzie shouted. "Don't you know what could happen?" She wasn't anywhere near finished with her scolding, but the bell jingled in the white folks' dining room, interrupting her. Lizzie closed her eyes and exhaled to get ahold of herself, then faced her daughter. "I got to go see what the missus wants. You finish putting their food on serving plates, then start washing them frying pans. We'll talk about this when your papa gets here." For once, Roselle had the good sense to do what she was told.

Lizzie hurried into the dining room, and there they all sat with their pretty dishes and their white tablecloth and fancy napkins, just like the old days. There wasn't anything to eat but slave food and hardly enough of that, but Miz Eugenia still wanted it served up on a silver platter like it was Christmas dinner.

"Bring us a pitcher of water, please," she said.

"Yes, ma'am."

Lizzie returned to the kitchen and told Roselle to find a pitcher, then sent Rufus and Jack out to pump water. Otis arrived while Lizzie was running back and forth from the kitchen to the dining room, and she saw him washing up outside. When the white folks were all fed, Lizzie was finally able to sit down at the kitchen table with her own family, even though she'd have to jump right back up again if that bell started ringing.

The moment Otis finished blessing the food, Lizzie turned to him. "You want to know what Roselle did today? She and her friends took off after lunch and didn't go back to school." She turned to her daughter, shaking her finger at her. "Now, you better start telling us why. And you better have a real good reason, too."

Otis held up his hand to calm Lizzie. He had warned her before that bossing and yelling didn't help matters. It only made Roselle boil up just like Lizzie did when Miz Eugenia started bossing and yelling. Before Roselle had a chance to reply, Otis began speaking quietly to her.

"You know the difference between being a slave and being free, Roselle honey? The difference is knowing how to read and write. If you learn them things, you can be whatever you want to be someday. Nobody will ever own you. But if you stay ignorant, you'll always be a slave."

"Besides," Lizzie added, "you should of heard them white folks laughing and making fun of you for going to school. They're thinking you'll never learn anything. You gonna prove them right?"

"Trust your mama and me, Roselle. We want you to have all the things we never did."

Roselle finally looked up from her plate. "I know you ain't my papa," she told Otis. "I remember when it was just Mama and me, before you came along."

Lizzie bolted to her feet, ready to reach across the table and slap her. Why did Roselle have to bring that up in front of her brothers and hurt Otis's feelings? "He's your papa now, and you're gonna do what he says!"

Otis held up his hand again. "Not having my blood doesn't stop me from loving you like you're my own, Roselle. Now, kindly tell your mama and me what was more important than going to school today."

Roselle shrugged. "Nothing . . . I just wanted to get away where nobody's telling me what to do. Lulu and Corabelle and me didn't go nowhere. We just walked around town trying to decide what we'd like to do now that we're free. Lulu says that my skin is light enough that I could 'pass.' She says if I went where no one knows me, I could marry a rich white man."

Lizzie's skin prickled. "Is that all you want for your life? Marry a white man?"

"Why not? It's better than this."

"That's all that those useless white girls in there want, too," Lizzie said, gesturing to the dining room. "So, tell me—after you marry this rich man, then what? You gonna sit around all day like they do, cackling like chickens?"

"It's better than emptying slops. Besides, what else is there?"

Lizzie didn't know. She had only been free to dream of a different life for a short time. But as she looked at Otis and her sons, seated around the table together, she suddenly knew exactly what she wanted. "Listen to me, Roselle. There ain't no shame in doing good, honest work. But the 'something better' is doing it in my own house, for my own husband and family. It's being able to look out at that garden and that flock of chickens and know they're mine. All mine. It's knowing we'll get the cream *and* the milk, not what's left over when the butter's all churned. Best of all, it's building something together with a good, decent man, a man you really love, not some pasty-faced white man you married because he's rich."

Otis reached for her hand. His grip felt warm and rough. "We can't stop you from doing whatever you want to when you're older," he told Roselle. "But for now, please stay in school."

"Because even if you do find a rich white man to marry," Lizzie finished, "he'll know exactly who you are if you can't read or write."

"Was my real father a white man?"

For a second time, Lizzie nearly bolted from her chair to slap her daughter's face. Otis's steadying hand kept her seated. "Never mind about him right now," she managed to say. "You learn everything they're teaching you at that school, and someday when you're all finished I'll tell you about your father."

"Promise?"

Lizzie swallowed a wad of fear before replying. "Yes. I promise. Now help me clear the table and wash up these dishes."

The bell jangled in the dining room just as Lizzie started to stand up. Her shoulders sagged. She couldn't face Miz Eugenia's nonsense right now, she just couldn't. "You go see what she wants," she told Roselle, "while I toss these scraps to the chickens." A few minutes away from everyone helped Lizzie slow down and calm down.

She came inside again just as Roselle was returning from the dining room with an armload of dirty dishes. "I hate working for Miz Eugenia," she grumbled. "I wish I could get me a job someplace else."

Lizzie knew exactly how her daughter felt. And as badly as she needed Roselle's help around here, she realized that maybe it would be better for both of them if Roselle got away and worked for somebody else for a while. Lizzie went to the dry sink where her daughter was scraping dishes and put her arm around her slender shoulders.

"Miz Eugenia asked me today if I knew somebody who could work for her friend, Miz Blake. You want me to tell her you'll go over there for a few hours after school every day? Maybe earn a little money?"

"I'll think on it," she said with a shrug.

When the day's work was finally done, Lizzie closed the door to the Big House and went down to her cabin with her family. Some nights they'd talk for a while, but not tonight. Everyone was too tuckered out. Lizzie lay down beside Otis and held him close.

"What're we gonna do about Roselle?" she whispered to him in the darkness.

"We're gonna pray and trust the good Lord, that's what."

"I'm scared for her."

"I know. Me too. But Roselle's gonna be okay, Lizzie-girl. We just gotta work here a little while longer."

Lizzie sighed and made up her mind to be patient. She would let the eggs grow into baby chicks, and someday she and Otis would have an entire hen house of their own.

10

A week ago, if someone had asked Josephine what she wished for, it would have been to escape from her family's constant complaining. Now her wish had come true, and she was sorry. The moment she awoke on Sunday morning and saw the satchel she had packed to take with her to Mrs. Blake's house, she realized her life had gone from bad to worse. Josephine would rather live in the woods than with Harrison Blake.

She did feel sorry for his mother, though. Priscilla didn't deserve all the sorrow that had befallen her. Josephine wouldn't mind helping her with the household chores until they could hire a new servant, or with planting a kitchen garden so the Blakes would have food to eat. Jo had enjoyed helping Lizzie with the kitchen garden, and she went out there nearly every day when she wanted to get away from her mother and sister. Spending the evening hours with Mrs. Blake would be pleasant, too, since she didn't complain nearly as much as Mother or continually correct Josephine's posture or her manners. But how could she stand living with Harrison Blake? Visiting him for a mere hour was like crawling into a badger's den.

Josephine sighed and climbed out of bed to get ready for church. For some reason, she thought of the Yankee she'd found hiding in her tree house four days ago. What had he said was the secret to happiness? Gratitude. *"When you take the time to be grateful for the little things, then those little joys all add up to make you happy."* It couldn't possibly be true, could it? But as Jo buttoned up her bodice and slipped into her skirt, it did make sense to her that being thankful was the opposite of complaining. Maybe she should try his advice. If Mother complained about not having bacon, Jo would tell her to be grateful they had eggs. When her sister complained about her well-worn dresses, Jo would tell her to be grateful she wasn't wearing rags like Lizzie.

Josephine opened the bedroom curtains to let in the sunlight and saw that the apple tree down by the garden had burst into bloom. She could certainly be grateful for that. Not only would they have apples to eat in a few months' time, but the tree was as beautiful as a ruffled bride, her skirts stiff with petticoats. Who needed lace on their dresses when they had an entire tree wrapped in lacy blooms, right outside their door? Maybe she would pick a handful of blossoms and bring them inside to decorate their table.

Then Josephine remembered she was moving in with bitter, miserable Harrison Blake today. How could she possibly be grateful for that? She turned away from the window, staring at nothing as she tried to think of an answer. She could be grateful that he wasn't related to her, which meant she didn't have to see him again after her work there was finished. And she could be *very* grateful that Harrison Blake wasn't her husband! The thought made her smile. Maybe gratitude did work, after all.

"What are you grinning at?" Mary asked. She yawned and stretched her arms, thin and pale as new tendrils.

"Nothing. I'm just . . . grateful," Jo said with a shrug.

"Mother says we mustn't shrug our shoulders."

"Mother has too many rules." Could Josephine be grateful for those, too? She thought about it for a moment and decided that following the rules had helped Mother remain strong—and her strength had kept their family alive throughout the war. So, yes, maybe she could be thankful for Mother's rules. She gave her sister

Mary's feet a shake and said, "You'd better get up or we'll be late for church." Then she sat down in front of the mirror to brush her hair.

Mary climbed out of bed and let out an aggrieved sigh as she peered into their wardrobe. "I have nothing to wear to church except the same old worn-out dress I wore last week."

"Be grateful the church didn't burn down during the war," Josephine replied. "And that we have a horse and carriage to take us there."

"What are you talking about?"

"Never mind. I can't explain it." Josephine twisted her hair into a bun and pinned it in place. Then she hurried downstairs to pick a bouquet of apple blossoms for their breakfast table. She would attend church with her family to avoid an argument with her mother, but she would spend the long hour daydreaming, not praying. Prayer had proven to be a waste of time.

Daniel took so long getting ready that he made everyone late for church. Josephine kept her head lowered, embarrassed as she tiptoed into a worship service well under way. How could she be grateful for their tardiness? Now their family would be forced to sit in the rear of the sanctuary among the restless whisperers.

Jo was still trying to find something to be grateful for when she spotted Emma Welch sitting across the aisle from them. She and Harrison had been so in love when they'd announced their engagement five years ago. Jo wondered if Emma had been heartbroken about the canceled engagement or relieved. As the sermon droned on and on, Jo realized that arriving late to church this morning had provided an opportunity to talk to Emma. If her love for Harrison could be rekindled, maybe Josephine wouldn't have to move in with the Blakes, after all. The moment the service ended, Jo pushed her way out of the pew and crossed the crowded aisle. "Hello, Emma. How are you?" Up close, Emma's dress looked just as threadbare as Josephine's did.

"I'm well. And you, Josephine?"

"I'm fine. Listen, can we talk? It's important." Jo knew she should chat about the weather and other polite topics for a few minutes instead of blurting everything out right away, but she wasn't very good at small-talk, much to her mother's disappointment. They stood aside to allow the other parishioners to move into the aisle, then sat down in the empty pew.

"Mother and I stopped by to visit the Blakes the other day," Jo began.

"Oh. I see." Emma looked away, scanning the departing crowd as if wishing someone would call to her so she would have an excuse to leave. "How is Harrison?" she asked.

"He's still bedridden and requires a great deal of nursing care."

"I'm sorry to hear that. Listen, I need to leave. Will you excuse me, please?"

"Wait. I understand you're no longer engaged, but Harrison's spirits are so low and you loved him at one time—"

"Don't ask me to visit him, Josephine. I confess that I find it very difficult to see him crippled that way. He was so tall and handsome, and now . . . well, his injuries are so horrid."

"But don't the Scriptures say that 'Love beareth all things, endureth all things'? Harrison is still the same man whether he has one leg or two."

"You're wrong. He isn't the same man. The Harrison I knew before the war was kind and loving and full of laughter. The man who returned home from the war isn't anything like him."

"But you loved him. Maybe if you took care of him a little longer and nurtured him—"

"I tried, Josephine. I told him I didn't care about his injuries. But I wasn't the one who ended the engagement. Harrison was. He said he didn't want to marry me, and he ordered me to go away. He said terrible things—like he never really loved me to begin with and . . . and I don't even want to repeat what else he said. He said he would never be able to work or support a wife and a family, and he told me to leave and never come back."

Josephine could easily imagine him saying all of those things and more. But she continued to argue with Emma, desperate to avoid caring for Harrison herself. "Can't you give him one more chance? Sooner or later he'll stop being angry, and maybe he'll be his old self again."

"It's too late. I've decided to see other suitors."

"But if you loved him—"

"Look, I want what every woman wants: a husband and a home and children."

"But—"

"Josephine, stop! The truth is . . . Harrison told me that he can never have children because of his injuries." Emma's cheeks had turned the color of cooked beets, and Jo felt the heat rising to her own cheeks, as well. Such topics were never discussed.

"I have a widowed aunt in Norfolk," Emma said, looking away again. "I'm moving there in a few weeks to help care for her children. There are more opportunities to meet people in a new city where no one knows that I was once engaged."

"Won't you at least say good-bye to Harrison before you leave?" Maybe another visit would rekindle a spark of love or hope.

But Emma shook her head as she rose to her feet. "I'm sorry, Josephine."

"I wish you well in Norfolk," she called after her, then sighed in frustration. Why did other people get to move on while Jo remained stuck here like a fly beneath glass? She stood and hurried up the deserted aisle in the opposite direction, fleeing the church through a side door, slamming it behind her. "Gratitude doesn't work!" she said aloud. "I have nothing to be grateful for!"

She stomped across the church lawn, ignoring the chatting groups of people, pausing only when she saw her sister, Mary. "Tell Mother I'm walking home," she called to her.

"But it's too far! Your shoes—"

"I'll stop when I get tired. You can pick me up along the way." Josephine's shoes might be a problem. They were her mother's and much too small. But Jo wasn't wearing hosiery, so she was able to slip the painful shoes off her feet and walk barefoot, like a slave woman. She would have to cram them back on before her family caught up with her in the carriage or endure another lecture.

It felt good to get away from everyone and be by herself. Maybe she would walk all the way home—except she wasn't going home, she remembered. Daniel had loaded her satchel into the back of their carriage. Her spirits sank. What in the world was she going to do about Harrison? If only she could get him out of bed and working his plantation again, then she could return home.

She pushed Harrison out of her mind, trying to be grateful for a sunny day and a few minutes all to herself. But when she rounded a bend in the road, she saw she wasn't alone. A young man, as tall and thin as a lamppost, was walking slowly down the road ahead of her, stopping every few yards to bend over and pick up a stone or to pluck a blue chicory blossom from alongside the road.

She didn't recognize him until she got closer and saw clumps of fuzzy sideburns sprouting below his ears. It was the Yankee from the tree house. What was his name? Mr. Chandler, from the Freedmen's Bureau. The thought struck her that maybe he could help Harrison. Josephine paused long enough to cram on her shoes, then called out to him, "Mr. Chandler! Mr. Chandler, wait!"

He whirled around, as if surprised to hear his name, and waited for her to catch up to him. He didn't seem to recognize her at first. Then he grinned and pointed at her. "I know! You're the young lady with the torn shoe."

"Yes." At least he hadn't mentioned her embarrassing tirade or her tears. "I need to ask your advice, Mr. Chandler."

"Of course, Miss . . . I don't believe I learned your name the last time we met."

"It's Josephine Weatherly, not that it matters. My question is in regard to a neighbor of mine, Harrison Blake. His family is in need of help to rebuild their plantation. You said that was the purpose of your agency, didn't you?"

He nodded. "Your friend is welcome to come into my office and—"

"That isn't possible. Mr. Blake is still recovering from the wounds he suffered during the war. He's crippled. Bedridden."

"In that case, I'll be happy to ride out to his place and speak with him. Where does he live?"

"If you continue down this road toward our plantation, he owns the very first plantation you'll come to on the right."

"Would Wednesday morning be a good time to visit?"

"Wednesday will be fine. Thank you."

Now that she had made the arrangements, Josephine didn't want to talk with this Yankee a moment longer. She was about to bid him good day when he asked, "Will you be there to make the introductions? I would hate to arrive unannounced. Some people take potshots at Yankees who step onto their property uninvited." His smile made him look younger than he probably was. And unlike her brother and Harrison Blake, Mr. Chandler seemed buoyant and good-natured, as refreshing as a tin cup of spring water on a hot day. But then Mr. Chandler had been on the winning side of the war. He hadn't lost nearly everything he owned.

"I'll be there," she told him. "I'm staying with the Blakes for the time being. I should warn you, though, that Mr. Blake may not be amenable to the idea. Or friendly towards you. But if you could simply explain some of the options he has for getting workers to return to his plantation, I'm sure his mother would be very grateful."

"Certainly. I'll be happy to. And if you—"

"Thank you. Good day." She turned around and hurried away before he could say more, heading back the way she had just come.

"I'll see you on Wednesday," he called to her.

She knew it was impolite to leave so abruptly, but she had no wish to hear more from him, nor did she want to be seen talking to him. She passed him again a few minutes later after climbing into her family's carriage, but she ignored him as they rode past, leaving him alone by the side of the road, holding his dusty bouquet of chicory blooms.

Dread tugged on Josephine's stomach like a fretful child as her driver dropped her off in front of the Blakes' pillared porch a few minutes later. It no longer seemed possible to be grateful for anything. Then Mrs. Blake greeted Josephine with a hug that melted her heart. How starved she must be for someone to hold, someone who could give her a shred of human affection and hope. Heaven knows she wasn't getting either from Harrison.

"It's so kind of you to stay and help us, Josephine. I hope your mother didn't force you to come."

"Of course not. I'm happy to help. It must be so lonely for you here."

"Yes, it has been lonely." Priscilla continued to talk as she led Josephine into the foyer, then up the stairs to a dusty, airless bedroom. "I apologize for not airing out your room properly, but we've been without help since Minnie quit, and I simply couldn't do it all alone."

Josephine nodded in sympathy. "You mustn't worry about it. I'm here to help you in any way I can."

"If I could just get one of our slaves to come back and clean and cook for us . . ."

"I might be able to help you find someone. There's a new government office in the village that helps with such things. I've already spoken with one of the agents on your behalf."

"You're an angel, Josephine. A godsend."

Jo laid her satchel on the bed and dug inside it for the little tin box she'd packed. "I brought you some chamomile blossoms I picked and dried. Shall I make tea for us, Mrs. Blake?"

"Yes, thank you. I'll go downstairs and see if Harrison is awake. He would enjoy some tea and some company, too."

Into the badger's den, Josephine thought as she carried the tea tray into his room a few minutes later. She hadn't known him well before the war because of the difference in their ages, but he had never looked as angry and unkempt back then as he did now. His skin was as white and fragile as eggshells beneath his black, untrimmed beard and overgrown hair, his dark eyes as frightening as a nightmare. Jo forced a smile. "Good afternoon, Harrison."

"Go away. I don't want you to read your insipid books to me. I'm perfectly capable of reading if I decide I want to waste my time with ridiculous imaginary stories."

"I've brought you some tea," she said, setting the tray on his bedside table. "And my brother Daniel sent over some newspapers if you'd like to read them."

"I wouldn't. Why read about a world that I'll never be part of again?"

"Is that what you've decided to do? Cut yourself off from the outside world?" It wasn't like Josephine to be so outspoken, but her thoughts and words, like the upstairs bedroom, had been locked up and unaired for much too long. If Harrison could be blunt, then so could she.

"I don't have any choice in the matter!" he shouted. "Look at me! How am I supposed to live a normal life?"

She took a slow, deep breath for courage. "I heard Dr. Hunter say the other day that there's nothing wrong with you."

"The doctor is a fool who still has two perfectly good legs! Look at me!" He threw back the covers to show her the ugly stump of his leg, severed above his knee. It resembled a chunk of raw meat, scarred and bitter red. "Does this look like there's nothing wrong with me?"

Josephine looked away, shocked. But she quickly met his gaze again, refusing to let him win. "You aren't the only man who was grievously wounded. If you wanted to, you could hire workers to plant your crops and get your plantation running again."

"Are you really that stupid? I have no slaves to do the work and no money to hire workers. I've lost everything!"

"No one has slaves, Harrison. But we still have to get our crops planted so we won't starve to death. I've spoken with the agent from that new government bureau in Fairmont. He's coming here later this week to talk with you about—"

"You have a lot of nerve. Get out of my house! Get out!" He knocked the tray off his bedside table, smashing the teacup, before picking up a book and throwing it at her. Josephine ducked just in time. She had never been treated this way in her life. Part of her wanted to run out the door and never come back, but another part of her was tired of being chased away by fear, and it made her angry enough to fight. She picked up the book and threw it back at him, missing his head by mere inches. It thumped against the wall and tumbled to the floor.

"There! How do you like it?" He glared at her, his expression as dark and deep as a well. She didn't know why she no longer felt afraid of him, but she didn't. "Are we going to continue this throwing match, or are you going to be civil to me?"

"Go home, you stupid child. I don't want you here."

Josephine shook her head. "I'm not here for your sake. I'm here for your mother's. Maybe you deserve to live all alone, but she doesn't."

"My mother will be better off without me."

"What a stupid, selfish thing to say!" She moved closer to the bed, lowering her voice so his mother wouldn't overhear. "Have you ever stopped to consider her feelings? You just told me how you've lost everything, but she has, too, Harrison. You're all she has left, and I don't think she can bear another loss. You're the only reminder she has of your father and the life she used to live. I don't care how miserable you are, but the least you can do is try to rebuild your life for her sake."

Josephine turned and left the room. She was trembling so badly that she needed to sit down, but she felt relieved by her outburst, the way a thunderstorm clears the air on a humid summer night so that everyone can breathe again. She had held her feelings inside for much too long, and had finally found her voice again. And for that she was grateful.

11

May 17, 1865

Eugenia ran her hand along the railing as she descended the stairs to the foyer. The wood was bone-dry. The mahogany banisters and railing needed to be oiled and polished or they would grow brittle and splinter in the summer heat. The same was true of the furniture in the parlor, languishing beneath layers of dust that made Eugenia sneeze every time she walked in the room. The floors felt gritty beneath her shoes. The floorboards hadn't been scrubbed and waxed in ages, nor had the few remaining rugs been beaten or the draperies and feather bedding aired. Cobwebs dangled from the crown molding above her head. Eugenia watched her once-beautiful home falling into ruin around her and felt helpless.

The deterioration wasn't only on the inside of the house. When Eugenia reached her morning room and gazed through the streaked windowpanes, she could see weeds growing in the distant fields instead of cotton, outbuildings in need of paint and repair, a vegetable garden that should be properly watered and tended if her family ever hoped to eat a decent meal again. She had finished breakfast only an hour ago but the continual aching rumble in Eugenia's stomach refused to go away. Her daughters looked as spindly as field hands.

She picked up the framed photograph of Philip she kept on her writing desk and studied his handsome face. Sometimes when she looked at him, she could almost hear a melody from happier days playing in the background, a waltz they had once shared or music from a recital they had attended together in Richmond. But she heard no music today as she stared at his picture. Instead, she felt a rush of anger toward him for deserting her. She laid the photograph facedown on the table.

Philip had held Eugenia's world together during the early years of the war, running the plantation, keeping the Negroes working, supporting the Confederacy by contributing money and supplies. He hadn't left to join the fighting until the war crept dangerously close to their land and all the men his age had been drafted into the Home Guard. In the end, he hadn't died in battle but of pneumonia during the last long winter of the war. A month later the Yankees had come, and she'd been forced to flee to Richmond. She and her family had been barely scraping by ever since, surviving on a hidden cache of money that Philip had wisely kept in reserve.

Eugenia had been so relieved when Daniel arrived home three weeks ago, certain he would take care of them all. But as she watched him wander around the plantation with dragging footsteps and drooping shoulders, it was clear the war had killed something vital in him. He had no idea what to do or where to begin to restore their plantation. His depression and lack of initiative frightened Eugenia more than the Yankees had. What was she going to do?

She moved away from the window and stumbled toward her armchair as she felt the familiar pressure begin to build behind her breastbone. Sometimes the sickening nausea swelled inside her until she couldn't breathe. Eugenia hadn't told anyone about the "spells" she'd been having. Why add to their worries? If she simply sat down for a few minutes and took her mind off her difficulties, sipping a little tea to calm her, the pain would eventually go away. She rang the bell beside her chair and closed her eyes while she waited for Lizzie to respond. She opened them again when she heard the maid's shuffling footsteps.

"Yes, ma'am?" Lizzie's aggrieved tone and impatient stance made the pressure in Eugenia's chest tighten as if winding a clock spring.

"I would like a cup of tea, Lizzie. Kindly use some of the mint leaves that Josephine picked and dried."

"Yes, ma'am." Lizzie slouched away, her annoyance obvious.

The tea helped soothe Eugenia, and so did the cheerful bouquet of apple blossoms Josephine had arranged in a glass on the writing desk. Eugenia hadn't realized how much work Josephine used to do around the house and how dependent they all were on her until she'd gone to stay with Priscilla and Harrison four days ago. The house seemed empty without her, even though Jo had always been quiet and withdrawn. Her nature was so different from Eugenia's that she sometimes wondered if the midwife had switched her real daughter with another baby at birth.

By the time Mary joined Eugenia in the morning room a few minutes later, the pain in her chest had eased. "What shall we do today, Mother?"

Should she ask Mary to do household chores or work in the garden the way Josephine had? Maybe Lizzie could teach her to do simple things like dusting the furniture or polishing the woodwork. But no, it would be much harder to find a suitable husband to take care of Mary and provide for her future if she had work-callused hands or skin that had browned in the sun. Eugenia forced herself not to think about the future, knowing the pain would begin all over again if she did.

"I think we'll visit Priscilla today and see how she and Josephine are getting along."

Mary made a face. "Do I have to go with you?"

"I do not like that whiny tone, Mary Louise. You must learn to ask for things without whining."

"Please, I would rather not go, Mother."

Eugenia couldn't blame her. Harrison could be gloomy when he was in one of his moods. In fact, Eugenia couldn't remember a visit when he hadn't been gloomy. "You may stay home, but you must promise to study your lessons while I'm gone." The war had forced Eugenia to become her daughter's schoolteacher, too, since they could no longer afford a private tutor.

"I promise I'll study. Please, Mother?"

"Very well. Kindly tell Daniel that I'll need the carriage and a driver."

Otis drove Eugenia the short distance to Priscilla's house. She had never handled the reins of a carriage in her life and she wasn't about to, no matter how many other jobs seemed more pressing to their one and only field hand. "Come back for me before lunchtime, please," she told him.

Another horse was already tethered to the hitching post when Eugenia arrived at the Blakes' plantation. "Am I interrupting something?" she asked when Priscilla came to the door. "Do you have company? Shall I come back another day?"

"No, please come in. I need your help, Eugenia. I don't know what to do."

Eugenia was still outside the front door when she heard Harrison bellowing at someone in his bedroom, yelling at the top of his voice.

"I'm sorry . . . I'm so sorry," Priscilla said, glancing in his direction. "You shouldn't have to witness such an uproar, Eugenia, but—"

"What's going on? Who's here?"

"A gentleman from some government agency in town. Josephine invited him here to talk to Harrison about hiring help for the plantation, but—"

"Get out!" Harrison's furious shout interrupted her, followed by the sound of shattering glass. Josephine emerged from the bedroom a moment later, trailed by a tall young man. He appeared shaken.

"I'm so sorry, Mr. Chandler," Josephine was saying as they proceeded down the hall toward Eugenia, "but if Harrison doesn't want to listen to you, maybe you should explain everything to Mrs. Blake and me. As you can see, she needs your help and . . . Oh, hello, Mother."

Josephine introduced Eugenia to Mr. Chandler, explaining that he was an agent with the Bureau of Refugees, Freedmen, and Abandoned Lands. He looked much too young and inexperienced to hold a government position. What must the Yankees think of them to send someone so young? Did they believe plantation owners were all uneducated bumpkins?

"How do you do, Mrs. Weatherly." The agent extended his hand, but Eugenia ignored it. She didn't blame Harrison one bit for kicking him out. What was wrong with Josephine that she would welcome him here? If this were Eugenia's home, she would order him out immediately, but it wasn't. She was Priscilla's guest. And this wasn't the time or the place to chide her daughter.

Eugenia sat down in the parlor with the others, half listening as the Yankee explained how plantation owners could get their work force back by an arrangement called sharecropping or by hiring Negroes as tenant farmers. Eugenia hadn't planned to pay much attention, but the more Mr. Chandler talked, the more she realized that Daniel needed help with White Oak just as badly as Harrison and Priscilla did. But like Harrison, Daniel would never swallow his pride and ask a Yankee for help.

"The plantations need laborers and the Negroes need work," Mr. Chandler finished. "This is really the best solution for everyone."

"Could Mrs. Blake also arrange to hire house servants?" Josephine asked. She looked directly at Eugenia, as if to make sure her mother was listening to his reply.

"Most Negro families want to stay together," Mr. Chandler said. "So, yes, we often arrange for the wives to work in the manor house in exchange for room and board."

Josephine was still staring at Eugenia, eyebrows raised as if to say, *See, Mother?* She was right, of course. Lizzie did need help.

"Would you like some time to think about it?" Mr. Chandler asked. "I could come back again."

Priscilla looked to Eugenia as if shifting the weight of the decision to her. "What do you think I should I do, Eugenia?"

Josephine spoke before Eugenia could reply. "You should sign the contract, Mrs. Blake. It's the only way to get the help you need."

Eugenia stared at her daughter. How had she suddenly become so strong and decisive? So unladylike?

"But shouldn't Harrison be the one to decide?" Priscilla asked. Her fingers fluttered to her throat and plucked nervously at her collar. Neither she nor Eugenia had been raised to take charge this way. Eugenia wondered if her friend also felt moments of irrational anger toward her husband for dying and leaving her in this predicament. Their husbands had vowed to take care of them.

"Harrison is unable to decide anything," Josephine said, "until he is out of bed and feeling better. In the meantime, planting your crops is a matter of life and death."

"You should listen to her, Mrs. Blake," Mr. Chandler said. "Miss Weatherly has a very good head on her shoulders. I'll be available to advise you along the way, of course, and to make sure your laborers are working hard and fulfilling their contracts. It's my job to see to everyone's best interests."

"How soon can she hire workers?" Josephine asked.

"Right away. I'll go back to my office and start the process—if that's what you want, Mrs. Blake."

Again she looked to Eugenia. Deciding for her friend was much easier for Eugenia than deciding for herself. "I think you should do it, Priscilla."

Mr. Chandler smiled. "Good. I'll talk to the workers and come back in a few days. Good day, ladies." Josephine rose and walked to the door with him.

While they were gone, Eugenia leaned back in her chair and gazed around the parlor for the first time since she'd arrived. It looked different than it had just a week ago, yet Eugenia couldn't put her finger on what made the difference. Was it because the draperies had been opened to the sun? Had the furniture been polished? If so, Josephine must have done all the work—but why? Eugenia hated seeing her daughter stray so far from her aristocratic upbringing to labor like a common woman, even though her hard work was saving all of them. The thought struck her that if Daniel had even half of his sister's gumption, Eugenia wouldn't be so fearful of the future.

"Do you think I'm doing the right thing?" Priscilla asked, interrupting Eugenia's thoughts. "I would hate to have Harrison angry with me, but what Josephine says makes sense. I'm so confused."

"It isn't in our nature to oppose our men's decisions," Eugenia said. "Jo doesn't understand how you feel, but I do. After Philip died, I was forced to make many decisions, and so I know how difficult it is. But until Harrison is well again, it's as if you're still at war, Priscilla. We must do whatever we need to do in order to survive and to reclaim what we've lost."

When Josephine returned to the parlor a few minutes later, the doctor was with her. "We have another guest," she said. "Dr. Hunter is here."

"Good morning, ladies," he said, following Jo into the parlor. He chatted with Priscilla for a moment, then walked over to where Eugenia was seated. "And how are you, Mrs. . . . I mean, Eugenia?"

"I'm fine, thank you. And yourself?"

He didn't reply. Instead, he seemed to be studying her, and so she studied him in return. His fair hair was turning gray and needed to be trimmed around his ears, but of course he had no wife to remind him of such things or to take care of him. And his blue eyes looked sad to her, as if they could still see all he had witnessed during the war. When he finally spoke, his words surprised her. "You look pale to me, Eugenia."

Should she tell him about the spells she'd been having? She longed to lean on him and to hear his assurance that it was only anxiety causing the pain, that it would disappear when things returned to normal. But then Josephine would hear about it, too, and Eugenia didn't want her daughter to worry. She smiled at the doctor and rested her hand on his arm for a moment. "I only seem pale alongside my daughter. She insists on working outside in the garden, and see how brown her skin has become?"

He didn't smile. "Is everything going well at home?"

"Yes, everything is fine, David." She waved her gloved hand, dismissing his concern.

"Good. I'm glad to hear it. Well, if you ladies will excuse me, I'll go look in on Harrison."

"Things aren't fine at home, Mother," Jo said when the doctor and Priscilla were gone. "Daniel can't run that huge plantation with only Otis to help him. And Lizzie can't do all the housework, either. Daniel needs to talk to Mr. Chandler and hire the help we need."

"Let's wait and discuss this in private," she whispered. Priscilla was returning to the parlor after escorting the doctor to the bedroom. But Josephine shook her head.

"Not until you promise that you'll tell Daniel what Mr. Chandler just explained to us."

"That's enough, Josephine. We won't spoil our nice visit by arguing. Now, tell me, ladies. How have you two been getting along?"

"Jo has been a godsend!" Priscilla gushed. But as she and Eugenia began to chat, Josephine rose and quietly left the room.

On the way home, Eugenia's thoughts seemed to wage war inside her. On one hand, women simply didn't take over unless their men were as ill as Harrison was. Daniel may not have been wounded, but something inside him was broken, and he wasn't taking proper care of the plantation or his family's needs. Should she go against her upbringing and take charge the way Josephine and Priscilla had? Or should she be patient and wait for Daniel to find himself again—and risk starving? Eugenia longed to have a man she could turn to, someone to rescue her. Men were stronger than women and always knew exactly what to do. But as Eugenia remembered turning Philip's photograph facedown, a niggling voice told her the men were the ones who had decided to go to war in the first place and had lost everything.

She got her driver's attention as her carriage arrived home and drew to a halt near the front porch. "No, kindly drive me down to the stables. I need to speak with my son."

"Yes, ma'am."

She found Daniel gazing into an empty horse stall, doing nothing as far as she could tell. He looked surprised to see her. "What are you doing down here, Mother?"

"I just had an interesting conversation at the Blakes' plantation." Eugenia told him what the bureau man had explained and wasn't at all surprised when Daniel reacted the same way that Harrison had.

"You expect me to trust a Yankee? A government man? Never! And we can't trust the slaves, either. They'll kill us in our beds and steal everything we own."

"The Negroes already outnumber us, Daniel. They might kill us anyway if we let them all go hungry. And if the work doesn't get done around here, we'll all starve."

"We have to protect ourselves, Mother, first and foremost. There's already a bunch of shiftless Negroes living down in the woods, and I'm worried for your safety." Daniel talked on and on, as if he had been brooding about this for a long time. "My friends and I have decided that it's up to us to keep the slaves under control."

"Is *that* what you've been meeting with your friends to discuss?" Eugenia wanted to grab him by the shoulders and shake him, but she kept her voice calm. "I'm glad you're getting together with your friends, but I had hoped it would lead to something more productive, like planting cotton. Wouldn't it be better for everyone if you hired the slaves to work for us instead of chasing them off?"

"How can we hire them? We can't afford it!"

"You need to listen to Mr. Chandler. There are ways of getting the money we need. Please, Daniel." It went against Eugenia's nature to be so direct, to argue with her son this way. But if the decision was right for Priscilla's plantation, then it was right for theirs, too.

Daniel turned away from her and stalked to the stable door. "I'm not Father," he said with his back still turned. "And I'm not Samuel."

"I know, darling. But—"

"I have to do this my way."

He strode out the door, heading toward the weed-choked cotton field. Eugenia didn't follow him. Instead, she slowly made her way up to the house, lifting her black skirt to keep her hem from trailing in the dust.

She could ask Otis to drive her into town. She could sign a contract with Mr. Chandler herself. Then the cotton could get planted, and they would have a crop to sell in the fall. But even as she considered the idea, Eugenia felt the pain in her chest begin to build. She needed to go inside and sit down. She needed to give Daniel a little more time.

12

May 20, 1865

Lizzie had been trying to ignore the signs for two days. The sickening way her stomach rolled in the morning before she even crawled out of bed. The way the stench of the chamber pots made her gag when she emptied them. The way she had to drag herself around, feeling weary all day long. She kept hoping she was wrong, praying she was wrong, but there was no mistaking the truth. Otis had come home one month ago and now she had a baby growing inside her.

She should be happy. This child would be born free, not a slave. He would belong to her and Otis, not to Miz Eugenia and Massa Daniel. Lizzie would never have to worry that this baby would be sold away from her. But oh, this was a terrible time to bring a child into the world! There was hardly enough to eat. She already had more work piled on her shoulders than one person could possibly do, especially with Roselle working for Miz Eugenia's friend after school every day. Another child would make it harder for her and Otis to move out of here and get their own place someday. Lord knew Lizzie loved all three of her children, but she didn't want another one. Yet she was going to have a baby whether she liked it or not. Faced with the truth, she sank down on the back step, lifted her apron to her face, and wept.

Long before she had a chance to cry out all her sorrow, Lizzie heard Miz Eugenia's bell ringing in the morning room. *Not now! Please! Leave me be!* she groaned. She waited, but the bell rang again. There was no one else who could go, and if Lizzie didn't hurry, things would be a lot worse for her. She wiped her eyes, drew a breath, and went to see what the missus wanted. She knew that if Miz Eugenia spoke one harsh word to her, she would burst into tears again.

"Yes, Miz Eugenia?" Lizzie stared at her feet, willing her tears to go away.

"You need to make time today to rub beeswax and furniture oil on the banisters and stair railing. The wood is bone-dry and it's going to be ruined if it isn't taken care of soon. In fact, all the furniture needs to be polished."

Lizzie bit her lip, waiting until she was sure she wouldn't cry. This was one more task on an ever-growing mountain of work that she just couldn't climb. "Maybe I can get to it today, ma'am," she said. "Or maybe tomorrow."

"Tomorrow is the Sabbath."

"Oh. On Monday, then."

"I would prefer today. And don't forget about it. It simply must be done."

"Yes, ma'am." Lizzie's tears started falling again before she reached the hallway. She let them fall as she worked all afternoon, putting a meal together from whatever she could find. She had to prepare twice as much food today so the white folks would have something to eat tomorrow and she could get her half-day off on Sunday afternoon. She wasn't expecting Otis to come up to the kitchen before the dinner bell rang, but when he arrived earlier than usual, he caught her crying as she was mashing the potatoes.

"Lizzie-girl? What's wrong? Has the missus been picking on you?"

"No . . . no more than usual." She tried to laugh about it but couldn't. Otis took the wooden masher from her hand and pulled her into his arms.

"Tell me what's wrong, then."

Lizzie knew this baby was her own fault. If only she didn't love Otis so much. Hadn't her mother warned her not to fall in love? She rested her head on his chest and heard his heart beating, strong and steady. Just like him. "I'm gonna have another baby."

He pulled back so he could look at her. He was smiling. "Well, that's good news, ain't it? Why're you crying over good news?"

"Because it ain't good news, Otis. There's so much work to do, and I can't do it all alone, and now we'll never be able to get a place of our own, and we'll have one more mouth to feed, and—"

He pulled her close again. "Shh . . . shh . . . Lord knows all that, Lizzie. And He still saw fit to send us another baby to love. We'll manage, I promise we will."

"How?"

"Well . . . I'm not sure yet. But maybe I can talk to Saul and the others again about coming back here to work. I should've done it a lot sooner, Lizzie. I'm sorry."

"What if Miz Eugenia kicks us out when she sees I'm having a baby? I can't do all the work now as it is. How am I gonna do it when my belly grows clear out to here?" She held her hands in front of her to show him where her belly would be. Otis laid his hand on her middle, patting it as if patting a baby.

"If Miz Eugenia don't want us, then we'll talk to that Yankee fellow in town and ask him to find us another place to work. Don't you cry no more. We'll be fine. A baby is good news, Lizzie."

His words gave her hope, and she managed to finish all the cooking and dishwashing by bedtime. But she never did get the banister polished like Miz Eugenia had asked her to. Nor did she have time to do it on Sunday morning. She barely got the table set and the food all ready before the white folks came home for their Sunday dinner after church. The polishing would have to wait until Monday.

Lizzie was grateful for a chance to sit down that afternoon and take a rest. Otis, Rufus, and Jack had gone fishing earlier that morning, and now Lizzie sat on the front stoop of their cabin, watching Otis clean the two fish they'd caught. Fish scales were flying everywhere as he scraped, and he'd given Rufus a small knife so he could learn how to do it, too. Lizzie basked in the sun and in the sight of her family, laughing and talking together. She didn't think she could be much happier, and when she looked up and saw Roselle coming down the little hill toward them, Lizzie couldn't help smiling.

"Hey, Roselle, honey!" she said, waving to her. She longed to leap up and give her daughter a hug, but she had kept her motherly instincts in chains for so many years, afraid of loving her daughter and then losing her, that she was still held captive.

"Did they give you the day off, too?" Lizzie asked.

Roselle nodded. "Missy Jo told me I could walk home and pay you a visit." Roselle held her arms tightly folded against her chest, a gesture she'd learned from Lizzie, holding her emotions back, afraid to show her love.

"How is everything going over there?" Otis asked.

"Fine. I like working for Missy Josephine. She's real nice to me. Massa is as mean as a rattlesnake, though. Missy Jo says to stay away from him."

Otis stopped scraping scales and looked up at Roselle. "I hope you're still going to school every day."

Roselle rolled her eyes. "Yes, I'm going. I like school a lot."

Lizzie knew it was the truth because she'd been asking Rufus and Jack about their sister when they came home from school. Lizzie still couldn't quite believe that her children were learning to read and write. It didn't seem possible. She'd heard of slaves who'd been whipped and sold farther south for learning such things, and so Lizzie had never dared to consider it. But it seemed as if every time she had something to be happy about, like her kids going to school, something bad would happen to make her lose hope again. This time it was remembering that she was pregnant, remembering all the fears and heartaches that went with having another child to love. Roselle looked happy for once, but Lizzie knew she was about to rain on that happiness.

"I'm sorry, Roselle, but you need to tell Missy Jo that you can't work for her no more."

"What! Why?" So much anger in those two words.

"Because you have to come back here and work with me."

"No! I don't want to! I hate working for Miz Eugenia, with her chin up in the air all the time. If you try and make me come back, I'll . . . I'll run away!"

Lizzie jumped to her feet as her temper flared. "You're always thinking of yourself, Roselle! You're telling me 'no' and threatening to run away before you even bother to ask me why I need help." Lizzie turned her back and walked away, hurrying down Slave Row to let off steam, like a pot that had just boiled over.

All of the cabins were vacant except for the one where her family lived, making the Row seem desolate. Some of the doors had been left open, and as Lizzie strode past she glimpsed stripped beds, a table and chair, things that had been too heavy to carry away when everybody went off to be free. Beyond the last cabin were the empty cotton fields and the big wooden shed where the cotton bales were stored. Lizzie sat down on the step of a smaller shed where they used to dry tobacco when Massa Philip was alive, and as soon as she was out of sight of the others, she began to cry. This time her tears weren't because of the baby but because of Roselle's threat to run away. Ever since her daughter had been born, Lizzie had worried that Massa would sell her, and now Roselle herself was threatening to leave. It made Lizzie's heart ache to try to hang on tight to her children while trying to hold them loosely at the same time.

A few minutes passed before she heard shuffling footsteps on the path. She looked up, expecting to see Otis, but it was Roselle. "Mama . . . ?" Roselle was still hugging herself as if she was cold. "Otis told me about the baby. I'm sorry, Mama. I'll come back and help out."

Lizzie stood and pulled Roselle into her arms. "Only in the afternoons, though. We won't let Miz Eugenia or anybody else keep you from going to school, okay?"

Roselle nodded. Lizzie kept her arm around her daughter's thin shoulders as they walked back to the cabin. Roselle wrapped her arm around Lizzie's waist, so lightly and carefully that it might not have been there at all.

Rufus ran to meet them, holding a chipped dinner plate in his hands with the cleaned fish piled on it. "Look, Mama! The fish is all ready to cook!" Lizzie held her hand over her mouth to keep her stomach from turning inside out as the fishy smell reached her nostrils.

"Thank you, Rufus, honey. I'm sure it's gonna taste real good."

"I'm cooking it," Otis said, "so you won't have to."

"Anyway," Roselle said with a sigh, "Missy Jo said they'll be getting lots more help soon, so they won't need me much longer. Bunch of their slaves are coming back and working the land for themselves. No overseer or massa or anything."

"Did Mr. Chandler and that bureau of his arrange it?" Otis asked.

"I don't know the man's name. But he's the same Yankee I see sitting in the office where the school is. He's been coming out to talk to Missy Jo sometimes. We should all go work over there. It's much better than here."

"I'm gonna try and get us some more help here first," Otis said. "Maybe I'll go back and talk to my brother and the others again tonight. Some of Miz Blake's slaves must be camping out in the woods with Saul and the rest. Everybody must know about Mr. Chandler and his arrangements by now. We should be able to work White Oak the same way they're doing."

"Do you think Massa Daniel will let you do that?" Lizzie asked. "With no overseer or anything?"

"I don't know, but Massa Daniel ain't planting cotton and it needs to get done pretty soon or it'll be too late. It's nearly June. We'll walk over to see Saul tonight after the boys are in bed."

"In the dark?" Lizzie shivered, remembering their last trip into the gloomy woods. "Why not go when it's still light out?"

"Because this is our only day off and I want to spend it with our kids." He rested one hand on Rufus's shoulder and the other on Roselle's. "They're gonna tell me what all they're learning in school, aren't you?"

"I can count," Jack said. "Wanna hear me?" He began saying his numbers, his little face as serious as a preacher's calling down hellfire.

Rufus had set the plate of fish down and was pulling on Otis's shirttail. "Can we come with you tonight to see Uncle Saul?"

"Not tonight. Maybe next time. Now let's get this fish fried up. I'll bet it'll taste real good cooked over a campfire. Roselle, run up to the kitchen and get me the biggest frying pan you can find. Jack and Rufus, you need to gather us some firewood."

The boys skipped off to the woodpile, with little Jack still reciting, "Thirty-seven, thirty-eight, thirty-nine . . . What comes next Rufus?"

"Forty." Their voices faded in the distance, still counting together.

Roselle was gone for such a long time that Lizzie began to grow worried. Was she having trouble finding the pan? Did Miz Eugenia call her to do something? She decided to head up the path to the Big House and see what was keeping her. But just as she reached the top of the rise, she saw Roselle running toward her shouting, "Mama! Mama, something terrible has happened!"

Lizzie felt her knees go weak, imagining the worst. "What, honey?"

"I haven't looked at my ducks all week, and so I decided to go look at them now—and they're gone! Mama, they're gone!"

Lizzie's strength returned with a rush of relief. There wasn't a crisis, after all. "Those eggs probably hatched open, honey. It's been a while, hasn't it?"

"Yeah . . . The shells are all broken open, and the mama and papa duck and five of the babies are gone, but three of them got left behind. They're all alone, Mama! I watched and waited and looked all around, hoping the mama and papa duck would come back for them, but those poor little babies are all by themselves. They're wandering all around the nest and peeping like their hearts might break, and they're all alone!"

That was the way of nature, Lizzie wanted to say, the way of life. It was hard, and sometimes innocent creatures were left to fend for themselves. It would be a hard lesson for Roselle to learn, but it couldn't be helped. "Listen, honey. From what I know about ducks, they head for a pond or a stream just as soon as the babies hatch. That's where they live—in the water—when they ain't setting on their nest."

"What about the last three babies? Will the parents come back for them?"

"Far as I know, ducks can't count. They don't understand that three of them are missing. Maybe those three eggs hatched open a little later than the others or maybe the babies dawdled behind. Either way, they're out of luck, I guess."

Roselle began to cry. From the time she was just a little girl she'd always had a tender heart. She wouldn't hardly let Lizzie step on an ant, and she would cry if you swatted a fly. Now she was heartbroken over three baby ducks. "They'll die, won't they?" Roselle sniffed. "What if a raccoon or a hawk catches them and eats them?"

"That's the way things work in nature."

"I don't like nature!" she said, stomping her foot. "I have to do something!"

Otis and the boys came running up the hill to see what all the fussing was about. Lizzie told them about the three little ducklings who'd been left behind. "Can't I bring them home with me?" Roselle asked. "I'll take care of them."

"Now, how you gonna feed them and take care of them?" Lizzie asked. "You taking them with you to school all day?"

"I have to try, Mama! I have to!"

"Wait just a minute now," Otis said in his calm voice. "I think I have an idea. Let's go find those babies and put them in the coop with the chickens. They'll be safe from the raccoons and they'll have food to eat, and maybe the hens will take care of them for you and keep them warm at night until they can be on their own."

"Will the chickens hurt them?" Roselle asked, still tearful.

"Let's try it and see."

"I think it's a good idea," Lizzie said. "Them chickens have been wanting to set on their eggs and hatch out some babies in the worst way, but Miz Eugenia keeps eating all the eggs every morning."

Roselle showed them where the duck nest had been, and after chasing the scared babies around for several minutes, Otis fetched a burlap sack and used it to catch all three ducklings. He carried them up to the chicken yard and set them inside the fence. Everybody watched for a few minutes, but the chickens didn't seem to pay them any mind at all. They were more interested in seeing if Lizzie was bringing them some crumbs to eat.

"Let's leave them alone now," Otis said, "and go eat our fish. The ducks will be fine. You'll see."

He and Lizzie left for the shantytown later that night after the fish was eaten and the fire had gone out and the boys were in bed. They took the shortcut through the cotton field this time, a bright quarter moon lighting their way. "How many stars do you think are up there in heaven?" Lizzie asked, looking up.

Otis laughed. "I don't even know numbers that go that high. Maybe Jack can tell us after he finishes learning how to count."

The shantytown looked like it had grown since the last time Lizzie had visited, with even more tents and campfires and makeshift shacks nestled in the woods. Someone was playing a fiddle, and folks were having a good time, singing and clapping and laughing. Maybe it would be better to live out here and cook for her own family instead of wearing herself out, ironing tablecloths and polishing furniture for Miz Eugenia. Her kids could still walk to school from here, couldn't they? She was about to ask Otis about it when he spotted his brother and hurried ahead to greet him. Lizzie went over to talk with Dolly and Cissy, who used to work in the Big House with her.

"Hey, Lizzie! Sit down here and talk awhile," Dolly said. "Tell us what's new."

Having a baby growing inside her was still in the front of Lizzie's mind, but she didn't want to tell the others about it yet. "Are you happy living out here in the woods?" she asked as they made room for her around the campfire.

"Well, there's things that take getting used to," Dolly said. "Like trying to cook without pots and spoons and bowls and such."

"And there sure are a lot of mosquitoes," Cissy added, swatting the air.

"Are you and Otis thinking of joining us?" Dolly asked. "Are you finally fed up with Miz Eugenia?"

"No, Otis wants to ask Saul and the rest of you to come back and work at White Oak again and live in your old cabins."

"Honey, we're all free now. Why you want to keep working for them Weatherlys?"

Lizzie didn't know how to reply. "I . . . I don't want to work for Miz Eugenia, but Otis says it's for the best that we stay there for now." Lizzie watched Cissy add another piece of wood to the fire and poke at the coals with a long stick. "Did you hear that some of the people from Miz Blake's plantation are going back there to work for her?"

"Yeah," Dolly said with a shrug. "I know a few of them folks. But Pete and me are waiting to get our own land out West. We'll be moving away from here just as soon as it comes through."

"Why you wanna go and move someplace you never seen before?" Lizzie asked. "Otis says there's a way you can come back to work for yourself at White Oak, without a massa or overseer."

Dolly shook her head. "I don't believe it. Ain't Miz Eugenia still telling you what to do?"

Before Lizzie had a chance to reply, she heard a loud rustling in the woods, like dry leaves being churned up and dead sticks cracking. "Shh!" someone said. The fiddler stopped playing. Everyone grew quiet, listening. Lizzie heard a horse snorting, and when she looked in that direction, she saw the light of a torch flickering back among the trees. It was moving closer. She turned her head and saw another torch a stone's throw away from the first, then another beside that one, and another . . . until the lights formed a ring around the campground. They were surrounded.

Lizzie and the others instinctively rose to their feet, getting ready to run. The sound of horse hooves stomping through the underbrush grew louder as the ring of torches drew closer.

Suddenly a gunshot rang out with a *bang* that made Lizzie jump. Then a volley of shots were fired, one after the other, until the woods echoed with gunfire.

The women screamed, children and babies cried out in fear, men scrambled in the dark, searching for their families, looking for a place to run to for cover. Lizzie crouched into a ball and covered her ears, terrified. Was she going to die out here? Who would take care of her children? Then she felt Otis's arms around her, shielding her.

"Lord help us!" he whispered.

"Don't anyone move!" someone shouted when the gunfire finally stopped. "Stay right where you are!" Lizzie dared to look up and saw a ring of masked riders on horseback surrounding them, aiming their rifles at them, torches blazing. She heard weeping and moaning all around her.

"You people have to move on out of here!" the voice shouted. "Every last one of you! You can't live in these woods anymore, understand? This is private property. If we have to come back here again to get rid of you, we'll shoot to kill next time."

Some of the riders dismounted and began tearing down the shanties with axes and clubs and the butts of their rifles. Others rode their horses overtop of the makeshift tents, trampling them into the mud. The stunned slaves froze where they were, not daring to stop the men, afraid of the loaded rifles pointing at them. When the armed men finished destroying the camp, they turned their horses around and rode off.

"You okay, Lizzie?" Otis's voice was shaking.

"Just scared. How about you?"

"I'm all right." He helped her to her feet. Lizzie felt numb as she gazed around, watching the others sift through the debris, salvaging whatever they could. Thankfully no one seemed to be hurt.

"Why do they hate us so much?" she asked Otis.

"They're mad because they lost the war. They can't kill Yankees anymore, so they're taking it out on us, blaming us." He reached down to help Dolly to her feet, too.

"You expect us to work for people like that?" Dolly asked.

"We have no place else to go," Lizzie said. "You heard them. You can't live here in the woods anymore. At least you'll have cabins and food on the plantation. Besides, Massa Daniel isn't one of them."

"You don't know that."

It was true, Lizzie didn't know that for sure. The thought sent a shiver of fear through her. They had left Roselle and Rufus and Jack all alone. "Let's go home, Otis. Please."

They held on tight to each other as they hurried back through the woods and crossed the deserted cotton field. Lizzie couldn't stop shaking. Freedom was supposed to mean a brand-new life, a life without fear. Why then was she still so afraid? She looked up at the moon and the stars glimmering in the night sky and wondered how the world could be so beautiful yet so ugly at the same time.

13

MAY 23, 1865

Dew soaked the hem of Josephine's skirt as she walked through the grass toward the cotton fields. Her feet were getting wet, too, as the dampness seeped through her torn shoe. She didn't care. She savored the freedom she had at the Blakes' plantation, freedom to walk around the grounds in the morning, listening to the birds and watching spring's renewal in the greening earth. This plantation wasn't nearly as large or as pretty as White Oak. There was no forest at the edge of the property and none of the towering oaks that gave her plantation its name. The house was smaller, too, and less elegant. But Harrison Blake had done well with the property after his father died, and the plantation had prospered—before the war, that is.

Josephine stopped when she reached the rail fence and looked out over the weed-choked fields. Soon the land would begin to prosper again. Mr. Chandler from the Freedmen's Bureau had arrived yesterday with five Negro families, who had contracted to become sharecroppers on the Blakes' land. Josephine had stood on the porch and watched as the former slaves walked up the road toward their new homes, their possessions tied up in bundles and carried on their backs or balanced on their heads. She felt a tiny prick of hope, the first in a very long time, as she'd watched the workers arrive. She wondered if they felt hopeful, too. Three of the women had gone to survey the basement kitchen right away and soon had a fire kindled. The men had talked and laughed amongst themselves as they'd searched for tools in the shed.

This morning Josephine watched a pair of robins tend their nest in a nearby tree and felt . . . almost happy. If it weren't for Harrison's perpetual misery, she would be in no hurry at all to return home. She liked the peace and quiet here without her family's constant complaints and Mother's reminders to watch her posture or tidy her hair. She liked the freedom she felt to work in the garden if she chose to or walk around the grounds. She and Mrs. Blake had been preparing simple meals together, and Jo enjoyed eating what her own hands had prepared, meals that didn't have to be served in a formal dining room with china and silver and a damask tablecloth. Priscilla Blake was much more realistic about her losses and her future. And unlike Mother, she was willing to get her hands dirty and do the necessary work to survive.

Josephine turned when a mumble of voices disturbed the quiet morning. The new workers were emerging from their cabins to begin their labors. A knot of children—Jo counted nine of them— carried sack lunches as they left together to walk the mile or so into Fairmont to attend school. Two of the men headed toward the cotton fields, pausing when they saw Josephine to remove their hats in respect. She waved and then watched as they bent to scoop up clumps of soil and crumble it in their fingers. How must it feel to know they would be working the land for themselves for the first time? Maybe it gave them the same satisfaction she'd felt when she'd tasted the first spoonful of soup she and Mrs. Blake had cooked. Jo was fond of Mrs. Blake, and she was accomplishing something useful here for the first time in her life, instead of existing merely to attract a beau or waiting for her parents to make decisions for her. She liked this new, stronger self.

"Oh, your hem is all wet," Mrs. Blake said when Josephine finished her stroll and returned to the house. It was an observation, nothing more, carrying none of the censure that Mother would have added.

"I know. But it's so lovely outside in the morning that I couldn't resist a nice walk, even if the grass is damp."

They sat down together to eat the simple breakfast the servants had prepared, marveling at the lightness of Mable's biscuits, laughing as they compared them to the ones they had struggled to make. Jo saw color in the older woman's cheeks replacing her pallor, and a hint of happiness in her pale fatigue-rimmed eyes. When they finished eating, Mrs. Blake prepared a breakfast tray for Harrison, but she returned with it in her hands a moment later.

"Harrison is still sleeping, and I didn't want to disturb him. Would you mind bringing him his breakfast when he wakes up, Jo?"

"Not at all. You need to get an early start so you'll have enough time to get all the way to Richmond and back."

"Thank you, dear. I hate to leave him for an entire day, but I know you'll be good company for him while I'm gone."

"Yes, of course." In truth, Josephine dreaded spending time with Harrison. He was moderately civil if his mother was in the room, and Jo didn't mind reading aloud to both of them while Mrs. Blake did embroidery or mending. But it was much too depressing to spend time alone with Harrison. He didn't want Josephine's company at all and would pretend to fall asleep so she would leave—which she was happy to do. This morning she waited as long as she dared after his mother left, steeling herself before going into Harrison's room alone. He lay on his back with his hands behind his head, staring at the ceiling.

"Good morning," Jo said, trying to sound cheerful. "I've brought your breakfast. Our new cook made the biscuits, and I think you'll find them much improved over the ones I made." She waited as he slowly pulled himself up into a seated position, then she set the tray on his lap. She would need to stay and make sure he ate everything, suspecting he was deliberately starving himself. He was already so thin that she could see the outline of his bones beneath his skin. In fact, he looked so ghoulish in this dark, shadowy room that she hurried to open the draperies and let in the sunlight.

"Don't open those!" he said. "Leave them closed. I've told you before that it hurts my eyes." Josephine ignored him. He would have to get up and close them himself if he wanted them shut.

"Mr. Chandler from the Freedmen's Bureau is coming again today," she said. "He agreed to help out as much as he could to get your new workers started."

"What does a Yankee know about running my plantation?"

"I have no idea. Would you like to speak with him today? You can ask him yourself how much he knows."

"I don't want anything to do with him."

"Fine. Suit yourself." She watched him mop up a puddle of egg yolk with a biscuit and take a tiny bite.

"I can't believe you expect me to tolerate a Yankee on my land. Or to be pleased that I have slaves and Yankees running my plantation for me."

She pointed to the crutches Dr. Hunter had brought, propped against the wall, collecting dust. "Why don't you get out of bed and start using those? I'll help you, if you'd like. You could go outside and run things yourself, you know." His eyes narrowed in rage and he picked up his cup as if considering throwing it at her. "I'll throw it right back at you, Harrison."

"Get out!"

She shook her head and sat down in her usual chair, just to be contrary. "I'm not a slave who you can order around. And if you won't take charge of your land and your life, then someone else will have to do it for you. You can't expect everyone to stand by and watch your mother starve to death just because you're too angry and prideful to take care of her yourself."

"You're a fool for raising my mother's hopes. How do you expect her to feed all these people she just hired?"

"The bureau will supply rations until everyone gets settled. And as I explained before, the workers will each get a portion of land to farm and a cabin to live in. They'll share part of the harvested crops with you this fall."

"You're an even bigger fool for thinking those slaves are going to get any work done without an overseer. You'll see just how lazy and shiftless they are."

"Or maybe you're the one who'll be proven a fool, Harrison. The Negroes know they're working for themselves now. I watched their children leave for school this morning, hoping for a better future. And three of their wives are in the kitchen right now, cooking for us."

"Tell them to stay out of my room."

"Oh, believe me, I already did. Your mother and I are very grateful for their help, and the last thing we need is for you to start throwing things at them and running them off again."

She watched him take another bite of egg-soaked biscuit, holding it in his pale, skeletal fingers. Unhappiness clung to him like a uniform. "You'd better bring me my gun," he said, not looking up at her. "I'll need it to protect you and my mother."

"These are your former slaves, Harrison. They aren't dangerous. You treated them well before the war, didn't you? They aren't holding any grudges."

"Are you really that naïve? They think they own everything now. I want my gun."

All her life, Josephine had done whatever the men in her life had told her to do, following the rules like a good girl, including God's rules. But everyone in authority over her had disappointed her—especially God—and she was tired of doing what they said. "No, Harrison. If you want your gun, you'll have to get up and fetch it yourself." She had never spoken this way in her life. But if she'd learned anything in the months since the war ended, it was that she had a voice and an opinion, and that it felt good to say and do as she pleased.

"Where's my mother?"

Jo hesitated, knowing the truth would likely upset him. But he was bound to find out sooner or later, and he was perpetually upset. "She went to Richmond."

"Alone?"

"She has a carriage driver now."

"What is she doing in Richmond? I thought the city burned down."

"Not entirely. She didn't want to tell you ahead of time for fear it would upset you, but since everything seems to upset you these days, you may as well know the truth. She's talking to your banker about a loan. She needs money to start planting and to buy mules and other farm animals."

Harrison lowered his head and closed his eyes. She felt sorry for him as she watched him struggle with his emotions. For a man like Harrison, accustomed to being in charge of his life, it must be devastating to lose control and be forced to lie helplessly while others made the decisions. She waited for Harrison's angry response, expecting him to toss the tray of food onto the floor or to throw it at her. But he continued to sit with his head lowered, his eyes closed, his shoulders slumped.

"I'm sorry, Harrison," she said quietly. And she was. "Dr. Hunter says he'll help you learn to walk on crutches. With a little practice every day, you'll eventually get stronger. There's no reason to remain bedridden. You could have gone to Richmond with your mother if you had made up your mind to get up." She paused again, waiting for his reaction, waiting for the explosion of temper that was sure to come. He remained quiet for so long, never moving, that she finally said, "Harrison? Are you all right?"

He looked up at her, his face serene, his dark eyes shining. She tried to read what she saw in his eyes but couldn't. "You're right," he said softly. "I need to change."

She stared at him, shocked. Had she finally gotten through to him? How was that possible when neither his mother nor his fiancée had been able to do so? "I-I'm glad to hear that," she said. She managed a smile.

"I believe I'll start changing by shaving off this beard." He ran his bony hand over his face. His hair and beard had become long and unkempt, adding to his frightening appearance. "The weather is getting warm, and I'll be hot and itchy if I don't shave."

"Do you want me to find someone to help you?" She was still stunned by the sudden change in him.

"No! There's no need!" He answered quickly, harshly, then sighed and softened his voice again. "I'm sorry. But you're right. I shouldn't remain dependent on everyone. If you'll bring me my razor and shaving soap, I can manage myself. Everything I need is in my rucksack. Just bring the whole thing to me. I believe Mother put it upstairs in my room."

"Won't you need a mirror and a basin of water, too?"

He nodded and turned to gaze out the window. He must have found it frustrating to watch his plantation becoming overgrown these past few months. Now, with the workers back, he would soon have a view of cotton plants growing and blossoming.

Josephine hurried upstairs and found a straight razor and leather strop in the tattered pack he had carried throughout the war. There was no soap, so she took a cake of it from beside the washbasin in her room along with her own hand mirror, and carried them down to him. "Would you like me to hold the mirror for you?" she asked after one of the servants brought the basin of water she had asked for.

"No, thank you, Josephine. Leave me alone, please." It was the first time she ever remembered him asking nicely or saying please. He even gave her a faint smile. If only these changes would last and Harrison would truly begin moving forward again.

She smiled in return and did what he asked, closing the door as she left his room. She had just gone outside to sit on the front porch when Mr. Chandler arrived on horseback.

"Good morning, Miss Weatherly." He swept off his hat before dismounting, greeting her with a grin. "How are you this beautiful day?" She was growing used to his Yankee accent and no longer had trouble understanding him. But like all Yankees, he spoke much too fast, running all his words together. Josephine still thought of him as a Yankee and her enemy, but that opinion needed to change. He had been extremely helpful to Mrs. Blake, and there was no reason to be unpleasant to him.

"I'm fine, thank you, Mr. Chandler. And you?"

"Just fine." He tied his horse to the hitching post and halted at the bottom porch step. "Are the new arrangements going well so far?"

"Yes. I can't tell you how grateful Mrs. Blake and I are for all your help. We had breakfast cooked for us this morning for the first time. We've been coping rather poorly up until now, I'm afraid, since neither of us has any experience in a kitchen."

"I'm very glad I could help. The Blakes are the first family in this area to take advantage of the bureau's services, and it has been very gratifying for me, too. I hope your enthusiasm catches on." He continued to grin like a schoolboy who had just been given a peppermint stick.

"I hope it does, too. My plantation could use more help. I wish my brother Daniel would listen to what you have to say and—"

Josephine stopped. As she looked at Mr. Chandler's boyish grin, she suddenly realized how false Harrison's smile had been, how abrupt his change of heart. People rarely changed that quickly. Dread washed over her like icy water.

"Miss Weatherly? Is something wrong?"

"I . . . excuse me." Josephine ran into the house and into Harrison's bedroom, her heart leaping wildly, her feet stumbling in her torn shoes. The first thing she saw when she opened the door was a swath of crimson splashed across the bed sheets, as if a child had spilled a container of paint. But it wasn't paint, it was blood. Harrison's blood. It gushed down his arm and spilled onto the bed from a deep gash in his wrist. He was transferring the razor to his left hand, about to cut his other wrist when she cried out, "No! Stop! Harrison, stop!"

Josephine leaped on top of his bed, grabbing the hand that held the razor in both of hers, wrestling with him as she tried to take it from him. His hands and forearms were slippery with warm blood, and it quickly soaked her hands, too.

"Leave me alone! Go away!" he yelled, the angry, bitter Harrison she knew only too well. She continued to grapple with him, desperate to take the razor away, to make the bleeding stop. He was surprisingly strong. She felt a sharp pain as the blade accidentally sliced into her hand. Harrison was going to win. He would get his wish. He was going to die.

"Help! Somebody help me!" she screamed, hoping one of the servants would hear her. They had been told to stay out of Harrison's room, but surely they would come to her aid, wouldn't they? "Help me! Please!"

At last, she heard running footsteps, then Mr. Chandler's voice. "Miss Weatherly? What . . . ?"

"Help me take the razor away from him! Hurry!"

Mr. Chandler ran to her side and grabbed Harrison's arm, opening his fingers and prying the razor from his hand. Josephine heard it hit the wall beside the bed and clatter to the floor as Mr. Chandler flung it aside. He was stronger than Harrison, stronger than she was, and she could finally let go and step back as he pinned down Harrison's flailing arms.

"Get out of here!" Harrison bellowed, cursing at Chandler. "Leave me alone! Let go of me!" He struggled in vain. The Yankee was too strong for him. But blood continued to gush from Harrison's wrist, and the sight made Josephine sick with fear. She didn't know how to stop it. He was going to bleed to death.

"Miss Weatherly, please . . ." Chandler said, breathing hard. "I need you to unbuckle my belt and pull it off." It was an outrageous request. When she didn't move, he said, "Please, we need to use it for a tourniquet to stop the bleeding. Otherwise he could bleed to death." Both men were covered in blood. So were Jo's hands and the front of her dress. "Hurry!" he pleaded.

She forced herself to move, crouching next to Mr. Chandler who was kneeling on the bed. The buckle was hard to undo with shaking fingers and sticky hands, but she finally managed to release it and pull it free from the belt loops. All the while, Harrison groaned and growled like a crazed animal, cursing and struggling.

"Wrap it around his arm and buckle it, Miss Weatherly. . . . Good. Pull it tightly. . . . Tighter!"

At last, the bleeding seemed to slow. "Good . . . good," Mr.

Chandler soothed. "Now, see if you can find me something to use for a rope. Is there a necktie or another belt handy?" Jo found Harrison's bathrobe and removed the sash. Chandler instructed her to tie Harrison's uninjured arm to the bedpost while he kept both arms pinned down. Harrison was no longer thrashing and seemed to be weakening from loss of blood, but he still moaned and cursed. His blood had gushed everywhere, soaking the sheets. Josephine's dress and the bed linens were probably ruined.

"If you can find something to tie his other arm, Miss Weatherly, I can ride back to Fairmont and fetch the doctor."

"Yes . . . of course." Josephine stumbled from the room and grabbed the first thing she spotted—the cord to the living room draperies. Two servants, Beulah and Mable, stood in the hallway, their eyes wide with fright at the sight of her.

"Is everything all right, Missy Josephine?" Mable asked. "You needing help?"

"I-I'm fine. This isn't my blood." She hurried back into the bedroom and watched in a daze as Mr. Chandler fastened Harrison's other arm to the bedpost. When he was sure the bonds were secure, he rested his hands on Josephine's shoulders for a moment as if to steady her.

"You'd better stay right here and watch him. I'll be back as soon as I can. Make sure the tourniquet stays tight." She heard the front door close, then the sound of a horse galloping away. She sank down on the edge of the bed, her knees too weak to support her any longer. Harrison pulled against the restraints for a moment as if testing them, then lay still. He resembled a corpse. This was how he would look lying in his coffin, she thought. Exactly like this.

Now that she was sitting down, Josephine became aware of the throbbing pain from her cut finger. It was still bleeding. She put her finger in her mouth, tasting blood, then took it out again and wrapped it tightly in a fold of her skirt. As her shock gradually began to fade, anger took its place.

"Why would you do such a stupid thing?" she asked him.

"Why do you think?" He glared at her for a long moment before looking away. "I would have done it a long time ago, but I didn't want my mother to be the one to find me."

"You ignorant . . . selfish . . . self-centered man!"

"You have no idea what it's like to lose everything."

"Oh yes, I do! In case you haven't noticed, your mother and I and everyone else in Virginia have suffered losses, too. We've had to learn how to adjust to a new life, and so can you."

"I have nothing to live for."

"You could have plenty to live for—your plantation, your home, a fiancée who loved you. It's your own fault for driving Emma away."

"I had nothing to offer her."

"You know what? I am sick to death of listening to you. When are you going to stop seeing everything through your own selfish eyes and start thinking about someone else for a change? The Yankees didn't have to kill you the way they killed my brother. You're letting your own selfish self-pity do the job."

"Don't you understand? I don't want to live this way!"

"Do you think any of us do? Don't you think we wish our lives were the way they used to be? We all have to get on with it, though, every last one of us."

"But you aren't crippled! You don't know what it's like to feel like you're no longer . . . whole."

But perhaps she did. Something was missing in Josephine's life, something invisible, and she didn't know what it was. There were holes in her soul like the spaces on the floors at White Oak where the rugs used to be, like the spots left behind on the wallpaper when the Yankees stole her family's paintings. Something inside of her had been stolen away, and she didn't feel whole, either. Harrison often complained of feeling pain in his missing leg, and Josephine's heart felt that phantom pain, too. If only she knew how to make the aching stop.

"None of us are whole, Harrison. But if you would stop trying to die, maybe you could start living. You keep pushing everyone away, acting mean and hateful, hoping no one will care if you live or die. Hoping we'll say good riddance. Well, it won't work. I'm not going to give you the privilege of dying. I've had to figure out how to hang on to hope after losing my father and my brother and our way of life, so you'd better figure it out, too. You were brave enough to go into battle and fight—why can't you be brave enough to live with the results of your stupid war?"

"I was willing to die for the South."

"Then it's time you mustered the same courage to *live* for the South. If you don't like Yankees coming down here and taking over and telling you what to do, then fight back by *living*, not by taking your own life."

"I have no reason to live," he said, pulling weakly against the restraints. "Slaves and Yankees are running my plantation . . . my mother has you to console her . . ."

"I'm only here temporarily. I hope to go home after you make up your mind to get out of bed."

"Go home now, then . . . and leave me alone." He closed his eyes.

"I would love nothing better than to leave you alone. And believe me, I will just as soon as Dr. Hunter arrives."

She folded her shaking hands in her lap and gazed out the window instead of at him, waiting in silence for help to come.

14

Josephine didn't know how much time passed before she finally heard Mr. Chandler galloping back with the doctor. She stood, smoothing her bloodied skirt, and looked down at the pitiful man in the bed.

"Harrison, listen to me." She waited until he looked up at her. "I've been thinking. I don't ever want your mother to know what you tried to do today. We're going to clean everything up before she comes home, and if she does see the blood or the gash on your arm, I want you to tell her you cut yourself by accident."

"What difference does it make if she knows the truth?"

Josephine stepped closer to him, glaring at him. "Don't you understand? If she finds out that you tried to kill yourself, she'll know you don't love her enough to rebuild this place and take care of her. Maybe you don't mind hurting her, but I refuse to stand back and allow you to do it." She heard the front door open and close, footsteps in the hallway. Then Dr. Hunter and Mr. Chandler strode into the room.

"Harrison, you fool!" the doctor said. "After everything we did to save your life, this is how you repay us? What were you thinking?" He lifted Harrison's arm, still tied to the bedpost, and examined the wrist. "Someone did a good job with this tourniquet. It saved his life."

"It was Mr. Chandler's idea," Josephine said. Harrison would hate the irony of being saved by a Yankee.

"We had to learn how to use tourniquets during the war," Chandler said. "This wasn't the first time I had to make one, I'm sorry to say."

The doctor's shoe crunched against something—Josephine's mirror, lying on the floor. He bent to pick it up and handed it to her. The glass resembled a spider's web, casting dozens of reflections instead of one. In every image, Josephine saw herself covered with blood. The sight made her dizzy. She closed her eyes to stop the room from whirling and groped for something to hold on to, to steady herself.

"Mr. Chandler, please take Josephine outside for some air," she heard the doctor say. She was only dimly aware of Mr. Chandler's arm around her waist as he helped her from the room, leading her outside to sit on the front step.

"Are you all right?" he asked after she was seated. "No, of course you're not. You're shaking!" He took off his jacket, stiff now with dried blood, and draped it around her shoulders, then sat down beside her. She laid the mirror in her lap and unwrapped her throbbing finger to look at the cut. "You're injured. How did that happen?"

Josephine shrugged. "I don't know. In the struggle, I guess." He pulled out his handkerchief and wound it tightly around her finger, squeezing her hand for a moment before letting go. Why was he being so kind? "I'm sorry for the way Mr. Blake acted," she told him, "and for the terrible names he called you."

"I'm used to it. You, Mrs. Blake, and Dr. Hunter are just about the only people in Fairmont who are civil to me. I don't blame the former slaves for not trusting a white man, and I'm trying to figure out how I can win their trust. I think the new school has been slowly winning them over. But sometimes I doubt if I'll ever get men like Mr. Blake to trust me."

"He's hateful toward everyone, including me. He's barely civil to his own mother." She lifted the shattered mirror from her lap, gazing at her multiple reflections. Mr. Chandler gently took it away from her and set it on the step.

"I would hate for you to cut yourself," he said.

"That mirror was a present from my father . . . and now it's broken." She was afraid she might cry. After everything else she had endured, was she going to cry now, over a silly mirror?

"I'm so sorry," Mr. Chandler said.

"Why? It wasn't your fault."

She heard him take a deep breath and slowly let it out. "What is your relationship to Mr. Blake? . . . If you don't mind me asking."

"Our families have known each other for ages. Harrison was my brother's best friend. They were together when Harrison was wounded and Samuel was killed. Mrs. Blake was here all alone with him, so I agreed to stay and keep her company—well, it was my mother's idea really. Heaven knows Harrison isn't good company for anyone."

"I thought maybe you were his fiancée."

"Never! Why would you think that?"

"You seem to care about him. You knew him well enough to figure out what he was about to do, and you cared enough to stop him."

"I couldn't stand by and let him die. His mother would never get over it. She's nearly lost all hope as it is. She's starting to revive now that she has servants again and me for company, but his suicide would kill her."

"How about your own family? Are they doing all right? Your mother never came to my office for help. I was certain she would after advising Mrs. Blake to work with me."

"My brother Daniel is home now. He's the one who's running the plantation. He may have survived the war, but he hasn't recovered from it any more than Harrison has, if you know what I mean."

"I'm not sure any of us will ever recover."

"My family is slightly better off than the Blakes, because two of our servants agreed to stay with us. And my mother is a very strong woman. She's determined to have her life back the same as it used to be—except for my father and brother, of course. I haven't been able to convince her that our lives can't possibly be the same. We'll never get back what we lost." Josephine halted, embarrassed to be baring her soul to this stranger—and a Yankee at that. What had gotten into her? "I'm sorry. I'm keeping you from your work." She started to lift his jacket from around her shoulders, but he stopped her.

"Please, keep it for a while longer. And I'm not in a hurry to start working. I want to make sure you're all right first." She wasn't. She was trembling all over, and she wondered if she would ever stop.

"There was so much blood!" she said with a shiver. "I can't imagine being desperate enough to do that. I'll never forget the look on Harrison's face when he was lifting the razor—" To her horror, Josephine started to cry. Mr. Chandler slid closer to her and wrapped his arm around her shoulders. His embrace was so comforting that Josephine forgot who he was for a moment and leaned against him, grateful for someone to hold on to, someone who would listen to her and care about her.

"After everything that Harrison has been through," she wept, "all the bloodshed he's seen, you would think life would be precious to him. That he'd consider himself fortunate to be alive at all. Instead, he wants to die."

"Unless you've been to war, Miss Weatherly, you can't understand what men like Harrison and your brother have really been through and how it changed them." He spoke quietly, gently, and she felt the strength in his arm as if he were holding her together. "After a while you see so much death that you become numb to it. You start to realize how close we are to dying every single moment of the day. We're just a heartbeat or a bullet away from it. In war you face death day after day, watching your friends die, facing it yourself, and you stop fearing it. It seems inevitable. You become a walking dead man."

"Harrison watched my brother die. Samuel was his best friend."

"We all watched our friends die. In one battle right here in Virginia, they ordered us to attack an enemy entrenchment at the top of a hill. One squadron after another had to run straight into enemy fire, and they got mowed down like hay. Men I had marched with and lived with and laughed with lay on that hill, dead, dying, screaming in agony. But as fast as they fell, the commander simply ordered the next squad to charge up the hill right on top of them. I watched five thousand men fall in twenty minutes. I was lined up with my squad, waiting for my turn, waiting for them to order me to die next, and it seemed so inevitable that I simply didn't care."

He paused, and when he didn't continue right away, Josephine looked up at him. Tears shone in his eyes.

"Someone finally saw the stupidity of it and called a halt to the slaughter. But I can understand why your friend would stop caring whether he lived or died. Death is nothing. It's an ordinary, daily occurrence during wartime. A razor across your wrist is nothing after what he faced."

"I don't know how to help him. How do I get him to move forward?"

"He never will as long as he remains bitter. Bitterness is one of the deadliest emotions we ever feel. You can't look forward when you're bitter, only backward—thinking about what you've lost, stuck in the past, despairing because it's gone. In the end, it devours all hope."

He was describing how Josephine felt about her unanswered prayers: bitter. And she suddenly remembered that she was talking to her enemy. She shouldn't be sitting here alone with him. It wasn't proper. Josephine sat up straight and slid out of his embrace, shrugging off his jacket. "What are you even doing here in Virginia, Mr. Chandler? Don't you have a home and a family up north somewhere?"

"When I first returned home from the war, I felt the same bitterness that Mr. Blake does and—"

"I doubt that very much! You were on the winning side."

"Nobody wins a war, Miss Weatherly. We all lose in one way or another. I lost my family, the girl I hoped to marry, my self-respect . . . but I don't want to bore you with my story."

"No, please. I would like to hear how much you think you lost."

"Well," he said with a sigh, "my family belongs to the Society of Friends—we're Quakers. I was raised in that faith and became deeply involved in the abolition movement. I couldn't understand how people could *own* someone, like a possession. I had read *Uncle Tom's Cabin*, and we all heard the terrible stories about slavery in the South. My faith teaches that it's wrong and inconsistent with Christianity to live a life of wealth and ease while making others suffer and toil. We also believe that God is greatly displeased by slavery."

"My father was always kind and fair to our slaves. He never whipped or mistreated anyone." She pulled his handkerchief off her finger and handed it back to him.

"But he *owned* people, Miss Weatherly. Human beings. I just didn't understand that, and I hated Southerners for it."

"Did you even know any of us?"

"No, of course not. Did you know any Yankees when you started hating us?"

"We had good reason to hate you. Your army invaded our sovereign nation and destroyed our land."

He held up his hands for peace, briefly waving his handkerchief as if in surrender. "I understand. I'm sorry." He paused for a moment. "Quakers teach nonviolence. We're pacifists—or at least we're supposed to be. But I wanted to fight. Other men my age were putting on uniforms and learning how to fire weapons and marching off to war, and they made it seem so manly and courageous. I could have claimed conscientious objector status and become a noncombatant when I was drafted, but I didn't want to. I told my father my motive was to help set the slaves free. He said I was fooling myself, and I was. In truth, I was twenty years old and I wanted to travel and fight like everyone else my age and earn glory. As you can imagine, my family was horrified. The woman I hoped to marry wanted nothing more to do with me."

"Was it worth it? Was killing us everything you hoped it would be?"

"It was hell," he said, shaking his head. "Or the next closest thing to it. The first time I went into battle and had to aim my rifle at another man and pull the trigger, I couldn't do it. I knew I had made a huge mistake. But I had to shoot. I had to kill or be killed. If I didn't participate but I somehow managed to live, I'd be branded a coward. If I walked away, I'd be shot as a deserter. If I didn't kill my attackers, I would likely be killed by them—and I didn't want to die. I had created an impossible mess for myself, and there was nothing I could do but follow orders and shoot."

"And when the war ended?"

"My home may not have been invaded like yours has been, but I had nothing to return home to. I understand how you and Mr. Blake and your families feel. I may have won the war, but I lost everything that was important to me. My old way of life was gone forever, everything I took for granted. Worse, I'd made a shipwreck of my Christian faith. And so I wallowed in bitterness, thinking about what I'd lost and despairing because it was gone."

He paused for a moment, twisting his handkerchief. "It's hard enough to come home when you're on the winning side. I can only imagine the bitterness and shame of defeat for the Confederates. The South fought hard and well, and that's the truth. Men like your brother and Mr. Blake lost this war through no fault of their own. The Union simply had more weapons and men than they did. And you're being made to suffer for their defeat."

"So why are you here, Mr. Chandler?"

"The Bible says we're supposed to love our enemies, so that's what I came down here to do."

"How very righteous of you." Josephine heard the scorn in her voice.

"I'm sorry if it sounds that way, but it's true. Everywhere I went, the Lord kept speaking the same words to me: 'Love your enemies, love your enemies.' I didn't know what it meant at first. I knew love couldn't be a feeling in this case; it had to be an action. I had seen all the destruction down here. I had taken part in it. I had seen how the Negroes had been set free with no place to go and no way to support their families, so I decided the best way to love my enemies was to come back here and help. Believe me, I didn't want to, but I was compelled to. So, here I am."

"I suppose you know there are a good many other Yankees down here who are just trying to steal what they can from us, even though most of us have nothing left."

"You may believe whatever you'd like about my motives, Miss Weatherly, but I don't want anything from you or your family or even Harrison Blake—except forgiveness."

"Forgiveness for what?"

"For being part of the army that killed your fathers and brothers and husbands. Forgiveness for ruining your land and causing you sorrow and hardship. Forgive me for picking up a gun and going to war against you. And forgive me for living when so many others died."

Josephine couldn't reply. He was asking the impossible. Neither she nor anyone else in her family could ever forgive him. Could this be why her brother refused to talk to Mr. Chandler? And why Harrison would rather die than accept his help?

"The only way our anger and bitterness are ever going to fade is if we forgive each other," he said, as if reading her thoughts.

"I'm not only angry with you and other Yankees like you—I'm also angry at my father and my brothers for getting us involved in this stupid war in the first place. What was it all for? If I forgave you, I'd have to forgive them, too. And I'm not ready to do that."

She was surprised by her own confession. She had never allowed herself to think such thoughts before. She was about to take back her words, saying she had spoken in error, when he asked, "What do you want, Miss Weatherly, for your life, for your future?"

Before she could respond, she heard Dr. Hunter's voice behind her. "Miss Weatherly?"

She stood, bending to pick up Mr. Chandler's jacket from the step and handing it to him. "Thank you for your help. Excuse me, please, Mr. Chandler."

"Wait. Before you go . . . won't you please agree to call me by my given name, Alexander? And may I call you . . . ?"

"Josephine."

"Yes. Thank you, Josephine."

She followed the doctor inside and into Harrison's room. He was no longer tethered to the bedposts but lay with his eyes closed, looking more dead than alive. "I was able to stitch up his wound," Dr. Hunter said. "Let's hope it heals properly. But the bigger issue, I think, is that his spirit needs to heal."

Josephine's stomach turned when she looked at Harrison's wrist. The wound was raw and purple, with black stitches like spider legs holding the two edges of skin together. Harrison's mother would faint from horror when she saw him—not to mention all the blood. The bed sheets were a mess, the blood drying stiff and brown.

"Harrison and I talked," the doctor continued. "I don't believe he'll try something like this again, but you never know." Josephine could only stare at Harrison and at the mess, feeling dizzy again. The doctor rested his hand on her shoulder, bringing her back. "If you'll fetch some soap and water, Miss Weatherly, I'll help you clean up."

"Yes . . . thank you . . . I don't want Mrs. Blake to find out."

"This is none of your business," Harrison mumbled.

"Well, I care about her, even if you don't," Josephine said. "If she finds out, it will be as if you slapped her in the face and told her you hated her. I won't let you hurt her that way, I won't!" She felt the doctor's hand on her shoulder again.

"She's right, Harrison. I'm going to move you over to that chair for a few minutes so we can clean up your bed." The doctor was not a large man and a head shorter than Harrison was, but he lifted him effortlessly and set him on the chair where Mrs. Blake usually sat. Harrison seemed too weak to resist.

Jo quickly stripped the sheets off the bed and crumpled them in a ball. The servants would have to boil them in lye soap, and even then the stains may never come out. She found clean sheets in the linen press and quickly remade the bed, knowing the doctor would have to leave soon.

"I'm going to bring you a wheelchair," she heard him telling

Harrison. "Otherwise you're going to get bedsores, lying here all day. I've already written to a friend at Chimborazo Hospital in Richmond, asking to borrow one. But there's no reason at all why you can't walk with crutches someday."

"You expect me to limp around here like a miserable cripple?"

"You can learn to walk again, Harrison. Why not let the limp remind you of the courage you and the others displayed against enormous odds?"

Josephine offered to leave the room while the doctor helped Harrison change into a clean nightshirt. "Put a long-sleeved one on him," she said, "so his mother won't see the stitches." She carried the ball of soiled sheets downstairs to the servants and returned with a basin of warm water, then helped Dr. Hunter wash Harrison's face and arms. He didn't resist. But she didn't want to scrub too hard, and the black, caked blood around his fingernails wouldn't come out.

"He'll be very weak for a few days after losing so much blood, so he shouldn't give you too much trouble." The doctor washed his own hands and then rolled down his sleeves. "You have blood on your face, Josephine. Would you like me to stay with him a little longer so you can wash and change your clothes?"

"Yes. Thank you." She hurried from the room to ask the servants for more warm water as Dr. Hunter sat down in the chair to wait.

She would have to change into her Sunday dress. And she would have to think of a way to explain to Mrs. Blake why she was wearing it. Tomorrow she would go home and find something else to wear. This dress and her mirror would have to be thrown into the garbage.

The servant knocked on her bedroom door before coming inside to fill her washbasin and pitcher. "Everything all right, Missy Josephine?" Jo saw concern in Beulah's eyes.

"I'm fine. Mr. Blake . . . had an accident. All this blood is his. But please don't say anything about this to Mrs. Blake when she comes home. We tried to clean it all up so she wouldn't see. I don't want to upset her."

"Yes, ma'am."

The water felt warm and soothing as Josephine splashed it on her face and neck and arms. She scrubbed her fingernails until they felt raw in order to get out all the dried blood. She felt so alone, weighed down beneath the weight of Harrison's terrible secret. It would do no good to pray. God wasn't going to help her. She would have to find another source of strength to keep moving forward. She should be used to this lonely feeling by now.

"It's very kind of you to help the Blakes this way," the doctor said after Josephine returned to the downstairs bedroom. Harrison was in his bed again, lying very still with his eyes closed. "Listen, Josephine. I can see that today's ordeal has taken a toll. You look shaken. I hope you'll try to get some rest this afternoon."

"Yes . . . thank you. I will rest. Mrs. Blake has servants to do the cooking and cleaning now. The agent with the Freedmen's Bureau made all the arrangements."

"It's good work that Mr. Chandler is doing. He's a good man."

"I wish my brother Daniel would listen to him. We could use more help at White Oak, too."

"Who's working your plantation?"

"No one, really. We only have one house servant and one field hand left, and he can't possibly do all the planting. Daniel won't ask for help, and so Mother is still carrying everything on her shoulders. She was here when Mr. Chandler explained about sharecropping, and she agreed it was a good idea, but Daniel won't listen to her."

"Would you like me to talk to him? I could stop by White Oak before I head back to the village, if you think he and your mother would be home."

"Yes, I believe they are. Thank you."

"I'll let myself out."

Josephine remembered Mr. Chandler's question as she sat down in Harrison's bedroom again. What did she want for her life, her future? She hadn't had time to think about it or to answer him. But what did she want? Today her wish would be for all of the drama to stop. For everyone to stop complaining, to stop looking back at the past and to put aside all the bitterness—and just live.

And for her own future? Josephine was afraid to dream, afraid to name anything she might want such as marriage or children or a home of her own. She had learned to extinguish her feelings and not think about the future. Her only wish would be for the hole inside to go away, but that was probably as unrealistic as expecting the Yankees to bring back Mother's rugs so the bare places on the floor would be filled again.

She suddenly remembered her broken mirror, remembered how Mr. Chandler—Alexander—had taken it from her and laid it aside on the front step. She had left it there where Mrs. Blake might see it.

Josephine hurried out to the porch intending to find it and throw it away, and to thank Mr. Chandler for his help. Had she remembered to thank him?

But the mirror was gone and so was Mr. Chandler.

15

Eugenia searched the morning room in vain, looking for the sterling silver bell she used to summon Lizzie. What had become of it? When she failed to find it, she was forced to walk all the way outside to the kitchen to fetch Lizzie herself. Eugenia wouldn't be at all surprised if the girl had stolen the bell to avoid being summoned. She had always been one of the slowest slaves.

"There you are," she said when she found Lizzie peeling potatoes in the kitchen. "Do you know what has become of my silver bell?"

Lizzie looked up with an expression of surprise. "Ain't it on the table in the morning room?"

"No. I've searched everywhere for it. Are you certain you haven't seen it?" Lizzie shook her head. If she had taken it, she was doing a masterful job of feigning innocence. "Listen, I asked you three days ago to rub furniture oil on the wooden stair rail and banisters, but I see the work still hasn't been done. Did you forget?"

"No, ma'am. But Missy Mary needed me to fetch something for her this morning, and Massa Daniel needed a clean jug filled with water right away, and I had to get this soup cooking for dinner, and I ain't even had time to wash the breakfast dishes. There's hardly enough time in a day for me to do everything."

Eugenia controlled her temper with great effort. Lizzie not only had a bad attitude about her work, she failed to show the proper respect. "Well, leave what you're doing and come take care of the wood for me right now."

"What about these potatoes, ma'am? They'll turn all black if I don't put them in water."

"I don't care. Leave them."

"Yes, ma'am." Were those tears in Lizzie's eyes? Eugenia was trying to keep her voice calm and her tone undemanding, even though she had been taught to be unyielding and firm when dealing with slaves. *They aren't slaves anymore*, Jo would remind her. Eugenia sighed.

"I'm not asking for the impossible," she said as she led the way into the house. "Just simple, basic housekeeping duties to keep my home from deteriorating any more than it already has."

"Yes, ma'am." Was she wiping a tear?

Eugenia kept a close watch on Lizzie for the next few minutes until she was certain she had found the beeswax, furniture oil, and a clean rag, and had begun to work. The stairs were right outside Philip's study, where Daniel was visiting with his friends Henry Schreiber and Joseph Gray. The two young gentlemen had both shown an interest in Mary as she'd greeted them at the door an hour ago. Heaven knows Eugenia couldn't wait for Lizzie to come and open the door for their guests, so she had sent Mary to greet them and entertain them with polite conversation as they'd waited for Daniel to come up from the stables. It had occurred to Eugenia that either of these men would make a wonderful match for Mary. Young Mr. Gray in particular came from a very fine family.

As Eugenia stood in the foyer, keeping an eye on Lizzie, she decided to take a moment to speak with the men. She rapped lightly, then opened the study door. Daniel and Joseph were reciting the names of local planters and their sons while Henry wrote them down on a list. "Excuse me for interrupting," she said, "but I thought I would say hello." They jumped to their feet to greet her like proper gentlemen. She waved them down into their seats again. "How is your family doing, Joseph?"

"I won't lie, Mrs. Weatherly, things have been hard on all of us. My father even talked about selling our land, but we won't let him."

"Please tell your mother that I would love to see her. In fact, why don't you bring her along the next time you come? Your mother should come, too, Henry."

"Thank you," Joseph said. "She would like that. She doesn't get out very much."

"What are you gentlemen up to today? It sounds like you're writing a guest list for a party."

The men exchanged glances like conspirators. "Oh, it'll be a *party*, all right," Joseph said with a sly wink.

"Better than the last one," Daniel said before turning to Eugenia. "No, Mother, we're planning for the protection of our community. This is a schedule of men who can take turns patrolling the roads at night the way we did before the war."

"Why would you need to patrol the roads? We don't have runaway slaves to recapture anymore."

Joseph sat forward in his chair. "The situation is worse now, Mrs. Weatherly. Now we have vagabond Negroes wandering all over the area at night. We need to send a message that we intend to protect ourselves and make sure the slaves remember their place."

"People are afraid to travel the roads alone, even in daylight," Henry Schreiber added. "The Yankees and their occupation army aren't doing anything about it, so it's up to us to protect our families and our property."

"Remember that shantytown in the woods that everyone was so afraid of? We broke it up." Joseph grinned in satisfaction. "We warned them not to camp there anymore, or else."

"Well, if they're no longer living in the woods, where did they all go?" Eugenia asked.

"What difference does it make?" Joseph shrugged. "They're gone and that's all that matters. Our women can ride past the woods now without being afraid for their lives."

The news upset Eugenia. If Philip were alive, he would have searched for a better solution than the one these boys had found.

"Did it ever occur to you that we may have been safer when we knew where they were living? Everyone knew to avoid that area at night. Now the Negroes could be hiding anywhere. And looking for revenge against the men who drove them off."

"You let me do the worrying, Mother. You don't need to concern yourself with such matters anymore."

Her son was dismissing her, brushing her off. He had the nerve to believe that by sitting in Philip's chair, he now had more wisdom than her years of experience with slaves. She stood up straight, lifting her chin.

"I am not a shrinking violet, Daniel. Nor do I worry unnecessarily. Who do you think has been running this plantation in your absence, standing up and protecting our home after your father died? I have remained brave throughout the war, and I am perfectly capable of looking out for my own safety now with a loaded pistol." She took another step into the room, moving closer to the men. "I'm not worried about the Negroes. But what does worry me is the fact the planting isn't getting done."

Daniel spread his hands. "What do you expect me to do without slaves?"

"You could very well hire them to work for you like Priscilla Blake did. It seems to me that if the Negroes are working hard and have their bellies full, they won't be discontented or roaming the roads at night."

Daniel gave her a patronizing smile. "I know how brave you were during the war, Mother. But you can leave all the decisions to me now."

Eugenia was about to react to being given the brush-off a second time when she heard the sound of a horse approaching out front. "Are you expecting someone else?"

"No." Daniel stood and looked out the window. "It looks like Dr. Hunter."

"Excuse me," Eugenia said. "I'll see what he wants." She needed to leave the room and allow her temper to cool before she had another spell. She could feel the telltale pressure beginning to build behind her breastbone, and she couldn't afford to have an episode in front of her son. As it was, he obviously thought of her as weak and incapable of giving sound advice.

Before opening the front door, she glanced up the staircase to make sure Lizzie was still working and saw that she was partway to the top. "Don't be too sparing with the furniture oil, Lizzie, or the wood will dry out again in no time." Eugenia checked her appearance in the foyer mirror and saw an unpleasant frown on her face. She made a conscious effort to replace it with a smile before opening the door. "Good day, David. What brings you to White Oak?"

He finished tying his horse to the rail before removing his hat and walking toward her. "I was just visiting the Blakes' plantation and Josephine asked me to stop by."

"Is everything all right? Are Priscilla and Harrison well?"

He seemed to hesitate for a moment before saying, "As well as can be expected."

"Please, come inside. I'm sorry I have nothing to serve you—unless you'd care for some chamomile tea."

"No, thank you." He followed her into the foyer looking rumpled and weary, as if he had remained awake all night or had slept in his clothes. Perhaps he had. "I just spoke with Josephine. Your daughter is doing a commendable job of helping out over there, but she is wearing out, Eugenia. She needs a rest and a chance to get away for a few days. I told her she should consider returning home now that Mrs. Blake has help."

"If that's why you've come, tell Josephine it's fine with me. I'm not forcing her to stay."

"Good. But that's not the only reason I came." He glanced around as if to see who might be eavesdropping, then said, "Josephine also asked me to talk to Daniel about getting more help for you here at White Oak. I understand you're aware of the work contracts the Freedmen's Bureau is arranging? Everything seems to be going very smoothly at the Blakes' plantation so far."

"I'm so glad."

"Could I talk to Daniel about it? Is he home?"

"Yes, he is. Please come this way." She led him into Philip's study, listening as the men greeted him and offered him a seat. Eugenia knew she should leave and let the men talk in private, but she didn't want to. Dr. Hunter supported everything she had just told Daniel, and she wanted to make sure her son knew that. Maybe Daniel would heed the advice of a man.

She stood by the door, listening as Dr. Hunter explained what he had just seen at the Blakes' plantation. Eugenia couldn't resist adding, "We were just talking about putting the slaves back to work here at White Oak, weren't we, gentlemen?"

"I believe it would be in everyone's best interests," the doctor concluded, "to give the bureau's plan a chance."

Daniel scraped back his chair as if he was about to leap out of it. "This so-called Freedmen's Bureau is from Washington, right? Do you honestly expect us to trust anything the U.S. government does? The name alone should tell you the bureau is looking out for the Negroes, not us. For all we know, we could be signing our life and our land away with one of their contracts. The Yankees would take everything, and we'd have nothing!" Daniel's friends muttered their agreement, looking as angry as he did.

The doctor held out his hands, as if trying to soothe everyone. "It's time to let go of the attitudes and opinions that started the war in the first place. Where did it get us? Everything has changed and we need to change, too."

"No. What we need to do is kick the Yankees out of Virginia for good," Daniel said, "not take orders from them. They're encouraging the slaves to take over. The Yankees don't have our experience with Negroes. They don't realize that they were better off with the way things used to be. Slaves are like children. They need guidance and hard work to keep them out of trouble. They can't plant crops by themselves and run their own farms any better than a child could."

"And the Yankees are wasting everyone's time with that school," Joseph Gray added. "In the first place, those slaves will never be able to learn a thing. And in the second place, what good will it do them if they do learn to read and write? Negroes can't do the same jobs as white men. Have you ever heard of a Negro physician, Dr. Hunter? God created them for hard labor, and that's all they're good for."

"That's simply not true," Dr. Hunter began, but all three boys began talking and arguing with him at once, drowning out his words.

Eugenia was growing more and more upset as she listened. The opinion that Daniel and his friends expressed was what she had always believed to be true, yet it sounded so cold and harsh coming from them. "I share your low regard for Negroes in general," Eugenia said when the men finally quieted. "But Philip always believed we were better off—safer, in fact—if we treated them with fairness and looked out for their welfare instead of enraging them by our cruelty. Now that they're free, what makes you think they won't retaliate if we don't make an effort to get along with them?"

"I heard some of those vagrants saying they're sticking around here because of the free school," Joseph said, ignoring her question. "We need to close that place down so the Negroes will have to move someplace else."

"Violence isn't the answer," Dr. Hunter said. "Haven't we learned that lesson yet?"

"This new government agency isn't the answer, either," Daniel said. "It's nothing but a Yankee trick to give the Negroes the upper hand. They want us to let our guard down. Well, I'm not signing away my plantation or letting them sharecrop my land."

"But nothing is getting planted!" Eugenia said. "How will we live?"

"If those slaves get hungry enough and start needing a warm place to live this winter, they'll come running back to us, begging for work. We don't need any Yankee interference."

Her son's stubbornness infuriated Eugenia, and she longed to shout at him to make him listen. Her gold coins were nearly gone, and her jewelry, too. They would have nothing left to live on if

159

Daniel didn't start planting crops and raising animals soon. Did he want them all to starve? But she could barely breathe, let alone shout at him. The pressure and pain in her chest had surged beyond her ability to control them, and she needed to leave the room and sit down somewhere before anyone noticed that she was ill. She stumbled toward the door, feeling light-headed, holding on to the doorframe, the wall, a bookcase to steady herself. She was nearly across the foyer to the safety of the parlor when she heard the doctor's voice behind her.

"Eugenia! Eugenia, are you ill?" He gripped her arm, supporting her and leading her to the nearest chair.

"I'm fine," she said through gritted teeth. "Don't make a scene . . . please."

"I'm so sorry. We never should have upset you that way."

"You didn't. I just . . . I just felt a little light-headed all of a sudden. It will pass. I'll be fine." But she wasn't fine. The pain was so intense that she feared she might faint, even though she was seated. "Go back in there and talk some sense into my son. Please, David."

"I'm not leaving you. I can clearly see you aren't well." He knelt in front of her with his face close to hers, staring into her eyes as if trying to read her like a book. Drops of dried blood speckled his shirt collar. "Shall I fetch my bag? It's right outside."

"No. Really, David. You're making too much of this. I . . . I didn't eat . . . and I . . ."

"Eugenia, you can barely breathe! Unbutton your bodice and loosen your belt. I would do it for you, but I don't care to be slapped."

She managed a smile at his attempt at humor and did as he said. Loosening her clothes didn't help. She pressed both hands against her chest to push against the pressure.

"Are you feeling pain in your chest?"

"A little . . . it will pass . . ."

"Where does it hurt? Here?" He rested his hand over her heart. Now he would feel how erratically it was pounding, as if trying to rip free from her chest. He would know something was wrong. "You've had this pain before?"

"It always goes away . . . after a moment. It's nothing."

"That's for me to decide. How long have you had it? And how long does it last?"

She couldn't reply, couldn't speak past the overwhelming pain. She hated that it had brought tears to her eyes. Part of her longed to surrender her pride and lean on David for help, yet she was humiliated to have him witness her weakness.

"Good heavens," he murmured as he felt her heartbeat. He stood and lifted her from the chair and into his arms, carrying her to the sofa so she could lie down flat. She did find it easier to breathe lying down, and the panic that always accompanied her spells slowly began to subside. David crouched beside her, gripping her hand, waiting until her breathing eased. "Eugenia, talk to me. Tell me what's going on."

"Once or twice . . . when I've become upset . . . I've had a little spell like this. It always goes away again. It's nothing."

"Eugenia, you don't need to pretend with me. I won't think any less of you. You are one of the strongest women I have ever known. How else could you have kept going after everything you've suffered? I admire you. Most women would have fallen apart a long time ago."

"I cannot fall apart until White Oak is thriving again, and I recover everything that I've lost."

"Everything?"

Eugenia nodded, closing her eyes.

"All by yourself?"

"Well, I had hoped to get a little help from Daniel now that he's home, but he has disappointed me. As you can see, he isn't up to the task yet."

"Restoring White Oak is too much for you to accomplish, no matter how strong you are."

Eugenia had heard enough of his well-intentioned advice. She sat up and discreetly turned away to re-button her bodice. "Thank you, David. I appreciate your concern, but you don't need to worry about me. I'll be fine."

"I don't believe you."

She looked at him and lifted her shoulder as if to say, *Too bad.*

"Listen, Philip was my friend. The very least I can do for him is take care of you. I wasn't able to do anything for his pneumonia, and I had to watch him suffer and die. But I won't watch you die, too."

"I'm not going to die. I have too much work to do." She managed a smile. "And Philip's death wasn't your fault."

"I feel like it was." He rose from his knees to sit down beside her on the sofa. "Ever since the war began I've been doing the best I can to take care of everyone under horrible circumstances . . . and getting nowhere. So many of my patients suffered and died. Now that the war is over, I find I'm still watching people get sick and die. I nearly lost another patient earlier today, and now you've collapsed. I'm at war with death, Eugenia, and I'm tired of losing."

"Maybe you're the one who is trying to do too much."

"No! I'm hardly doing enough and—" He stopped. They looked at each other and both smiled. "We're cut from the same cloth, aren't we, Eugenia?"

"Maybe so." She studied his worry-lined face, his kind, tired eyes, and resisted the impulse to embrace him. "But I truly am feeling better now. See? I told you it was just a passing spell."

"You need more help. Your daughter was wise enough to seek out that government agency and get help for your friend Priscilla. Neither one of them tried to do it all alone. Josephine asked me to come and talk sense into Daniel, but maybe I need to talk some into you, too."

"You don't need to convince me. I heard what Mr. Chandler had to say, and I agree that it makes sense. But you heard Daniel's reaction when you mentioned it just now."

"You could sign the contracts yourself. That's what Priscilla did. She didn't wait for her son's approval."

"That's different. Daniel isn't crippled. And he's trying to fill

Philip's shoes, which are very large ones to fill. I could hire more household help, I suppose, but I don't know anything about planting cotton. I've been trying to convince Daniel, but he makes all the final decisions."

"Then I'll talk to him for you. This situation isn't good for your health."

Eugenia gripped his arm. "Don't you dare say a word to Daniel about my health! I don't want him or anyone else to know."

He studied her in silence for a moment. "I'll agree on one condition, Eugenia. You must let me come here and check up on you on a regular basis."

"And have everyone know I need medical attention? Never!"

"I'll attend you in secret, then. I'll take you for a carriage ride or something. The fresh air will be good for you, as will getting away from all the pressure for a while. We could use some normal activities in our lives again."

"But carriage rides?" she laughed. "Everyone will think we're courting."

He looked away, but she saw his cheeks turn pink. "Would you prefer they thought you were my patient?"

"Heavens, no! I'd rather they gossiped about us than about my health. And please, David. I don't want my children to know. They would be frightened to death after losing Philip."

"I understand. I promise it will remain our secret." He paused, rubbing his jaw as if in thought. "I promised to check on Harrison Blake more often, so I could easily call on you while I'm out this way. Let's say . . . three times a week?"

"That's absurd! The gossips would have us engaged and married if you came that often!"

"Well, I'm coming to take you for a ride at *least* twice a week, Eugenia, and I won't take no for an answer." He pulled himself to his feet but stopped her as she started to rise. "Nothing doing. You sit there and rest for at least thirty more minutes. Take a nap, even. I'm going back to the study now to see if I can talk some sense into Daniel and his friends."

"But I need to check on my servant and make sure she is still working."

"No, Eugenia. You stay right here. I'll see what she's doing." He was gone for a moment, then returned to say, "She's polishing your banister. Is that what you want her to do?"

"Yes. Thank you. And please remember your promise?"

"Will you be ready for a carriage ride on Thursday?"

She nodded, smiling. She could always find an excuse to change her mind when the time came.

"Good. I'll see you then."

Eugenia leaned back against the sofa cushions and closed her eyes. If only she could get Daniel to put aside his resentment and be happy again. Obsessing about the Negroes and mistrusting the government had led to the disastrous war in the first place. It was how they had lost everything. Daniel and his friends should be settling down and starting families. They should be courting their sweethearts, going to dances. As Dr. Hunter said, they could all use some normal activities in their lives.

The more Eugenia thought about it, the more convinced she became that a dance was precisely what Daniel and the others needed to take their minds off their defeat. What better way to forget their troubles and move on? If Daniel fell in love, he would quickly see the need to start planting cotton.

She would do it. She would organize an event right here at White Oak. It didn't have to be as lavish as the balls she used to hold before the war. Just a simple dance. But it would lift everyone's spirits and bring Eugenia one step closer to recovering the life she had lost. And who knows? Maybe she would find husbands for her two daughters, too. Of course, Mary and Josephine had nothing at all to wear—neither did she, for that matter. But no one would see their frayed hems and worn lace in the candlelight. She would call it a candlelight dance or maybe a moonlight dance.

Eugenia would start by making social calls and talking to the other planters' wives. They could plan it together. No one had much these days, but if they each added what little they did have—some homemade dandelion or elderberry wine—it could be a wonderful evening. She would hold it in her drawing room where she used to hold balls. Maybe Priscilla would let her borrow her servants for a day to get the room dusted and ready.

Eugenia was feeling happier already. Yes, it was time for laughter and love to fill the rooms of White Oak once again.

16

The best part of Lizzie's day was when Rufus, Jack, and Roselle arrived home from school. The boys would chatter on and on about all the things they were learning, both of them talking at once as they shared their day with her. Lizzie wished she could sit down and pull them onto her lap and take it all in, but there was always too much work to do to get dinner on the table. Besides, she wanted Otis to hear all their stories, too. He was so proud of his children.

"I know you want to talk about your day," she said, shooing them out of the kitchen. "But you need to go do your chores. You can tell your papa and me all about it at dinner."

They skipped off to gather kindling wood and pump water, and Lizzie turned back to the hearth, poking the coals and giving the soup a stir. She called to her daughter over her shoulder. "Roselle?"

When she didn't reply, Lizzie turned around. Roselle had sunk down on a kitchen chair like a rag doll that had lost all its stuffing. "I know it's a long walk home from town," Lizzie said, "and I hate to put you to work right away, but there's just so much to do. Go take the wash off the line, then see if we have clean napkins for the table. You can start setting it for dinner, too, and—"

Roselle interrupted with an angry huff. "I thought we were supposed to be free?"

"I know how you're feeling, honey, Lord knows I do." Lizzie rested her hand on Roselle's head, smoothing back her hair, caressing her cheek. She was such a pretty girl, even when she frowned this way and got that tiny little crease between her brows. "But before you do all of that, go see if you can find that bell Miz Eugenia's always ringing. It's supposed to be in the morning room, but she's been looking for it all day. She's gonna nag me to death until we find it."

Roselle's frown changed into a sly, sweet smile. "I know exactly where that bell is."

"You do? Where?"

"I took it and I hid it from her."

"Roselle! You can't do that!"

"Well, I got sick and tired of hearing her ringing it all the time and bothering you. You need to take it easy because . . . you know . . ."

Lizzie's hand went to her middle. Yes. The baby.

"Listen, all you're gonna do is make Miz Eugenia mad," Lizzie said, shaking her head. "You know how she loves ringing that bell."

"I don't care. Maybe if she has to get out of her chair once in a while and she sees what you're doing and how hard you're work-ing, she'll quit bothering you all the time."

Lizzie tucked a strand of hair behind Roselle's ear. She hoped her daughter never did find out just how pretty she was. "That's awful sweet of you, honey, it really is. But you need to go put her bell back now. Pretend you're finding it under a chair so she'll think it rolled there by mistake. You'll get on her good side for finding it, that's for sure."

"But she's so lazy, Mama. She won't lift a finger to wait on herself. When I was at Miz Blake's house, she and Missy Josephine didn't mind doing things for themselves. They cooked and washed dishes and everything."

"I know, honey. I know. But I found out today that Miz Eugenia's sick." Lizzie lowered her voice to a whisper. "She had some kind of spell when the doctor was here, and I heard them talking about it in the front room. She don't want anyone to know, but the doctor sure seemed worried about it."

"What's wrong with her?"

"I don't know, but maybe she keeps ringing that bell because she's too sick to get up. We gotta try to keep her happy, Roselle. Something happen to her, no telling what will happen to us."

"She's never happy, Mama."

"Don't I know it? But give her back her bell, honey. Then come help me finish supper."

Roselle struggled out of the chair, still looking as floppy as a rag doll, and went into the house to put the bell back where it belonged. She was a good girl, Lizzie knew. Even if she was much too pretty for her own good.

Lizzie tried not to worry about the other things she had overheard while she was polishing the staircase earlier today, but they sat in her stomach like spoiled meat. It was all she could do to wait until later to tell Otis about what those men were planning. After the kids were bedded down for the night, she pulled him outside their cabin so they could talk. Even then she kept her voice to a whisper.

"I overheard Massa Daniel and his friends talking today about how they was the ones who broke up the shantytown and chased everyone out of the woods. He was one of them, Otis!"

"Are you sure?"

"I could hear every word they said from where I was working. They were also talking about doing something to the school to try and close it down and scare us all away. They said they don't want our kids learning to read and write."

"We need to go see Mr. Chandler and warn him." Even in the dark, Lizzie could see the worry on his face.

"I know, but how can we? It's too dangerous to go to town at night. That's the other thing they talked about. They're starting night patrols, like they used to have in the old days, remember? Anybody caught out on the road after dark's gonna get a good beating—or worse!"

"They can't keep us from going where we want. We're free now. They got no right to stop us. Are you sure you heard right?"

"I was listening to every word and I know what I heard. That's what they were doing in Massa Philip's room all afternoon—making up a list of men who could take turns patrolling."

"This is bad . . . we gotta do something . . ."

"I know, I know!" Lizzie twisted her hands together like she was wringing water out of cloth. "Oh, I wish we could leave White Oak and go work for somebody else! And I wish we could send our children to school without looking over our shoulder all the time, waiting for something bad to happen."

Otis took her hands in his to soothe her. "We have to talk to Mr. Chandler. Maybe we can go into Fairmont this Sunday on our half-day off. Think he'll be there?"

"I don't know, but we better try. I don't want them white men to close down the school."

Otis pulled her into his arms. "The Lord knows what to do," he murmured. "He'll show us." Otis knew a lot more about the good Lord than Lizzie did. His daddy used to be a preacher-man before he passed on, and he would hold meetings in the woods on Sunday afternoons. All the slaves would flock there to hear him. Otis's faith seemed to grow stronger every year, like the big oak trees that gave this plantation its name, in spite of all that he'd been through. His dream, Lizzie knew, was to learn to read and to own a Bible of his very own.

Lizzie was airing the bed linens the next day when she saw Missy Josephine arrive at the house in the neighbors' carriage, wearing her Sunday dress. Lizzie waited until Missy Jo finished talking to her mother and sister, then followed her upstairs to her bedroom.

"Anything I can do to help you, Missy Josephine?"

"I don't know . . . probably not." She was rummaging through her wardrobe as if searching for something. When she didn't seem to find it she sighed and sat down on the edge of her bed. "Can you sew, Lizzie?"

"No, ma'am. That's one thing I can't do. You need Ida May for that."

"But Ida May is gone." She sighed again. "I came home because

I need something to wear, but there aren't any clothes that will fit me."

Lizzie liked Missy Josephine. She wasn't nearly as pretty as her mother and sister were, so she didn't walk around with her chin up in the air the way they always did. She had been kind to Lizzie after the other slaves all left, helping her in the garden and talking to her. And Roselle said Missy Jo had treated her real nice when she'd worked at the Blakes' plantation. Lizzie decided to take a chance and ask her for help.

"Can I ask you something, Missy Josephine?"

"Certainly, Lizzie, what is it?"

"Otis and I need to talk to that Yankee man about something. Do you ever see him? Roselle says he comes to Miz Blake's house sometimes."

"He's there today, in fact."

Lizzie looked around to make sure no one was listening. She didn't see anybody, but she lowered her voice just in case. "When you see him, could you ask him to stop by here to see Otis and me? It's important."

Missy Jo's expression changed, and Lizzie could tell that her answer would be "no" before she even spoke. "That's not a good idea, I'm sorry." Lizzie nodded and started to leave, unwilling to let Missy Jo see her disappointment. "No, wait, Lizzie. I want to help you, but if my brother sees a Yankee riding up our lane he'll get out his gun. But I can give Mr. Chandler a message, if you'd like."

Lizzie hesitated, remembering her mother's warnings about never trusting the white folks. She had made that mistake once before and was afraid of what might happen if she made it a second time. "Thank you, Missy Jo. But never mind."

"You can trust me," she said, "even if it concerns my family. I promise I won't say a word about it to them."

Lizzie was in deep water now and didn't know how to get out. If she didn't confide in Missy Jo, it might make her mad. But Massa Daniel was her brother. She wouldn't listen to bad things about him, would she? Besides, Lizzie would have to admit that she'd been eavesdropping, and that would cause a whole peck of trouble. She searched for a way out of the mess she had made and decided to tell Missy Jo only part of the story.

"We can't go into town and talk to Mr. Chandler ourselves because we have to work all day and there's men patrolling the roads at night."

"They're not patrolling anymore. . . ."

"Yes, ma'am, they're gonna start again. Ask Massa Daniel. Otis and I will get into trouble if we go out at night. That's why we need Mr. Chandler to come see us."

"He can't come here, Lizzie. I'm sorry."

"Only other time we can go see him is on Sunday afternoon, and what if he don't work on the Sabbath day?"

Missy Josephine seemed to think for a moment. Lizzie held her breath. Was she really going to help solve her problem or would she answer like a white person? And what if she asked how Lizzie knew about the patrols? Oh, she wished she had never started down this winding road in the first place!

"Listen, Lizzie . . . how would it be if I told Mr. Chandler that you wanted to see him and asked him to wait in his office on Sunday? Could you do that? That way you'll be sure he's there to see you that afternoon."

Lizzie could breathe again. "Thank you, Missy Jo. Thank you."

In the meantime, Lizzie continued to worry about whether or not it was safe to send her kids to school. The men wouldn't come around in the daytime and scare them all away, would they? Were they that mean? "Maybe we should keep the kids home from school for a few days," she told Otis that night. "Tell them we need their help around here. Lord knows it's true enough."

"No, Lizzie. We can't let the white men scare us off and get their own way."

So Lizzie whispered a prayer as she sent Roselle and Rufus and Jack off every morning and prayed some more as she waited outside in the garden every afternoon, watching and worrying until she finally saw them walking down the path toward home. Could she ever make herself forget the old days and start believing that nothing or no one could take her husband and children away from her? Lizzie should have listened to her mother and never dared to love anyone so much.

Sunday couldn't come soon enough. As soon as she and Otis finished their work, they got ready to walk into town. "Why can't we go fishing this afternoon?" Rufus asked. Sunday was the only day the boys could spend time with their papa, but Lizzie knew this was much more important. Otis crouched down to face him, resting his hands on his son's shoulders.

"I'm sorry, but your mama and I got some important business to take care of in Fairmont today."

"Can't we go with you?" Jack asked.

"Not this time, but we'll go fishing next week, Lord willing. I promise."

Lizzie wondered how he dared to make promises. No one knew the future. Their lives were like that ball of white fluff on a dandelion—one breath and *poof*, it could blow apart and scatter to the winds. Otis couldn't know what would happen tomorrow or how quickly everything might change. But if she asked him how he dared to talk about the future, he would tell her to trust God.

Lizzie was tired when they reached town. This was supposed to be a day of rest, but she wasn't getting any, that's for sure. Otis had followed the railroad tracks for part of the way to stay off the roads, and they were still walking down the tracks as they approached Massa Chandler's square brick building near the station. The front door to his office stood wide open on this warm spring Sunday, and Massa Chandler himself was standing in the doorway as if he'd been waiting for them. Lizzie had never used the front door of a white man's house in her life, but there he was, beckoning to them. It didn't seem right.

"I heard you wanted to see me," he called. "Please, come in." The tiny office seemed even more cramped than the last time, with crates and barrels and boxes crammed into every space. Piles of papers covered his desk, and he had a book lying open on top of one of the piles as if he'd been reading it before they arrived. "Please, have a seat," he said, gesturing to the two empty chairs.

Neither Lizzie nor Otis made a move to sit. It was just as hard this time as it had been the last time to forget everything she'd ever been taught and sit down with a white man. There were probably a lot of things she would have to learn now that she was free, but it sure was hard getting started.

"Please sit down, I insist," he said. "You've had a long walk to get here."

Lizzie looked at Otis. He gave her a nod and they both sat down, afraid to disobey a white man. But Lizzie perched on the very edge of her chair so she could jump up again real quick. She stared at her shoes, too nervous to start the conversation, hoping that Otis would do it.

"Thank you for waiting to see us, sir," Otis began. "We'll try and be quick so we won't take your time. It seems my wife heard the white folks talking about something the other day. She didn't mean to listen in on them, but she was working in the hallway and she overheard what Massa Daniel and the other men were saying."

"You don't need to call him *Massa* anymore," Mr. Chandler said. "But please continue. I'm sorry for interrupting."

"Well, sir, they was making plans to start up the night patrols, like they used to have before the war—"

"I don't understand. What are night patrols?"

"They used to take turns riding the roads at night with their rifles loaded to make sure none of us slaves escaped. But now that we're free, they're thinking we're dangerous and so they want to keep us off the roads after dark. That's why we had to come and see you in the daytime. They'll probably give a good whipping to anyone they catch."

"They can't do that! It isn't legal!" Mr. Chandler said, raising his voice.

Otis stared at his shoes. "Well, sir . . . that's the way things are around here," he said quietly.

"I see. Thank you for telling me. I need to let someone in

Richmond know about this right away." He looked as though he wanted to jump up and ride there this very minute. His willingness to help gave Lizzie courage.

"That ain't the worst of it," she said, barely able to stay seated. "Them men was also talking about doing something to the school to close it down—your school." She gestured toward the back of the building where the classroom was. "They said they didn't want Negro children learning to read and write, so they're planning to shut it down for good so we'll move someplace else."

He stared at her, and for a moment she saw fear in his eyes. She didn't think he was afraid for himself, but for his school. Why had the Yankees sent someone so young to do this job? Why not send someone older or stronger or fiercer? Mr. Chandler was a nice man, but he looked like a schoolboy in a grown man's uniform. Lizzie knew that Yankees like him had won the war, but he didn't look as though he would stand a chance against Massa Daniel and all his friends. Mr. Chandler opened his mouth as if to speak, then closed it again. Lizzie waited.

"I don't know what to say," he murmured. "A threat against the school is very serious. I can't imagine why they would . . . Did they say what they planned to do, exactly? I'll need to take precautions. I'm concerned for the safety of our students and our teacher, Miss Hunt."

"You need to be careful for yourself, Mr. Chandler," Lizzie said. "Them men all have guns, and they ain't afraid to use them. They broke up the shantytown back in the woods where some of our friends were living. We were there visiting Otis's brother the night they came, and they warned us that they'd shoot to kill the next time."

"We don't know what became of Saul and the others," Otis said, "or where they all moved to, but somebody needs to warn them about the night patrols. I tried to tell Saul he should settle down and sign one of your contracts, but he says you're gonna move him and his family to a piece of land out West someplace."

"Yes, I'm sorry but that program might take a little longer to get started than I had hoped. My bosses in Washington have a lot of other things to argue about first."

"What about the school?" Lizzie asked. "Is it safe to keep sending our kids here?"

"These men will be attacking a U.S. government institution if they do try anything," Mr. Chandler said with a frown.

"They don't care about that," Otis said. "They took on the U.S. government once before, didn't they? Ain't that why they fought the war?"

Mr. Chandler's shoulders sagged. Lizzie felt sorry for him. But then he sat up straight again as if collecting his courage. "I'll go to Richmond and see about getting some protection."

"Thank you, sir. We appreciate it," Otis said. "My family means the world to me." He looked relieved, but Lizzie didn't share his relief.

"We want to work someplace else," she blurted out. "Massa Daniel is the ringleader of these men, and I . . . do you have a place we can move to? Somebody else we can work for instead of the Weatherlys?"

"The Weatherlys? Is . . . is that who you work for?"

"Yes, sir."

"Is Josephine Weatherly their daughter?"

"Yes, sir."

"And her brother is the man you overheard? The man whom you call the ringleader?"

"Yes, sir."

Mr. Chandler leaned back in his seat and let out his breath in a rush. Lizzie's heart began to pound. Was he going to get mad at them for telling on Massa Daniel?

"Did we say something wrong?" Otis asked. He was squeezing his hat so tightly in his hands that he was going to punch his fingers right through it.

"No . . . no, you didn't say anything wrong. I'm just . . . surprised, that's all. I should have made the connection when Josephine asked me to see you today. Does she know about the threat to the school?"

"No, sir. I was afraid to tell her because then she'd know I was listening outside the door."

"I understand. And I understand why you'd want to work someplace else. But the Blake plantation is the only one that has signed a contract for sharecroppers, so far. They have all the help they need for now. I'm sorry. But as soon as someone else asks for help, you'll be the first ones I ask."

Otis reached for Lizzie's hand as he rose to his feet. "Thank you, sir," he said. "Let's hope it ain't too late to plant cotton by then."

"Listen, I can't thank you enough for sharing this information with me. And as long as you're still working at White Oak, maybe you can continue to help the others—and me—by listening in. If you happen to hear anything else, I hope you'll pass it along to me. Perhaps you could send a note with your children?"

Lizzie nodded, but she knew that was impossible. Had he forgotten that she and Otis couldn't read or write? They said good-bye and started walking home, but Lizzie didn't feel any better or safer than she had on the way into town. And it was tiring to walk along the tracks. The rough gravel poked her feet beneath her tattered shoes.

"I feel like we're rabbits caught in a snare," she said. "We can't work someplace else, can't live in the woods, can't leave or we'll all go hungry."

Otis looked worried, too. "I sure wish I could warn Saul and the others about the night patrols."

"We got some time before it gets dark. Maybe we can go look for him. Rufus says he sees Saul's boys at school sometimes, so they can't be living too far away."

Otis halted. "Let me think. Where would he go? . . . I do know where his favorite fishing spot is, and it's on the way home. You mind going there with me to see?"

They found Saul and a couple of others from the plantation fishing by a creek that fed into the Pamunkey River. The glade was hidden by a tangle of weeds and vines and wasn't visible from the road until you got right up to it. "Am I glad to see you," Otis told his brother. "We didn't know how to get ahold of you."

Lizzie sat down to rest on a large rock near the edge of the creek. It was so quiet and peaceful here that she wished she could build a little cabin and live right here, far away from all the trouble. She dipped her fingers in the creek and quickly pulled them out again. The water was icy cold.

"Are you living here now?" Otis asked his brother.

"No, we're still in the woods. Farther back from the road, though."

"That ain't very smart. You heard what those men said. They won't fire their rifles over your heads the next time—they'll shoot to kill. And they'll probably get away with it. No one's gonna believe a Negro's story over a white man's."

"We won't be there much longer. We're gonna get us some land soon and move away from Virginia for good."

"You better talk to Mr. Chandler again. Lizzie and me were just there, and he said it might take some time for that land deal to come through."

Lizzie closed her eyes, listening to the gurgling sound the water made as it flowed over the rocks. If only every day could be as peaceful as this. Meanwhile, Otis told Saul and the other men about the night patrols and the threat to the school. Their voices sounded far away.

"Make sure you tell everybody to stay off the roads after dark."

"We ain't afraid and you shouldn't be, either. We're free men now."

"The law might have changed, but Massa Daniel and the others are still thinking the same old way. They're mad about losing the war and looking for somebody to blame, so they're blaming us."

When Lizzie opened her eyes again, the sun was touching the tops of the trees, painting the sky red. She stood and went to where the men were still talking and tugged on Otis's hand. "We need to get home before dark."

They walked a little faster as they made their way home, and the peaceful feeling Lizzie'd had by the creek was gone. "Do you think Saul and them will listen to us?" Lizzie asked.

Otis shook his head. "Saul always was muleheaded."

The shadows were long and purple when they arrived back. The boys were playing a game in front of the cabin using sticks and stones, but they dropped everything and ran to meet them as soon as they got close to home. "Where's Roselle?" Lizzie asked, looking all around.

"She went for a walk up to the chicken coop to see her ducks."

Lizzie's stomach twisted like an old rag. "When did she leave?"

Rufus shrugged. "Not long ago."

"You boys stay here!"

Otis stayed right beside Lizzie as they hurried up the hill. "Every day after school she runs to that coop," Lizzie panted. "Her baby ducks are growing bigger and doing good with their chicken mamas. But when they see Roselle, they run to her like they know she was the one who rescued them." Fear was making her babble. She should have warned Roselle not to wander too far from their cabin, but she didn't want her kids to feel scared all the time the way she did. Now she wished she had warned her.

They reached the top of the rise, and Lizzie's heart stood still. Roselle stood on the walkway between the house and the kitchen, talking to Massa Daniel. Roselle was smiling and looking all shy and pretty, but the way Massa was looking at her made Lizzie's blood run as cold as creek water through her veins.

"Otis! Otis, get her away from him!" She held her hand over her mouth to keep from screaming.

"Hush. Don't say a word, Lizzie. Stay right here."

Lizzie couldn't breathe. She wanted Otis to run the rest of the way, but he walked calmly toward Roselle as if he didn't have a care in the world. Massa Daniel turned and saw him coming and his expression turned as hard as ice in January. Roselle turned around and saw Otis, too. Her smile vanished.

Otis removed his hat in respect and looked down at his feet, not at Massa, the way he'd been taught. Lizzie couldn't hear what they were saying, but after a minute he and Massa Daniel walked off toward the stables. Lizzie beckoned to Roselle and waited for her to walk back down to Slave Row.

"What did Massa Daniel want?" Lizzie asked. Her heart was still pounding much too fast.

"Nothing. We were just talking. He wanted to hear all about my ducks."

Lizzie could see the outline of Roselle's maturing body beneath her thin cotton dress—and Massa would have seen it, too. "Stay away from him, Roselle. And if you have to go near him, you be real careful. You hear?"

"He's our massa. We have to do what he says, don't we?"

"Listen to me. He ain't our massa no more. Your papa works for him, Roselle. But we work for Miz Eugenia."

"Otis isn't my papa."

Lizzie grabbed Roselle's arm as she started to walk away and pulled her back. "Don't start with all that, you hear me? Otis loves you like his own child. There ain't a thing he wouldn't do for you."

"When are you going to tell me about my real father? You promised, remember?" Roselle was so pretty, even when she was pouting, that it scared Lizzie half to death.

"I'll tell you about it when the right time comes. But this ain't it. In the meantime, I'm warning you to stay as far away from that man as you can."

17

MAY 28, 1865

Josephine stood before Mrs. Blake's hall mirror adjusting her hat. It looked so faded and bedraggled after being worn every Sunday for the past five years that she longed to toss it into the trash. The style might have suited her as a girl of seventeen, but it seemed too childish for a young woman of twenty-two. Jo would rather not wear a hat at all, but she lacked the courage to defy convention or the patience to listen to her mother's rebuke if she came to church without a hat.

"Isn't it wonderful to have a carriage driver again?" Mrs. Blake asked. "And to be able to attend church on Sunday?" Josephine could see Priscilla's reflection in the mirror behind her, securing her own hat in place with a hatpin.

"Yes . . . wonderful," Josephine murmured. But in truth, she had been perfectly happy to avoid church these past weeks. Mother had offered to pick her up every Sunday, but Jo gave the excuse that she didn't want to leave Mrs. Blake alone—and Mrs. Blake didn't want to leave Harrison alone. Now that they had servants again, they were both free to attend, much to Josephine's dismay.

"When Dr. Hunter brings the wheelchair, we must convince Harrison to come with us," Mrs. Blake said. She looked so happy and so hopeful that Jo nodded in agreement. But Harrison would never go. A man as bitter as he was would have nothing to say to God. Jo knew because she had nothing to say to God, either.

"Are you certain you don't want me to stay home with him, Mrs. Blake? I would be happy to, you know."

"He'll be fine. He said he would ring for one of the servants if he needed anything."

Josephine still worried that he would try to end his life again if she left him alone. The servants knew the truth and had promised to keep it a secret—how could they not know when they had seen all the blood? Josephine made sure she went into his bedroom before Mrs. Blake whenever he'd been alone for a while. His mother should never have to face the horror that she had witnessed.

Jo savored the carriage ride into Fairmont on such a beautiful spring day. But as she walked up the church steps, she realized it had been a mistake to come. The tidy little building with its prim pews and colorful windows reminded her of the hours she had spent on her knees here in fervent prayer during the war. And how God had mocked those prayers with His cruel lack of concern.

"Would you mind if I sat in the back?" she asked. "I'm feeling very warm. I'm sure my mother would love to have you sit with her." Thankfully, Mrs. Blake didn't argue.

Josephine found a seat in the very last pew. She stood when everyone else did and opened the hymnal to the right hymn, but the cold anger that filled her made her unable to sing a note. If she could just get through the service today, she would make up a string of excuses to never come back. The minister talked about faith as if it were as colorful and clear-cut as the scenes portrayed on the stained-glass windows, but Jo knew it wasn't true. The Savior who looked down on her from the windows seemed as flat and cold and lifeless as the glass. The world, as it turned out, was not as neat and orderly as Josephine had been led to believe—*simply follow the rules, do what's right, and your life will be happy. . . . Good people are blessed, bad people are punished. . . . Ask and it will be given unto you. . . .* None of it was true. God didn't answer prayer.

Josephine's anger churned and swelled inside her until she couldn't breathe. What was she doing here if she no longer believed any of it? As the congregation stood to recite the Apostles' Creed, she pushed her way to the aisle and hurried out.

Fresh air! It smelled of hay and woodsmoke and horses, but at least she no longer felt trapped. She hurried down the church steps and away from the building, longing to walk all the way home. But it was too far and her shoes were in terrible condition. She would have to wait for the service to end.

A row of carriages stood parked by the hitching posts, the horses flicking insects with their swishing tails, the Negro drivers relaxing in the sunshine, talking quietly. Josephine decided to follow the path around to the rear of the church and visit the cemetery. The hinges on the rusted gate squeaked loudly as she opened and closed it. The air felt cool in the shade beneath the trees, and she pulled her shawl tighter around her shoulders.

Some of the graves dated back a hundred years or more, their stone markers barely legible after a century of wind and rain. But there were far too many new ones, all casualties of the war. She knew that for every soldier buried here, two or three more young men had been laid to rest in cemeteries far from home, never to return. She followed the path to her family's burial plot where Daddy and Samuel were buried alongside three generations of Weatherlys. She sat down on Granddaddy Weatherly's blocklike tombstone with her back to the church, waiting for the service to end.

She had only been seated a few minutes when she heard the cemetery gate squeak open and shut behind her. Jo didn't turn around, hoping whoever it was would have sense enough to respect her grief and leave her alone. She didn't want to talk to anyone or explain why she had left the service. She waited, holding her breath.

"Are you all right, Miss Weatherly?"

She exhaled in dismay, recognizing the voice behind her. It was the Yankee. She had seen him as she'd hurried out of the church, standing against the rear wall near the door. He had watched her as she'd walked past him.

"I'm fine," she lied. "I needed some fresh air, that's all." He didn't reply, but she could tell he was still there, standing a short distance away. "I would like to be left alone, please." Instead, she heard him moving closer. He stopped and crouched down beside her. He wore a plain dark suit and white shirt instead of his Yankee uniform. "Didn't you hear me? I said I would like to be alone."

"I know. That's what people always say when what they need more than anything else is someone to talk to."

"Please go away, Mr. Chandler." But she said it softly, without conviction.

He took it as an invitation and sat down cross-legged on the grass in front of her. "You promised to call me Alexander, remember?"

"I came out here to be alone . . . Alexander."

"When I first came back from the war, I couldn't bear to go to church, either. I felt as though I had no right to be there worshiping God. I had broken His commandment 'Thou shalt not kill' and gone against all the tenets of my faith by taking up arms. Surely God would never welcome me back after I'd broken His rules. And I didn't feel welcome in my congregation back home, either. But as you can see, I've finally made it through the door of a church again, even if I do stand alone in the back." He paused, waiting, plucking up a clover blossom and tearing it into bits.

Politeness dictated that Josephine respond, but she was tired of being polite. She wanted to shock him into leaving. "I don't believe in God anymore."

"Why not?" He sounded curious, not shocked.

"Are you truly that dense? Look right in front of you! That's my father's grave, and that's my brother Samuel's. We lost the war! You have no idea how hard I prayed—how hard everyone in that church prayed—for protection for our loved ones, for victory over an enemy who had invaded our land. But does it look to you like God answered us? Or that He was even listening? Either there is no God, or else He doesn't care about us and our needs. As far as I'm concerned, going to church, sitting in there, going through the rituals . . . it's nothing but a sham."

"Have you ever read the book of Job in the Bible?"

"Please leave me alone."

"I'm sorry, but I can't do that any more than you could leave Harrison Blake alone when he wanted to kill himself."

"I assure you that I do not intend to kill myself."

"Maybe not in the same way that he tried to do it. But despair will have the same result, Josephine, if you let it run its course. You might still be walking around like the rest of us, eating and conversing, but you'll be dead inside."

"You don't know anything about me." But he was dangerously close to describing how she already felt. How did he know? And what right did he have to speak to her about it?

"I may not know much about you, it's true. But I do know we were all created to love and serve God. He loves us deeply and passionately. And so any time one of His children decides to walk away from Him, it can only lead to despair. And spiritual death."

"Should I sit in there and go through the motions, even though I no longer believe any of it? Wouldn't that make me a hypocrite?"

"Not at all. It would make you His child. If you sensed that your real father was angry with you, if he stopped talking to you, stopped giving you things, wouldn't you want to at least sit down with him and ask him why? That's all I'm suggesting you do. Sit down with God and ask Him the reason for your suffering, the reason why He didn't answer your prayers."

"Am I supposed to expect a voice from heaven?" She couldn't help sounding scornful.

"No, you probably shouldn't wait for a voice from heaven." He smiled as if she had been making a joke, not speaking sarcastically. "But—"

"If God never answered any of my previous prayers, what makes you think He would answer me this time?"

"Because now you would be asking the right questions. And while I've never heard an audible voice, God does speak to me through the words of Scripture—which is why I suggest that you read the story of Job. And He sometimes chooses to speak through your friends . . . and I beg you to consider me your friend. When we cut ourselves off from God and from other people, it always leads to despair. Isn't that what happened to Harrison Blake?"

"He has even more reasons to be angry than I do. He lost his leg. He'll never walk again."

"And yet you're trying to convince him to keep on living, aren't you? That's all I'm saying, Josephine. Give God another chance. He was gracious enough to offer me a second chance."

The windows of the church were open, and Josephine heard music as the organ started up, then the sound of the congregation singing. The service was drawing to a close. "You need to leave, Alexander. We shouldn't be seen alone together without a chaperone."

"I understand . . . I'm the enemy, right?"

"Yes. I'm surprised you have the nerve to show up in church."

"It's difficult, I assure you. This is only the second time I've come. But I'm trusting that at least a few people will respond like Christians."

"You may be disappointed."

He sighed and rose to his feet. "I've enjoyed talking with you, Josephine. I hope we'll have an opportunity to talk again."

She watched him saunter away, hands in his pockets. She couldn't help thinking that it was easier for him to believe he had all the answers since he had won the war.

Even so, Jo decided to take his advice. Later that afternoon she borrowed Mrs. Blake's Bible and carried it up to her bedroom to read while everyone else napped, opening it to the book of Job. It was a heartbreaking story, one she couldn't stop thinking about after she finished it. She felt angry and upset with Mr. Chandler and was anxious for him to return to the plantation. But he didn't come on Monday. Or on Tuesday, either.

On Wednesday morning Josephine carried her sewing box out to the front porch where the sunlight was bright to try her hand at sewing a seam. As she suspected, Harrison's blood hadn't washed out of her dress, but she had scavenged some of the lace and enough cloth to fashion a skirt. It couldn't be much different than embroidery, could it? All she had to do was sew in a straight line.

She was making headway with her task when she looked up and saw Mr. Chandler riding up the road on horseback, his dark Yankee uniform stark against the green trees. She laid her sewing aside as he tied his horse to the hitching post and hurried down the steps to talk to him, unwilling to have Mrs. Blake overhear them. She saw a smile forming on Mr. Chandler's lips as he swept off his hat, and she quickly said, "I've been waiting to speak with you."

"Oh, dear. You don't look very happy about it, either." His smile faded. "Is it the workers? Aren't they cooperating? I would have come sooner to check up on them, but I had to make a trip to Richmond and—"

"It has nothing to do with the workers. I'm angry about that story in the Bible that you told me to read."

"You mean Job? What about it?" He looked as though he wanted to smile but was afraid to. He stood idly patting his horse's neck.

"The Bible says that Job was a good man, a righteous man. God loved him and he loved God. So how could God stand by and allow Satan to take everything away from him? His wealth, all his children, his health. That's horrible, Mr. Chandler!"

"Please, it's Alexander—"

"Why should I trust in a God who is so cruel? Does He truly allow us to be pawns in a stupid contest?" Josephine felt so much pent-up anger, she could barely speak. "It's a terrible story!"

He looked around as if the answer to her outrage might be found in the yard, then beckoned for her to follow him. "Please, let's walk toward the barn as if we're talking about the workers or something. You don't want to risk being overheard talking to a Yankee as if we're friends, do you?"

"I'm . . . I'm still not at all certain we are friends. I found the story you suggested very upsetting." But she moved toward him just the same, and they slowly began walking toward the cotton field.

"Did you read the entire book, Josephine?"

"No. Some of it was incomprehensible—men arguing endlessly

with each other. Job's friends were supposed to be consoling him, but instead they condemned him. Who needs friends like that?"

. "But I imagine you could relate to his suffering, couldn't you? How he'd lost everything?"

"Yes. But so can Harrison—and he wants to die. Why shouldn't we both be angry with a God who treats people that way?"

"Exactly! That's why I advised you not to stop going to church or talking with God. People walk away and stop believing because they're taught that it's wrong to get angry at God. It isn't wrong! Job takes his suffering straight to Him. He yells and complains and protests. He tells God it isn't fair, just as it isn't fair that you were forced to suffer even though you had nothing to do with the decision to go to war. What Job shows us is that it's all right to argue with God. God understands our pain. He can handle our anger."

"You expect me to argue with God?"

"Yes!" he said, laughing. "Just like you're arguing with me."

Josephine had no idea why he found that so funny. "I have been taught not to show anger toward those in authority over me, Mr. Chandler—"

"It's Alexander."

"—nor am I supposed to argue with them. Most especially, I am not supposed to argue with my father or with God. So for you to tell me to get angry with Him and argue with Him, it's . . . it's absurd!"

"You're already angry with God, and He knows it. You may as well talk to Him about it."

She halted when they reached the rail fence, but she refused to look at him. "I'm sorry, but yelling at God is not something I can easily do."

"Prayer isn't just about asking for things. It's taking time to hear what God is saying, too, just like any good conversation. Once we finally stop talking and demanding and begging for things, it's easier to hear what God is trying to say to us. Give it a chance, Josephine. And please read the end of the book."

"I already read the end. God made sure that Job got everything back. Is that supposed to make him feel better? God even gave him a new set of children, but that won't ease the pain of losing the ones he had. My mother is trying to get back everything she lost, too, and I've told her she's expecting the impossible. Do you honestly believe God will give her a new husband to replace my father? Or a new son to replace Samuel?"

"No, of course not."

"I think it's asking too much to tell someone to keep on praying when none of her other prayers have been answered."

"Josephine, I don't know how to say this, or if I even should . . ."

"Just say it."

"I believe I know why your prayers weren't answered the way you wanted them to be."

"Is that so?" She finally looked up at him, and he seemed older than his years, wiser than he had a right to be. He had an inner serenity and sense of purpose about him that she didn't understand. She had seen him in action the day he had taken charge of Harrison, stopping the bleeding and riding into town for the doctor. Now he was gazing out at the field, at the newly plowed earth scored with furrows, at the men bending as they worked, and she believed he did know the answer—unlike Job's hapless friends. "Tell me," she demanded.

He shook his head. "I'm not sure you're ready to accept the reason yet."

"What's that supposed to mean? Am I supposed to suffer even more before I'm ready to hear it? Or are you going to be like Job's friends and tell me that I must have committed a great sin and this is God's way of punishing me?"

"It has nothing to do with sin. We all sin—North and South, men and women, all of us."

"Then why didn't God answer my prayers?"

He finally turned to look at her. "Okay, I'll tell you what I think is the reason. But I need you to promise that you won't argue about it with me right now. Promise you'll think about it for a few days, and then we'll talk about it again. Promise?"

She reluctantly agreed. Mr. Chandler took her shoulder and gently turned her around to face the cotton fields. "Look. See those people laboring out there?"

Josephine saw Negroes plowing, raking, working. It was a familiar sight, one that she had seen countless times in her life. She grew impatient. "Of course."

"What do you suppose they were praying for during the war—and even before the war began?"

She knew the answer he expected to hear, but she was too stubborn to reply.

He answered for her. "I think they were praying the same thing the Israelites prayed for when they were slaves in Egypt—they wanted to be free. They wanted their children to belong to them, not to their masters. They wanted hope and a future here on earth and not just in heaven. Don't you think?"

Josephine had been taught that God created the Negro race to be laborers. The curse of Canaan was upon them, and they were destined to serve the white men. But that was before she had befriended Lizzie and Roselle, before she had worked alongside them and Mrs. Blake's servants. Deep inside she knew that what she had believed all her life was wrong. "Probably," she conceded.

"Now, God heard the prayers of those slaves and He heard yours. Can you think of any way at all that He could have answered both of you and given you both what you asked for?"

"So the South was wrong and God decided to punish us with defeat. Is that what you're saying?"

"Not at all. I'm saying there are reasons why God doesn't answer our prayers the way we'd like Him to. Remember Jesus's prayer in the Garden of Gethsemane? He didn't want to suffer any more than we want to. But He said, 'Nevertheless not what I will but what thou wilt.' And it was God's will that Jesus would die. God didn't even answer His own Son's prayer! But Jesus trusted that God's will was better than His own."

"So Jesus gave in to God's will. Is that what I'm supposed to do? It was His will that we lost the war and my daddy died and my family and I have to suffer?"

"He didn't necessarily want the South to suffer. But it is always God's will that the people He loves are set free. It's why He sent

Jesus. So we'd have freedom from sin, freedom to be what He created us to be, freedom to serve Him. Of course it's going to be His will to answer the slaves' prayer. Since the Garden of Eden, it has been His plan to restore all things and all people to himself. Unfortunately for your father and brother, they opposed God's plan and went to war. And when we go against God, we end up walking a very hard road. It was not God's will for me to fight in the war. But I went against Him and my Quaker heritage and joined the army anyway. I can't blame God for all I endured these past five years. It was my own fault for opposing Him."

Alexander's words seemed like heresy to Josephine. The way he talked about God seemed much too personal and direct, like an impertinent slave chatting and arguing with his master. This wasn't the way faith was portrayed in her church. But then, her pastor had never given a reason why the congregation's prayers had gone unanswered. And everyone continued to pray just the same after the war—except for Josephine. "But I don't see how—"

"Wait. You promised you would think about it for a few days, remember? And by the way, I have something for you in my saddlebag. Walk back with me."

She had to hurry to keep up with him as he strode back the way they had come. They stopped beside his tethered horse. Josephine couldn't imagine what he wanted to show her and was stunned when he unbuckled the pouch and pulled out her hand mirror. The looking glass was in one piece again. "You . . . you had it fixed for me?"

"Yes, when I was in Richmond. You said it was a gift from your father, so I knew it must be special to you."

She turned it over and over in her hands. It was as good as new. "I don't know how I can thank you." She feared she might cry.

"The best way to thank me is to be my friend. I could use one, Josephine. It gets very lonely with no one to talk to."

"How can you ask such a thing? If I become your friend, my family will consider me a traitor. Everyone will turn against me the way they've turned against you."

"Do you really care what people think? Because you strike me as the sort of woman who doesn't."

"Why do you say that?"

"I've watched you work in the garden and the kitchen, doing all sorts of things that women in your social position aren't supposed to do. I've never seen you sitting around expecting a servant to wait on you. And if you cared about what everyone thought, you never would have enlisted my help with the sharecropping agreements. No one else in town has been brave enough to do that."

She saw the truth in his words. She had been rebelling against social mores ever since the war ended. "My behavior gives my mother fits," she said, smiling slightly.

"Also, the fact that you're angry with God and you say you no longer believe in prayer makes you different, too. I imagine that really goes against your upbringing. Wouldn't the people around you be shocked if they knew?"

"They don't know."

"But I know, Josephine. And I don't think any less of you. I consider you my friend. Think about what I said, and we'll talk again." He sauntered away before she could argue.

Josephine thought about her odd friendship with Alexander Chandler as she carried her mirror upstairs and laid it on the dresser in her bedroom. For the first time in her life she had found someone she could talk to freely, someone who didn't censure her for saying exactly what she felt and believed. What a relief it was.

But it was also dangerous. Not only because he was a Yankee but because there would never be another situation in her future where she would have such freedom again. Women didn't speak that way to their husbands, and certainly not to their fathers. If she was fortunate, she might find an ally in a sister or a friend, but even a good friend might be tempted to divulge a secret in a moment of anger or weakness.

She couldn't say she was entirely comfortable talking with Alexander Chandler, but she knew she would continue to do it, if for no other reason than for the chance to speak her mind freely. But she had no doubt at all that the time would come when even the guilty pleasure of his friendship—if that was truly what it was—would be taken from her, as well.

18

MAY 31, 1865

Every morning and afternoon for three days, Eugenia traveled to the neighboring plantations to invite everyone in her social circle to her spring dance. It would be held in White Oak's drawing room a month from now on the first Saturday in July. Most people reacted with surprise to hear that she would plan such an event when everyone still struggled to recover from the war, but they promised to attend just the same.

When Eugenia stopped at the Blakes' plantation to invite Priscilla, a servant brought them a lovely tea tray with china cups and pressed linen napkins. "I confess I'm envious of your servants," Eugenia whispered as the girl finished pouring and tiptoed from the room.

"It's only chamomile tea, Eugenia. I don't know about you, but I think we're all sick of having nothing but mint and chamomile. And that dreadful chicory! But what can we do? I'll be glad when we have real tea and coffee again. And sugar, of course."

"It doesn't matter," Eugenia said, waving her hand. "I find the ritual very soothing, don't you? Porcelain teacups and a warmed pot, polished silver and embroidered napkins? And a servant! Those are all wonderful signs we're getting back to normal. So is the dance

I'm planning. I won't call it a ball because . . . well, we're not ready for a ball yet. But a simple dance will be lovely, don't you think?"

"Do you really think this is the best time for it, Eugenia? Everyone is still suffering."

"That makes it the perfect time. Don't the Scriptures say there is 'a time to mourn and a time to dance'?"

"But I'm not certain the mourning has ended."

"No, but we can allow ourselves to be happy again—if only for an evening. It doesn't mean we don't miss our loved ones. Heaven knows I still grieve for Philip and Samuel. I've worn mourning for as long as I can remember, and I will continue to wear it because it's all I have. But life must go on . . . for our children's sakes, if not for our own."

"But look at us! We have nothing but weeds in a cup." Priscilla held out her teacup as if to display the evidence before replacing it in the saucer. "Any dance you hold now can only be a shadow of happier times. Won't we feel worse after comparing it to the old days?"

"Of course the first dance will be difficult—remembering how it used to be, remembering all the young men we'll never see again. But we have to begin somewhere. No one is expecting it to be the same. But I do believe it will lift everyone's spirits a little after so much grief."

"Please don't be angry with me, Eugenia, but I don't think I'll come."

"Priscilla! Of course you will! You're my best friend, and you're also the only person who has refused my invitation. You must come. I could use your help."

"I'm afraid I won't be much help."

"Nonsense. You'll be invaluable to me by simply standing at my side. We've both lost our husbands. We need each other." She reached for her friend's hand and squeezed it before letting go. "And I was also hoping you'll let me borrow your servants for a day. Lizzie will need help cleaning the drawing room and moving the furniture aside. I've been warning everyone that I won't be serving a midnight dinner like I did in the old days, but I do think if everyone brings a little something, it will turn out to be very festive. It's like that old children's story *Stone Soup*. Remember? They started with a pot of water and each person added something to it, a carrot or a potato, and pretty soon they had soup."

Priscilla managed a smile. "I wish I had your strength—and your optimism."

"Well, you could have both. It's your choice, you know. I cheered myself up enormously simply by planning this dance. Imagine how we'll all feel the night of the party? Please, Priscilla. Say you'll come."

"Very well. You've been so good to me, sending Josephine to help me."

"Harrison must come, too."

Priscilla's smile vanished like smoke. "You can't ask a crippled man to attend a dance. That's horribly cruel. He won't come."

"I'll tell David to encourage him."

"Who?"

Eugenia laughed to hide her embarrassment. "David Hunter . . . *Dr.* Hunter. As you've probably heard, he's been taking me for carriage rides occasionally." Eugenia had gone out with him several times and each time they had encountered people she knew. No doubt the gossip had spread.

Priscilla reached for the teapot and refreshed their cups. "Now that you mention it, I did hear that you were seen together. Millicent Gray mentioned it after church last Sunday, but I didn't believe her. You're not courting Dr. Hunter, are you, Eugenia?"

"No, of course not. He's hardly from our social circle. But he knows the people of our community very well, and he's been kind enough to allow me to air my ideas with him. He's as concerned about restoring the South as we all are."

"He has been an enormous help with Harrison."

"I can think of several other men besides Harrison who were wounded in the war, and they have agreed to come to my dance. Harrison won't be alone. Tell him the music will lift his spirits."

"Where in the world will you get music?"

"I've been asking everyone I know who can play an instrument if they would kindly volunteer. Laurence Schreiber plays the violin—did you know that? He promised to ask a few other people he knows. Josephine and Mary will play the piano, although not for the entire evening. They deserve a chance to dance. We'll have quite a nice little ensemble of musicians. Don't you feel happier just thinking about it?"

Priscilla smiled. "You're right. You always are, you know."

"I have another motive, too. I want to see the young people getting together again. The men are still so gloomy. They need to fall in love and start thinking about their futures, their families—to look ahead instead of back. Daniel is the gloomiest one of all, and the best remedy I can think of is for him to dance with a pretty girl and fall in love. I'm also hoping to find husbands for my two girls. Since there is a shortage of men, I intend to make the first move by holding this dance before any of the other mothers do."

"You are incurably romantic, Eugenia."

"Oh, I hope so! I hope we have moonlight and starlight that night. They make an evening so romantic, don't you think?"

Eugenia looked up as the morning room door opened, expecting to see Priscilla's servant. But it was Josephine. "Hello, Mother. I didn't realize you had come for a visit until I saw our carriage outside."

Her appearance appalled Eugenia. She had obviously been doing some sort of work outside and her face was sweaty, her dress soiled around the hem. She hadn't even arranged her hair properly but wore it pulled loosely back with the hairpins falling out. Her disheveled state highlighted her plainness and made her look like a common girl. This could not continue. It was time for Josephine to come home and behave like a proper lady again. Eugenia started to speak, to chastise her, then changed her mind. She would have plenty of time to deal with her daughter's appearance once she returned home.

"Would you care to join us for tea?" Priscilla asked. "Shall I call the servant?"

"No, thank you. I don't care for any right now." She remained in the doorway instead of taking a seat, leaning against the door-frame. She wasn't wearing stockings, and Eugenia could see bare toes peeking through the sole of her ruined shoe. Eugenia forced herself to remain calm and not scold.

"Josephine, dear, I've come to invite you and Priscilla and Harrison to the dance I'm giving in July."

Jo gave a short laugh. "A dance? That's ridiculous!"

Again, Eugenia held her temper with great effort. "Kindly tell me why it's ridiculous, Josephine."

"Oh, never mind," she said, shrugging—another bad habit. "I can never win a debate with you, Mother. But I hope you don't expect me to attend. I think it's absurd."

"I want you to tell me why."

Jo gave a huff of frustration. "Because, as I've been trying to tell you for weeks, we can never go back to the old days. Things are never going to be the same, and it's a waste of time to try. We would be like little children, playacting."

"That's your opinion, dear. I don't happen to share it."

What had gotten into her? Josephine used to be such a quiet, compliant girl. She never used to talk back this way. Eugenia drew a breath to remain composed. "I believe I know what's best for my family, and I happen to think it will be good for you and Daniel and Mary to meet other young people your age. A dance is the perfect place to do that."

"Our future spouses, right?"

"It occurred to me that it might happen."

"Well, I don't care if I ever get married."

"Now you're being ridiculous."

"No, Mother, I'm resigned to it. I know I'm plain—and besides, there just aren't enough eligible men to go around."

Eugenia was certain now that it would be in Josephine's best interests to return home. She had too much freedom here and had acquired too many bad habits and attitudes. "I will need your help with the dance, Josephine. It will be an excellent opportunity for you and Mary to practice your hostess skills. I know you remember how to make our guests feel welcome, am I right?"

"I have nothing to wear."

"Neither does anyone else, dear. We're all going to wear our Sunday dresses. Fancy clothes don't matter. Getting together with friends and neighbors is what's important."

Josephine didn't reply; she was gazing through the window with a distant look in her eyes. She may have stopped voicing her rebellious thoughts, but Eugenia knew she was probably still thinking them. "Listen, dear, now that Priscilla doesn't need you full time, I think you should move back home."

She jerked to attention and stared at her mother. "But I . . ."

"Of course you will come over to visit Harrison and Priscilla often, but Dr. Hunter tells me that Harrison will soon be getting out more. I think it's wonderful that you are no longer needed here."

Josephine sighed as if aware it was useless to argue. Eugenia was accustomed to having her own way.

By the time she arrived home again, Eugenia felt tired. Arguing with Josephine had wearied her, but her daughter had agreed to move home by the end of the week. The driver stopped the carriage in front of the house and helped Eugenia down. But she was surprised when he stood in front of her, blocking her way up the porch steps.

"Miz Eugenia? May I please have a word with you?" He was hemming and hawing, staring at his shoes. He was a courteous, docile slave, the kind every owner preferred. Why did Daniel insist that she needed to be afraid of him?

"Yes, Otis? What is it?"

"I may be out of line and I'm sorry if I am . . . but we need to start planting cotton soon, and Massa Daniel won't listen to me."

"Yes . . . Go on."

"Planting cotton is what I know how to do best and my hands are just itching to get started." He paused, shifting his weight from one foot to the other. "Now, I know that Massa Daniel was away before the war, and he never did have a chance to learn how to grow cotton like Massa Samuel did. And that's okay. I just want to borrow a piece of land that he ain't using and grow cotton on it by myself. And maybe another little patch of land where I can grow food for my family and extra vegetables I can sell. I'm willing to work hard in my spare time when you don't need me to drive you around. I may even know a few others who can help me out."

"Have you talked to Daniel about this? What did he think of your idea?"

"He won't listen to what I have to say, ma'am."

Eugenia looked down, frustrated. Why was Daniel being so stubborn? Was it from fear of filling Philip's shoes? Was he afraid he would fail?

"I'm grateful that you give my family a place here and provide for us," Otis continued. "But I want to provide for them myself, like the Negroes are doing over at Miz Blake's place."

"My son will never sign one of those contracts. He won't work with a Yankee."

"Well, ma'am, maybe we don't need the Yankee. Massa Philip always kept his word, so I know you will, too. I could maybe find a few more workers if you let them live here. My Lizzie could use some more help in the house."

"Yes, she certainly could. And I would be very grateful to have Ida May back, if you can find her." Eugenia's initial reaction to her servant's proposal was one of relief. At last, someone else was as concerned about restoring the plantation as she was, even if he was a mere slave. With more household help she could begin to restore her home, too. But how would she get Daniel to agree?

"I'll think about your idea, Otis, and let you know my answer soon." She started to move forward to go inside, but he stopped her again.

"Ma'am? . . . Excuse me, but the other thing is animals. We sure could use a mule to help with the plowing. And we could do with some pigs and maybe even a cow, too. I'm willing to take care of them, ma'am. All I ask for my pay is maybe some of the milk for my boys and some salt pork for my family come slaughtering time."

His initiative surprised her. Eugenia would love to tell him to go ahead and plant cotton and buy farm animals, but she feared Daniel's reaction.

"I mean no disrespect, ma'am, but Massa Daniel won't hear me out. He has his own things he's busy doing . . . but I wanted to let you know I'm willing to work hard if you give me a chance." He was begging now, and it made Eugenia uncomfortable.

"As I said, I'll have to think about it. I'll let you know."

He had the grace to back away, bowing in respect. "Thank you, ma'am. And thank you for hearing me out."

Eugenia went into the house and removed her hat and gloves in the front hallway. She had been so happy and excited about her dance, but her enthusiasm had been dampened, first by her daughter and now by this reminder of her son's stubbornness. How was she supposed to accomplish her goals if they kept fighting her? Didn't they realize she was making plans for their own good and for the good of White Oak?

She barely had time to remove her hat and gloves when Dr. Hunter arrived out front, driving himself, of course. His carriage wasn't enclosed, and her clothing had become coated with dust every time she went riding with him. He saw her in the doorway as he climbed down and called to her.

"Are you ready for our ride?" He gave a shy smile, hat in hand, reminding her so much of a young suitor coming to call that he made her feel like a girl again. Dozens of men had pursued her when she was young, coming to court her in a steady stream. It had been such a happy time in her life, so long ago.

She walked out onto the porch to talk to him. "I'm sorry, David, but not today." His smile changed into a frown of concern.

"Are you unwell?"

"I'm fine, but I have been riding all over the countryside these past three days, and I just returned home a few minutes ago. Would you be terribly disappointed if I didn't ride with you today?"

"Not if you invite me inside and tell me how you've been. You've been well, I hope? Not overdoing it?"

"Shh . . ." She glanced behind her as she descended the porch steps. "My children are home. I can't invite you inside because Mary or Daniel might overhear us."

"Then we'll go for a stroll." He offered his arm and she took it, feeling like a girl again. But they didn't progress very far before weeds and fallen branches stopped them, strewn across the pathway.

"This walk used to lead to the rose arbor. Remember how lovely it was, David? Now look at it. Maybe we should go inside, after all. It always upsets me to see how overgrown everything has become."

"Is that a bench?" he asked. "Let's sit there." He took a moment to brush off the dirt and dead leaves, then they sat down together. "Are you certain you've been feeling well? You looked . . . preoccupied when I arrived."

Eugenia hesitated before deciding to confide in him. "I just had a conversation with one of my slaves. He wants to begin planting cotton . . . sharecropping I suppose you'd call it. Daniel wouldn't listen to him, so he approached me. He says he knows all about it and he even offered to find more workers."

"It sounds like a good idea. Will you take him up on it?"

"I don't know. It will make Daniel angry if I do."

"It's his own fault, not yours, if he won't listen to reason. He'll change his tune next fall when you have a cotton crop to sell."

"You're right. I think I will do it." She smiled up at him and noticed his fair hair was too long and curling over his ears. She resisted the urge to tuck it back for him or to suggest a haircut. Both gestures seemed too intimate. David went against current fashion by not wearing a beard and a mustache, and she could see by the stubble that they would be gray if he did. Philip's beard had also turned gray during the last terrible years of the war.

"Have you had any more episodes with your heart?" David asked, interrupting her thoughts.

"No, none at all, now that I think about it." The realization surprised her. "I have been planning a dance here at White Oak, and I believe it has done me good. I took your advice, you see, and decided to participate in what you called normal activities. You know how I adored entertaining before the war."

"So I heard. The parties and balls at White Oak were legendary."

Eugenia realized her mistake. The doctor and his wife had never been invited to any of Eugenia's formal affairs. With only a moderate income and no family history to speak of, the doctor was beneath her, socially. Philip enjoyed playing chess with David but would never dream of inviting the doctor to a social event. David and his wife had neither the wardrobe nor the social manners for a ball. But he had been kind to Eugenia these past few months, and she wanted to invite him. She enjoyed a high enough standing in the community that she could go against society's norms if she wanted to.

"You must come to my dance, David. Bring a date, if you'd like."

He laughed, a wonderfully rich, rumbling sound that brought a smile to her face and made her want to hear it again. "A date? Then people would know I'm not courting you. That was our plan, remember?"

She squeezed his arm. "Let's keep them guessing. They'll think you must be a very eligible bachelor indeed to be courting more than one woman at a time." He wasn't nearly as handsome as Philip had been, but he had a gentle nature and a tenderness that were endearing. He would make some fortunate widow a good husband—and there were plenty of widows for him to choose from. But if he did remarry, the woman would have to be a hard worker like his first wife had been. The Hunters had never owned slaves.

"Are you certain it won't cause you too much stress to hold a dance?" he asked.

"Never! I used to love entertaining, and this is my way to get back a little of what I've lost. I'm doing this for my children's sakes."

"You're a strong woman, Eugenia, accustomed to getting what you want and accomplishing your goals. But may I offer you a piece of unsolicited advice?"

"If you'd like." She felt her guard going up and released his arm.

"Before you fight to get your old life back, I advise you to examine it carefully to see if everything is worth getting back. I remember how there used to be a . . . a falseness about it, an attitude of keeping up pretenses that wasn't healthy for any of us. Now that the Negroes are free, people no longer have the manpower to live as they did in the past. Nor do most of them have the finances for it."

"So I should let everything fall apart?"

"Of course not. It's fine to reclaim what you can, Eugenia. I don't give up on my patients as I work to restore their health. But it's unrealistic to expect things to be exactly the same as before—just as it would be unrealistic for me to expect my patients to live forever with proper doctoring."

"Why are you telling me this?"

"I don't want you to be hurt or disappointed when things don't go the way you'd hoped. And I would hate to see you take on too much and destroy your health."

"Thank you for your concern, David. The dance will be on the first of July. Promise you'll come?"

"I'll try. In the meantime, please don't overdo it. Ask for help when you need it. It's not a sign of weakness to know your limits."

After the doctor left, Eugenia made up her mind to talk to Daniel about Otis's proposal. She must keep calm, she told herself, and not risk having a spell. She found her son in Philip's office, where he was taking apart his rifle to clean and oil it. She watched him from the doorway for a moment, the smell of the oil pungent, reminding her of Philip. Should she simply tell Daniel that she had decided to allow Otis to plant cotton, or suggest that Daniel listen to what he had to say for himself?

He looked up when he saw her in the doorway. "Hello, Mother. Did you need something?" He didn't smile. How she missed his carefree smile.

She paused, deciding how to begin. She had tried making suggestions once before and he hadn't listened, so Eugenia made up her mind to announce her decision and let him get angry. He may stop speaking to her, but at least the cotton would get planted.

"We need to talk, Daniel."

"What now?" His look was angry, stubborn.

"I have decided to make arrangements with some of our former slaves to work the land. They're going to plant cotton."

"Don't start badgering me again about talking to that Yankee. I won't hear it."

"This has nothing to do with him. We will make the arrangements ourselves. Tomorrow is the first of June and cotton must get planted. Since the slaves know how to do it, I've decided to let them."

He dropped the rifle onto the desk with a loud thump. "We can't pay them. And I'm sure they won't work for nothing."

"We'll arrange to keep a portion of the harvest in return for the use of our land. The slaves are free to sell the rest of the cotton themselves. It's the same arrangement the Yankee is making, only we won't go through him."

"You're naïve if you think you can trust the Negroes."

"Maybe so, but I believe we have to try. We have nothing to lose. How would we be any worse off for trying? If we let them plant cotton, we might make a little profit. If we don't, we're certain to have nothing at all."

Daniel shoved the rifle away from him and leaned back with his arms crossed. "As long as you're taking charge of the plantation, Mother, are you planning to stand out in the field and be their overseer, too?"

She remained calm, but his anger sat like a weight on her chest. "We're going to let them work without an overseer. They know what they're doing, and they're motivated to do it. They don't want to starve to death any more than we do."

"You don't think I can run this plantation, do you? Why don't you just say it?"

The pressure in Eugenia's chest sprouted tentacles that wrapped around her ribs, squeezing painfully. She willed the pain away. "I never said that, Daniel. But I do know you weren't raised to run White Oak the way Samuel was. Neither of us is happy about the tasks we've been left with, but let's give this a try, shall we?"

"Do whatever you want," he said, throwing up his hands. "I

don't care." His sullen attitude made Eugenia's pain flare, white hot. She needed to sit down. She couldn't let him see her weakness, nor could she let him win. She drew a tight breath.

"I intend to make an agreement with Otis. I don't need your permission. And as long as you're angry with me, you may as well know I plan to purchase some farm animals, too. We'll need a mule, some hogs, maybe a cow so we can have butter again."

He shot to his feet and strode to the window, standing with his back turned. "You make me feel like such a failure, as if I've disappointed you."

"Not yet, you haven't. I understand that you need time to adjust to being home. But if you continue to be uncooperative, you will disappoint both of us."

She hurried away, trying to hold her head high. But the pain was taking over, winning the fight. She went to her morning room and closed the door, praying that Daniel would change his mind, praying that the crushing pain would stop.

19

Otis burst into the kitchen where Lizzie was busy mixing biscuits, shouting, "Lizzie! Lizzie, she said yes! Miz Eugenia said yes!" He picked her up in his arms and spun her in circles, squeezing the breath out of her.

"Put me down, you fool," she said, laughing, "and tell me why you're acting like a crazy man." He obeyed, but Lizzie still felt the room tilting as she looked up at Otis's grinning face.

"I asked Miz Eugenia yesterday if I could have a patch of land we could plant for ourselves, and this morning when I finished driving her all around, she said yes! Now we can plant cotton, Lizzie, and all kinds of food to eat, and maybe even have enough vegetables left over to sell."

Lizzie's eyes filled with tears of joy. "I never did see a man who looked so happy about working hard."

"The good Lord answered our prayers. We'll be working for ourselves from now on. I'm gonna go talk to Saul and the others and get some help and, Lord willing, you'll get some help here in the house, too."

"I'm scared to believe it."

"You better believe it, Lizzie, because I ain't making it up." He bent to steal a kiss from her, and she couldn't help glancing at the door, worried Miz Eugenia would come in and catch them.

"I gotta get back to these biscuits," she said, shooing him away. Otis sat down on the kitchen stool, talking up a storm as he watched her work.

"I been making plans ever since I asked her about it, Lizzie, hoping and praying she would say yes. I even got out the plow blade, and I been sharpening it on the grindstone so it's all ready. I took a walk out through the fields, too, deciding which ones are best for cotton and which one I want for our vegetable patch. I know exactly where I'm going to start just as soon as I get some seed and a mule. Did I tell you she's getting us some farm animals, too? But the best part of all is that nobody will be cracking a whip over my head all day. It's almost as good as owning my own land."

"Sounds like a dream come true." She wiped a tear with her floury hand.

"I guess it is, for me. What are you dreaming of, Lizzie?"

She glanced at the kitchen door again, then back to her mixing bowl. "I never been a dreamer, you know that. I just keep taking one day at a time and see what happens."

Otis shifted his muscular body as he relaxed on the stool, his long legs stretched out toward the hearth. "Come on, Lizzie. Take a chance and dream of something. It might come true, you know. Did you ever think we'd have this much? That we'd be free and that our kids would be learning to read and write?"

"No, sir. That's more than I ever thought would happen, so now I don't even know what else there is to wish for."

"Maybe wishing is the wrong word. What about a prayer, Lizzie? I prayed real hard before I talked to Miz Eugenia, and I asked the Lord to please let her listen to me. And He did! What would you ask the good Lord for?"

Lizzie scooped a spoonful of biscuit dough onto the baking griddle as she thought about his question. She scooped another and another, putting them in neat rows. "I guess I'd pray that my children could grow up to be themselves and not what somebody else tells them to be, that they'd have a better life than I had." She paused, adding another spoonful, her eyes filling with tears again. "And I'd pray not to be so afraid we're gonna lose it all."

Otis sprang to his feet and took her in his arms. "Hey now. We been to the very bottom and the Lord was there, wasn't He? He won't leave us now."

Lizzie longed to stay in the comfort of his arms, but she couldn't help glancing up at the kitchen door. "Don't you have work to do?" she asked, freeing herself from his arms, wiping her eyes.

"I got plenty of it. I just wanted to tell you the good news. And after supper tonight, I'm gonna go tell Saul, too. Maybe he and the others will come back and plant cotton with me."

Lizzie went stiff with fear. "You can't go out at night! What about the patrols? No, sir! You have to think of some other way to talk to him."

"There is no other way. The sooner I talk to him, the sooner we can start planting. It's gotta be done, Lizzie. I'll be careful."

She backed up and sank onto the stool, her knees weak. "Do you even know where Saul is?"

"He and the others are living way back in the woods where we used to hold prayer meetings. I won't have to take the road."

"Oh, Otis, please don't go. Please!"

"I have to, don't you see? Miz Eugenia's gonna let me take over the planting and I told her I could do it, but I can't do it alone. I need Saul's help."

"Then I'm going with you."

"No," he said, shaking his head. "You need to stay home and rest. I don't want anything to happen to that baby you're carrying. It's bad enough, you working hard all day with barely enough to eat. I don't want you walking in the woods all night, too."

Lizzie wanted to grab him and shake him and plead with him, but fear made her too weak to rise from the stool. "You can't fool me, Otis. It ain't safe for you to be going out at night, and you know it. That's why you don't want me coming along."

He stepped toward her, resting his hands on her shoulders.

"Listen. Why would the Lord go to all the trouble to answer my prayer and move Miz Eugenia's heart if He wasn't gonna look out for me?" He bent and kissed her forehead, then left before Lizzie could argue with him further.

He kissed her again when he left after supper, saying, "Don't you worry now. I'll be back before long." But the sky grew dark and the stars came out, and Lizzie watched through the cabin window as the moon traveled across the night sky—and Otis still wasn't home. Roselle and Rufus and Jack were sleeping, but Lizzie didn't even bother crawling beneath the covers.

She sat in the wooden chair for a while, wide awake. Sat outside on the stoop until she got too cold. Sat inside again. And all the while she couldn't stop worrying and praying. Fear made her so restless that she paced the cabin floor, even though she was bone tired from working all day. She walked to the window and looked out in one direction, then to the door to look out the other, her stomach writhing like a nest of snakes.

Hours later, she thought she heard the low rumble of men's voices. Otis and Saul! She hurried outside, gazing down the path, then jogged up the rise toward the house. Lizzie halted when she saw it was Massa Daniel and a group of his friends, just riding back home from somewhere. Night patrols! He stood talking with the others for a few minutes, then the men rode off as Massa Daniel led his horse into the stable. She saw the long, thin outline of a rifle in his hand.

Had they caught Otis already? Was he lying injured somewhere, bleeding, dying? Lizzie ran back to her cabin on trembling legs and fell down on her knees, praying and pleading, worrying and weeping. Maybe he'd seen the patrollers in time and had decided to hide out until morning. *Please, Lord! Please!* The night had turned into one of the longest ones in Lizzie's life. Waiting had become unbearable, but what else could she do? Why had she ever dared to hope for a better life?

When the rooster crowed, she knew the night was finally coming to an end. The sky grew lighter until the sun dawned at last. Still no Otis. It was time to go up to the Big House and start the fire, gather the eggs, dry her tears. She felt soggy and limp from not enough sleep and too much crying, and much too exhausted to work. But Miz Eugenia wouldn't care what her night had been like. Lizzie would be in big trouble if she didn't get all her work done.

Otis still wasn't back by the time Lizzie finished cooking breakfast. He usually woke the kids up, so she had to hurry down to the cabin to shake them awake. "Come on, Rufus . . . Jack. Time to get up and get ready for school."

Rufus rolled over to look at her, yawning. "Where's Papa?"

"You'll see him later. Better get going, Roselle. Can you make sure the boys get dressed? I got to get back to the kitchen."

"Is Papa up already?" Jack asked.

Lizzie felt sick. "Come up to the kitchen and get some breakfast when you're dressed. I'll go fix your lunches for school."

Dear Lord . . . where's my Otis?

She came out of the cabin and there he was, limping across the cotton field from the woods. Saul and another man were holding Otis up between them. His shirt was stained with blood and he had a bloody rag tied around his head.

"No, no, no . . ." Lizzie ran toward him, relief and anger boiling together inside her. Up close, his swollen face didn't even look like his own, and he had a deep cut on his head, still oozing blood. His clothes were torn and bloody, and he stumbled along like an old, old man. "Who did this to him?" Lizzie cried. "Who beat him up this way?"

The other men had cuts and bruises, too, but neither had taken a beating as bad as Otis had. Saul told her the story as they slowly made their way to the cabin. "The night riders found our camp in the woods and started shooting their rifles and destroying everything. Most of us scattered and ran off, but Old Willie couldn't move fast enough, so one of the riders started beating on him with his rifle butt. Otis ran back to help him and took the beating for him."

"I saw Massa Daniel coming back with his friends in the middle of the night," Lizzie said. "It was them, wasn't it?"

"They had handkerchiefs tied over their faces and it was dark," Saul said.

"But I know that horse and that horse knows me," Otis said. His words all ran together in a funny way as he spoke through swollen lips. "Massa Daniel was there."

"They said we was all troublemakers and that we better leave town before something worse happens to us," Saul added. "But I don't know what can be worse than getting shot at. They was shooting at us for no reason!"

They reached the cabin. The children had come outside to see what was going on and they watched, wide-eyed, as the men helped their papa inside. Jack and Rufus started to cry. Roselle grabbed the water jug and poured some into a cup for him. "Thanks, Roselle, honey," he murmured. Then he tried to soothe the boys. "I'll be all right, don't you worry. . . . It ain't nothing that won't heal. . . . Hey, shouldn't you be heading off to school now?"

"I don't want to go, Papa."

"I'm scared!"

Lizzie was scared, too. If they could do this to Otis—big, strong Otis—what would they do to two little boys or to her beautiful Roselle? She didn't even want to imagine it.

"You'll be fine," their father assured them. "The good Lord will watch over you."

"Like He watched over you?" Lizzie blurted.

"Yes, Lizzie. I'm still alive and I'll be fine. Just a little banged up, that's all."

She rushed out of the cabin and up to the kitchen feeling as worn and wrung out as an old rag. She might have been sleepwalking as she set the table for breakfast, put food on platters, and served it to Miz Eugenia, Missy Mary, and Missy Josephine, who had moved back home from the Blake plantation a few days ago. Lizzie kept her head lowered the entire time, afraid she would say something terrible if she had to look at their white faces. Thankfully, Massa Daniel didn't come down to eat with the others. He was all tired out, no doubt, from beating up defenseless people.

Lizzie never could have forced herself to serve the man who had hurt her Otis.

At last the meal was over. Lizzie's kids ate breakfast in the kitchen and headed off to school, huddled close together like little lambs as they walked up the road toward town. Lizzie had just sat down to eat when Missy Jo walked through the open kitchen door. Lizzie sprang to her feet again. "Did you need something else, Missy Jo?"

"No, no. Please, sit down, Lizzie, and finish your breakfast. I just came to ask . . . are you all right? You seemed . . . upset."

What could she say? She didn't dare tell Missy Jo that her brother was a horrible man, who beat up innocent people for no reason. "I'm fine." Lizzie kept her head lowered and turned away from Missy Jo so she wouldn't see her red eyes, her sudden tears.

"Please tell me, Lizzie. Is there something I can do to help?"

Lizzie decided to take a chance. "I'm worried about my Otis. He had a bad . . . accident . . . last night. If that doctor comes today, do you think he can come take a look at him?"

"Do you want me to see what I can do for him?"

She shook her head. Missy Jo was Daniel's sister, raised in the same house. Could they really be that different? "No, thank you, Missy Jo. Your mama won't like it, and I don't want to make her mad. She promised to let Otis farm the land, did you know that? He went out last night to see about getting more workers and that's when . . . when he got hurt."

"But if he's injured, maybe I could help."

"Could you tell Miz Eugenia that we're real sorry, but Otis won't be able to drive her today?"

Missy Jo seemed to study her for a long moment before saying, "Of course, Lizzie. Why don't you go down and take care of your husband now. I'll explain everything to my mother. And please let me know if there's anything I can do."

"Thank you, ma'am. I'm grateful for that. I'll just finish these breakfast dishes first."

"I'll do them. Don't worry about my mother. Take your breakfast with you, Lizzie, and go."

"Yes, ma'am. Thank you, ma'am."

But Lizzie left the plate of food behind and hurried down to the cabin, feeling too sick to eat. Saul and the other man were gone and Otis was asleep. She stood by the side of the bed, gazing down at him, longing to get a basin of water and tend his wounds, wash away the blood, but she didn't want to wake him. She was furious at God for allowing the white men to beat him up this way—but thankful to God that He had spared Otis's life.

Lizzie was still standing there, gazing at the wonderful, terrible sight of him when the cabin door opened and Roselle and the boys crept inside. "What are you doing here?" she whispered. "Didn't I tell you to go to school? Your papa needs to rest."

"There is no school, Mama," Roselle said. "There was a fire last night and everything burned!" She ran into Lizzie's arms, weeping on her shoulder.

"A fire? . . . At the school?" Lizzie shouldn't have been shocked, but she was. Hadn't she heard Massa Daniel and his friends planning to do something to the school? Hadn't she and Otis tried to warn Mr. Chandler?

"Miss Hunt said we . . . we can't have school until . . . until it's fixed," Rufus told Lizzie between sobs, "and . . . and she sent us home."

"Oh, Lord, no," Lizzie moaned.

The commotion woke Otis up, and he tried to sit. "What happened? How did the fire start?"

"Somebody piled all the schoolbooks and tables in the middle of the room and set fire to them," Roselle said.

"They did it on purpose, Mama!" Rufus said. He and Jack ran to their papa for comfort. Lizzie was afraid she might burst into tears herself.

"Was anybody hurt?" Otis asked.

"The Yankee's hands were all bandaged up," Roselle said, "and his voice sounded funny. From the smoke, he said. He and some others got the fire out before the building burned down, but the schoolroom is ruined, and there's still lots of smoke. We can't have school until he gets it fixed."

"And there's no more books!" Jack wailed. "How can we learn to read?"

"They can't shut down the school . . ." Otis said as if to himself. "That's the only way you'll have a better life. Maybe if we all help Mr. Chandler, he can get it started up again."

"Otis, no! It's too dangerous. You want them to hurt our kids the way they hurt you?"

"We'll be fine, Lizzie. Don't give up hope. If we ever stop hoping and believing, then they'll win." But Lizzie knew the white men would always win. She never should have begun to hope in the first place.

20

Something was wrong with Lizzie. The moment the servant had crept into the dining room this morning, Josephine saw that her eyes were swollen as if she hadn't slept all night. It was obvious she had been crying. As soon as Mother and Mary went upstairs, Josephine had snuck out to the kitchen to help her. Lizzie had been vague about her husband's accident, but Jo sent her home to tend to him, and now she was content to be alone in the kitchen for a few peaceful minutes. There was something about the smoky scent of the hearth and the aroma of biscuits baking that gave her comfort. Josephine had enjoyed working in the kitchen with Mrs. Blake, doing simple tasks like washing dishes and tending the fire—slaves' tasks. Now that she was home, she hardly dared to do those things anymore.

Jo finished washing the dishes, then swept the floor, glancing up guiltily as if expecting to see her mother. Eugenia would never understand the simple satisfaction these chores gave Josephine or how thoroughly weary Jo had become of living an idle life. She was on her way to the woodpile for another log when she saw Roselle and her two brothers walking toward the kitchen.

"Aren't you supposed to be in school, Roselle?"

214

"We can't go, Missy Jo." The girl was close to tears. "There was a fire at the school last night and everything burned up, the books and chairs and everything."

Josephine felt a moment of panic. Alexander Chandler lived in the rooms above the school. "Was anyone hurt?"

"Our papa was," Roselle's brother said. "Somebody hurt our papa."

"But that wasn't from the fire," Roselle said. She nudged him as if warning him to keep quiet.

Before Jo could ask more questions, Lizzie hurried up the rise toward the kitchen, tying her apron around her waist. "Don't you be bothering Missy Josephine now. Go on and get your work done." The children scattered, the younger boy to the woodpile, the older boy to the stables, Roselle into the kitchen. "I'm sorry they bothered you, Missy Jo. I'm giving them jobs to do since they don't have school today."

"How is Otis?"

"He's resting now. I can get some work done while he sleeps."

"Please tell me what happened. Do his injuries have anything to do with the fire at the school?"

"No, ma'am."

Jo waited, forcing her to say more.

"Like I said, he went out last night to ask his brother to help him plant cotton. Only time he could go was after dark, and the night patrols caught him."

"Night patrols? But—"

"We ain't supposed to be out after dark. Thank you for helping me, Missy Jo, but I got plenty of help now."

Maybe this was none of Jo's business. Was she intruding into their lives if she stayed? Lizzie seemed very uneasy with her here. Josephine was trying to decide what to do when she heard her mother's bell ringing inside the house. Lizzie sighed and turned to go, but Josephine stopped her.

"Let me see what my mother wants. I'll explain that . . . that your routine is a little off this morning." She hurried away before

Lizzie could protest and found her mother sitting at her desk in the morning room. "Did you need something, Mother?"

"Oh, good heavens, Josephine! Don't tell me you're going to start answering when I summon the servants, are you?"

"Of course not, but—"

"Where's Lizzie?"

"She has something . . . personal to take care of. I offered to come."

"Since when do her personal problems matter? She has work to do."

"Since the war ended, Mother, and the slaves were set free. They aren't our property to command anymore."

"I don't have time for this nonsense, Josephine." Eugenia pushed her chair back and stood. "I rang for Lizzie because I need my driver and my carriage. Daniel usually arranges all of that for me, but he isn't awake yet. He must not be feeling well."

"Otis won't be able to drive you today. He went out to find more workers for our plantation, and he was stopped by the men on night patrol. They beat him up for being out after dark—even though he is a free man and has every right to be out."

A strange look crossed Mother's face before she composed herself again. Josephine tried to read what it was. Not the anger or outrage that Jo felt but guilt, perhaps? Or shame? Was Mother involved somehow? "Do you know who's organizing these patrols, Mother? Is Daniel one of them? Is that why he didn't come down to breakfast?" Jo was appalled to think that her brother was capable of attacking innocent people, burning the school.

Mother shook her finger in Jo's face. "You remember who you are, Josephine Weatherly, and which side you are on! Our men are doing what they must to keep everyone safe. Do you want gangs of shiftless Negroes coming to our home in the dark of night, seeking revenge for their years of slavery? Daniel wouldn't be able to fight a mob single-handedly."

"But you know Otis. He isn't dangerous. Why would Daniel attack him?"

216

"That is none of our business."

Josephine saw her mother's raised chin, her folded arms, and knew it was useless to argue. Her mother was incapable of changing her ways. Fuming, Jo decided to approach the problem from a different direction. "Are you expecting Dr. Hunter today? Otis needs medical attention. Or maybe I could walk over to Mrs. Blake's house and see if he's there."

"First of all, you are not *walking* anywhere. And second, the doctor attends white people, not Negroes."

"Otis is your driver! He works for us. Why aren't you concerned about his injuries? Why aren't you furious with the men who beat him? Even if you don't care about the injustice of it, don't you need him to get well so he can work for you?"

"I don't know where you have acquired these strange opinions, Josephine, or how I can correct your thinking. You used to know better than to befriend our Negroes, and now you're expecting them to receive special treatment from a white doctor?"

Josephine exhaled. "Lizzie asked me if Dr. Hunter was coming today, and if so, would he please look at her husband's injuries. They must be bad if she's asking me for help."

"How can you expect him to take care of our families after he dirties his hands with them? He could spread contagion. Don't you dare ask him such a thing!"

"Dr. Hunter should be the one to decide who he helps, don't you think?"

As if on cue, Josephine heard a carriage arriving out front, and when she peered through the window she saw it was the doctor. She hurried to the door, but her mother followed right behind her, both of them watching as he climbed from the carriage and came up the steps.

"Good morning, ladies," he said, sweeping off his hat. He was about to say more, but as he looked from Josephine to her mother and back again he must have read the anger on their faces. "Am I interrupting something?"

"No, David. Do come in."

He remained on the porch. "Actually, it's such a lovely morning that I thought I would see if you wanted to go for a ride, Eugenia. And I didn't realize you had returned home, Josephine. Harrison's wheelchair has finally arrived, and I'm delivering it to him today." He gestured to his carriage where a wooden chair with large, spoked wheels had been tied onto the back. "I hoped you could help Mrs. Blake and me manage him the first time."

Jo hurried to reply before her mother. "I would be happy to, Dr. Hunter, but there's another matter first. Our Negro driver was injured last night. His wife, who is our housekeeper, asked if you could see him—"

"And I told Josephine that your patients are respectable white people. Please don't feel you have to placate my daughter. She has acquired some very odd ways of behaving lately."

Dr. Hunter seemed to be weighing his thoughts before answering. He was such a considerate man, a true gentleman, and they were forcing him to take sides. "Eugenia," he said, addressing her first, "there was a terrible outbreak of violence against some local Negroes last night, and several of them suffered very serious injuries. While you're correct in saying they aren't usually my patients, it might be wise if I do have a look at your servant. I know how very short-staffed you are right now and how much you depend on this man to work for you. Isn't he the one who's going to plant cotton on your land?"

"What kind of violence?" Jo asked before her mother could reply.

"Four Negroes who had been savagely beaten were brought to my office last night. Two more suffered gunshot wounds. One of the men died this morning, and I'm afraid the other one might, as well."

"Why the violence? What did they do?" Josephine asked.

"It seems they were living out in the woods, and the night patrollers came to break up the camp. Unfortunately shots were fired. The Negroes had been warned to leave the woods, but they didn't." He looked down at his feet for a moment, then up again. "There was also a fire last night at the school for Negro children."

Josephine swallowed. "Do they think the fire was deliberately set?"

"It looks that way. I woke up when I heard the fire bell ringing. I've known for some time that there are people in our community who don't want the Negroes attending school, and I find those sentiments very tragic."

"How bad was the fire? Was anyone hurt?" Josephine asked.

"The agent at the Freedmen's Bureau suffered burns and inhaled a great deal of smoke, but he'll recover."

Jo felt a rush of relief. She was surprised to discover that she cared about Alexander, that he had become a friend in a strange sort of way. "Lizzie's children told me the school had to be closed."

"Yes. Someone will have to see if the structure is still sound, and even if it is, it will be some time before it can be repaired, from what I could see."

Jo saw her mother standing with her typical haughty stance, head lifted with pride. How could she not be moved? She was a caring woman, capable of deep concern for others. Why didn't she care about the Negroes? But Jo knew better than to ask in front of their guest.

Dr. Hunter briefly touched Eugenia's arm as if pleading with her to understand. "If you'll excuse me, ladies, I'll go fetch my bag so I can check on your servant. I'll only be a moment." He was doing his best not to insult Mother. He respected her, Jo realized. Her opinion mattered to him. Perhaps too much.

Josephine started to follow him, intending to show him the way to Slave Row, but her mother pulled her back. "Don't even think about going down there with him."

Jo fought to control her temper, to be the dutiful daughter. She was walking the same narrow path that Dr. Hunter was, her conscience telling her one thing, her sense of duty and her ingrained respect for her mother telling her something else. "May I please go with him to help Harrison with his new chair?" she asked.

"Of course."

Josephine turned to go into the house, but her mother stopped her again.

"Josephine, I know you think I'm being harsh and unreasonable, but I want what's best for you. It's important that you continue to be accepted as part of this community, and that means you can't go against our established values."

"Even if those values are wrong?" She thought of Daniel, wondering again if he was involved.

"I don't want you to end up all alone. You'll be considered strange, an outcast."

"But it's my life—"

"Yes, and I won't let you destroy it. The war has left us in ruins, and we can't afford to act as individuals. We're part of a community. We need each other, especially now. If you go against the accepted social norms, your life will be so much harder, so much more painful. No one will accept you. Please understand that my criticism is intended for your own good. Your family needs you. I need you. I'm trying to direct you down a better path, an easier path."

"But so much has changed. The South isn't going to be the same as it was."

"All the more reason why we need to hang on to our traditions and to each other. The future will be less frightening if some things can remain the same."

"I don't understand why they had to attack Otis. Or set the school on fire."

Mother didn't reply. Instead, she seemed to be appraising Josephine, brushing imaginary lint off her shoulder, tucking back a strand of her hair. "You need to go upstairs and get ready to go, Josephine. Take more care with your hair, please, and take off that horrible apron. And while you're up there, please think about what I said."

Jo hurried up the stairs, not sure what to think except that she was angry. As she pulled out the hairpins and brushed her hair again, Josephine knew she didn't want to go against the community and live in isolation like Harrison. Hadn't she told him he was wrong to cut himself off from everyone? But why was Mother making her choose between one side or the other? Why couldn't she show concern for Lizzie and Otis, engage in conversation with Alexander Chandler, and still be accepted by everyone else? Why couldn't everyone work together? Get along with each other?

Maybe the men had gone on night patrols before the war, but Josephine had been sheltered from such things. Women had their concerns and men had theirs. But the war had changed everything.

She was on her way downstairs again several minutes later when she saw Daniel's jacket draped over the railing outside his bedroom. She bent to sniff it, then wished she hadn't. It reeked of woodsmoke and gunpowder. She wanted to burst into his bedroom and confront him, rage at him. But the doctor had returned to the house and was standing in the foyer, bag in hand, talking to Mother.

"How is Otis?" Mother asked him. Was she truly concerned, Jo wondered, or did she simply want her driver back?

"He's a strong young man. I stitched up a laceration in his scalp, and I think he'll be fine. He had no gunshot wounds or broken bones, thankfully. Some of the others weren't as fortunate. But you shouldn't expect him to drive you anywhere for a few days."

"Did he tell you what happened?" Josephine asked as she reached the bottom of the stairs.

The doctor shook his head. "No, but it was obvious he had been beaten just like the other men I treated last night. They're afraid to confide in me, I suppose because I'm white."

"I'm ready to leave, Dr. Hunter, if you are." Jo wanted to flee this house, her family.

"Won't you please come with us, Eugenia?" the doctor asked.

"Not today, if you don't mind. I have so much to do. Another time?"

"Certainly."

Once Josephine was alone in the carriage with Dr. Hunter, she decided to confess her fears. "I . . . I can't be certain but I think my brother Daniel was involved last night. He didn't come down for breakfast this morning, and I noticed just now that his jacket reeked of smoke. He hasn't been himself ever since he came back from the war and . . . and I'm not sure what to do. If the authorities come . . ."

"There won't be any arrests. If your brother was involved, he was one of dozens. Our young men are restless, trying to adjust to being home again. And in many cases they face huge new responsibilities—with women to care for and no resources, no money. They're angry and frightened. Their world has been turned upside down and they don't like it."

"None of us do. That's hardly an excuse for violence."

"You're right. But those young men have been through hell together, fighting together, living together. And so they're finding strength in what they know—guns and violence. Your brother grew to maturity in the middle of a war. His civilized life was interrupted. It's much too easy to make scapegoats of the Negroes and blame them for the war. They make easy targets because they're powerless and vulnerable. I don't condone what your brother and the others are doing, by any means, but I do understand what has led to it."

"What's the answer? How do we stop the violence?"

"The young men need good leaders, men they respect who can direct their energies toward something more productive. They're never going to accept the Negroes as equals, but maybe they can at least reach a compromise with them and learn to work together, the way they're doing at Harrison Blake's plantation."

The two plantations were close neighbors, and the carriage arrived a few minutes later. Josephine climbed down as the doctor untied the wheelchair, but he stopped her before going inside. "Josephine, wait. The reason I asked you to come today wasn't to help me physically move Harrison. It's because you're good for him."

"Me? That can't possibly be true. To be honest, Dr. Hunter, I can't stand him. It requires all of my patience just to stay in the same room with him. He's so bitter and nasty and ill-tempered—"

"I know, I know. But you're the only person besides me who has the guts to stand up to him. He needs that. If he's fighting with you and me, at least he's fighting and not giving up."

"You mean . . . you *want* me to argue with him?"

The doctor smiled. "Well, he doesn't exactly give you a choice, does he?"

"I have been worried it's unladylike to talk back to him. I can't imagine what Mother would say if she heard me."

"You are very much like your mother, Josephine. You have her great inner strength and courage, although you show it in different ways. I hope you'll continue to visit Harrison."

Josephine felt very confused as she went up the front steps to the house. Was she truly as strong as her mother? And if so, could she summon the courage to stand up to Daniel and risk being ostracized in the community? Her thoughts were interrupted when Mrs. Blake came out to greet them. Then there was a flurry of activity as Dr. Hunter carried the wheelchair into Harrison's room. "I'm not going to lift you in and out," the doctor said. "I'm going to teach you how to get into the chair yourself with just a little help." He made Harrison sit on the edge of the bed, and while the doctor held the chair steady in front of him, he instructed Harrison to brace his hands on the arms of the chair. For once he wasn't fighting their efforts or being abusive, but he remained quiet and sullen.

"Now stand up, pivot around, and sit down." Harrison followed the doctor's instructions, landing in the chair with a grunt.

"What if he falls?" his mother asked.

"You can call one of your servants to help him."

Harrison was as thin as a sapling and couldn't possibly weigh very much. Josephine remembered him as a stocky, broad-shouldered man before the war, strong and solidly built. Now Dr. Hunter, who was a much smaller man, could lift him in his arms and carry him. The doctor could have conducted a lesson on the human skeleton by pointing out Harrison's protruding bones. Yet Harrison didn't evoke pity in Josephine the way that Lizzie had this morning, creeping into the dining room with tired, red-rimmed eyes. Or the way Roselle had at the loss of her school. Jo wondered why not.

"As you get stronger," Dr. Hunter continued, "you'll be able to push the chair yourself by turning the wheels. But today I've asked Josephine to push you."

The chair barely skimmed through the bedroom door. Jo wondered how Harrison felt to be out of that dreary bedroom, his self-imposed prison, for the first time in months. "Where would you like to go?" Josephine asked. But Harrison, who hadn't spoken a word since she'd arrived, didn't reply.

"I think you should take him outside," Dr. Hunter said. "The rear entrance should be easier to manage than the front." Josephine wheeled him down the short hallway and through the door to the back porch. The doctor maneuvered the chair down the three short steps by tipping it backward and thumping down each one. "We'll get some boards and make a ramp so you can roll the chair in and out. This is just the beginning, Harrison. As you gain strength, you'll eventually be able to get rid of the chair altogether and use crutches."

Harrison still didn't reply. Behind his back, the doctor motioned for Jo to push him across the yard toward the barn and cotton fields. It was hard work since the ground was rough and uneven, but she wouldn't give Harrison the satisfaction of hearing her complain.

"Isn't it nice to be outdoors in the fresh air?" she asked. "The sun is so warm and comforting."

"Is that supposed to be a joke?"

"No. Most people enjoy being outside in such lovely June weather. I'm surprised you don't, too."

"I served in the army, in case you've forgotten. I lived outdoors in all sorts of weather for nearly five years. What's nice is to have a roof over my head and a bed to sleep in at night."

She paused beneath the shade of a maple tree, watching the workers laboring in the distant field. "Do you enjoy being contrary, Harrison?"

"You ask such idiotic questions! You have no idea what it was like for us."

"Why don't you tell me, then?"

"You couldn't handle it."

"Try me. Tell me what you remember about going into battle." She didn't think he would take the bait and was surprised when he began to talk.

"I remember how dry my mouth would get from tearing open the powder cartridges. How I would be dying of thirst but couldn't stop for a drink. And the weariness—it was bone deep. It wasn't courage that made us wade into enemy fire or stand beneath an artillery bombardment, but sheer fatigue. After a while you become indifferent to danger. You just don't care what happens anymore. Dying seems like a welcome escape from the horror."

"Another soldier told me that he became so accustomed to death it seemed inevitable, that he felt like a walking dead man."

"He's right. You even become used to seeing bloody arms and legs scattered all around you, heads without bodies, torsos without heads. Then one day you look down at a mangled, disembodied leg and you realize it's your own."

"Now you're deliberately trying to shock me."

"You asked for it. . . . For the last two years of the war, most of us were just waiting for our turn to die. I wasn't surprised at all when I was hit. It seemed long overdue."

"But you didn't die. You're home again. And now when you see your house and all your beautiful land, doesn't it make you grateful to be alive?"

"No. I don't have the will or the energy to start all over again. The only thing you're accomplishing with your stupid meddling is to set my mother up for disappointment. Our way of life depended on slavery. We can't make a profit on cotton if we have to pay our laborers. I know it and the other planters know it, too. This plantation can never be restored because I can't make enough money to run it the way I used to. It's impossible."

"So instead you're giving up?"

"Should I foolishly go through all that hard work knowing it will never pay? Or maybe you want me to take up a new profession? I'm not qualified to do anything else and neither is your brother or any of the other planters and their sons. Your mother and mine—and you—expect the impossible from us."

"That's not true. I keep telling Mother things will never be exactly the same, but that doesn't mean we shouldn't rebuild what we can." For a moment she thought of the story Alexander had told her to read in the Bible and how Job eventually got back twice as much as he had after God finished testing him. If only that could come true in real life. But the Bible was nothing but fairy tales.

She watched a lone rider gallop down the road, and, as if thinking of him had made him appear, Alexander Chandler arrived at the plantation.

"There's that ridiculous Yankee," Harrison said. "I wish you would tell him to go away and never come back. I don't need him checking up on my workers."

"Why don't you tell him yourself?" She pivoted the chair and started to push it toward the front of the house, but Harrison reached around behind him, grabbing Jo's arm.

"No! Stop right here, Josephine! Stop!" He was so upset that she did what he said, halting abruptly and nearly jolting him from the chair. "I have nothing to say to that man. Take me back inside."

"I don't know why you hate Mr. Chandler so much. He isn't like the other Yankees, you know. He came here to help, not to take advantage of us. I'm sure he could use your advice and assistance with the planting and so could your workers."

"Take me back to the house. I don't want to be anywhere near him—and neither should you. I see you talking to him all the time, and you need to stop. If you keep cozying up to him, you're going to ruin your reputation."

"Cozying up!" Jo started to defend herself and her odd friendship with Alexander, hating that she'd been ordered to stop talking to him—by Harrison, of all people. Then she realized it would make matters much worse for both her and Mr. Chandler if she tried to defend herself. She turned the chair around and began moving toward the house. They were close enough to Alexander to see the white bandages on his hands, so she decided to tell Harrison what had happened.

"Did you know that some men attacked the former slaves last night and broke up their camp in the woods? Two men were shot and one of them died. Then the Negro school was set on fire and it had to be closed."

"It's none of my business—or yours."

It suddenly occurred to Jo that Harrison could become one of the good leaders the doctor had said were sorely needed. Harrison had served as an army captain during the war and most of the local men had been under his command, including Daniel. Harrison owned one of the area's most prosperous plantations, which made him a man of influence in the community. "You could make it your business to get involved," she told him. "You could speak up on the Negroes' behalf. The other men respect you."

He gave a short laugh. "I don't even respect myself; how can I expect it from them? Look at me. I have women and Negroes running my plantation. They literally push me around whether I want them to or not. Is it any wonder I no longer feel like living?"

"Do you agree it's wrong to treat the former slaves that way? To beat them up and shoot at them and kill them? To burn down their school?"

"You have the gall to ask my opinion, Josephine? After running roughshod over all my wishes for the past month? You won't even allow me to take control of my life or my death and now you ask my opinion? And you ask me to speak up for *Negroes*, of all people?"

"Harrison, please."

"What do you expect me to do? About the Negroes and their school?"

"Talk to my brother and the others. Make them see that what they're doing is wrong. Tell them to stop, to make peace with their former slaves and get their crops planted. Haven't we had enough war and killing? Where did it get us?"

"You expect too much. People don't change overnight. And around here they'll always believe that slaves must be kept in their place."

"But we have to change because the laws have changed. Look at your new workers laboring out there. They're willing to start over . . . Why can't we? Please help me, Harrison."

"Since you and the other women want to be in charge, why don't you do something about it yourselves? But if you really want things to get back to normal, then you need to remember *your* place in the order of things and let the men be in charge. That means living with our decisions."

She pushed him the rest of the way to the house, too furious to speak. She got the doctor to help haul the chair up the stairs, then left the house again, hurrying to meet up with Alexander before he reached the cotton field.

"I heard what happened last night," she said, out of breath from running. "Are you all right?"

"I'm fine, just some burns." He spoke in a rough whisper that sounded painful.

"You've lost your voice."

"It's hoarse from the smoke." He pointed to his workers, bending to plant cottonseeds. "I came to see if they were all right and . . ." He stopped, closing his eyes for a moment before turning to look at Josephine. "That's not entirely true. I came because I wanted to see you and to tell you I won't be coming back to this plantation for a while. I have to rebuild the school."

"I-I'm not staying here anymore. I moved back home." She needed to change the subject. Her heart had gone from a canter to a gallop at his confession, and she didn't dare listen to any more talk of seeing each other. "Did you see the men who set the fire?"

"They wore handkerchiefs over their faces. And it was dark. The fire woke me from a sound sleep." He paused, struck by a spasm of coughing. "Excuse me . . . It all happened so fast."

"My mother's driver went out last night, and the men on night patrol attacked him and beat him for no reason. He isn't a violent man. He's a hard worker, not a troublemaker. He didn't deserve this."

"None of the injured ones did. They're all good people."

"Dr. Hunter told me a man was shot and killed."

"Yes. I'm leaving for Richmond to report the violence and to ask for help. I'm also sending our teacher, Miss Hunt, back home until we can rebuild. She wanted to stay and she said she wasn't afraid, but I can't take that risk. It's too dangerous." He paused to cough again and clear his throat. "Besides, it's going to take a while to repair the damage. All the books burned up. She may as well go home for now."

"But the children want to learn. You can't let those men win. Whoever they are, they beat up my servant!"

He lowered his head as if struggling to contain his anger. "I feel responsible for what happened because I was warned. Some folks told me they'd overheard a plot against the school. With nothing specific, it was hard to prepare for it. But I did report the threat to Richmond and asked for help."

"Didn't they believe you?"

"It didn't matter if they did or not. The occupation forces are already spread too thinly. There's more than enough trouble to deal with in Richmond. Fairmont is just a small country town."

"Well, if they aren't going to send help, I hope you'll take measures to protect yourself in the future." She said this, knowing one of the arsonists might be her brother.

"You mean arm myself?" Alexander shook his head. "I'll never pick up another weapon for as long as I live."

"Then I think you are a very foolish man. Good day, Mr. Chandler."

"Josephine, wait!"

She whirled around to face him, frustrated and furious—at him, at her brother, at her own helplessness. "What?"

"I know I'm not welcome at your plantation. How will I see you? How can we talk?"

She wanted to say, *We can't talk. I should never speak with you again.* Especially after Harrison's warning, and her mother's. But the thought of not seeing Alexander again made her feel lonely and empty inside. There was more she wanted to know about the book of Job and about her unanswered prayers. Alexander had asked her to forgive him, and she had never replied. And she still didn't know how to answer his question, *"What do you want for your life, your future?"*

Josephine looked down at her torn shoe, not at him. "Remember the tree house on our property? Where we first met?"

"Yes, of course."

"We can't meet often, Alexander . . . but maybe once in a while."

"Tomorrow?"

She couldn't breathe. "No . . . Tuesday. Early in the morning, before breakfast." She hurried back to the house as fast as her ragged shoes would allow, wondering what in the world she was doing.

21

Eugenia searched in vain for an envelope. She'd had trouble enough finding a nice sheet of writing paper and enough ink to compose a letter to her sister, but evidently she had used up her supply of proper envelopes during the war. Never mind. Olivia would understand. The important thing was the message she was sending, that Olivia and Charles and their daughters were invited to Eugenia's dance a month from now on the first of July. It would be a treat for them to get away from the devastated city for a weekend, away from the insufferable Yankee soldiers. Daniel would deliver her letter when he traveled to Richmond on Monday.

The house seemed quiet. Where were Mary and Josephine? She thought it might be wise to find out. Ever since Josephine had returned home from Priscilla's house, Eugenia had been forced to follow her around as if she were a toddler bent on mischief. Otherwise, she would find Josephine washing dishes in the kitchen or working outside in the garden or wandering in the woods or the cotton fields. Why wasn't her daughter content to behave like a proper young lady? She needed to fall in love and settle down as badly as Daniel did.

Eugenia looked through her morning room window to see if

231

Josephine was working in the kitchen garden. Thankfully she wasn't, unless she was out of sight, bending down to plant seeds or who knew what else. The morning mist that had draped over the landscape like a bridal veil had finally lifted and Eugenia could see the big, tall slave, Otis, repairing the pasture fence. The Yankees had dismantled many of the rails during the war, probably to use them for firewood. But now that Daniel had agreed to purchase a mule and some hogs and maybe a cow or another horse—as much as Eugenia's dwindling funds would allow—the fences needed to be mended. She would give Daniel the last of the gold coins that she and her girls had sewn into the hems of their dresses. Thank God, Philip hadn't invested every last cent they had in the Confederacy. At least they would survive for another year.

Eugenia wandered through the empty, dusty rooms of her home, grieving over their faded beauty, and found Josephine and Mary in the drawing room. They sat in a patch of spring sunlight with the French doors to the terrace thrown wide open, and the room was filled with the scent of damp earth and new leaves. Mary was reading aloud in her rabbit-soft voice while Josephine bent over a lapful of billowing green taffeta—one of the dresses she had outgrown during the war. She was sewing. Sewing!

Eugenia crossed the room and stood between Josephine and the doorway, blocking her light. "What are you doing?"

Mary looked up, holding her place in the book with her finger, but Josephine continued stitching. "I'm altering my old dress to fit Mary."

"But . . . but you don't know what you're doing. You'll ruin it."

"No, I won't. I've done this before. One of Mrs. Blake's new servants was an excellent seamstress, and she showed me how to take extra fabric and make gussets to make the bodice larger. And if I make the skirt a little less full, I can add the extra fabric to the hem to make it longer."

"Oh, Josephine." Eugenia was both amazed and appalled.

"I'm hoping to finish it in time for Mary to wear to your dance."

"But you aren't a common seamstress. Sewing is beneath you.

Why not give it to Priscilla's servant and let her do it for you? I'm certain Priscilla won't mind sharing her with us after everything you've done for her and Harrison."

Maddeningly, Josephine continued to stitch, poking the needle in and out, drawing the long thread through the shimmering green cloth. "Can you explain why embroidery is an acceptable pastime for young ladies," she asked without looking up, "yet sewing isn't? Don't you think making something useful to wear is a much better use of my time than embroidering pillow cushions and handkerchiefs?"

Eugenia controlled her emotions with great effort. "You girls descend from two of Virginia's finest families, the cream of Southern aristocracy. Our women have never labored at such menial tasks. Yet every time I turn around I find you in the kitchen, Josephine, or in the garden. And now you're sewing gowns? Who knows what you'll be doing next? It's unthinkable that we have been forced to stoop this low."

Josephine finally looked up, resting her hands in her lap. "Do you want Mary to have something to wear or not?"

Eugenia couldn't reply. Women were delicate creatures, cherished by their husbands and fathers and sons. Yet here sat her daughters, practically in rags, their toes sticking out of their shoes. How had they fallen this far? It wasn't fair! She was furious with Philip and Samuel and Daniel, furious with all the other misguided men for failing to find a more civilized answer than declaring war.

"Shall I sit here and embroider samplers, Mother, or fix something to wear?" Josephine's gaze never wavered.

"You've made your point. There's no need to belabor it. But promise me this won't become a habit, and that you'll stop as soon as we can afford a seamstress."

"What if I don't want to stop?"

"Josephine!" She had never talked back to Eugenia this way before or even stated an opinion, much less argued with her.

"I find it very satisfying to work with my hands, whether it's sewing a dress or preparing soup or mixing biscuits. Much more satisfying than sitting around reading poetry all day or brushing my hair for one hundred strokes or practicing good posture with a book on my head."

"I believe you are trying to upset me on purpose."

"I'm not. But I've decided I'm not going to wait for a savior to come and rescue us. No one else in heaven or on earth is helping us, so I've decided to do it myself."

"Are you planning to become a cobbler, too?" she asked, gesturing to Josephine's torn shoe.

She pulled her feet out of sight, hiding them beneath the chair and the hem of her long skirt. "I would if I knew how," she said with a smile.

"Why are you still wearing those terrible shoes? I thought I gave you a pair of my own to wear."

"They're too small for me. My toes feel so pinched I can barely walk. I would never be able to dance in them."

Eugenia had chosen to purchase farm animals and cottonseed with the last of her money. There was none left for shoes. Would her daughters end up barefoot?

"I'll make my hems longer so no one can see my feet," Josephine said. She resumed her sewing and a moment later pricked her finger with the needle. "Ouch!" She put her finger in her mouth to suck on it.

Eugenia reached for Josephine's hands, bending to inspect them. "Oh, look at these hands . . ." she said, her voice choking. The new needle prick sprouted a dot of bright blood, and she saw a partially healed cut on one hand that looked as though it had been deep. She had blisters on her palms, presumably from hoeing the garden, fingernails that were ragged and dirty, and skin as red and rough as a rooster's comb. "What in the world were you doing at Priscilla's house?"

"Whatever was necessary." Josephine pulled her hands free and hid them beneath the cloth on her lap.

"Promise me that you won't wash another dish or do any more work before my dance. Let your hands heal, for heaven's sake."

"I'll be wearing gloves, won't I?"

"That isn't the point. Don't frustrate me, Josephine. Besides, if I know you, you'll have your gloves off within the first hour. . . . Let me see your hands, Mary." She reached to inspect hers next, and while they weren't red or chapped or blistered, Mary had continued the nervous habit of biting her nails and the skin around her fingertips. Both girls would need gloves for the dance, but every pair they owned was worn or stained or patched.

"I promise I'll stop biting them," Mary said when Eugenia released her.

"Thank you."

"As long as we're speaking of work . . ." Josephine began.

"What now?" Eugenia asked with a sigh. She needed to sit down. She looked around for the nearest chair and pulled it over beside the girls.

"While I've been sitting here sewing, I've been looking out at this terrace and thinking what a shame it is that it has become so overgrown. Wouldn't it be nice to get it all cleaned up for your dance so our guests can stroll outside?"

"Don't you dare! I mean it, Josephine, don't even think about it! Oh, if I had money to spare I would pack you off to Richmond with Daniel on Monday and send you to finishing school."

"I'm not going to do the work, Mother. I thought we could ask Lizzie's two boys to pull the weeds. They aren't attending school anymore because someone tried to burn it down. You should have seen how upset Jack and Rufus were. They were just learning how to read."

"Slaves reading . . . who ever heard of such a thing?" Eugenia spoke without thinking. When she saw Josephine's surprise, she softened her tone. "I'm sorry, but literate slaves were something everyone feared when I was a girl. The adults used to talk about it as if it was something very dangerous."

"Why?" Mary asked. She had her fingers near her mouth again, and Eugenia reached over to pull her hand down.

"Because slaves who could read and write would use those skills to escape and to help others escape. Valuable property would be lost. They had to be severely punished, and so did anyone who dared to teach them." Josephine looked at her accusingly—or was it Eugenia's imagination? "I'm sorry, but you can't expect me to shed all those biases overnight. The war just ended two months ago, for heaven's sake."

"And those poor children only had a chance to attend school for a few weeks."

Eugenia looked away. She wished she had never overheard Daniel and his friends talking about closing down the school and breaking up the Negroes' camp in the woods. David Hunter said that a man had been shot and killed. Would Daniel do such a thing? He and his friends had claimed to be defending their homes and families, but shooting people and setting the school on fire seemed more like the actions of outlaws. Her own servant had been injured for no reason that she could see. When Philip had been alive, Eugenia sometimes overheard rumors involving the slaves, but Philip had always assured her that she was better off not knowing. Now she understood why. A sudden breeze blew in through the open doors, and Eugenia pulled her shawl tighter, shivering.

"The Negro school is none of our concern," she said, turning back to her daughters, "and I don't want to argue with you about it." She had felt good all morning and hadn't had the pain in her chest in days. "I agree with you about clearing the terrace, but we can't order the little Negro boys to do it, can we? You're always the first to remind me they aren't our slaves anymore."

"I've been thinking about that, too," Jo said. "I decided I could offer to pay them by giving them some of my old schoolbooks. They were heartbroken when theirs burned up. So . . . would you like me to ask them to do the work?"

"*Ask* them? They eat my food, they live on my property, and they don't do any labor in return—"

"They're children, Mother. Of course they don't do any labor."

"They used to in the old days." Eugenia remembered seeing children like Lizzie's young boys out in the cotton fields working alongside their parents. She exhaled. "The terrace would look much nicer without all the weeds. Yes, you may *ask* them, Josephine. Pay them however you'd like. Just don't become overly friendly with them or allow them to get the upper hand."

"The upper hand?" Josephine repeated. "They're children!"

"And do *not* engage in any of the work yourself."

"Of course not. Thank you, Mother." Josephine bent over her sewing to hide a smile. What else was she plotting?

"I can hardly wait to go to your dance," Mary said. "And I'm so happy I'll be getting a new dress to wear . . . well, new for me."

"Do you want to help me sew?" Josephine asked her. "You know how, Mary. Your dress will be finished sooner if you do."

Eugenia was relieved when Mary shook her head. She was such a good girl, such a lovely girl. She was still much too quiet and fearful after everything she'd suffered, but perhaps the dance would help give her confidence.

"Speaking of my dance, I'm inviting Aunt Olivia and Uncle Charles and their girls to come from Richmond and stay overnight with us. I thought you would enjoy spending time with your cousins again. Of course, that means the guest bedroom will have to be aired and made up. Remind me to speak with Lizzie about it. Or maybe Roselle can do it if someone supervises her. I'm so relieved we have her back as a house servant again, even if she is very young and inexperienced. You girls can share your bedroom with your cousins, can't you? It will be so much fun to have guests again."

Mary sat forward in her chair, her eyes bright with excitement. "I hope I'll have a chance to dance that night. Do you think any of the gentlemen you're inviting will want to dance with me?"

"Certainly! You're a very beautiful young lady, you know. Daniel's friend Joseph Gray seemed quite taken with you the last time he was here."

"But he's Daniel's age, and I'm Daniel's little sister. Won't he think I'm too young?"

"Not at all. I was your age when I began attending balls and parties. My mother would invite every eligible bachelor in Richmond so that Olivia and I could meet potential suitors and be seen by their families. I loved every minute of it."

Should she talk to her daughters about the fine art of flirting? Teach them how to be vivacious and intriguing to men? It had come so naturally to Eugenia that it had seemed like part of her personality, but she was aware her girls, as shy and nervous as baby mice, were not at all like her. They had grown up with too much fear and sorrow and uncertainty.

"The whole process of courting seems so artificial," Josephine said. "You mix young people together at parties and balls and expect them to make suitable matches? The idea makes me shudder." She bent her head to continue sewing.

"It isn't artificial at all! How else will you ever meet suitors if someone doesn't take the initiative to arrange it?"

"Is that how you met Daddy?" Mary asked. "At a dance?"

"Yes. I lived in Richmond, as you know, but distance was no obstacle for Philip. We had attended several of the same events together, so I knew who he was, but I had another serious suitor at the time. Then Philip's parents invited me here to a ball in this very drawing room. My sister, Olivia, came, too. The bedrooms were filled with out-of-town guests."

"I remember how they used to be before the war," Mary said. "I loved watching the ladies getting dressed in all their finery—like princesses. And I loved to watch the couples dancing."

"Your father was a wonderful dancer, and at his parents' ball that night he danced with me all evening. He wouldn't let anyone else have so much as a waltz with me. We talked and talked, not about meaningless things as I had been trained to do, or merely exchanging flatteries, but thoughtful conversation. He was so different from all the other men I knew. He treated me as . . . as his friend, which was unheard of, of course." Eugenia smiled as she let her thoughts drift back to that evening.

"I remember the lavish dinner your grandmother served, the dining room table set for dozens of people. That's how it was done in the old days. You always had a dinner with a ball. Philip switched the place cards so that I would be seated right beside him. Again, that was unheard of. The seating arrangement had been composed with care, and Philip's mother was very piqued with him. But no one could stay angry at Philip for long. You know how charming he was. He set the standard for Southern manners as if he had invented the word *gentleman*."

She paused to control a sudden rush of grief and looked out at the once-lovely terrace. Weeds filled the cracks between the paving stones, growing so high and thick that the stones were barely visible. Tall pillars along one side of the square had supported a lattice roof and wisteria vines, but the vines were densely overgrown and matted with dead branches. She remembered how the blossoms would fill the terrace with their sweet fragrance. The stone benches where people used to sit between waltzes were too filthy to sit on now, and the low railing around the perimeter of the square needed a coat of whitewash. Remembering how it had looked on that long-ago night brought tears to Eugenia's eyes. She turned back to her daughters. "Your father asked me to marry him that night."

"And you said yes!" Mary's dark eyes shone.

"Of course! Such a handsome, charming man, such a magnificent home—he swept me off my feet."

There was more to the story than Eugenia would dare to tell her daughters. As the party had been breaking up and the neighboring plantation owners leaving, Philip had pulled her aside. "Meet me on the terrace after everyone's asleep," he'd whispered.

Eugenia hadn't replied. It was a scandalous request. But she couldn't stop thinking about him as she retired upstairs to the guest rooms with the other young ladies from out of town. Philip made her feel like no other man ever had—breathless, every muscle and limb of her body on edge as if her skin had grown too small. It had seemed like torture to be held so chastely as they had danced. What would it feel like to be held closely, to hold his hand without gloves, to touch his skin? Such wicked thoughts made her feel as though her corset was laced too tightly.

The slaves had followed Eugenia and the other girls upstairs to help them undress and shed their jewelry and ball gowns and corsets and hoop skirts, unpinning their hair and brushing it. The girls would sleep in their chemises and bloomers. Eugenia climbed into the feather bed beside her sister, but she couldn't lie still, feeling so restless she feared she might crawl out of her skin.

"Why are you acting so strange?" Olivia asked. "First you spend all evening dancing with Philip Weatherly and hardly give anyone else a chance, and now you're kicking the covers like you have a grudge against them. What's wrong with you?"

"Nothing."

Everything. She couldn't confide in Olivia. Eugenia didn't understand what she was feeling or why, but she wanted go downstairs to be with Philip. Of course she couldn't go, shouldn't go. If anyone found out, her reputation would be ruined.

She was still wide awake after Olivia and the other girls had fallen asleep. And so Eugenia had climbed carefully out of bed, wrapped herself in a dressing gown, and tiptoed down the sweeping stairs to the drawing room. She didn't need a candle to guide her, having memorized every inch of the Weatherlys' beautiful home. She saw Philip's silhouette in the terrace doorway, bathed in moonlight. And ran to him.

"Eugenia, you came!"

He pulled her into his arms, no longer holding her at a chaste distance but pressing her close to himself, his strong arms holding her tight. Then he bent to kiss her, and the sensation of his lips on hers was more wonderful than she ever could have imagined. It was Eugenia's first kiss. Other suitors had stolen kisses by pressing their lips to her cheek or her hand, but this was a kiss of passion, desire. She felt the power of it and pulled away after a minute, giddy and afraid. They were both breathless.

"I have been longing to do that all evening," Philip said, "and for weeks . . . no, months before that. Ever since I first saw you at the mayor's home in Richmond, remember? On Christmas? Then at the ball at your father's house, and at the Sheffields' party, and . . . and I can't even remember all the other places. You are so beautiful, Eugenia. I've been captivated by you from the very beginning, but you were always surrounded by admiring men, and I feared I never would win your notice."

"I noticed you, Philip." His hands were still on her back, and the warmth of them sent shivers through her.

"Desire from a distance is one thing, but after talking with you all evening, dining with you, I've now come to know the woman behind the exquisite face and . . . I've fallen in love with you. Please say you'll marry me, that you'll be my wife."

His wife. The word carried many meanings to Eugenia: gaining the prestige of a good family name and performing the social obligations that went with it, leaving a father's protection for a husband's, and of course obliging him with marital duties to give him sons. But that night she realized that being his wife also meant being held in his arms this way, kissed this way, feeling his hands on her bare skin. She had heard her cousins and girlfriends speaking of such intimacies with fear and vague horror, but they had been wrong—such intimacy seemed wonderful, breathtaking.

Eugenia was no longer wearing gloves, and she reached up to touch Philip's face, his beard. He had removed his jacket and rolled up his shirtsleeves, and she trailed her hands down his bare arms until they stood hand in hand. She looked up into his eyes, longing to marry him this very night, this instant, but it wasn't her decision to make.

"You must ask my father," she said.

"I know, I know." He groaned as if in pain. "But you can convince him to give his consent, can't you? You've stolen my heart. See . . .?" He pressed her hand to his chest. "Feel it hammering? It's yours, Eugenia. I want to spend my life with you, this home with you." He pulled her close and kissed her again before she could reply.

She knew then that this wonderful, overwhelming feeling was love. Marriage shouldn't be simply the end of a well-played game but a commitment of love and passion. Eugenia no longer wanted to marry a man because he was the ideal social match or an economic advantage to both families, or choose the best home or most handsome man—although she truly believed that Philip was the most handsome. At that moment she would gladly forego the vast mansion in Richmond that belonged to one of her other suitors, John Sheffield, and forfeit all of his wealth.

"Yes, Philip," she breathed when they pulled apart. "Yes! I'll marry you!"

"Promise?" She was astounded to see that he had tears in his eyes.

"I promise."

"Forgive me, but I must have one more kiss." He held her chin in his hand for one more kiss, a soft, tender one this time, then he murmured, "Go to bed, Eugenia. I won't sleep but you must. . . . Good night."

She was surprised her legs could support her as she returned to her room. Olivia woke up when she climbed into bed. "Ooo! Your feet are ice-cold! And you're shaking! Where were you?"

"I went downstairs."

"Downstairs? Why? What were you doing?"

Eugenia couldn't hold her joy inside a moment longer. "I'm going to marry Philip Weatherly. He just proposed to me and I said yes."

"You . . . you *talked* to him? In your *dressing gown*? And with your hair loose?"

"Please don't tell anyone. It doesn't matter that he saw me this way because I'm going to marry him, Olivia!"

"But isn't it up to Father? Doesn't he want you to marry John Sheffield?"

"I'll convince him to change his mind. I'm in love, Olivia. I love Philip Weatherly."

"You can't be in love. That's for silly, common girls, not us. Mother says real love is something that grows over time out of mutual respect after you're married. What do you know about love?"

"I know I've never felt this way before about any other man—and I've met dozens. I don't have to pretend or talk about meaningless things with Philip. All of that seems ridiculous now, the flirting and game playing. I love him!" She remembered the tears in his eyes, remembered his passion and tenderness, and she buried her face in her pillow and wept.

"What's wrong with you?"

"You can marry John Sheffield, Olivia, I don't care at all about him. Philip is going to ask Father for my hand, and you have to help me convince him. I have to marry Philip!"

Two months later, Eugenia had gotten her wish when her father announced her engagement to Philip Weatherly. In the years since then, she had never doubted for a single moment that Philip loved her, only her. And her love for him had never wavered, never dimmed.

Now he was gone. The terrace where they had shared that first passionate kiss was overgrown with weeds. And Eugenia was alone.

22

Lizzie couldn't believe what she was hearing. She pulled her hands out of the washtub and wiped them on her apron as she stared up at her husband. His swollen face still bore bruises from the beating those men had given him, and she knew his bruised back and shoulders ached. But he was still going to Richmond with Massa Daniel on Monday?

"Why do you have to go?" she demanded. "How can Massa expect you to ride all that way with him? He was one of the men who hurt you!"

"He was part of the group, but not the one who—"

"Why can't we move someplace else? Our boys don't have school anymore. Why are we even staying here? I can hardly stand to serve that man his food every day after what he done to you."

"We're supposed to love our enemies. Jesus said—"

"Did He say to keep on working for them so they could beat you all over again?"

"He said that if your enemy hits you on one cheek, then turn and let him hit the other one."

"No, sir! I ain't never doing that! And neither should you!" She plunged her hands into the laundry tub again, pulling out a shirt and rubbing it so hard against the scrubbing board that she could have worn a hole clear through it.

"That's what Jesus said, Lizzie. I ain't making it up. He told us we have to forgive our enemies and pray for them, too."

"That's asking too much. Forgive the people who hurt you? Forgive a mean man like Massa Daniel for burning down our school? Uh uh. No, sir." She wrung the water out of the shirt with both hands, the same way she would like to wring Massa Daniel's neck.

"Listen, I have to go with him. Not just for our own sakes or because Miz Eugenia's letting me plant cotton, but because there'll be work for the others if we stay here at White Oak. Old Willy got hurt that night, too, and he needs a place to live. He's too old to be sleeping out there in the woods, and he'll die if they beat him up that way again. But if he starts driving Miz Eugenia around all day, I'll be free to work in the cotton fields. And Saul's thinking of coming back, too. His wife can help you out."

"Clara's a field hand. She ain't never worked in the Big House, never even been inside." Lizzie lifted Missy Mary's chemise from the water and scrubbed it against the board.

"You can show Clara what to do, can't you? Then Miz Eugenia will stop running you ragged all the time."

"I suppose so. But I ain't praying for Miz Eugenia, and I ain't praying for Massa Daniel, either."

Otis rubbed the scab on his head from that awful night. He'd told Lizzie that the stitches the doctor put in made it itch. "I know it's hard to forgive people like them," he said, "but Jesus forgave those men who put the nails through His hands, remember?"

Lizzie thought of Roselle's father as she squeezed the water out of the chemise. She could hardly stand to remember the day Roselle was conceived, even after all these years. How was she supposed to forgive? "I don't know the Bible like you do, Otis. But if you expect me to be forgiving and praying and all those other hard things, then you'll have to teach me how."

"We all need to learn how, all of us. That's why I want to start holding prayer meetings again like we used to have when my pappy was alive. Remember?"

"You expecting people to go out in the woods at night to pray? You trying to get us all killed?"

"It ain't against the law anymore for us to meet and read the Bible. And if we get together in the daytime instead of at night—"

"We're not doing it. No, sir. It's too dangerous."

He exhaled. He looked frustrated but not angry. Otis never got angry, even those times when he probably should get good and angry. Lizzie certainly didn't understand this business of forgiving and turning the other cheek, even if Jesus did say to do it.

"All right, I have another idea," Otis said. "That Freedmen's Bureau is supposed to be a place that looks out for us, right? What if we had our prayer meeting in town, right outside that office so Mr. Chandler can watch over us? Maybe he'll even read the Bible out loud until one of us learns how. Once the schoolroom is fixed, maybe he'll let us meet there in the winter." She could see his excitement growing.

"Those white men tried to burn that office down, remember? And Mr. Chandler couldn't even stop them."

"They won't burn a church, Lizzie."

"Ha! You sure about that?"

"I think my idea is a real good one. We'll hold our meetings on Sunday afternoons . . . maybe find us a preacher . . ."

"Not you! No, sir! It's too dangerous."

Otis grinned. "I know how to grow cotton, Lizzie-girl, but I don't know anything about preaching. But we can all pray, can't we? That's what we need the most right now, more than anything else. With all that's going on around here, we need to ask the good Lord to watch over us and help us figure out where to go and what to do until we get used to being free. We need Him to watch over our children, too."

Lizzie could only shake her head. She wished she had his faith, wished she could keep on believing like he did that everything would turn out all right. She reached into the soapy water to pull out a sock and slipped it over her hand to scrub it. "So your mind's made up that you're going to Richmond on Monday?"

He nodded slowly. "Massa Daniel wants to leave early in the morning."

Lizzie remembered the awful feeling she got in the bottom of her stomach, like she'd swallowed a pile of rocks, the last time she'd watched Otis drive away to Richmond. She remembered how long the days had seemed while she waited, how worried she got. At least this time Massa Daniel couldn't sell Otis for money. She knew she shouldn't worry. But she did.

She turned back to her laundry after Otis left, sighing when she saw it all piled up in the basket, waiting to be rinsed and hung up to dry. By the time the cotton fields would be ready to be picked next fall, she would be too heavy with a baby in her belly to help him out. How was she going to get all this work done with diapers to wash and a new baby to feed, too? Maybe Otis was right. If they stayed here and Saul and the others came back, they would both get the help they needed.

When the laundry was finally finished and hung out to dry, Lizzie walked over to the kitchen garden to see how Rufus and Jack were getting on with their chores. She had set them to work hauling water to pour over the vegetable plants, seeing as there hadn't been a good rain in a while. The boys had worked hard and the droopy bean plants had perked up with a little water. But both boys were soaking wet and she could see they'd been playing in the water and splashing each other while watering the plants.

"What you boys doing to get yourselves all wet like that?" she teased. "There a hole in your buckets?"

"No . . . Jack and me were just . . ." He shrugged.

Playing, Lizzie thought. They didn't hardly know the word. "That's fine. You could both use a good bath. You about finished?"

"Just two more rows, Mama, and—" He stopped. His smile faded and his little body went stiff as he looked past Lizzie to something behind her. She turned around and saw that Missy Josephine had come out the back door and was walking straight toward them, holding something in her arms. Lizzie felt her body go all stiff, too, like she'd been dipped in starch. Missy couldn't blame Lizzie for not trusting any of the Weatherlys, could she? Did Missy Jo know what her brother and his friends had done? If so, she should be ashamed to be his sister. Miz Eugenia knew the truth. She'd been in that room and heard the men planning to burn down the school. Oh yes, she'd heard them. Miz Eugenia knew.

"Afternoon, Missy Josephine."

"Good afternoon, Lizzie." She unlatched the garden gate and came inside. "I see your boys are here, too. Good. I have a proposal for all of you."

"A what?"

"I want to ask you a question. My mother is planning to hold a dance here in July, and I thought it would be nice to clean up the stone terrace off the drawing room so people could stroll outside. The weeds have taken it over, I'm afraid. I wondered if I could hire Rufus and Jack to help me restore it?"

"Your mother ain't letting you do that kind of work, Missy Jo, especially if it means working alongside us all day."

"I know. She already forbade me to do any of the work, but she said I could show Rufus and Jack what to do." She squatted down to talk to them, right to their faces, and they backed up a step. "I don't have any money to pay you for the extra work, but if you're willing, I thought I could teach you reading and arithmetic in return. I know you're sad about missing school. And I can pay you with these." She unfolded her arms and showed them two books.

Lizzie saw her boys' eager looks as Missy Jo held the books out to them. They knew better than to reach out or touch them, but they quickly wiped their hands on the sides of their pants, just in case.

"Go ahead, you may each take one," Missy Jo said. "They're yours if you're willing to do the work. And you can earn more books, too. What do you say?"

"Don't matter what they say. What will Miz Eugenia say?"

Missy Jo rose to her feet again. "She already agreed."

"She'll let you give away them books? And be their teacher?"

"It's all arranged."

"Can we, Mama? Please?"

"Please?"

They were looking from Lizzie to Missy Jo and back again as if Missy was offering them a pot of gold. "I guess so . . ." Lizzie finally said. The look on their faces as they each reached for a book brought tears to her eyes. She was afraid to hope that this would be something good, afraid to let them hope, too. "Now, you have to earn them books before you can keep them, you hear?"

"No, they may take them now, Lizzie. I insist. That way you'll know that I'll keep my promise." She looked right at Lizzie, as if she was trying to tell her something. Maybe she did know what her brother had done. Maybe she was trying to make up for it. Lizzie looked down at her feet.

"Thank you, Missy Jo. The boys will work real hard for you, I promise. Now, you boys better go take them books home so they'll stay nice."

"But bring them with you tomorrow when we start work, right after breakfast, all right? We'll practice reading them."

"What do you boys say for yourselves?" Lizzie asked as they raced toward the garden gate.

"Thank you, Missy Josephine."

"Thank you."

Later that afternoon, Lizzie and Roselle were cutting moldy spots off the last of the winter squashes to fix for dinner when Rufus burst into the kitchen. "There's a bunch of people coming, Mama. Slaves, like us. Coming across the cotton field."

"We ain't slaves no more," Roselle said. "And neither are they." Rufus tugged on Lizzie's hand until she left her work and she and Roselle went outside with him.

"See. Mama? See them?"

She shaded her eyes against the setting sun's glare and saw a little knot of people moving slowly across the field with bundles of belongings tied onto their backs and balanced on their heads. Even the children were carrying loads.

"That must be your Uncle Saul and Aunt Clara, coming to help us out. That's their three kids, ain't it? Looks like they brought a couple more people with them, too." Lizzie couldn't help feeling excited for Otis. His dream of growing his own cotton might finally come true.

Rufus tugged on her skirt. "Is that Old Willy, Mama? With the walking stick?"

"Sure enough, that's him. Your papa told me he might be coming back here to work." Lizzie saw another man helping Willy as he limped across the field. They were both toting belongings.

"I remember Willy," Jack said. "He used to let me feed apples to his horses."

"Can we run and meet them?" Rufus asked. "We could help them carry their things."

"Yes, go ahead. I don't see no harm. Just watch where you're running. Don't step in a rabbit hole." She knew her boys missed being with other children now that the school was closed.

"May I go, too?" Roselle asked. Lizzie saw her eagerness and remembered she was just a child, too.

"Yeah, go on."

Lizzie went back to the kitchen to finish fixing the squash, but she kept watch through the window, waiting for the group to arrive. Once she had the food cooking, she hurried down to Slave Row to greet them. Saul's wife and three kids were moving into the cabin right next to hers, and Willy and the lanky young man who was helping him were taking the cabin across from them. The kids were all running up and down the Row, flittering and chattering like a flock of birds.

"I brought Otis another field hand," Saul told her. "Name's Robert. Otis said he could use lots of help."

"That's the truth," Lizzie said. "Good to have you, Robert. And you, too, Willy. All of you."

"We didn't come empty-handed, either," Clara said. "Look what Saul and Willy caught this morning." She set an old tin bucket on the ground in front of Lizzie, filled with fish. The strong smell made Lizzie's stomach flop around the way it did every morning, but maybe it would settle down again when it was time to eat.

"Those fish look real good. Is that what you been eating out there in the woods all this time?"

"Not just fish," Saul said. "We've been snaring rabbits, too. And the other day we caught a wild turkey. That was good eating, let me tell you."

"I can help you cook this fish for dinner," Clara said. "You got any cornmeal?"

"We got some dried corn. Maybe the kids can grind it up for us. But I got to feed the white folks, too. I was just looking around for something for their dinner."

"How many of them are left?"

"Just Miz Eugenia, Massa Daniel, Missy Jo, and Missy Mary. But them two girls don't eat very much. They peck at their food like sparrows most of the time."

"I guess there'll be enough, then. Now if Saul can get this fish cleaned while I finish moving into my cabin, you and me can start frying it, Lizzie."

"I'll help you move in," Lizzie said. The cabin was small, their belongings few, so it didn't take long at all to stuff the straw mattresses and hang their jackets and extra clothes on the pegs.

"I thought it would be hard coming back here," Clara said, "and I didn't want to at first. But it ain't so bad. It seems different now, don't it?" She had a little smile on her face as she looked all around. Lizzie couldn't recall ever seeing Clara smile.

"No, it ain't bad," Lizzie said. "Miz Eugenia works us pretty hard—and make sure you stay away from Massa Daniel. But Missy Mary ain't no trouble and Missy Jo treats us real nice. At least that old slave bell won't be clanging every morning and no overseer's gonna be standing over us."

They came out of Clara's cabin just as Willy and Robert were leaving to walk up to the stables to find Otis. "He's getting ready to go into Richmond on Monday," Lizzie said. "If he ain't in the stables, he'll be out in his cotton fields somewhere. He likes the feel of the dirt in his hands, and he's been itching to start plowing."

The children had all gathered around Roselle, begging her to tell one of her stories. Saul and Clara's two girls, Annie and Meg, were about the same ages as Rufus and Jack, their boy Bill a little older.

"I'll tell you a true story," Roselle said, "but I want to show you something first." She led the way up the rise, and Lizzie knew she was taking the children to the chicken yard to see her ducks. "See them three little yellow ones? Them's mine."

"Those are awful funny-looking chickens," Bill said. "Their feet ain't right."

"That's because they ain't chickens, they're ducks. And they're my ducks. It's time for their bath. Want to watch?"

Every afternoon Roselle would fill an old basin with water to make a little pond for the ducks to play in. They splashed and frolicked, their little tail feathers waggling as they shook off the water, their funny flat feet slapping the surface. The children laughed and laughed as they watched, and Roselle told the story of how she'd rescued them. The sun was turning the sky red as it sank below the hills, and as Lizzie looked at the flaming sky and listened to the children's laughter, she felt almost happy. If only it would last.

That night after the white folks ate their dinner, Lizzie's new family all gathered around the table in the kitchen to eat theirs, using empty barrels and stools for chairs. The kids spread an old tablecloth on the floor and sat down to eat. "This sure is good fish, Clara," Otis said.

"The white folks seemed real happy about their dinner, too," Lizzie said. "Miz Eugenia said it was just as good as what Dolly used to fix."

"That's a real compliment," Clara said. "That gal sure could cook."

"Ain't it something, sitting here like free people?" Saul asked.

"We don't have to look over our shoulder, either," Otis said, "because we work for ourselves now. And by Monday night, there might be a cow in the barn and some baby pigs to fatten up. And a mule. I sure hope we can find a good mule."

"I'll teach all you young ones how to milk the cow," Clara said.

"That can be your job every day. And separating the cream and churning the butter."

"We already have a job," Rufus said. "Missy Jo hired us to pull weeds. She's going to teach us how to read while we work, too."

"And she's paying us with books!" Jack added.

"Can we help you?" Annie asked.

Rufus shrugged. "I guess so. We can ask Missy Jo tomorrow."

"Papa, she gave us each a book to keep," Jack said. "And we haven't even done any work yet."

Otis shook his head in wonder. "How about that? I can hardly wait until bedtime to see those new books. Maybe you can read them to me one of these days."

That night, Lizzie finished her work sooner than usual with Clara and her two girls helping. After she said good-night to the others, she and Otis went inside their own cabin and Jack and Rufus sat on their papa's lap to show him their books. It was too dark in the cabin to read the words, and they didn't have a candle or a lamp, but they squinted at the pretty pictures together in the moonlight.

"I already looked at the words while it was still light outside," Rufus said, "and I think I know some of them."

"I can't wait to hear that, son. I'm real proud of you."

"Roselle can read it better than we can."

Otis squinted at one of the pictures, then held it up to the faint light coming through the window. "Say, I just took a closer look at this picture and I think this must be a story from the Bible. See here? This looks like David and the giant." He and the boys bent their heads together to study it before turning the page. "And this looks like Jonah and that great big fish. And here's the story of when the walls came tumbling down—see the men blowing their trumpets?" He leaned back with a huge grin. "Pretty soon you'll be reading the Bible to us."

Lizzie felt content as she lay down beside Otis that night. "Today was a real good day, wasn't it?" he whispered. "We're gonna make this work, Lizzie-girl. All of us together, my brother and the others. Our families are happy and free. Yes, I thank God for this good day."

"I still wish you didn't have to go with Massa Daniel on Monday."

"Don't spoil today by worrying about tomorrow. Everything will be fine, you'll see."

Lizzie wanted to believe that good things were going to happen from now on, but she was afraid. Truth was, she still had to work for Miz Eugenia and Massa Daniel, and experience had taught her not to trust the Weatherlys. Not a single one of them.

23

On Monday morning, Josephine hurried through breakfast, eager to start the day. Cleaning up the terrace and secretly teaching the children would be new adventures for her, a break from her boring routine. She had been disappointed when she awoke to a damp, cloudy day with low-hanging clouds that threatened rain, but at least the children wouldn't broil beneath a hot sun. Daniel had already left for Richmond, and she was eager to get started, too.

"May I please be excused?" She rose from the breakfast table before Mother had a chance to reply.

"What are you up to, Josephine? You bolted down your food like a slave with a field of cotton to pick."

"I've hired the children to clear the weeds from your terrace, remember? I want to get started before it rains."

"Don't you dare lift a finger or I'll call off the whole project, do you hear me?"

"Yes, Mother. Now may I please be excused?"

Jo had to force herself not to race up the stairs and further annoy her mother, but she couldn't help feeling excited about the work ahead. She had enjoyed working in the vegetable garden, planting seeds and watching them grow into rows of leafy green plants. This project promised to be just as satisfying, taking an overgrown patch of thistles and weeds and making the terrace look clean and new again.

She put on her straw hat and an old skirt and blouse, and went outside to survey the work. How she longed to dig in and get her hands dirty, ripping out weeds and trimming vines, but Mother would be watching. Josephine had learned at dinner last night that the plantation had acquired more workers, and with them three more children. Now she saw all six children coming up the little rise from Slave Row, and they broke into a run when they saw her waiting for them.

"Can our cousins help, too?" Rufus asked. "They just moved back here and they want to learn to read, too." They were serious children like Rufus and Jack, with dark fear-filled eyes. Their thin little bodies reminded Josephine of sticks of kindling. The cringing way they looked up at her from lowered faces, not quite meeting her gaze, made her feel like an ogre in a fairy tale.

"Of course they may help. The more workers we have, the faster the work will get done." She would have to find more books to give away, but she didn't care. She led the way to the gardener's shed to gather tools, and the children soon went to work raking the leaves, pulling weeds, and gathering dead branches. Josephine had to stuff her hands into her pockets to resist the urge to help. She felt like the dreaded overseer standing idly by, issuing orders, brandishing a whip.

"See if you can lift some of the stones to get beneath them and yank out the weeds by the roots," she coached. Rufus and the older boy, Bill, competed to see who could lift the biggest flagstones, intrigued by the earthworms and scurrying insects and the maze of ant holes they found beneath them. The new girls, Annie and Meg, squealed.

"Can we keep these worms for fishing?" Rufus asked.

"They're all yours," Josephine said. Their curiosity excited her. She thought of the nature books in her brothers' room and couldn't wait to share them with the children.

Willy, their old carriage driver, had moved back to White Oak, too, and when he saw them working he limped up to the house with a saw to help. Josephine was glad to see the gentle old man with his wooly white hair and gnarled fingers. He pitched in to help, sawing dead branches and overgrown wisteria vines. Jack and Annie carried the branches to the kindling pile.

"These railings sure could use a coat of whitewash," Willy said as they began to clear away the bushes that had enveloped them.

"Where would we get whitewash?" There was so much that Josephine didn't know and wanted to learn.

"Most folks make it themselves, ma'am, out of crushed oyster shells."

"There's some shells down by the river where we go fishing," Rufus said. "Want me to get some for you next time we go?"

"Yes, please. That would be wonderful."

Willy took a handful of dead leaves and used them like a brush to sweep off the stone benches. "Be nice to clean these benches off real good, too."

"I'll ask Lizzie if she knows of something to scrub them clean."

It began to rain as they worked, a light, gentle mist, which no one seemed to mind at first. But as the morning wore on and Josephine began to feel the dampness soaking through her clothes, she knew it was time to quit—to avoid her mother's ire if for no other reason. "That's all the work for today," she said. "Now go wash your hands and meet me in the kitchen, and we'll have a reading lesson."

Josephine hurried inside, taking the back staircase to her bedroom to retrieve the books she had chosen to give away and a small slate to write on. She stopped at the door to her brothers' room on the way back. Should she borrow some of their books, too? Josephine rarely went into their room, not only because it made her sad to remember Samuel but because she had been avoiding Daniel, outraged by what he and his friends had done. But Daniel was on his way to Richmond with Otis. She turned the knob and went inside.

There was a scent in the room that reminded her of Samuel, the same way the scent of tobacco and leather in the downstairs study reminded her of Daddy. Samuel had been much older than Josephine and had always seemed like a grown man to her. But as she studied the treasure trove of books and other artifacts on his shelves—birds' nests and arrowheads and a woodchuck's skull— she saw her brother as the curious boy he'd once been. His life seemed much too short, his death such a waste. And now Daniel and Harrison, whose lives had been spared, were wasting theirs on bitterness and hatred.

She selected two of her brother's books to share with the Negro children today—one with pictures of insects, the other with plants native to Virginia—and hurried back to teach them their first lesson. It was raining hard now, and she held the books under her apron as she sprinted from the back door to the kitchen. She found the children waiting for her, seated on the floor in a semicircle in front of her empty chair. Lizzie's boys had their books on their laps, and when Jack saw her, he held out his hands to her to show they were clean.

"That's good, Jack. You did a good job washing them." She sat down, feeling nervous suddenly, and not only because Mother would be furious if she found out what she was doing. Josephine had tutors of her own over the years, but what did a spoiled rich girl like herself know about teaching school? The subjects she had studied were much different from what these children needed to learn. She glanced at Lizzie, busy at the hearth with Roselle and the new servant, Clara, then cleared her throat.

"I wish I knew of a better place to meet," she said, "so we're not bothering you while you're trying to work, Lizzie."

"That don't matter, Missy Jo. Maybe I can learn something, too. Roselle, you go sit down and listen. I'll answer the bell if Miz Eugenia starts ringing it." Roselle gladly dropped what she was doing and sat down with the other children.

"Let's begin with the alphabet," Josephine said. "Did you all learn that yet?"

After a very nervous start, Josephine soon lost herself in the work, surprised by how much the children already knew. She tried a few simple addition problems, using the slate and chalk, and discovered that Rufus was very quick with numbers. But the children loved books most of all and loved to practice their reading with her. She couldn't wait to teach them again.

"I'm afraid that's all for today," she said after an hour. She didn't dare go any longer or Mother would come looking for her—and would probably make good on her threat to send her to finishing school if she discovered what Jo was doing. Mother had agreed to the project of weeding the terrace and paying the children with books but not to starting a school in her kitchen with Jo as the teacher. She would be appalled.

Josephine gave each of the new children a book as their pay, then pulled Roselle aside. "I've noticed you learn much faster than the others, Roselle. Since I can't spend very much time teaching every day, how would it be if I taught you some things and then you could teach the younger children?"

"Really, Missy Josephine? I sure would like that. It's fun being a teacher. Before the school burned down, Miss Hunt used to let Cissy and me teach the younger kids, and she said I could be a teacher someday if I wanted to. Do you think that could ever happen, Missy Jo? Do you think I could be a teacher like Miss Hunt?"

Josephine didn't know what to think. She had been raised with the same prejudices as Mother, believing slaves were fit only for manual labor. Of course she knew it wasn't true, but could the world change fast enough to allow Negroes to be accepted as teachers? Jo thought it was ironic that while the war had forced her to do slaves' work, it allowed the former slaves to dream of doing white men's work. Once again she thought of Alexander's question, *"What do you want for your life . . . for your future?"*

"I think you would make a wonderful teacher, Roselle."

"Really, Missy Jo?" She beamed at Josephine, and for the first time Jo realized what a pretty girl she was, with features as fine and delicate as her sister Mary's, as fine as any white woman's.

"Miss Hunt said that up north where she comes from, Negroes do all sorts of jobs and live in nice houses and everything. Is that true, Missy Jo?"

"I don't know, Roselle. I've never been there." She would ask Alexander about it when she saw him tomorrow. Tomorrow! She had agreed to meet him beneath the tree house early in the morning before the Freedmen's Bureau office opened, before Mother and Mary noticed she was gone.

Jo awoke the next morning as soon as the rooster crowed and climbed out of bed. Her room seemed very dark as she tiptoed around, dressing quietly, and she realized it was raining again. The clouds seemed to touch the barn roof and looked like smoke among the trees as she stepped outside into a light drizzle. She had wrapped a shawl around her shoulders against the chill, and she lifted it over her head as she hurried down the path to the tree house as fast as her torn shoe would allow.

Alexander Chandler was already waiting for her beneath the tree, his horse grazing nearby. He held his saddlebag in his hands, and he broke into a smile when he saw her. She ran to join him beneath the tree house, which acted as a roof to block the rain.

"I'm glad you came, Josephine." She noticed his voice was no longer hoarse.

"Yes . . . me too." It was an awkward moment. Neither of them seemed to know how to begin. Rain pattered on the floor of the tree house above them and dripped from the leaves. Alexander broke the silence first.

"I brought you something. Here, have a look." He opened the mouth of his saddlebag, and she saw it was filled with shoes. She couldn't speak. "It was my fault you tore your shoe because you were running away from me," he said, "so I brought you some new ones. Well, they aren't actually new; they're secondhand. I hope that isn't insulting to you."

"Where did they come from?"

"They were collected by my church up north and donated to the Freedmen's Bureau for needy families. I didn't know your size, so I put several sizes in here. Maybe someone else in your family needs shoes, too?"

"My mother would never allow us to accept charity."

"She doesn't have to know."

"She isn't blind, Alexander. She's sure to notice me wearing different shoes."

"But you need them. Would she rather you go barefoot than to swallow her pride and accept charity?"

Yes, Josephine thought. She probably would.

"Please, try on a pair. Take more than one pair, if you'd like."

Jo looked into the bag and saw that although the shoes were used, they were obviously well made and in good condition. And she did need them. She was desperate, in fact. She selected a pair that looked to be her size and leaned against the damp tree trunk as she slid one of them onto her foot. It fit comfortably. So did its mate. They would keep her feet warm and dry.

"I'll think of something to tell my mother," she said. "Thank you, Alexander. I appreciate your kindness." He relaxed and smiled with relief. "And just so you know," she continued, "I don't blame you for my torn shoe that day. They were old and wearing out. It was my own fault running away so gracelessly. But thank you."

"You're welcome to take more than one pair."

"Not for me. But if I may, I'll take a pair for my sister, Mary." She rummaged through the bag and chose a pair of slim, dark shoes that appeared to be Mary's size.

"I can bring you other things, too. The churches up north are eager to help the South rebuild—"

"No, please don't. It will be too hard to explain. I think it's best to keep our meetings and our friendship a secret." There was another awkward silence. This time Josephine broke it, desperate to change the subject. "How are the repairs to the school coming along?"

"I'm afraid they've become mired in bureaucratic problems. I'm forced to wait for funds for the building materials, and the wheels of government move very slowly. They've promised to send more schoolbooks right away, but they haven't arrived yet."

"I've started a school of sorts on our plantation. We have three new children at White Oak besides Lizzie's three, and I promised to give them lessons in return for their help with some yard work. We started yesterday and it was fun. They are so eager to learn. And very bright, too."

"Hey! Why not come into town and teach all the children?"

"You said the school wasn't finished."

"Not yet. But once the new books arrive, you could hold classes outside the bureau office."

"My mother would never allow it. She doesn't know I'm teaching White Oak's children as it is. But Roselle told me that she would like to become a teacher someday. Do you think that's possible? Would I be wrong to encourage her?"

"Not at all. I've heard of Negro teachers in other bureau schools down here."

"Good. I'll encourage her, then." She looked up at Alexander, and the way he was gazing at her made her forget everything she had planned to say.

"I'm glad you came today, Josephine. I was afraid you might not because of the rain."

She looked away, suddenly self-conscious. "I only agreed to meet with you because you raised so many questions the last few times we spoke, and you still haven't answered them all."

"I don't know all the answers myself," he said with a laugh. "But go ahead and ask. I'll give it a try."

She dared another glance at him and saw that he was smiling. Josephine thought he was a nice-looking man, not as handsome as her father had been, but then few men were. But what made Alexander attractive to her weren't his looks, but the quiet inner strength he seemed to possess, and a maturity beyond his years.

"Well," she began, "I have been thinking about your comments on why God never answered my prayers. You said we could talk about it after I had time to think, remember?"

"Of course. Aren't you tired of standing, Josephine? Shall we sit down?"

"No, thank you. The ground is much too wet." And it made her heart beat in a funny way to think of squeezing close to him in the cramped space beneath the tree house. "Anyway, you said that God couldn't answer my prayers because He wanted to set the slaves free—"

"Not only the slaves. What if God wanted to set you free, as well?"

"What do you mean? I am free. I always have been."

He shook his head, impatient with her. "What do you suppose your life would have been like if the South had won the war? If your father hadn't died?"

"My mother was just talking about this the other day when she was discussing her dance. She and my father would have made sure I was courted by suitors from proper, respectable families. I would have married one of them and become a wife and mother. I might have moved to my husband's plantation, perhaps lived with my in-laws for a time. Eventually I would have become the mistress of my own plantation."

"How do you feel about that? Are you sorry it didn't happen that way?"

"To be honest, I feel relieved. I told Mother the old way of courting and arranging marriages seems so artificial now. But I wouldn't have questioned it if we hadn't lost the war and everything else."

"The war stripped away all those expectations. The old demands are gone and you—and the former slaves—are free to do what God created you to do, not what everyone tells you to do."

"But God created women to be wives and mothers."

"True, but women can fill additional roles, too. The Quakers believe in education for men *and* women. My two married sisters did some public speaking for the abolition movement. What if the war was about your emancipation as well as the slaves'?"

That was the other question he had raised, the one that haunted her. What did she want for her life, for her future? Jo realized she didn't know the answer because she had never been free to ask it. All the important decisions had been made for her, and she'd been expected to trust her parents' choices. She had never sampled another way of life.

"I don't know how to answer that," she finally said. "I would have been content to marry my father's choice and now I'm content not to marry. I realize I'm too different from other girls, too plain—"

"You aren't plain!"

She laid her hand on his damp jacket sleeve to silence him. "Please don't. I wasn't fishing for a compliment. I-I need to go. Mother will wonder where I've been and why my hair and clothes are wet. Thank you again for the shoes."

"But . . . we didn't finish talking. When will I see you again?"

She wanted to say *never*, knowing she shouldn't have come in the first place and shouldn't be talking to him at all. "A week from today," she said.

"The same time?"

"Yes, the same time and place." She hurried away into the cold morning rain.

24

Every time Josephine talked to Alexander Chandler she would spend the rest of the day thinking about his words. He always challenged the things she had been taught, challenged her to think differently. It was the same this time, his words shadowing her as if Alexander himself was following her through the house.

It rained all day, frustrating her. She and the children couldn't work on the terrace, nor could Jo find an excuse to sneak away to the kitchen to teach them another lesson. She had nothing to do all day but think about Alexander.

She waited until the following day to show the shoes to Mary, trying to dream up an explanation for them—and failing. "Come upstairs to the bedroom with me," she said after breakfast. "You need to try on your dress so I can pin the hem." Josephine waited until Mary had buttoned on the unfinished dress, then handed her the shoes. "Here, I thought you could use a pair of shoes to wear to the dance with your new dress."

"Josephine! Where did these come from?"

"Try them on. See if they fit."

Mary sat down on the bed and slipped the shoes onto her feet. "Where did you get them?"

"They're a gift from someone who saw that we needed them. I

have a new pair, too. See?" She lifted the hem of her dress to show Mary her shoes.

"You shouldn't have accepted them. Mother won't like us taking charity." Her soft voice was little more than a whisper.

"But we need them, don't we? Do they fit you?"

"Yes. Very well, in fact."

"Good. Mine do, too. Let's just wear the shoes and enjoy them for now. We can deal with Mother once she notices them."

Mary looked doubtful, as if afraid to go against their mother's rigid code of rules. She had been a mere child, eleven years old, when the war began to dismantle their comfortable life, and Josephine could see the lasting effects it had left on Mary. "Do you remember the old days, Mary, when we took things like shoes and new dresses for granted instead of considering them luxuries?"

"Yes . . . I never had to worry about outgrowing my shoes or my dresses or wonder what I would do if I did. But things just keep getting worse and worse until it seems like every day we lose something else." She started to take off the shoes, but Josephine stopped her.

"No, leave them on and climb up on that chair so I can measure the hem. How does the dress feel? Does it fit you?"

"Yes. Perfectly. How did you ever learn to sew like this?"

"It isn't difficult. You—" She started to say, *You could do it, too*, but changed her mind. "You would be surprised how easy it is."

She helped Mary climb up, then sat cross-legged on the floor below her with a cushion of dress pins as she started to work. She remembered her sister's terror as she'd huddled at Aunt Olivia's house in Richmond. Mary was a beautiful girl with porcelain skin like their mother's, her delicate cheeks still rosy and childlike. But she was so fearful, talking softly, walking softly, as if afraid she might do something to trigger the next disaster. What would her future be? Josephine stopped pinning for a moment and looked up at her.

"Someone asked me, not long ago, what I wanted for myself, my future. How would you answer that question, Mary?"

"I want the same things every woman does: marriage, a home of my own, children. What else is there?"

Josephine didn't know the answer herself. "Would you ever marry a man for love?"

"What do you mean?"

"Suppose you fell in love with a man who Mother thought unsuitable? Someone who couldn't afford to hire servants, and you had to do all the cleaning and cooking and everything that Lizzie does. Would you marry him anyway?"

"I don't even want to imagine such a thing! It won't happen. I know that people around here don't have much right now because the Yankees stole it all, but Mother says that by the time I'm old enough to marry, we'll have everything back again. We already have some of our slaves back, don't we?"

"They aren't slaves, Mary."

"You know what I mean. Mother says she's going to train Roselle to be my lady's maid and teach her how to fix my hair and get dressed in the morning. She said Roselle could even move with me and be my maid after I marry."

Roselle, who dreamed of being a schoolteacher. Josephine sighed, realizing the hopelessness of trying to change her sister's way of thinking—the way Alexander Chandler was changing hers. "Stand still so I can pin the hem."

"Will my dress be done after you finish the hem?"

"I'm afraid not. The side seams are just basted. I wanted to be sure it fit you first. I'll need to re-sew them with a backstitch before you can wear it, or you'll rip them all out the first time a gentleman whirls you around the dance floor."

Josephine was nearly finished when Mother walked into the room. "That dress looks lovely on you, Mary. Josephine, must you sit on the floor? I'm sure there's a footstool you can use. Anyway, I've come to tell you girls that we're going to visit the Blakes today. I've asked Willy to bring the carriage around."

That meant visiting Harrison. Josephine hadn't thought of him in days and certainly hadn't missed seeing him—although she did miss talking to Mrs. Blake. Mary stepped down from the chair to change her dress. "She didn't notice our shoes," she whispered to Jo after their mother left.

When they arrived at the Blakes' plantation, Josephine was surprised to see Harrison sitting on the front porch in his new wheelchair. "Hasn't he made wonderful progress?" Priscilla whispered to Jo after she greeted her. "He can wheel himself all around now, in and out of the house."

"I'm so glad," Josephine said.

While Mother and Mary went inside to visit with Priscilla, Josephine stayed on the porch to talk with Harrison for a moment, leaning against the railing. It had begun to rain again, drumming on the porch roof, dripping from the eaves, reminding her of her visit with Alexander beneath the tree house.

"I'm glad we're getting rain, aren't you, Harrison? It will be so good for your crops."

"It won't matter if it rains or not. Those Negroes will never make a profit from cotton."

"Well, I see you're still your same old cheerful self. I also see you've had a haircut and trimmed your beard. You look much better."

"And you look like Eugenia Weatherly's daughter today and not like the scrub maid."

Her face went hot with embarrassment. "That was unkind."

"I meant it to be unkind."

"Why? Why do you enjoy insulting me and hurting my feelings? Does it make you feel better to speak to me that way? More like a man?"

"Shut up, Josephine. Just . . . shut up."

"Don't tell me what to do. You have no right." It made her tremble from head to toe to talk to him this way, but it also felt good to speak her mind. Hadn't Dr. Hunter encouraged her to argue with Harrison? And if her friendship with Alexander had taught her anything, it was to ask questions, to say what she thought, to speak up for herself.

Alexander. She would see him again next Tuesday. It seemed like a long time to wait. "Do you believe in God, Harrison," she asked suddenly, "and that He answers prayer?"

"What?"

She stopped leaning against the railing and took a step toward him. "I asked if you still believed in God after everything that happened."

"Of course I do. I'm not a heathen."

"Do you believe He answers prayer?"

"Why do you want to know?"

Josephine decided to tell him the truth. "Because I no longer believe He does, and I wondered if we had something in common. Heaven knows, we don't agree on anything else."

Harrison laughed out loud. He actually laughed! In all the weeks she had lived with him, all the hours she'd spent with him, Jo had never once heard him laugh. She expected his mother to come running out to the porch to see what that unfamiliar sound was or who the jolly visitor could be. Surely it couldn't be Harrison who was laughing. But it was.

"You are something else!" he said, shaking his head.

"Are you going to answer my question?"

"Sure. I'll answer it. Unfortunately I still believe in God. I believe He allowed the Yankees to blow my leg off as payment for my sins. He turned me into a mangled, grotesque cripple to torment and punish me."

She couldn't reply. Alexander said that suffering wasn't God's punishment. Wasn't that the lesson from the book of Job?

"I tried to end it all and take the shortcut to hell," Harrison continued, "but God sent you and that ridiculous Yankee to stop me. The two of you make a fine pair of hell's messengers, sent for the sole purpose of torturing me and punishing me here on earth for a little while longer. I guess the price of my sins hasn't been paid in full yet."

Josephine had no idea what to say.

"Have I shocked you? Aren't you going to ask me what my unforgiveable sins are?"

"That is none of my business."

"Ah! But you've made the rest of my miserable life your business. Why is that, you little hypocrite?"

"I'm not a hypocrite. A hypocrite is someone who claims to have faith but lives an entirely different life. You weren't listening to me, Harrison. I said I no longer believed in the sort of God they taught us about in church, who's always there listening to our prayers and—" She stopped. If what Alexander said was true, if God had better reasons for not answering her prayers, wanting to set the slaves free, to set her free, then could she begin to trust Him again?

"Go on . . ." He was waiting for her to finish.

"Never mind. I'll give you your wish now. I'll go inside and leave you alone." And she did.

But Harrison's words haunted her. Would God really turn him into a cripple to punish him?

Josephine asked Alexander about it the moment she met him beneath the tree house the following Tuesday. "You said the book of Job proved that suffering isn't a punishment. But does that mean God never punishes people for their sins?"

"No, what the book of Job shows is that even good people sometimes suffer for reasons only God can see. . . . Shall we sit down, Josephine? We don't need to visit standing up today. It isn't raining."

Her heart sped up at the thought of sitting beside him. "No, thank you. My skirt would get all dirty."

"I'll bring a blanket or something to sit on next time. I should have thought of it, I'm sorry." His smile disarmed her. It seemed to come from a source deep inside him that filled his entire body, instead of a smile that was a mere social pleasantry. They remained standing beneath the floor of the tree house, as close together as they had the last time even though it wasn't raining.

"Please, go on," Josephine said. "I want to understand about Job and suffering."

"If we believe God is good, then we can trust that if He brings suffering into our lives or if He doesn't answer our prayers, it's for our ultimate good."

"Harrison thinks he lost his leg because God was punishing him. Could that be true?"

Alexander moved his shoulders in a halfhearted shrug, as if to say there was no simple answer. "Sometimes our suffering is a consequence of our own choices, going our own way, fighting against God. Losing his leg could be the result of Harrison's decision to fight, not a punishment. God takes no joy in our suffering."

"Why does He allow it, then?"

"Sometimes it's His way of coaxing us to come back to Him. God used the war to draw me back to Him. People do more praying on the battlefield than they ever do in churches."

"But if that's true, I would have to believe it was good that Daddy died, good that my family and I suffered during the war and lost nearly everything we had."

"You can never know for certain what your life would have been like if the war hadn't happened. Suffering is part of living in a broken world. Your father might have died another way. Your family might have lost their fortune in some other kind of disaster. We're wrong to expect our lives to be perfect on this side of heaven. And it's wrong for parents to shelter their children and make them believe that the most important thing is to be happy."

"If life isn't supposed to be happy, then why live it? Why not end it like Harrison tried to do?"

"Because there's a big difference between happiness and joy. Happiness is external and can change when your circumstances change. If you believe that money will make you happy, for instance, and then you lose all your money, you'll be very unhappy. But joy is deep inside us and isn't dependent on circumstances. Even poor people can have joy. Didn't you tell me that doing simple chores like working in the garden brought satisfaction?"

"Yes . . . and it gives my mother fits. She claims the work will ruin my hands, among other reasons."

Alexander reached for her hand and held it, looking at it before looking up at her. "When we walk away from God, we walk away from any chance of joy. Joy doesn't come from circumstances but from God."

His touch warmed her entire body as if she stood beside a flaming hearth. So did the way he was looking at her. Her heart began to gallop, and she had a sudden memory of how her brothers used to race each other down the lane on Daddy's horses, hooves thudding on the dirt, pounding faster and faster. That's what her heart felt like right now. She wanted Alexander to continue holding her hand, which was why she pulled it free. She forced herself to look away from his intense gaze, looking down the path toward home.

And there stood Mary, a stone's throw away, watching them.

How long had she been there? Josephine turned her back on Alexander and hurried toward her. "Mary! What are you doing here?"

"I saw you get up and get dressed. I heard you leave the other morning, too. I wondered where you went, so I got dressed and followed you."

"I needed some fresh air and—"

"You came to be with that Yankee. I saw you with him." Jo turned to look back, but he and his horse were gone. She linked arms with Mary to walk home.

"You were spying on me?"

"Is that why you asked me about marrying someone unsuitable? About marrying for love? Are you in love with *him*?" She said the word in a disparaging way, as if Alexander were nothing, less than nothing.

"No, I'm not in love, don't be absurd! We were just talking."

"He was holding your hand, Jo."

"He wasn't—"

"I saw you!"

"Listen. He's trying to help me understand things about the war—"

"What does a Yankee know about our side of the war?"

Jo couldn't begin to explain their strange friendship, nor could she tell her sister that she'd lost her faith and could no longer pray. Mary would never understand. "Are you going to tell Mother that you saw us?"

"That depends. Are you going to keep sneaking out to see him?"

When Josephine hesitated, Mary said, "Jo, you can't! It isn't proper! People will think . . . I mean, he's the enemy, and I saw him holding your hand. I saw the way he was looking at you."

"Stop it. He's not our enemy. And I swear we were simply talking. It's not what you think." But Mary was right. The way Alexander looked at her made her heart race like a thoroughbred pounding down the track. She drew a deep breath and let it out. "Please don't tell Mother. I sewed you a new dress, I brought you new shoes—that's where they came from, by the way. From Mr. Chandler's church up north."

"You're sweet on him, aren't you? And don't tell me you aren't because I can see it on your face."

"Mary—"

"What will our neighbors think if they find out? Mother is having this dance so we can find husbands—proper, gentlemanly husbands—and you can't ruin it for me, you can't! Maybe you don't want happiness, but I do."

Jo drew Mary to a halt near the stables, afraid Mother would hear them arguing if they went near the house. She recalled Alexander's words about happiness and joy and wondered if she could explain the difference to Mary.

"Happiness is what we had before the war, when Daddy was alive. It was based on being wealthy and having servants and a beautiful home, and it didn't last. When our circumstances changed, we weren't happy anymore. But we can have joy, now and in the future, even if we don't have a beautiful home again or dozens of servants or rich husbands."

"You aren't making sense." Mary looked so much like Mother when she stood this way, with her hands on her hips and her chin in the air.

"Have you ever watched Lizzie and Otis with their children? They have nothing—no house, no money, they wear rags and walk barefooted—but they have love and joy."

"And you think you can have that with your Yankee?"

"No, Mary. No. I need someone to talk to, that's all. I can't stand being trapped inside the house all day with nothing to do. I'm bored. That's why I started sewing your dress and cleaning up the terrace. Mr. Chandler is someone new to talk to, that's all. But please don't tell Mother. She won't understand. She'll turn me into a prisoner."

"If you promise not to see him anymore, then I'll promise not to tell."

"Fine. But I'll have to see him once more to explain why—"

"No! Just stop going to the tree house. He'll figure out why."

"But he'll think—"

"What? What will he think?" Mary planted her hands on her hips again.

Josephine had been about to say that Alexander would think she didn't care for him, but she didn't dare say that out loud. Because she did care for him. Against all reasoning, all logic, all propriety, she did care for him. Perhaps too much.

She took Mary's hands in her own, looked her in the eye. And as much as Josephine hated to do it, she said, "I promise. I promise I won't see Alexander Chandler again."

25

JUNE 17, 1865

"I would like this room thoroughly cleaned," Eugenia said as she surveyed her guest room. "That means the bedding must be changed, the floor swept, and the room dusted. Those curtains will need to be taken down, washed, starched and ironed. Leave all the windows open while you work so the room gets thoroughly aired."

"Yes, ma'am." Roselle had given the proper answer, but Eugenia caught her looking out the window, not at the work that needed to be done. The two little Negro girls who would be helping Roselle looked suitably frightened of Eugenia, yet they were mere children and much too young to be proper servants yet.

"Pay attention now, Roselle. I want it done right. We have company coming from Richmond in two weeks."

"Yes, ma'am."

Josephine, who also had been following Eugenia all around, moved close and whispered, "You can't order them around, Mother. They aren't—"

"I know, I know. For heaven's sake, Josephine, quit pestering me about it."

"Well, servants should be paid for their work and—"

"I'm providing room and board, aren't I? The very least they can do is help me with a few simple chores once in a while."

"But when they helped me with the terrace—"

"I never should have agreed to let you pay those children for their work. Now they'll expect it all the time."

Josephine sighed. "At least let me help them take down the curtains. I'm taller than everyone else."

Eugenia agreed, but only because they were running out of time and there was still a great deal of work to be done before her dance. Thank heaven she finally had Clara for another house servant so Josephine didn't feel compelled to help Lizzie do everything. Clara was proving to be a much better cook than Lizzie and nearly as good as Dolly had been. Of course, their menu was still severely limited, but they would have fresh produce from the kitchen garden in a few more weeks. Roselle and these two new little girls were very young, but that meant Eugenia could train them herself, the right way—if they weren't too dull-witted, that is.

"Can I leave you under Josephine's supervision?" she asked. "Can I expect the work to be done properly?"

"Yes, ma'am," Roselle repeated.

"Promise me you won't do any of the work yourself, Josephine."

"I'm simply taking the curtains down." She had already moved a chair in place beneath one of the windows and was lowering the rod. As Jo stood on tiptoes, Eugenia noticed her toes were no longer sticking out from her shoes. She moved closer for a better look.

"Josephine? Where did those shoes come from?" Jo turned around so fast, still holding the unwieldy curtain rod, that she nearly fell off the chair. Eugenia reached to steady her.

"My shoes? . . . Um . . . Someone noticed I needed new ones and—"

"Does this someone have a name?"

"They wish to remain anonymous. Everyone knows how you feel about accepting charity."

"But you accepted charity just the same?"

Josephine drew a deep breath, then exhaled. "Yes. I did. And you may as well know that I accepted a pair for Mary, too. We need them, Mother. And someday when we get everything back, as you're so convinced we will, we'll be able to repay the good deed and be charitable to someone else in need."

Eugenia couldn't argue with her daughter's logic, nor could she explain the pain it caused her to be unable to meet her children's needs herself. "I'll be downstairs if you need any more instructions," she said. "Priscilla promised to send two of her girls over to help me rearrange the drawing room, and they should be here any minute."

Eugenia was gazing at her newly restored terrace when Priscilla's servants arrived. The flagstone courtyard had turned out even better than Eugenia had dared to hope, with the weeds cleared and the railings newly whitewashed. Of course she knew what Josephine had been up to, sneaking around trying to teach those children to read. But at least the work was finished and the terrace looked wonderful. Now if only Josephine would meet a nice young man at the dance. Surely one of them would take a fancy to her, someone who wanted his family name associated with the Weatherlys.

She put Priscilla's servants to work, rearranging the drawing room furniture, pushing chairs and end tables against the walls to create a dance floor, sweeping and mopping the huge room. They were just finishing when Lizzie entered, carrying a dusty bottle of elderberry wine in each hand. "Look what I found, Miz Eugenia."

"Where in the world did those come from?"

"I found them in the root cellar, ma'am. We hid them from the Yankees after you left, and I forgot all about them until I got to the bottom of the potato bin today. There's a few more bottles just like these."

"Wonderful! Now make sure you remember to wash and dry all the wineglasses for our guests."

"Yes, ma'am."

The next two weeks flew past with a bustle of activity that White Oak hadn't seen since before the war. Eugenia could barely fall asleep the night before her dance, and by the time her guests began to arrive, she felt as giddy as a schoolgirl. Her sister, Olivia, had arrived from Richmond that afternoon with her family and would be spending the night in the guest room.

"You're very brave to open your home to entertain guests this way," Olivia said as the first carriages began to arrive that evening. They stood in the foyer together in their well-worn gowns, wearing the few pieces of jewelry that hadn't been sold. "To tell you the truth, Charles and I still can't afford to entertain this way. We're forced to go to bed when it gets dark most nights to save lamp oil."

"I checked the almanac and planned the dance on a night with a moon. Thank heaven the weather cooperated and there aren't any clouds. Lamp oil and candles are scarce here, too, but I asked everyone who could to bring a candle with them."

"Everything looks lovely."

"Thank you. I was afraid the . . . shabbiness of this affair would be embarrassing, especially compared to the lavish parties Philip and I used to give."

"Not at all. I think you'll win everyone's admiration for being brave enough to move forward."

That admiration proved to be enough for Eugenia. It felt like the old days as she greeted guests at her door and welcomed them into her home. Some of her friends had tears in their eyes as they told Eugenia how much they needed this diversion. Their gratitude cheered her, and the happiness on her neighbors' faces made all the hard work and planning worthwhile. Eugenia had hoped this would be a tiny step toward restoring her old life, but it was turning out to be a huge one.

Soon her volunteer musicians arrived and began to play. Mary and Josephine took turns on the piano. Guests whirled around the dance floor, the women in their best gowns, many of the men in their Confederate uniforms. Laughter and music filled the room.

For the next few hours Eugenia made the rounds like a good hostess, talking to her guests, attentive to their needs. They showered her with compliments. She saw Daniel waltzing, and he was smiling for once. An admiring group of young men, including

Joseph Gray, hovered around Mary and her cousins. Mary looked beautiful in the dress Josephine had remade for her. But Eugenia couldn't understand why Josephine hadn't sewn one for herself. When she had asked, Jo had simply shrugged and walked away.

Josephine wasn't even trying to meet a beau. In fact, as the evening wore on it looked as though she was going to spend the entire time playing the piano. Eugenia waited until the song ended, then went over to the piano and took Josephine by the arm. "Come, dear. Let someone else take over for a while. You need to mingle with our guests." She saw young Henry Schreiber conversing with Daniel near the open doors to the terrace and towed Josephine over to them.

"Are you gentlemen enjoying yourselves?"

"Yes, Mrs. Weatherly. Very much so," Henry said. "Thank you for inviting me." Eugenia lingered long enough to help Josephine start a conversation, then discreetly left when Henry invited Josephine to dance. She saw Priscilla Blake just coming through the drawing room door and hurried over to greet her.

"Where's Harrison? Didn't he come?"

"I told you he wouldn't."

"I'm so sorry to hear that. But I'm glad you came, dear. Everyone has been asking about you."

"I'm sorry I was late. I was trying to convince Harrison, but . . ."

"Never mind. There's some elderberry wine over on the sideboard. Dolly, our former cook, made it. Come, I'll fetch a glass for you."

They met Leona Gray by the refreshment table, and Priscilla was soon engrossed in conversation with her. Eugenia surveyed the room to see who else might need attention and to make sure her guests were mingling. Olivia and her husband were waltzing together, and Eugenia felt a stab of jealousy when she saw them—and then a rush of anger toward Philip for supporting the war, for dying, for leaving her alone. He'd been such a powerful, dynamic man, always strong and in control, filling any room he entered with his presence. She felt the pain of his absence now as if her arm or her leg had been severed or her heart gouged from her chest. As she struggled to stop her sudden tears, she felt a tap on her shoulder.

"May I have this dance, Eugenia?" She turned, surprised to see David Hunter. He had cut his hair at last and looked slender and handsome in his Confederate uniform. For a moment she forgot her manners and simply stared at him. He smiled shyly. "Please don't say no, Eugenia. It has taken me all evening to gather up my courage to ask you."

"Of course I'll dance with you. I just . . . you took me by surprise, that's all. I didn't realize you had arrived, I'm sorry."

"Your daughter Mary met me at the door. Shall we?" She moved into his arms, and he led her around the dance floor in a graceful waltz. Eugenia had always loved the company of men, loved their strength and masculinity and the way it complemented her femininity. She had enjoyed the game of flirtation when she'd been Mary's age and the command her beauty gave her over men. She envied her daughter, just beginning to discover her power.

David turned out to be a wonderful dancer, graceful and smooth. "Where did you learn to waltz so beautifully?" she asked as they glided around the room.

"My mother taught me. She said it was something every gentleman should learn." Eugenia wondered how a common physician's mother had learned to waltz, but she didn't ask. "If you're wondering how my mother learned," David said with a smile, "she was born into a privileged life like yours. She married 'down' because she fell in love with my father, a physician like myself who had treated her for scarlet fever."

"Really? How interesting."

"Theirs was a very romantic story, so I've been told. My mother was a Blandford from Fairfax County."

"I know the name. They are a very fine family." No wonder David had always displayed such good manners, with one of the Blandfords for his mother.

"You picked a beautiful evening, Eugenia, with moonlight and starlight. Your home looks magnificent."

"I wish you could have seen the galas we used to have. This gathering is a pale shadow in comparison."

"Does it make you sad to compare this night with the past?"

"It doesn't matter. We're allowing ourselves to be happy again, to put the war behind us. Today is a better day than yesterday, and that's what counts. We've given ourselves one night to dance and visit with old friends and not worry about tomorrow."

What she missed the most, Eugenia realized, was the freedom from worry, the contentment of knowing that Philip was in charge and that he would take care of her. Ever since he'd died, she'd been forced to run the plantation herself, making the arrangements with her former slaves, making sure the crops were planted and the vegetable garden tended. Daniel had turned out to be a great disappointment to her. She didn't know what he did with his time every day, but he wasn't running White Oak. She glanced around for him as she and David covered the dance floor but didn't see him.

"We're a bit like one of my patients," David said, "whose fever and pain have gone away for a day or a night, and he can finally sleep in peace. Perhaps the fever will return tomorrow, perhaps he'll become worse and die. But for today, he can celebrate life—and so will we."

"You're right. All these fine families have suffered these past few years, and many continue to suffer. But we're coming together as a community and enjoying each other's company tonight."

"You called them 'fine families.' Even after the war, Eugenia, do you still put people into categories the way you were taught to do—rich and poor, socially acceptable and not, black and white?"

"I haven't placed them there. Life has."

"But people are all the same in God's eyes, don't you think? Or do you believe there will be segregated divisions in heaven like the ones we've created here on earth?"

"What an odd question to ask. I guess I've never thought about how it will be in heaven."

"No. Because we were taught that there was the Southern aristocracy and there were common men. That the Negroes were little more than beasts with souls. But what I'm wondering is, do you still believe that?"

"I'm not sure what I believe. Why are you asking me these things?"

"Because it's time we thought about these issues here in the South. The old aristocratic system has been destroyed, and now we have a chance to rebuild it. Are we going to make it the same as it was? Or, as Christians, are we going to start seeing people the way God does?"

"Are you trying to shock me, David? Make me angry?"

"I'm trying to change you. For selfish reasons, I confess. Perhaps I'm wrong to try to do that tonight."

Eugenia had long suspected that David Hunter cared for her. If this was his clumsy attempt to see if he stood a chance of courting her, she would pretend not to understand. "I know all about change," she said. "I've had to accept more than my share of it already. But I still believe that some things shouldn't change. Some traditions need to remain in place for our children's sakes."

"I think you'll find our children's values will be different from ours. They'll see that slavery was wrong and that it had to end. They've seen the futility of war. They're learning to live without wealth and privilege. I would hope our sons and daughters would also learn to look for other qualities in each other besides money and social position."

She thought immediately of Josephine and the odd habits and opinions she had developed. This conversation was making Eugenia extremely uncomfortable, and she fidgeted in David's arms, wishing the waltz would end.

"Your daughters, for instance," David continued. "Suppose one of them decided to marry for love, as my mother did?"

That would be the last straw, Eugenia thought. She would never allow it. "I was fortunate to have both love and respectability with Philip," she replied. "I pray my daughters will, as well. Women who marry outside their station in life find that it leads to heartache and disappointment."

"My mother was very happy."

"I doubt that was possible. After the love fades, what's left? There must have been times when your mother missed her privileged life—I confess that I miss mine. There are days when I ache to have it all back the way it was. But I didn't choose the changes I've been forced to live with. Your mother did."

Eugenia realized her words had come out sharper than she'd intended when David said, "I didn't mean to make you annoyed with me. I'm sorry. Thank you for the dance, Eugenia."

"My pleasure."

He gave a courtly bow and strolled away from her, through the open doors to the terrace.

Eugenia busied herself with her guests again, and with making sure Lizzie and Clara kept the wineglasses washed and the sideboard refreshed. A few other gentlemen asked Eugenia to dance, including Daniel and her brother-in-law, Charles. She saw Mary waltzing with Joseph Gray. Couples were also enjoying the warm evening outside on the moonlit terrace, but when she went out there herself to cool off for a moment she was appalled to see Daniel talking to the little chambermaid Roselle. He was laughing with her, of all things. Eugenia strode over to him and linked her arm through his.

"Daniel, do remember our guests, please. I see several young ladies who haven't been invited to dance yet." She gave Roselle a stern look before steering Daniel back inside. She would reprimand the servant later.

As the evening wore on, Eugenia realized she had lost track of David Hunter. Their conversation had left a sour taste in her mouth, and she wanted to be certain she hadn't insulted him. She made a circuit of the room but couldn't find him. "Have you seen Dr. Hunter?" she finally asked Josephine.

"He left. He saw that you were busy, and he asked me to thank you for inviting him. He said he was sorry, but he had to leave early."

"Oh. That's too bad." Eugenia felt a deep disappointment that she couldn't explain. She needed to get away from the merriment for a moment and went out into the front hallway, hoping she might find David there, that she wasn't too late to convince him to stay or to bid him good-night. But the foyer was deserted. She was fighting tears again and didn't know why. She paused in the doorway of Philip's darkened study, longing to see her husband seated in front of the window, smoke curling from his cigar as he played a game of chess with Dr. Hunter. But Philip was never coming back, she told herself for the hundredth time. Eugenia wiped her tears and put on a brave smile, then returned to the drawing room and her guests.

When the last candle died, when the last note of music had been played, when the last guest had thanked her and bid her good-night, Eugenia sank down on a chair in the deserted drawing room, tired but happy. It had been a wonderful evening, the first step toward reclaiming her life. The only sad note had been David's conversation about social divisions. Had he been flirting with her? Was he asking about her attitudes because he wanted to court her? Eugenia had grown accustomed to receiving men's attentions in the past, but was he really daring to hope that she would fall in love with him, marry him? No, it was impossible to expect her to marry down, even for love. He had asked if she would allow her daughters to do that, and the answer was firmly no.

Perhaps she should stop spending so much time with him, even as his patient. After all, she hadn't felt the pain in her chest in weeks. She had to admit she enjoyed his company, his admiration. But maybe it wasn't fair to David to encourage his hope that something more might develop from their relationship. Yet was she prepared to spend the rest of her life alone, never held or loved by a man again? She was only fifty. Would she have to attend a dance in order to feel a man's arms around her? She wiped a tear. She was working so hard to get her old life back, but in the end she would be alone and she couldn't bear the thought.

She gazed around the room, feeling sad that her long anticipated dance was over. The room was in disarray, but at least she now had servants to clean it up. She should go to bed. She rose from the chair and was about to close the doors to the terrace when she saw Olivia and her husband, standing in the moonlight with an arm around each other, sipping the last drops of elderberry wine. They would go upstairs together, hold each other close.

Olivia turned and saw her. "We were just saying how glad we were to see you getting on so well, Eugenia. Your cotton fields are growing, you have servants again. . . . But I knew you would be all right. You've always been strong."

"Thank you. I haven't had a chance to ask how things are for you in Richmond?"

Charles sighed. "I confess that I find it difficult to begin all over again at my age. The Yankees are making it as hard as they possibly can for us to govern ourselves again, requiring loyalty oaths and a new constitution for the commonwealth, and all that other nonsense. They seem determined to rub defeat in our faces."

"Let's not talk about that tonight," Olivia said. "This has been such a wonderful evening, Eugenia. Thank you so much for giving us and our daughters this gift."

Eugenia climbed the stairs to her bedroom feeling weary but content. She heard whispering and giggling as she passed the girls' room and opened the door a crack to peek inside. The girls were dressed in their nightclothes, talking about the young men they'd waltzed with and brushing each other's hair. Even Josephine was laughing. When one of the girls admired Mary's dress, which she'd hung on her wardrobe door, Eugenia held her breath, praying Josephine wouldn't tell her cousins that she'd sewn it. It would be so humiliating. But Mary saw Eugenia in the doorway and ran to give her a hug.

"Thank you, Mother! Thank you so much for a wonderful evening."

"You're welcome, dear. I only wish it could have been as lavish as in the old days. Good night, girls."

Eugenia thought about David Hunter again as she took off her jewelry and hung up her dress. What had he been trying to say? He'd said that he wanted to change her for selfish reasons, but Eugenia knew if she tried to bend any more, she would break in two like a brittle stick. She liked his attention and enjoyed being with him, but should she continue seeing him? She looked at herself in the mirror as she unpinned her hair, and the thought of not seeing David Hunter brought tears to her eyes.

Her bed felt very cold and empty. Cold pillows, cold sheets, even on a warm July night. Eugenia had been so happy during the party, but now she began to weep.

Why did you do this to me, Philip? Why did you ever involve us in that terrible war?

26

Lizzie walked around the deserted drawing room, gathering empty glasses on a tray to take out to the kitchen. The candles had all burned out, but there was still enough moonlight streaming through the terrace doors to see what she was doing. She felt tired clear down to her bones after all the hard work of preparing for the dance, but she needed to clean up a little or Miz Eugenia would complain about it in the morning. Tomorrow was Sunday, Lizzie's only half-day off from work. She and Otis were planning to walk into town in the afternoon for the first prayer meeting at the Freedmen's Bureau.

Lizzie's tray was full, and she didn't see any more glasses. She was about to leave when Roselle came in from the dining room. "Got the table all set for breakfast?" Lizzie asked her. "Extra places set for their company?"

"Yes, Mama."

"You go on to bed, then. I'll be down shortly."

Instead, Roselle stood in the doorway to the courtyard and leaned against the frame. She had a dreamy look on her face, and she seemed reluctant to leave, as if she could still hear the music playing. "Wasn't it beautiful tonight?" she asked. "I have never heard music like that before. I would love to wear a beautiful gown like the one Missy Jo made for Missy Mary and dance with a handsome man." She spread her arms and made a little twirl in front of the doors as if she was dancing with somebody.

Lizzie shook her head. "Don't even think about it, Roselle. And don't bother wishing for it. Put it all out of your head."

"Why? I could go to a dance someday. People tell me I'm pretty, you know."

Lizzie's stomach made a slow, sickening turn. "Who does? Who tells you that?"

"My friends, Lula and Corabelle."

"Don't you go getting all proud now. Nothing worse than a pretty girl who acts like she's better than everyone else just because the good Lord made her pretty."

Even in the dark, Lizzie saw Roselle give a shy, blushing smile. "And Massa Daniel told me I was pretty, too."

Lizzie went cold all over as if someone had stepped on her grave. "When did he say that?"

"Tonight. At the dance."

Lizzie nearly dropped the tray of glasses. *Oh, Lord, no . . . please . . .* She had to sit down. She made her way to the nearest chair, but Roselle didn't seem to notice as she kept on chattering.

"He said I was as pretty as any white girl, and he wanted to dance with me. I told him I didn't know how to dance and he said that's all right, he would teach me how. So he took me right outside there on the paving stones so we could practice."

No . . . Lord, no . . .

"Then Miz Eugenia came along and took him away and ruined it all."

It was the first time in Lizzie's life that she'd ever been grateful for Miz Eugenia. Lizzie couldn't breathe, couldn't speak. It felt as if someone was sitting on her chest, squeezing all the air out of her.

"And remember that night when I went up to see my ducks," Roselle continued, "and I ran into Massa Daniel up by the kitchen? He asked me my name and said, 'My, don't you look pretty?' He remembered my name tonight, Mama. He said Roselle was a very pretty name for a very pretty girl."

Lizzie set the rattling tray of glasses on an end table and leaped up from the chair as anger surged through her. For the second time in her life she understood how someone could be angry enough to kill another person. She grabbed Roselle by the shoulders and began to shake her, desperate to shake some sense into her. "No! No! No! You stay away from him, you hear? Stay away!"

"Mama . . . don't!" Confusion and fear filled Roselle's eyes.

Lizzie stopped. What was she doing, shaking her this way? Roselle had been so happy only a moment ago. Lizzie pulled her daughter into her arms, hugging her fiercely. "I'm sorry, honey. I'm sorry. Don't cry . . . But you got to stay away from Massa Daniel. Don't you ever go near him again."

Roselle wiggled out of Lizzie's arms, glaring at her like she didn't believe a word of Lizzie's warning. "We're free now, aren't we? We're not slaves who never dare to talk to our massa—or dance with him if he invites me."

"Listen to me! You can't dance with him. You can't do anything but bring him his food or wash his clothes. And don't you ever believe a word he says to you."

Tears filled Roselle's lovely dark eyes and rolled down her cheeks. "I just wanted to see what it was like to dance like Missy Mary and all the other girls were doing. Just once, Mama."

"You're not like them other girls. If you want to dance, then you find someone like yourself, not a white man. And especially not Massa Daniel. He was one of the men who beat up your papa, don't you remember?"

"That's not true! You're just saying that because you don't like him."

"Ask your papa, then. He'll tell you. And you know Otis don't tell lies. He saw Massa Daniel there that night with the other men, beating on poor old Willy and shooting their rifles."

"Otis isn't my papa. My real papa was white, wasn't he? Is that why you hate white men? Because my father was white?"

"Don't you dare talk to me like that!"

"That's why you won't tell me who he is, isn't it? You don't want me to know that I'm white, too." She turned away, but Lizzie grabbed her arm and yanked her back.

As mad as she was, Lizzie still couldn't tell Roselle the truth. She didn't want to remember her own foolishness. Or her shame. But she had to tell Roselle something. "I'll tell you this one thing about your father, and that's all. He started wooing me with sweet talk, just like Massa Daniel's doing. Carrying on and telling me I was pretty. But do you see your real father anywhere around here? Did he stay and love you and me or be a papa to you like Otis is?"

Roselle looked down at her ragged shoes as her tears continued to fall.

"No sir! Otis has been a papa to you in all the ways that count. And he's a good husband to me, too. You find yourself a good God-fearing man like Otis. Someone who's gonna stay with you and help you raise his babies after he puts them in your belly. You think Massa Daniel's ever going to marry the Negro girl who empties his slop pail every morning?"

A sob shuddered through Roselle. "I just wanted to dance," she said softly.

"I know, honey. I know. But there are bad men in this world who would take advantage of you for that." Lizzie pulled her into her arms again. She understood how Roselle felt. She had been innocent and trusting, too, all those years ago, but it had ended so badly. Would it take a tragedy before Roselle would stop trusting? Lizzie released her daughter and picked up the tray again to take to the kitchen. "Let's go to bed. The rest of this mess can wait until morning."

As tired as Lizzie was, she couldn't fall asleep. Her mind whirled around like the people on the dance floor as she tried to figure out what to do about Roselle. She didn't trust Massa Daniel. If he ever hurt her daughter, she would kill him. She would. Same as she should have killed Roselle's father.

Before she knew it, the rooster started to crow and Lizzie had to get up and make breakfast for everybody, had to try and make the food stretch to feed Miz Eugenia's company from Richmond.

Thank heavens she had Clara to help her now, and she could let Roselle sleep. Lizzie didn't want to face her. And for sure she didn't want Roselle waiting on the white folks in the dining room.

On Sunday afternoon, when the work was done, everybody got ready to walk into Fairmont for their first prayer meeting at the Freedmen's Bureau. Lizzie was so tired from her sleepless night that she would have liked to stay home and take a nap, but she couldn't hurt Otis's feelings that way. He and Saul and a few others had talked to Mr. Chandler, and he'd agreed to let them meet on the grassy slope alongside the tracks. He even said he would read the Bible out loud to them. Lizzie and Clara packed a simple picnic lunch for their families to eat afterward, and everyone set off for the walk to town, following the road, even though the path through the fields and along the railroad tracks was shorter. Old Willy wanted to come and he couldn't walk that far, so Robert had offered to push him in the wheelbarrow.

"Look at that sight!" Otis said as they passed the cotton fields. "The good Lord's been blessing us with sunshine and rain and making our cotton grow." In fact, the plants were so thick and green they could hardly see the pathways between the rows.

But Lizzie's eye was on Roselle, walking ahead of them. The smaller children crowded around her like a mama hen with her chicks as she played schoolteacher with them and made them say their ABCs. One minute Roselle was a child, skipping down the road just like the other little ones, and the next minute she was wanting to wear a fancy gown and dance with Massa Daniel. Lizzie thought of what might have happened last night if Miz Eugenia hadn't interrupted, and she felt the fear return. She reached for Otis and tugged on his arm.

"Otis? I think Roselle should work with you from now on instead of me."

"You mean out in the fields? Lizzie, why would you want such a thing?"

"Because Miz Eugenia's trying to make her into a fancy lady's maid for Missy Mary, and Roselle is too good for that. I want a better life for her than combing some spoiled gal's hair and lacing her corset."

"You ain't making sense. How is working in the fields any better than working in the house?"

Lizzie decided to tell him the truth. "We need to keep her away from Massa Daniel. He was sweet-talking her last night at the dance, saying she was pretty and asking her to dance with him."

Otis stopped walking. He stared at Lizzie. "Why would he want to dance with a colored girl when he hates us so much?"

"You know exactly what he wants. Roselle doesn't understand what can happen, Otis. She's too trusting. I don't want her in the Big House anymore. That place is so big, it'd be easy for Massa Daniel to get her off someplace by herself. She won't like working in the fields, that's for sure. But it's for her own good."

Otis sighed and started walking again. "If only the school would start up again. I thought maybe we could all help Mr. Chandler rebuild it, maybe work on it at night or whenever we have an afternoon off. But nobody has time when there's corn and vegetables to plant and so much other work to do. And you know we don't dare go out at night."

"What are we going to do about Roselle?"

"Bring it to the Lord, Lizzie. That's why we're having this prayer meeting. We'll bring all our troubles to the Lord."

Mr. Chandler stood in the doorway of the little brick building that housed the Freedmen's Bureau, greeting everybody. It looked just fine from the front, but when Lizzie walked around to the back, the room where the school had been looked like the inside of a fireplace, all black and charred and filled with burnt wood. That's how much the white folks hated them, and Lord help her, Lizzie hated them in return for making her feel so helpless. She had to turn her back on the sight to keep the anger from twisting around inside her like a nasty vine.

Dozens of other families had already arrived, and Lizzie tucked her feelings away as she greeted Dolly and Ida May and the others who used to work at White Oak. The children chased each other and took turns balancing on the tracks and jumping the railroad ties until the prayer meeting began. There were too many people to count, even if Lizzie knew how.

Otis came up alongside her, interrupting her thoughts. "I need to talk to Mr. Chandler about the part of the Bible I want him to read. I'll be right back and then we'll get started."

"Wait. I'll go with you." The size of the crowd had given Lizzie courage, and as soon as Otis finished speaking to him, Lizzie made up her mind to speak to Mr. Chandler herself. He was as slender as a bean pole, and she had to look up to see his eyes, which were as pale as a faded blue shirt. "Massa Chandler, sir? We need to get the school going again right away. Our kids don't care if it's finished or not. They don't mind sitting outside on the grass. But they need to learn how to read and write."

"I'm sorry, but the new books haven't arrived yet. And there's no teacher."

"Can't you ask Miss Hunt to come back? Please? It's the only way my kids will ever have a better life. Every day that the school stays closed they're forced to work on the plantation, and they're learning how to be slaves again instead of learning how to be free."

"I understand, but—"

"I heard Miz Eugenia say she's making my Roselle into a lady's maid for her spoiled daughter. It's bad enough I have to empty her slops, but I don't want my daughter to have to do it all her life, too. If Roselle and my boys don't go to school, they'll always be slaves, no matter what the law says, no matter who won the war. Please open it again. Please!"

He nodded and pressed his fist to his mouth as if he was thinking. She saw pity in his eyes and that gave her hope. "Give me a little time to think of something, Lizzie. Right now, I know Otis wants to get this meeting started."

"Yes, sir. Thank you, sir."

Otis had walked to the top of a little rise and stood in front of the group, holding up his hands for silence. A shiver of fear ran through Lizzie. He didn't need to be coming forward as the leader of everybody. He'd only get himself in a mess a trouble. She hurried over to him and whispered, "I thought you said you weren't preaching."

"I'm not. I'm just getting things started this first time. Go save me a place to sit. I'll be right there."

Lizzie went back and sat down on the sun-warmed grass. Jack climbed onto her lap, and she put her arm around Rufus as he leaned against her. Roselle sat in front of them with her friends.

"I asked Mr. Chandler to read something to us from the Bible," Otis said when the crowd finally quieted. "Something I remember my pappy reciting. Then we can take turns praying and talking to the Lord."

Mr. Chandler was still paging through his Bible as he walked over to stand beside Otis. The pages were as thin as onion skins and rustled in the breeze. "I think I found the verses Otis wants me to read," he began. "It's actually two passages that he mixed together. One is from Psalm 126, the other from the book of Galatians." He cleared his throat and began to read in his odd Yankee accent, speaking loud enough for everybody to hear: "'When the Lord turned again the captivity of Zion, we were like them that dream. Then was our mouth filled with laughter, and our tongue with singing: then said they among the heathen, the Lord hath done great things for them.'"

Someone in the crowd shouted, "Amen," and Mr. Chandler looked up, smiling.

"'The Lord hath done great things for us; whereof we are glad,'" he continued. "'They that sow in tears shall reap in joy. He that goeth forth and weepeth, bearing precious seed, shall doubtless come again with rejoicing, bringing his sheaves with him.'"

"Thank you, Lord!" someone else shouted. The pages of the Bible rustled again as Mr. Chandler turned them, looking for the second place.

"'Whatsoever a man soweth, that shall he also reap. For he that soweth to his flesh shall of the flesh reap corruption; but he that soweth to the Spirit shall of the Spirit reap life everlasting. And let us not be weary in well doing: for in due season we shall reap, if we faint not.'"

"That's just the ones I wanted," Otis said. "Thank you, sir." He drew a breath and began talking to the crowd in the same calm, steady voice he used when he told bedtime stories or when he prayed. "Now everybody here knows that if you plant cottonseeds in the ground, you get cotton. Put corn seeds in and a corn plant grows. And like that verse just said, if you sow hatred year after year you're gonna reap a war, like the one that just ended.

"Now I know it seems like the only seeds we slaves ever get are things like hard work and pain and suffering. But if we give them to God, He can do a miracle under that ground. We see it every day. Put in a tiny seed, get a big green plant with blossoms and leaves and cotton. We can't do it ourselves. We got to trust the Almighty. But today we can take all our suffering and give it to God, and you know what we'll reap when the time comes? Joy!

"They can burn our school and take everything else away from us, but they can't take away Jesus. He's with us always, and He promised us a better life with Him in heaven someday. Today we're here to pray and bring all our trials to Him. But don't be planting seeds of hatred. Give Jesus our tears and someday we'll reap a harvest of joy."

To Lizzie the words felt like a warm shawl around her shoulders on a cold day. She wished she could trust Jesus the way Otis did, but she forgot how to trust a long time ago. Even so, her prayer today would be, *Protect my Roselle. Keep her safe. Don't let anything bad happen to her.*

Otis started to come over to sit down beside her, then turned back and said, "Oh, and one more thing. Don't forget that Jesus said we're supposed to pray for our enemies, too."

Pray for Massa Daniel? Or for Roselle's father? Lizzie couldn't do it. The words would stick in her throat like a mouth full of flour.

Everyone bowed their heads and began to pray. Sometimes one person would pray out loud, sometimes everyone would pray at the same time, sometimes somebody would start singing a song.

And though their cries were mournful and pleading at first, the afternoon ended just as Otis promised it would, with singing and laughter and joy. Most people had brought food along, and they spread everything out on the grass and shared it with each other in a great big picnic.

Mr. Chandler had gone inside the building to let them worship alone, but late in the afternoon he came outside again and stood at the top of the rise to get their attention. "Please don't leave yet. I have an announcement to make." He waited until the crowd grew still. "As you know, it's my job to take care of the freedmen—that's all of you—looking out for your interests, seeing to your needs. Today I have to ask for your forgiveness because I haven't done a very good job of that. A while back, several of you suffered a vicious beating in the woods, and two good men died of gunshot wounds. I'm determined to get justice for all of you, and especially for the two murdered men. But I can't do it without your help. I talked to the authorities in Richmond about the violence, and they told me they can't prosecute without witnesses. Please, I need everyone who was there that night, everyone who was injured, to come and talk to me. Tell me everything you remember. If I can combine all your pieces of information, we'll stand a better chance of finding the men who were responsible and bringing them to justice."

"They're never going to take our word as the truth," Old Willy said, shaking his head. "Especially against a white man's word."

"I'm going to hound everyone in the Freedmen's Bureau, all the way to Washington, until I get justice. That's my job. That's why this bureau was created. Please, those of you who were there, come and talk to me."

"You gonna tell him it was Massa Daniel?" Lizzie whispered to Otis. He didn't reply.

"And one more thing," Mr. Chandler added. "I've realized I allowed a group of evil men to keep me from seeing to one of your greatest needs—an education for your children. I'm sorry. Please send them here tomorrow morning for school. We'll hold classes out here where you're sitting or in my office if it rains. As of tomorrow morning, the school is officially open once again."

Rufus had been sitting at Lizzie's side, but he leaped to his feet, too excited to sit. "Hear that, Mama? We're having school again!" Jack jumped up, too, and they held hands and did a little dance right there on the grass.

Otis reached for Lizzie's hand and squeezed it tight. "See? The Lord is answering our prayers already."

"What about telling him about Massa Daniel and his friends?"

"I need to pray about it first. There's a difference between justice and revenge, and I need to make sure I'm doing it for the right reasons. I know Massa Daniel's horse was there. I don't know if he was riding it. And I don't know if he was the one who shot those people."

"But Mr. Chandler said everybody needs to tell what they know."

"Mr. Chandler don't understand the way things are here in the South. If we accuse a white man to his face, chances are the white man will still go free—but we'll all be dead men."

"But it ain't fair."

"Life won't be fair until we reach heaven, Lizzie-girl."

On Monday morning, Lizzie was serving breakfast to the white folks in their dining room when Miz Eugenia looked all around and asked, "Where is Roselle? She needs to go up to Miss Mary's room when we're finished. It's time she learns how to be a lady's maid."

No, ma'am! Lizzie wanted to say. *She needs to learn how to read and write!* She bit her lip to keep from saying the words out loud, then answered quietly, "Roselle ain't here, ma'am. She went to school this morning."

"You're lying!" Massa Daniel said. He looked so angry he could have breathed out fire. "I know for a fact the school is closed."

"It's the truth," Lizzie said, feeling scared and happy at the same time. "The school just opened up again. Today is the first day." She risked a glance at Missy Josephine and saw that she was holding back a smile.

Miz Eugenia looked like a woman who had just been robbed and didn't know where to turn. "I suppose those two new girls went to school, too?" she asked. "What are their names?"

"You mean Annie and Meg? Yes, ma'am, they're gone off to school, too."

Lizzie quickly turned her back and carried the empty platter out to the kitchen so nobody would see her smiling. She told Clara about the white folks' reaction when she got to the kitchen, and they both had a good laugh. Clara had just finished churning the cream from their new cow into butter and was pressing it into the butter molds.

"You'd think she'd be happy to have butter again and cream in her tea. She say anything about that?"

Lizzie shook her head. "They ain't never happy. The more Miz Eugenia gets, and the more it's like the old days around here, the more she wants." Lizzie took a bucket out to the pump to fetch water for the dishes. She could see Otis and the other men out in the cotton field, and to her far left, rows of new green corn plants sprouting from the dark earth. She'd told Otis that she was willing to help him. She'd been a field slave like her mother, before moving up to the Big House, and in some ways she wished she still was, especially now that there was no overseer cracking his whip. But Otis wouldn't hear of it.

"That baby is gonna start kicking before we know it," he'd said, pressing his hand against her middle. "You stay in the Big House where at least you can sit down once in a while and get out of the sun."

Rufus and Jack wouldn't have to work in the fields, either. Lizzie smiled, remembering the looks on their faces as they'd carried the books they'd earned from Missy Jo to school to share with the others. No sir, Lizzie wasn't going to let Miz Eugenia or Massa Daniel spoil her day. She was going to take all of those seeds they kept throwing at her and hand them over to Jesus so they could grow into joy.

27

July 3, 1865

Lizzie's children were back in school. Josephine rejoiced when she heard the news at breakfast, even though she would miss teaching them. They had been bright, alert pupils, eager to soak up everything she taught them. She wondered who Alexander had found to teach them and felt a little sad that it wasn't her. Of course, it was impossible to do such an outrageous thing. Mother would banish her to Richmond before ever allowing Josephine to become a common schoolteacher, much less teach a classroom full of Negro children.

The hot July day stretched endlessly before Josephine, as long and empty as all the others. She missed her days at Mrs. Blake's house when they had learned how to cook together and when Josephine would work in the garden in the morning before the sun grew too hot. Now her only guilty pleasure was sewing. She had decided to try fashioning a skirt and bodice for herself from two worn-out dresses. "If I'm going to entertain suitors, I'll need something nice to wear," Jo had told her mother to pacify her. She didn't dare take out her needle and thread too often, though, or appear to be enjoying her labor, or Mother would become upset.

Jo was sitting in the parlor that afternoon stitching a side seam, the slippery taffeta rustling beneath her fingers, when she saw the children coming home from school. The boys chased each other in a game of tag; the little girls fluttered around Roselle like hummingbirds. Jo put aside her sewing and went outside to talk to them, standing in the back doorway as they raced into the yard. She could hear Lizzie and Clara working in the kitchen and smelled sweet potatoes baking. "How was school? Did you have a new teacher?" Jo asked.

"Mr. Chandler taught us today," Jack said as he made a game of jumping on and off the wooden walkway. "But he doesn't teach the same way Miss Hunt did."

"He said maybe our old teacher might come back," Rufus added. "But we liked you teaching us the best, Missy Jo."

She ran her hand over Rufus's wooly hair. "That's sweet of you to say so, but I'm not a real teacher." She was glad the children felt free to talk with her and even laugh with her after they'd all worked together. She missed being with them and had even considered hiring them to tame a few other portions of the badly overgrown plantation grounds, just to spend time with them again. But going to school was much better for them than doing yard work.

The children skipped away and she was about to go inside when Roselle called to her, "Missy Josephine, wait." Roselle took Josephine's hand in both of hers and pushed a piece of paper into it, closing her fist around it. "Mr. Chandler asked me to give that to you," she whispered.

Josephine opened her hand as Roselle hurried into the kitchen and found a crumpled, folded note with *Miss Weatherly* printed on it. Jo glanced all around, then quickly walked to the terrace on the side of the house to read it. Her heart pounded as if she had run circles around the house instead of walking slowly. She found a patch of shade and leaned against the newly whitewashed railing with her back to the house. Alexander's handwriting was as tall and slender and angular as he was, and it made her smile. She pictured his blue eyes and fuzzy brown whiskers and heard his Yankee accent as she read:

My dear Josephine,

Can we meet? I long to be assured that I didn't get you into trouble with your family, and . . . well, the plain truth is that I miss talking with you. I'll be at the tree house tomorrow, just after dawn like the last time. Then the same time the following day in case you cannot come tomorrow for some reason. Or you can always send a note back to me and ask Roselle to deliver it. I anxiously await your reply.

Yours,
Alexander Chandler

She should throw the letter away. No, she should burn it in the fire so no one would ever see it. Instead, she put it in her pocket where she could reach in to touch it every now and then.

For the rest of the day Josephine thought about his request and tallied all the reasons why she shouldn't go. She should send a message back with Roselle, explaining the promise she'd made to her sister, explaining there was no point in continuing their friendship. But Jo was wide awake the next morning before the rooster had a chance to crow, and after making sure Mary was sound asleep, she carried her clothes into the guest room to get dressed. She didn't take time to pin up her hair, letting it fall loose down her back so she could say she had been to the privy if anyone caught her outside.

The air was already warm when she slipped through the back door and hurried down the path to the tree house. She wouldn't stay long, she told herself. Just long enough to see him again.

Alexander was already standing beneath the tree house waiting for her. As soon as he saw her, he broke into a grin and jogged up the path toward her, his hands outstretched. "Josephine! I'm so glad you came." She had the irrational urge to run into his arms and hold him tightly. Instead, she reached for his hands and took them in hers, squeezing them briefly before letting go. She hoped he wouldn't say awkward things like he had missed her. She was afraid of what she might say in return, and so she hurried to speak first.

"I can't stay long. I promised my sister I wouldn't meet with you again, and I'm breaking my promise." She glanced back, determined to keep her eye on the trail this time. And she wouldn't let Alexander hold her hand no matter how warm and strong and wonderful it felt.

"Did I get you into trouble with your family?"

Jo shook her head. "I convinced Mary not to tell, but I had to promise not to see you." The morning air was still, without a breeze. She heard the new cow lowing in the barn, waiting to be milked, the rooster crowing to be fed.

"How have you been, Josephine?"

"Fine, thank you." Her words came out more stilted than she intended, but her feelings were in such a state of confusion that she didn't know what to say or how to say it. "We can't be friends anymore, Alexander. I mean, I'll always consider you a friend, but we can't meet anymore. I came today because I wanted you to know that it wasn't because of anything you said or because I was angry with you, but . . . well, because . . ."

"I'm a Yankee."

"Yes. And a man. I'm not sure how things are done where you come from, but down here it isn't proper for an unmarried man and woman to be alone together without a chaperone."

"My intentions are honorable, I assure you."

"I know. I'm not worried. But I'm risking my reputation by coming here." There. She had said it plainly. She was also risking more confusion and sorrow if she continued to see him because their friendship was impossible. And she was running the risk of caring for him even more than she already did. "What have you been doing? How is your work progressing?" she asked.

"I'm sure you've heard that I've reopened the school."

"Yes. The children were very excited about it. I didn't realize the building had been repaired."

"It hasn't. But I decided to hold classes outside since the weather is so nice. It's not ideal, but it's better than nothing."

"What made you change your mind?"

"Your servant Lizzie begged me to reopen it—and she's right. The only way the next generation of freedmen will ever have a better future is if they can get an education."

"Roselle told me you're teaching the children yourself."

"I admit I'm a terrible teacher. I wrote to the Missionary Society and asked them to please send Miss Hunt or someone else right away, but it will still take a few weeks. And so I was wondering . . . is there any way at all that you could teach them in the meantime? I know I asked you before, and I understand why you had to refuse, but—"

"Nothing has changed." She took another glance down the trail. "Unlike the women you know up north, I'm not free to go wherever I want to and do whatever I choose. That's the way it is down here. I'm sorry."

"I'm sorry, too. I have a goodly amount of other bureau business to attend to, and it won't get done while I'm tied up with teaching. I need to return to Richmond, for one thing. An important part of my job is to get justice for the freedmen, so I'm trying to arrange an investigation into the beatings and the two murders and the fire. The school is government property, and the arsonists must be brought to justice."

Josephine didn't know what to say. She suspected that Daniel was one of the men responsible for the fire and for the beatings in the woods. What he and the others had done was wrong, but she didn't want the Yankees to send him to jail. Could they try him for murder? Hang him? What would become of White Oak?

She shouldn't be here, Jo realized. She shouldn't be talking to a Yankee. She was being disloyal to her family and to the South. "Was there something else you needed to tell me?" she asked, taking a small step away from him. "I can't be gone long. I shouldn't have come at all, but . . ." But she had wanted to see him. She had missed him. Being here was wrong in every possible way, yet she thought of Alexander every single day, thought of him when she lay in her bed at night. On the evening of the dance she had foolishly wished that he would walk through the door, tall and handsome, and ask

303

her to waltz with him. She had pretended it was Alexander she'd waltzed with instead of Henry Schreiber.

"I understand," he said. "Since we don't have much time, I also wanted to ask if you're still mad at God, still unable to pray?"

"I avoid God altogether," she said, looking down at her feet and the shoes he had given her. "I go to church with my family because it's expected of me, but I'm simply going through the motions." She took another small step away from him. Maybe if she did it in small increments, it wouldn't hurt so much when she finally turned her back and walked away.

"Have you tried yelling at God? Getting angry? Telling Him what you think?"

She gave a short laugh. "I'm just beginning to do that with real people like Harrison Blake. I have even talked back to my mother a bit—something I never would have dared to do before I met you. But I still don't have the nerve to yell at God."

"You don't really have to yell," he said, laughing. "Just talk freely, like you and I always do."

"He doesn't answer my questions out loud the way you do." She looked up at him, and his grin made her smile. "You've acted as His spokesman, Alexander, giving me a lot of things to think about. I'm grateful."

"You look so pretty with your hair that way," he said softly. "I've missed you, Josephine." He hadn't stopped looking at her since she arrived. She closed her eyes, longing to say that she missed him, too, but there was no point at all in doing so. Their friendship was impossible. Anything more than friendship was scandalous.

"I need to leave. I'm so sorry. I feel bad about breaking my promise to Mary."

"Wait!" He reached for her hand, and she let him take it. She kept her head lowered, hiding the tears she didn't want him to see. "Could we write to each other? That wouldn't be breaking your promise, would it? We could send letters to each other through Roselle."

"I don't have any paper. I used it all up writing letters to my brothers during the war. I know that sounds like a feeble excuse but it's true."

"Then I'll send you some paper. And ink, too, if you need it. I'll send it this afternoon, in fact. Please, Josephine? You could ask me questions in your letters, and I'll try to answer them. I need to know how you're doing."

She shouldn't agree to write to him. But if she said good-bye today and walked away, she might never see him again, never speak to him again, and she couldn't bear the thought. "I suppose we can try writing for a while."

Even that seemed deceitful to her. She would have to do it in secret or Mother would want to know where the writing paper had come from and who the letters were for. But Josephine couldn't deny the relief she felt at having a way to continue their friendship.

"Thank you, Josephine." His words came out like a sigh of relief. He squeezed her hand before letting go. "And one more thing . . . ?" he asked as she started to walk away. She turned to look at him. "Please give God another chance?"

Josephine made it all the way back to the house without being seen and was sitting at the dressing table in their bedroom, pinning up her hair when Mary awoke. They went down to breakfast together, but Jo avoided her sister's gaze, certain she would read the guilt in her eyes. Or maybe the happiness.

"I have good news, girls," Mother announced at breakfast. "I have invited Mrs. Schreiber and Mrs. Gray to tea today. I expect both of you to be there, of course, and to make our guests feel welcome. Their sons would make very good matches, as you know."

Josephine stared at the tabletop, trying to quell a rising sense of panic. Her father had once explained to her how he and the other men hunted pheasants by getting the slaves to move through the brush in an ever-tightening circle, chasing the birds into the hunters' path. She felt like one of those helpless birds now. Her mother was a strong, determined woman. Her plans left no room for escape.

"But . . . but Joseph Gray is nearly ten years older than Mary," Jo blurted. "She's much too young for him."

"I'll be seventeen in August." Mary's cheeks were as bright as ripe apples. She had spent a lot of time with Joseph at the dance, and Jo could see that she was sweet on him already.

"Mary is the perfect age," Mother said. "And as you know, your father was a few years older than me. The young men in our community are ready to settle down after the war. We can't afford to wait too long."

"Why don't you just say it, Mother: I'm twenty-two and plain and practically a spinster already. Go ahead and find Mary a husband, but please leave me alone."

"Leave you alone? To do what, dear?" Mother kept her voice pleasant, but Josephine heard the hard edge behind her words. "Do you plan to immerse yourself in religion like Great-Aunt Hattie did, reading the Bible all day and moralizing? I know you don't believe me, but being the mistress of your own home, raising children and having a good man to take care of you is very satisfying. There are few other options that will give you that satisfaction."

Josephine knew it was true. She looked down the long, lonely road of spinsterhood and saw nothing—no home of her own, dependent on her family's goodwill for her support until the day she died. Alexander had insisted the war had set her free, and while that might be true for women up north, it was not true for her.

"What do you think of Henry Schreiber, Josephine? You talked with him at the dance, didn't you?"

"He seems pleasant enough. I hardly had time to get to know him."

"That's what courtship is for. You might at least give him a chance before you give up. And the place to start is by being pleasant to his mother."

Henry was one of Daniel's friends, one of the men who had attacked Otis and Willy and burned the school. Alexander had reminded her again this morning that two Negroes had died that night. Might she or Mary end up married to a murderer? Would she always look at her husband and wonder if he was capable of killing an innocent man—and never dare to ask?

"And, please, Josephine," Mother finished, "let's hear none of your radical ideas about doing your own gardening or cooking or sewing."

At her mother's tea that afternoon, Josephine felt like an item on display. She had attended similar teas before the war with the same object of snaring a husband—that much hadn't changed. But the war had changed Josephine. She was finding her voice, and she longed to speak up, speak out, to choose her own husband or choose not to marry at all. But she remained quiet, demure, doing what was expected of her for her mother's sake and for Mary's. A portion of the Schreibers' land adjoined White Oak, and as Josephine listened she realized that Daniel and Henry were scheming to create an empire by combining their families and their two plantations. She wouldn't be allowed to stand in the way of her brother's plans by refusing a marriage proposal.

The afternoon couldn't end soon enough for Josephine. The moment Roselle returned from school with a supply of writing paper and ink for her, she went upstairs to hide in the guest room and write to Alexander.

Dear Alexander,

I don't understand why you believe that God intended for the war to set me free in the same way that it gave the Negroes their freedom. My mother has embarked on a campaign to see me happily married, a campaign I am not at all in favor of. But the alternative, spinsterhood, is also unattractive. I am not as starry-eyed as my sister, dreaming of romance with a handsome, wealthy husband—not that any men in our community are wealthy these days. And while I have protested that I don't care if I ever marry, the truth is that spinsterhood is a very lonely life, where single women are shuttled from one relative to the next for the rest of their lives, becoming a somber, powerless presence in each unfortunate household they visit.

You asked what I wanted for my life and my future, and

I still don't understand the question. Don't you know that I'm not free to want anything for myself, any more than the slaves were free to dream of their futures before the war? If you could kindly explain what you meant—

She stopped. Was her tone too harsh, too demanding? She had a sudden memory of Alexander gazing at her this morning and saying, "*You look so pretty with your hair that way.*" She forced back her tears and continued writing.

I'm sorry if I sound strident, but I'm so confused. The future I once expected to have with marriage and a family now seems unacceptable to me, but I don't like the alternative, either. I would greatly appreciate your advice and wisdom.

> *Sincerely,*
> *Josephine*

She sent the letter with Roselle the next morning and received one in return:

My dear Josephine,

I can feel your frustration and your sense of being trapped. I do suggest a third alternative that is neither an arranged marriage to someone you have no feelings for nor spinsterhood. It's an option that may seem impossible at the moment but can surely be achieved with God's help. It is to marry a man you love and make a new life together as partners, the way God intended it to be when He made Eve "bone of Adam's bone, flesh of his flesh."

I understand that the desire to please your family and to make an alliance with a man of their choosing must be very strong and ingrained. But the truth is, the only One we are required to please is God. Your mother's intentions are honorable in that she wishes to see you in a secure situation with all your needs met. But if we serve God and honor Him, He has promised to meet all our needs. That is the very definition of faith—to walk in hope, trusting in what you can't see or control.

I urge you to take your situation to God, confiding in Him as you have with me, and asking for His guidance and His will. He will show you what to do. Write Him a letter if you must, just as you are writing to me. You need more wisdom than I am able to give you. Stay well, dear Josephine—and please try prayer.

> *Yours,*
> *Alexander*

Prayer? He expected her to pray? Josephine folded the letter and stuffed it into her pocket, unwilling to risk more disappointment by turning to God. Her prayers were as certain to go unanswered now as all the others had in the past.

A week after she and Alexander began exchanging letters, Josephine and her mother were invited to tea at the Blakes' plantation. As their carriage drew to a halt out front, Jo was amazed to see Harrison hobbling across the yard on crutches, slowly making his way toward the rail fence that marked the boundary of the cotton field. She paused to stare for a moment before going in to tea and felt a surge of happiness for Priscilla—and for him.

"It's so nice to see Harrison walking around," she said as she spread her napkin on her lap.

"I have you to thank for it, Josephine. You and Dr. Hunter." Mrs. Blake smiled as she poured tea into each of their cups.

"Does the doctor still come by?" Mother asked.

"Not every day. It isn't necessary now that Harrison is doing so much better. He stops in maybe once a week. More if he happens to be out this way."

Josephine wondered why Mother was asking, then realized that Dr. Hunter hadn't paid a visit to White Oak lately. Not since the night of the dance, in fact. In the weeks before that, he seemed to visit quite often, even taking Mother for carriage rides.

Mrs. Blake moved to the edge of her seat, as if too excited to sit still. She hadn't touched her tea. Josephine could tell by her flushed cheeks that she had something on her mind. "Eugenia, dear . . . I understand your girls have been seeing suitors. No, that's not the right word. But you told me, didn't you, that you wanted to see your girls happily married? And I saw both Josephine and Mary dancing with young men at the gathering, and . . . well, I will be blunt. I would be so happy if you would consider Harrison as a suitor for Josephine."

Jo set down her cup, fearing it would slip from her shaking hands and shatter on the floor. This couldn't be happening. It couldn't!

"As you can see," Priscilla continued, "Harrison is doing so much better now. He walks everywhere with his crutches, and he even rode a horse the other day. The work on the plantation is going smoothly; we have servants and workers and livestock again."

Josephine wanted to shout, *No!* But she couldn't speak, couldn't move.

Marrying Harrison would be even more horrible than marrying Henry Schreiber.

Mother replied for her. "Why, Priscilla! I never imagined! What about his engagement to Emma Welch? Might she return now that he's doing so much better? I wouldn't want Josephine to be accused of stealing another girl's beau."

"It's over between him and Emma. She moved to Norfolk, and her mother tells me she is seeing other suitors." Priscilla reached to take Jo's hand, which had fallen limp on her lap. "I grew so fond of you while you stayed with us, Josephine. You helped me through the most trying time in my life. I already think of you as my daughter. You've been so good for Harrison and me. And, Eugenia, you're my dearest friend," she said, touching her arm, as well. "This match would be the answer to my fondest wishes."

Jo still couldn't speak. She loved Mrs. Blake and was glad she'd been able to help her. But she could never marry Harrison. Never. The thought made her want to throw up.

"I think it's a wonderful idea!" Mother said. She looked happier than she had in a very long time.

"What do you think, Josephine?" Mrs. Blake asked. "No one is going to make you marry against your will. But when I heard that you were considering Henry Schreiber, I wanted to ask you to consider Harrison, as well. I feel as though you already belong here with us."

The two women looked at her, waiting for her answer. She tried to speak but nothing came out. She cleared her throat and tried again. "W-what does Harrison say about it?"

"I talked it over with him and he promised to think about it. But it's up to the parents to get things started, don't you think? Nudge things along? Eugenia, I know you've been trying to turn Daniel's thoughts in the direction of marriage, and I feel the same about Harrison."

"That's true," Mother replied. "It's what needs to happen in order to move forward and get things back to normal. What could be more normal than joining two families in marriage?"

The women chatted on and on about weddings and shared grandchildren, but Josephine was too horrified to say anything at all. She could barely keep a pleasant expression on her face, barely avoid bursting into tears. She wouldn't hurt Mrs. Blake's feelings for the world, but the conversation seemed like something from a nightmare, and she wanted to wake up.

They were nearly finished with their visit when Josephine heard the back door open and close, then the scrape and thump of Harrison's crutches on the wooden floor of the hallway. She could tell that he had halted in the parlor doorway, though she couldn't bring herself to turn and look up at him.

"Harrison! Come in and say hello to our guests," Priscilla said. Again Josephine heard the scrape and thump of crutches as he entered the room.

"Good afternoon, ladies. How are you today?"

Josephine finally looked up as her mother greeted him, hoping to see the same revulsion for this idea that she felt, hoping he would think of a way to dissuade his mother without hurting her. Instead, Jo was surprised to see that he had managed to smile. He had gained weight since she'd last seen him and no longer resembled a skeleton, his skin healthy-looking from the sun.

She shuddered as she remembered wrestling with him to get the razor away, his blood pouring out along with his curses. Alexander had come and saved them both, stopping the blood, helping her subdue him . . . piecing her shattered mirror together. He was trying to help her piece her life back together in the same way, but it was proving to be impossible. As impossible as a marriage to Harrison would be. As impossible as her feelings for Alexander.

Her mother and Mrs. Blake continued to talk and plan as they headed toward the door to say good-bye. Josephine managed to pull Harrison aside in the hallway and whisper, "Are you aware of what they're planning for us?"

"Yes, my mother mentioned it. And just look how happy she is." He gestured to Mrs. Blake at the same moment that a burst of her laughter filled the foyer.

"You agreed to this?" Jo knew that she had left herself open to his scathing reply, that he might try to hurt her the way he always did, but she needed to know.

"Why not?" he said with a shrug. "I'm shocked that you would need to ask. This is what you've wanted for me all along, isn't it? Aren't you always telling me to get on with my life and, most of all, to be nice to my mother, to make her happy? You have to admit that the idea of our marriage has made her very happy."

Jo turned to go, too upset to reply, but he gripped her arm to keep her beside him. "If you refuse this marriage, you will be the one who is hurting her this time."

She saw that the glint in his eyes was sparked by anger, not happiness. He would go through with this marriage so that his mother would have a companion, then probably kill himself as he'd wanted to do all along. Alexander wouldn't be able to save either one of them this time. "Do you truly hate me that much, Harrison?"

"Hate you? I'm simply returning the favor. You saved me from suicide; now I'm saving you from spinsterhood. You made an important choice for my life, and now I'm choosing for you. We should both be grateful to each other, don't you think?"

She pried his hand off her arm. "I hate you," she whispered.

"Well, I don't hate you, Josephine. In fact, I admire you. It's my own life that I hate."

She struggled to hold her feelings inside during the ride home, trying not to cry, half listening as her mother talked on and on about Jo's good fortune and how Priscilla was such a dear, dear friend. As the carriage pulled into their lane, Jo realized her mother had asked her a question, and she didn't know what it was.

"I-I'm sorry. I'm not feeling well. What did you say?"

"I asked what you thought about courting Harrison."

Once again, Josephine feared she might vomit. "I-I have no feelings for Harrison."

"Well, of course you don't. Not yet. Do you have feelings for Henry Schreiber?"

"No."

"Well, see? It will be a luxury to consider more than one suitor. Your brother and Harrison were so close. I can't help thinking that Samuel would be pleased if you married his friend."

Josephine's legs felt unable to hold her as Willy helped her down from the carriage. All she wanted to do was run upstairs to her room where she could finally let herself cry. But she carefully removed her gloves and hat in the foyer so Mother wouldn't ask questions, then made her way slowly up the stairs to her bedroom.

Mary and Daniel were waiting for her, sitting on her bed. Her letters from Alexander Chandler were in Daniel's hand.

All of Josephine's pent-up rage and anguish exploded from her, and she leaped at her brother, trying to tear the letters from his grasp. "What are you doing with those? They're mine!" He was too strong for her. He easily fended her off as he rose to his feet and held them above his head where she couldn't reach them. She turned to her sister and grabbed her shoulders, shaking her. "How could you, Mary! How could you touch my private things? You have no right!"

"Stop it, Jo!" Daniel said. "Stop it!" He pushed between them and shoved Josephine away from Mary. He had stuffed the crumpled letters into his pocket. "Just sit down and calm down. Do you want Mother to hear you?" He forced Josephine backward until she sank down on Mary's bed, her trembling legs no longer able to hold her. "Mary showed me the letters because she was worried about you. She says you've been meeting that Yankee in the woods, all alone. These letters prove what's been going on—'My dear Josephine,'" he mimicked. "'You should marry for love . . . Yours, Alexander.'"

The thought of Mary and Daniel sitting together, reading her private letters, filled Jo with outrage. She sprang to her feet and lunged at him again. "You have no right! My life is none of your business!"

"Stop shouting," Daniel said. His voice was low and unnaturally calm as he restrained her. "We're the ones who have a right to be furious, not you. You've been carrying on shamefully with one of our enemies. So listen to me now. You will never see him or talk to him or write to him again, do you understand?" He tightened his grip on her wrists. "Because I'll place you under lock and key if I have to, to make sure that you don't. You're a disgrace, Josephine!"

"No! You're the disgrace! I know what you've been doing. You set the school on fire and beat Otis and Willy and those other helpless people out in the woods. You murdered two defenseless people! You'll be sorry, too! Alexander Chandler is investigating everything, and he has witnesses. He's going to find out that it was you!"

"Are you accusing me?"

"Yes! It was you and your friends who did all those terrible things." She turned to her sister, wanting to hurt her, as well. "Joseph Gray was one of them, Mary. He's just as guilty as Daniel is. Do you want to marry a man who is capable of murdering innocent people?"

"That's a lie!" Mary said. "You don't know what you're talking about!"

"Where's your proof?" Daniel asked. "How dare you make accusations without any proof?"

"I know that you and the others went out that night. Your jacket smelled of smoke the next day."

"That could have come from any campfire or even from a fireplace," he said with a shrug. "But I have proof of what you're doing, right here!" He pulled the letters from his pocket and waved them at her. "Shall I show these to Mother?"

"Go ahead. They're just letters. I've done nothing to be ashamed of."

"I saw you with him in the woods," Mary said. "You were holding his hand."

"I'd say you have plenty to be ashamed of," Daniel finished. "But listen to me. You've not only put your own reputation at risk, but you're jeopardizing your family's safety. Do you know what they do to people who collaborate with the enemy? Do you?"

"Get out of here, both of you! Go away and leave me alone!"

Daniel shook his head. "I've decided not to tell Mother what you've been doing because it would kill her, Josephine. You'll break her heart. She has suffered enough already. But from this moment on I'll be keeping a very close eye on you. There will be no more meetings and no more letters."

Someone knocked on the bedroom door, and a moment later Mother came inside, still glowing from her visit with Priscilla. "Well, here you all are! Did Josephine tell you her good news?"

"No, what news?" Daniel broke into a smile, casually sliding the letters back into his pocket.

"Harrison Blake is interested in courting Josephine!" Was Mother truly that blind? Couldn't she see the anger on their faces or feel the tension in the room?

"That's wonderful news, Josephine," Daniel said, turning to her. "No wonder you look so happy. See, Mother, she's crying tears of joy. I certainly give my approval to the match. Harrison is an even better catch than Henry Schreiber."

Daniel finally managed to herd Mother and Mary from the room, leaving Josephine alone at last. Her world had been shaken to pieces just as it had been shaken during the war. The devastating losses had already begun: the loss of her freedom, her independence, the loss of her friendship with Alexander . . . and there was nothing she could do about it.

She would write one last letter to him and give it to Roselle to deliver tomorrow morning. Daniel had taken away her writing paper, but she tore a scrap from the margin of one of her books and wrote on it:

Dear Alexander,
  Our letters have been discovered. We cannot see each other or write to each other anymore. I'm so sorry.

Josephine

28

JULY 13, 1865

"Where is Josephine?" Eugenia asked at breakfast. "Isn't she coming downstairs? Her food is getting cold."

Mary stared at the tabletop. "Jo said to eat without her," she mumbled. "She doesn't feel well." The dance had put new life into Mary and she had seemed so happy and confident in the days that followed. Eugenia hoped she wasn't going to turn back into a frightened rabbit again.

"Are you ill, too?"

"No."

"Then kindly stop sitting there like a wilting flower and eat your breakfast. And please stop chewing your fingers." Mary pulled her fingers out of her mouth and picked up her fork, but her shoulders were still hunched. "Must I add you to my list of worries, too?"

"No, Mother."

"Josephine didn't come down for supper last night, and now she's skipping breakfast? It isn't like her to get sick."

The meal seemed very subdued with neither Mary nor Daniel saying much. They had been quiet at dinner last night, too. As soon as Eugenia finished eating, she went upstairs to Josephine's room and found her still in bed with the pillow over her head, the curtains closed.

"Are you all right, dear?" Eugenia parted the mosquito netting and lifted the pillow off her face. Josephine's eyes were red and watery, her nose congested. "You've been in this room since yesterday afternoon."

"I don't feel well."

"What's wrong?"

"It's just a summer cold. I'll be fine."

"Do you have a fever?" Eugenia laid her hand on Jo's brow. It felt warm and clammy, but then the entire bedroom was humid and stifling even though the day had just begun. "Why don't you come downstairs? It's cooler in the drawing room where there's at least a breeze from the terrace."

"No, thank you. I don't want to make everyone else sick. "

"Well, you've caught this cold at a very bad time. With two eligible suitors showing interest, you should be paying visits and accepting callers."

"I'm sorry," Jo said. Her nightgown and hair were damp with sweat. The bed sheets, too. She did indeed look miserable.

"I am simply thrilled about your prospects, dear. Someday you'll look back at this as one of the happiest times in your life."

Josephine didn't reply. She covered her eyes with her hand.

"You never told me what you thought about Harrison as a suitor? I don't want to rush you into anything, but you do know that Priscilla and I would be overjoyed if you two decided to marry."

"I haven't been able to think about anything. I've had a very bad headache since yesterday."

"I realize you're probably not in love with either man yet, but I hope you remember what the alternative is."

"Of course I do."

"Good. Should I send Lizzie up with a tray? Would you like something to eat, something to drink?"

"No, I don't want anything. I just want to sleep."

Eugenia heard sounds of activity downstairs. She listened for a moment and thought she heard the front door opening and closing, then men's voices in the foyer. Had someone arrived? David Hunter, perhaps? She used Josephine's mirror to tidy her hair before hurrying downstairs to the foyer. The hallway was empty; whoever it was had come inside and then vanished without any proper greetings at all. She heard voices in Philip's study and listened at the door. It sounded like Joseph Gray's voice, but it was much too early in the morning for him to call on Mary. Eugenia hoped nothing was wrong.

She was about to go into the study and greet him when she heard Daniel say, "This is serious, Joseph. That Yankee at the Freedmen's Bureau is going to investigate the fire. And he's determined to find out who killed those two Negroes. He has witnesses."

"Does your slave know it was us? What about that other slave, your driver? Wasn't he there, too?"

"I don't know if they recognized us or not, but we need to get everyone together and decide what to do. Spread the word. We'll meet here tonight after my family is in bed."

It had been a long time since Eugenia had felt the pain in her chest, but the heaviness began to build as she listened to Daniel's conversation, the pressure tightening, squeezing the air from her body. She staggered to her morning room, leaning against the walls for support and sank into her chair. Those foolish, foolish boys. She needed to stop them from making a very bad situation worse—but how? Daniel had dismissed her concern the last time she'd tried to reason with him. He'd told her not to worry, to let him be the man of the house. He likely would tell her the same thing now.

Eugenia wished she had someone to talk to about this, but who? Her friends would all tell her not to interfere, to let the men attend to their own business. That was what she used to do when Philip was alive. But the Yankees hadn't been occupying the South when Philip was alive. If Daniel and the others got caught, they wouldn't face a friendly judge who understood why the Negroes had to be kept in their place.

The only person Eugenia could think of to talk to was David

Hunter, but she hadn't seen him since the night of the dance nearly two weeks ago. She missed him—even though she now had more social activities to occupy her time. But as she closed her eyes against the pain, struggling to breathe, she longed to have him come to her rescue as he had once before. If only she could confide all her worries in him and ask him what to do. She longed to hand the problem over to him and let him take care of it for her the way Philip used to do. But she was too ill to ride into town and talk to him, too ill to visit Priscilla on the odd chance that David would be there with Harrison. If Eugenia sent a servant to fetch him, her children would learn about her spells.

She sat in her chair for a while longer, waiting for the pain to subside, before suddenly remembering that Josephine was also sick. Why not use Jo's fever as an excuse to send for Dr. Hunter? Eugenia groped for her silver bell and rang for one of the servants. It seemed to take forever for Lizzie to shuffle into the room.

"Yes, ma'am?"

"Tell Willy I need him to go into town to fetch Dr. Hunter. Josephine is ill, and I'm worried about her." Eugenia thought she saw a look of concern in Lizzie's eyes before she turned away.

"Yes, ma'am."

She heard Joseph Gray leave the house a few minutes later, but it seemed to take forever before Eugenia finally heard her own carriage leaving for town. Willy was old and slow. She should have sent Otis. Another eternity passed before Eugenia heard the carriage returning, and by that time the fire in her chest had eased into dying embers. She went to the door herself and saw David riding on the carriage seat beside Willy as if to remind her of his familiarity with Negroes and the gulf between the doctor's class and her own. Would it be a mistake to confide in him about Daniel?

"Good morning, Eugenia," he said as he stepped down. He untied his horse from behind the carriage and tethered it to the post.

"Will you be needing the carriage again, ma'am?" Willy asked.

"No, you may put it away." She turned to the doctor as the carriage headed back to the stables. "Thank you for coming, David.

I'm worried about Josephine. She hasn't eaten since yesterday, and summer fevers can lead to so many terrible things, as you well know. I don't think our family could bear another loss."

"I understand."

He was so quiet. He had barely looked at her or greeted her. Eugenia knew she had hurt him the night of the dance and she was sorry. She didn't know how to make it up to him.

"I'll show you to Josephine's room." She led him upstairs and knocked on the bedroom door. "Josephine? Please don't be angry with me, dear, but I've sent for Dr. Hunter. It will ease my mind if he has a look at you."

"Come in." Josephine rolled over to face them as they entered. Her eyes were terribly red and swollen. "Please leave us alone, Mother."

"Very well. Let me know if you need anything, Doctor."

Eugenia went downstairs to wait, pacing the front hallway, wondering what to do about her children. It almost seemed as if God didn't want her to be happy. Just when things were going so well and she dared to hope her life might one day be happy again, she had cause to worry about all three of her children. She was standing in the open doorway, gazing at the weeds that had taken over her yard, remembering how lovely this view of her plantation once had been when David finally came downstairs. She hurried to the bottom of the steps. "Well? Will she be all right? Do you know what's wrong with her?"

"There's no fever. I'm sure she'll be fine in a few days. Just let her rest until the illness runs its course. If she does develop a fever, send for me right away." He was moving toward the door. He was leaving.

"Must you leave? Do you have a moment to talk?"

He seemed to hesitate before saying, "I have some time."

"Would you like something to drink? Shall I ring for a servant?"

"Nothing, thank you."

Eugenia led him into the parlor. He chose a chair, not the sofa, and sat with his leather physician's bag on his knees. Eugenia remembered how he had lifted her into his arms and carried her in here after she'd had one of her spells. He had been so tender, so filled with concern for her that day. Now he acted as if they were strangers.

"David, I fear I have offended you, and I want to apologize. When you left the dance without saying good-bye, I knew—"

"No, I'm the one who should apologize. It was very rude of me to leave that way. I sensed that I had irritated you, and I didn't want to make matters worse. But I had a very nice time that evening. Thank you for inviting me."

"You're welcome." There was an awkward silence. Eugenia had been trained to avoid such silences, but she felt tears pressing against her eyes and didn't know why. Her throat felt so tight that she feared the tears would spill over if she tried to speak. David broke the silence first.

"How have you been feeling, Eugenia? Any more pain in your chest?"

She shook her head, lifting her chin to keep back the tears. "Planning the dance was like a tonic for me. I've never felt better. And the dance turned out to be the beginning of better days. My girls have attracted the interest of suitors, and I have been entertaining many of my old friends for tea—not that we have real tea, mind you. But we do have cream. And butter for our bread now. And more servants and a new cook . . ." She stopped, her throat tightening again. She hoped he wouldn't ask what was wrong because she really didn't know.

"Everyone could see how happy you were that night. I'm glad you're feeling better and that my medical services are no longer needed."

His words sounded so cold. But what did she expect? Why should he waste his time on a friendship that could never develop into something more? Hadn't she told him that she didn't think the traditional class barriers should be erased?

"You've worked hard, Eugenia, and I have no doubt that you'll accomplish whatever you put your mind to. In a few years, White Oak will be thriving again." She could only nod, and in spite of all her efforts to hold them back, her tears began to overflow. His features finally softened, and she saw tenderness in his eyes as he leaned forward. "Eugenia. What's wrong?"

"It's Daniel. I'm worried sick about him. Please don't tell anyone I said this, because I-I can't be certain . . . but I believe he may have been involved in the fire at the slaves' school. And now . . . I'm afraid he and his friends are planning something else. Joseph Gray is involved, too, and my daughter Mary has her hopes set on courting him and . . . How can I get them to settle down and forget about night patrols and all the rest of it? Why is Daniel wasting his time with all of this instead of helping me get our old life back?"

"If you want everything back the way it was, then the hatred and brutality toward Negroes is part of that picture. Daniel and his friends have lost control over their former slaves, and this is their way of getting it back."

Eugenia stared at her lap. She knew what David said was right, but it sounded so wrong.

"You have your definition of how you want the South to be," he continued, "and those young men have theirs. Didn't you tell me there have been too many changes already? Daniel doesn't want things to change any more than you do. The only people who want things to be different than they were before the war are the former slaves. They want the freedom to go wherever they please and live wherever they choose. They want to educate their children. But that's what Daniel and the others are fighting against."

"It's so complicated, isn't it?" she asked, blotting her tears, ashamed of them. "How do we untangle this mess?"

"Either we all change or none of us do. Either we start all over again with a new South or everything goes back to the way it was. No one will accept half measures."

"I don't know what to do. I've tried talking to Daniel, but he dismisses me. He wants to be in charge and—"

"Isn't that what you wanted? For him to be in charge? Isn't that the way things used to be, with your husband and your sons making all the decisions?"

"Yes, but how can I stand by and let him take part in violence? The Yankees are policing us, controlling the courts. They don't understand the South. I-I don't know what to do, David . . . what should I do?"

"I'll give you my opinion, but you won't like it."

He was showing no mercy, refusing to tell her not to worry, that everything would be all right. But she needed advice, and she had no one else to talk to. "Go ahead, tell me."

"We have to lead by example. Our generation has to make peace with the Negroes and with the Yankees. We have to show our sons and daughters that the old South was destroyed because it was flawed and that we're willing to embrace the changes. It will only lead to more suffering if we don't. We can show our children that many of the changes are good. . . . It begins with us—you and me."

Eugenia leaned back in her seat, smoothing her hair off her face with both hands. "How did this happen to us? How did we lose everything we once had?"

"Pride. We began to believe that we were little gods, expanding our empires, living well at the expense of an entire race of people. The Almighty finally had enough and showed us we were only human after all, that we would bleed and die from cannonballs and bullets. He reduced us to the same poverty and helplessness that we inflicted on the Negroes—but some of us just haven't learned that lesson yet. Young men like your son and his friends are still hanging on to the illusion of power, stubbornly refusing to let go of a way of life that has been judged as flawed. They've lost their possessions, their livelihood, their status as aristocrats—even the pride they once had in our beautiful South—yet they're still trying to be gods and exercise power over the fates of others."

Eugenia looked around at her once-beautiful parlor and saw the dust, the shabbiness and cobwebs. "We used to believe that our wealth and prosperity were God's blessings, signs of His favor."

"It's impossible to believe that anymore, isn't it? The war has exposed our false beliefs and the moral rot that accompanied slavery. All of our prideful decisions and the shameful way we treated the

Negroes have been exposed. We were flawed, Eugenia. God said so. It's time to let go of our old attitudes and rebuild the South with compassion for others and with the belief that's at the core of our Constitution—that all men are created equal. And it's up to us to lead by example."

Could she do that? Could she discard a lifetime of beliefs and suddenly pretend that she saw the Negroes as equals instead of as an inferior race that could never be educated or given responsibility? "How do I decide which changes are necessary and which ones will bring my world toppling down?" she asked.

David exhaled, taking a moment to think before he replied. "When the Yankee invasion came and you left for Richmond, you had to decide which things in your life were truly valuable and which things had to be left behind. Now is your chance to do it again."

"My family, my children were the most important things to me—then and now. That's why I'm so worried about Daniel not facing his responsibilities. That's why I'm trying to make sure my daughters find husbands who will provide for them and take good care of them."

David shook his head again. "That's the old way of thinking. You are a strong, intelligent woman who has proven that you don't need to be taken care of. You can decide for yourself what's best for White Oak, and you can teach Daniel that his way of thinking about Negroes is wrong. You can allow your daughters to think for themselves, too, instead of arranging marriages for them—especially with young men who think murdering Negroes is perfectly fine. Isn't your daughters' happiness more important than family connections and social classes and maintaining old alliances?"

"Change is so hard," she murmured. "I've endured too much of it already."

"I know. But some of the things that seemed so important in the old days just aren't worth dragging along into your new life. They'll hold you back and weigh you down. Ask yourself what's worth fighting for, what's worth hanging on to in God's eyes, and leave the rest. You'll be happier and freer without it." He stood, preparing to leave.

Eugenia rose to face him, resting her hand on his arm to plead with him. "Will you talk to Daniel for me? Stop him before he commits more violence? You can explain it to him just like you explained it to me."

David slowly shook his head. "He won't listen to me, Eugenia."

"Of course he will. Why wouldn't he?"

"Because he's a Southern aristocrat, and I'm not."

29

Josephine tossed in her bed, unable to sleep. The sticky summer night glued her skin to her nightclothes and plastered her hair to her sweaty neck. She was still furious with Mary, and the sound of her deep, untroubled sleep in the bed across the room added to Jo's restlessness.

After remaining in bed for two days, Josephine had no tears left to cry. She had mourned the loss of her friendship with Alexander and grieved the inevitable prison sentence of a marriage to Harrison Blake. Dr. Hunter had guessed that she was in bed because of grief, not illness, but she hadn't trusted him enough to confide the reason for her sorrow. "I wish I could help you," he had said.

When she couldn't stand the heat a moment longer, Josephine grabbed her pillow, pulled the gauzy netting from around her bed, and walked down the hall to the upstairs porch, hoping for a breeze. In the stillness she heard the low mumble of men's voices, coming from the porch below her.

For a moment she feared that a band of vagabond Negroes had come to break into her home and take vengeance on her race. White planters and their families had long feared this would happen and that they would be slaughtered in their beds. Jo remembered how terrified she had been in the chaotic weeks after her father went away to war, leaving her and Mother and Mary alone and outnumbered. But Daniel was here to protect them now, and as she listened she was relieved to recognize his voice among the others. She let her pillow and the netting drop softly to the floor and stood still, straining to hear.

". . . scare him off but not hurt him—"

"He won't scare! We've tried before, remember?"

"Shhh! . . . My family's asleep."

The floorboards creaked beneath her bare feet as Josephine crept to the edge of the porch and peered down. The men stood on the porch beneath her, out of sight. She could see a drooping clump of horses tied to the hitching post, but it was too dark to distinguish whose they were.

". . . Freedmen's Bureau out of town for good . . . I know for a fact that he's investigating the shootings and the fire."

"We have to keep the slaves from testifying."

Jo sank to the floor, sitting cross-legged, hoping to hear better, but the conversation was very soft and the incessant scrape and buzz of crickets and cicadas drowned out some of their words.

"Chandler has caused trouble since the day he arrived."

"We have to get rid of him for good. Agreed? The slaves will be too scared to testify when they see what happens to him."

Josephine heard murmurs of assent, and her heart began to race with fear.

"Okay, but how?"

"Accidents happen . . . look like an accident."

". . . make him disappear . . . bury the evidence."

"The bureau will send someone else, so what's the point?"

"Maybe they will . . . or maybe the others will be too scared to come."

"When should we do it?"

"Tonight. Why waste more time?"

Josephine heard more murmuring as several men talked at once.

"Enough! We're agreed," Daniel said. "So what's the plan?"

She listened in horror as her brother and the others discussed how they could murder Alexander Chandler in his bed tonight, then set fire to the bureau office, leaving no evidence. Their plan shocked her. Alexander hadn't done anything to deserve this. The war was over. He was no longer their enemy. How could her brother kill an innocent man, just to hide his own guilt?

Josephine stood and hurried into the house, determined to run downstairs and stop them. This was wrong! She would find out who the other men were and let them know that she had heard their plot. They wouldn't get away with it.

But when she reached the stair landing she halted, remembering her recent argument with Daniel and how furious he had been with her. She remembered lashing back at him in anger and realized then it was her fault that he had learned of the arson investigation. If they murdered Alexander, it would be her fault.

Daniel and his friends would never listen to her. Her brother had been outraged by her friendship with a Yankee, and his friends would be outraged, as well. If they knew she had overheard them, they would detain her here while they completed their plan.

She had to warn Alexander. He needed to run. Now!

Jo hurried back upstairs to her room. It seemed to take forever to wiggle into her clothing, her body damp with sweat and fear. She was finally dressed—but now what? She couldn't run all the way into town by herself in the middle of the night. Nor could she go by horseback. The stables were in plain sight of the porch, where the men were still plotting. Someone else would have to warn Alex, but who?

Lizzie. She would know who to send. She and Otis were Alexander's friends, too. Josephine slipped out the back door and hurried down to Lizzie's cabin. The night was feverishly hot and humid, the air as thick and suffocating as wet cotton. Even the insects rasped their complaints. She knocked on Lizzie's door and called softly to her.

"Lizzie! . . . Lizzie it's me, Josephine."

A moment later the door opened and Jo felt the heat billow from the cabin as if she had opened an oven door. "Missy? What's wrong?" Lizzie's bony face glistened with sweat. She looked disoriented and frightened, and so did her husband, Otis, who appeared in the darkness behind her. He wasn't wearing a shirt, and Jo averted her eyes from his lean, bare chest.

"Please! I need your help. I just overheard Daniel and his friends talking, and they're planning something horrible."

"Oh, Lord, help us!"

"Not against you, Lizzie . . . they're going after Alexander Chandler and the Freedmen's Bureau. Please, someone has to go into town and warn him to get out of there. He needs to hide!"

Lizzie glanced all around, her eyes wide with fright as she whispered, "Step inside, Missy Jo, so nobody hears you." She opened the door wider, and Josephine entered a Negro's cabin for the first time in her life. Lizzie closed the door behind her.

The single-room house, airless and stifling, smelled of woodsmoke and sweat. Lizzie's children lay on the floor in a row like logs, with no mosquito netting to protect them. Their bare arms and legs glistened with one of Lizzie's smeared concoctions to keep the mosquitoes from biting. Josephine could hear the insects' high-pitched hunger and see a wispy cloud of them hovering over the sleeping children.

"Now say that again, Missy?"

Josephine told her what she'd overheard of the patchy, whispered conversation. "Please! You have to go into town and warn Mr. Chandler. They're planning to kill him!"

Otis let out a deep groan like a man in pain. He shook his head. "We can't, Missy, we can't. Much as I'd like to help him, you know we ain't allowed out after dark. There's a curfew on all us colored folks. Massa Daniel and his friends will string me up for sure if they catch me out on the road or in town this time of night."

Josephine had forgotten about the night patrols. She couldn't ask Otis to risk his life for a white man, even though Alexander had set up the bureau to help the former slaves. Tears filled her eyes. "But I don't know what else to do! They're going to kill him!"

"When they gonna do this?" Lizzie asked.

"Now! Tonight! They're planning it right now. Someone has to stop them!"

"Well, it ain't gonna be my Otis," Lizzie said. She linked her arm through his as if locking a chain, and Jo knew by her uplifted chin that she would never give in. "Now, I sure hate to see anything happen to Massa Chandler because he's a good man. But if Otis or any of our folks try and warn him, those white men will do the same thing to us that they're planning for him. Otis ain't going and that's that. He has a family to look after."

"It's gonna have to be you, Missy Jo," Otis said. "Them men won't hurt you."

"But . . . but I can't go!"

Lizzie's chin seemed to jut out even further. "Why not?"

"All alone? I-I'm too scared!"

"Well, how do you think we feel?" Lizzie asked. "We're scared half to death every single day of our lives."

Josephine looked into Lizzie's eyes—maybe for the first time in her life—and saw the terror she hid behind her tough façade. No doubt she was remembering the beating Otis had already suffered.

"Time's wasting," Otis said. "If them men are gonna do this before sunrise, then you don't have much time. They riding horses?"

"Yes."

"Best way is for you to take the shortcut through the woods."

According to Daniel, a pack of dangerous, homeless Negroes still camped out in the forest between here and town, in spite of the night riders' efforts to dislodge them. Josephine shuddered and shook her head. "Those woods are too dangerous for a white woman, even in daylight."

Otis looked at his wife, and she finally nodded. He slowly pulled his arm free from her grip. "I'll go with you that far, Missy Josephine, but I can't go into Fairmont or onto the roads. I'm sorry."

Jo couldn't breathe. It would be dangerous for both of them. She longed to run back to her room and climb into bed and tell herself that this had all been a very bad dream. But she couldn't stand by and let them kill Alexander. She would be as guilty as Daniel and the others.

Otis put on his shirt and his broken-down shoes, making the decision for her. "Let's go, Missy Josephine."

The night was so dark, the woods so thick that she could barely see where she was going. Josephine couldn't remember ever being so scared. She not only feared the woods and the dangers it hid, but she was terrified she would arrive too late. Alexander would die, and it would be her fault. Otis strode along the path so quickly she had to jog to keep up with him. And as badly as she longed to stop and catch her breath, she grew frustrated with him for stopping every few minutes and looking around, listening.

"We have to hurry, Otis! Why do you keep stopping?"

"I'm listening for their horses. They might take this shortcut, too, and I'm scared of the night patrols. They catch me out at night, they'll do a lot worse than beat me this time."

Josephine didn't want to believe that her brother would hurt Otis if she was with him. But she'd heard him plot to kill Alexander, and he was a white man. "I'm so scared, Otis. If the riders get there before us, they're going to kill him!"

"Are you praying, Missy Josephine?"

Otis took off at a trot again before she could reply, but the truth was that she hadn't thought to pray. She hadn't prayed in months. Why bother when God didn't seem to hear her or answer her? Otis glanced over his shoulder as if to see if she was still behind him and said, "I'm praying, too, Missy Josephine."

Oh, God, please, she began to silently beg—then stopped. What had Alexander said about praying? He'd said that God couldn't answer if she prayed for something that was contrary to His will. Surely it wasn't God's will for Alexander to die, was it? Or for her brother and the others to commit murder?

Heavenly Father . . . The words brought tears to her eyes, reminding her of her own father. He had been stern when he'd needed to be but was also kind and loving, willing to give Josephine whatever she asked for if it was something that would do her good and not harm. And surely that was the way her heavenly Father was, too. She finally understood what Alexander had been trying to teach her: God couldn't answer her prayers during the war if it meant harming His other children, the slaves.

All at once, Josephine knew that God was with her and Otis in these dark, terrifying woods, and she silently cried out to Him as His child. *Heavenly Father, please help us. Please help us get to Alexander in time to save him. He's trying to help the Negroes, Lord. He loves you, and he's trying to obey you by coming here and loving his enemies and helping us rebuild.* She gripped Otis's shirttail, laboring to keep up with him as her tears fell faster, blinding her. *I love him, Father. I love Alexander Chandler and I know you do, too, and I don't want anything to happen to him.*

The maze of trees began to thin as they finally reached the other side of the woods. They were almost to town. Otis stopped again, but this time Josephine was grateful for the chance to rest. She was unaccustomed to so much exercise and she was exhausted, her clothing drenched with sweat from the heat.

"This is as far as I can go," Otis whispered. "I'm sorry, but there's too much open space from here on into town."

The night was so dark that Jo couldn't see any familiar landmarks. She didn't seem to be anywhere near the road. Could she do this all alone?

She had to. She didn't want Alexander to die. "I've never been to his office, Otis. I'm not even sure where it is."

"Stay on this path until you get to the railroad tracks, and—"

"Path? What path?"

"This is the trail that Rufus and Roselle and the others take to school. See it?" Josephine had to bend down and peer carefully at the ground in order to see the narrow dirt track that led out of the woods and through the weedy, overgrown field. "Keep your eye on that trail and it'll take you all the way to the railroad tracks. Then turn and follow the tracks to the office. It's a little brick building behind the train station."

She looked up at him, wishing she could beg him to go with her.

Tears choked her throat. Otis reached out and tentatively laid his hand on her head, then closed his eyes. "Oh, Lord, please watch out for Missy Josephine and guide her the rest of the way. Help her to get there before them men do. And, Lord, please keep Mr. Chandler safe. Amen." He opened his eyes again and removed his hand. "You'll be fine, Missy Jo. The good Lord will be watching over you."

"Thank you, Otis." She gripped the fabric of her skirt in her fists, lifting her hem so she wouldn't trip, and took off as fast as she could run in the dark, careful to keep her eyes on the trail. She hadn't run far when a sharp pain knifed her side, but she ignored it and kept running. The horses could cover the distance into Fairmont much faster than she could, even with Otis's shortcut.

By the time Josephine finally spotted the railroad embankment she could barely breathe. She stumbled up the gravel rise and turned toward town, following the tracks. Otis hadn't said how far she would have to follow the tracks, but at last she rounded a curve and saw the church steeple and houses silhouetted in the distance, including the long, low roof of the train station. Behind it was a small, two-story brick building, its back room damaged by fire.

Josephine slid down the embankment into the ditch beside the tracks and paused for a moment, panting for breath. She listened, like Otis had, for the sound of horses as she emptied the gravel out of her shoes. It was hard to hear anything at all above the pounding of her heart and her labored breaths. She waited until she was certain there was no sign of her brother and the others, then stood and sprinted across the open space to the Freedmen's Bureau office. The fire damage made it impossible for Alexander to lock the back door, so she hurried inside, dodging around the burned debris. Daniel could get inside just as easily.

She groped her way down a narrow hallway, not waiting for her eyes to adjust to the darkness, and came to a set of steps that led upstairs. "Alexander!" she called up to him. "Alexander, wake up!" She was so breathless, so frightened, that she could hardly get the words out. She pounded on the hollow wall of the stairwell, praying he would hear her. Her brother and the others could likely hear her, too, if they were outside, but at least Alexander could defend himself once he was awake. "Alexander! Please, wake up!"

Had the men beat her here? Was he already dead? She started up the steps, pounding on the wall with both fists, calling his name. She finally heard thumps and rustling noises above her, then a voice: "Who's there?"

She collapsed onto a stair with relief. "Alexander, it's me—Josephine. You have to get up! It's an emergency!" He came to the top of the steps looking sleep-tousled. He had pulled on his pants but wore no shoes or shirt.

"Josephine! What are you doing here? What's wrong?"

"They're coming to kill you! You have to get out! Right now!"

"What? . . . Who's coming?" He looked half asleep, and she could tell that her words weren't making sense to him.

"I don't have time to explain. Grab your gun and your shoes and get out!"

"I don't have a gun. Let me light a lamp—"

"No!" she cried out as he turned to go back in his bedroom. "No lights! You have to leave! Now!" He stared at her in sleepy confusion, and in the momentary silence Josephine thought she heard a horse whinny. She plunged up the stairs and grabbed his arm, pulling him toward her. "Please, Alexander! They're coming to kill you and burn down your office. They're on their way. They'll be here any minute. You have to run! Before it's too late!" The tears she had been holding back all this time began to fall.

He stared at her as if finally comprehending her words. "Okay, okay . . . Let me get my boots . . ." He ran into his room, and she heard him rummaging around.

Please, dear God. Please give us just a few more minutes to get away.

He returned a moment later with his boots on. He was shoving his arms into his shirt. "What's going on, Josephine?"

"There isn't time to explain. We have to get out . . . No, no, the front. Use the front door." She was certain she had heard another horse whinny out back.

He led the way into his office, then stopped for a moment to look around. "There are some files I should save—"

"There isn't time!"

"But the schoolbooks. I won't let them burn again." He picked up a wooden crate and dumped its contents onto the floor, then scooped up a stack of books piled on his desk and dropped them into the crate. Josephine pitched in, grabbing a second stack of books.

"Now, please, Alexander! Go!" She ran to the door ahead of him and opened it a crack to peer out, fighting the instinct to bolt out of the office as fast as she could run. The dirt road in front of the building looked deserted. So did the main street in front of the train station. Josephine spotted an alcove behind the station, where a baggage wagon was parked, and pointed to it. "Over there! We can hide there. Now run!"

She plunged out into the darkness, lifting her skirts, trying not to trip over her leaden feet. She felt like she was in a nightmare, trying to run and not being able to move. Alexander was behind her and moving even slower, burdened down with the heavy crate of books. A dog began to bark nearby, sending up an alarm, but at last they reached the alcove and sank into the shadows beneath the baggage wagon, breathing hard.

"Josephine, what in the world—"

"Shh!"

Two men had come around from the rear of the Freedmen's Bureau in the dark, crouching low. They went up to the door that she and Alexander had just fled through—the door they had foolishly left wide open—and looked all around. "If they find you, they'll kill you," she whispered.

She wondered how he felt to know he was being stalked, to know his enemies were trying to murder him. He had come to work for the Freedmen's Bureau, believing he was obeying Jesus's command to love his enemies. Was he questioning his faith at this moment?

Alexander refused to carry a gun or defend himself—did he regret that decision, too?

Josephine reached for his hand and gripped it tightly as two more figures appeared in the open doorway. They must have searched the house and found it empty. All four men stood still for a moment, studying the deserted rail yard. "We can't stay here," Josephine whispered. "They'll search the rail yard."

"Where can we hide?"

She hesitated for a moment, then said, "The church. Or the cemetery behind it if the door's locked." They left the box of books behind and crawled through the bushes surrounding the building until they were out of sight of the office. Two more dogs began to bark, giving them away as they ran the short distance to the church, trying to stay hidden behind trees and bushes and fences, stumbling, praying, holding hands as they ran.

"Not the front door," Josephine whispered. "There's a side door that leads to the vestry." *Please let it be unlocked*, she silently prayed. *Please keep us safe.*

The door was unlocked. Josephine exhaled in relief and felt a sliver of hope. God had answered all her prayers, so far. He had been with her, helping her, helping them. She closed the door behind them and stood still for a moment, catching her breath. Their eyes met, and in the next moment she was in his arms and they were holding each other tightly.

"Thank you," he whispered. "I don't know how or why you came for me, but thank you."

His arms were around her. Alexander was safe now, and so was she. Josephine closed her eyes, longing to stay here with him forever. But she could still hear dogs barking a warning in the sleeping village, so she slipped out of his arms and tugged his hand again. "Come on. We still should hide." She led him into the sanctuary, and they sank down together behind one of the pews in the choir loft, hidden from view.

"How did you know they were coming for me?" he asked. "Who are these men?"

"My brother is one of them. I couldn't sleep and I accidentally overheard him and the others plotting. They know that you're investigating the arson and the murders, and they're the ones who are responsible. They decided to kill you and destroy all your evidence."

"But you . . . you came all this way alone? In the dark?"

"Otis came with me part of the way. I prayed and asked God to get me here on time, to get you out of there on time, and He answered my prayer."

"Wait. You mean . . . you . . . you prayed?" Josephine nodded, as amazed as Alexander was. He took her in his arms again and held her.

"I love you, Josephine. Not just tonight or because you saved me, but . . . I've loved you all along."

He pulled back, and they looked at each other in the darkness. Josephine remembered the overwhelming emptiness she had felt after Daniel took her letters and she was cut off from Alexander forever. She remembered her terrible fear as she'd raced here to save him and the certainty she'd felt in her heart that she loved him.

"I love you, too," she whispered.

He cradled her face in his hands, smoothing her damp hair from her cheeks. Then Alexander leaned toward her and kissed her. His kiss was tender and beautiful, and she put her arms around him and kissed him in return. She thought her heart would burst from the wonderful, terrible mixture of love and sorrow. Her love for him was impossible. She loved him, wanted him, but she could never have him. When the kiss ended and he finally pulled away, she rested her head on his chest, and they held each other tightly.

"Remember in my letter," he murmured, "how I said that you should marry a man you loved? I meant me."

"I know . . . I know . . . but it's impossible. My family would never allow it. My brother is trying to kill you."

"We could run away together and get married. I'll take you home with me, and we could start a new life together, away from all of this."

Could she leave her home, her family? Josephine was still angry with Daniel and Mary and didn't know if she could ever trust them again. And Mother would persist with her matchmaking plans until Jo ended up married to Harrison Blake. Mother was strong and would have her way—she always did. But could Jo really run away from her family and White Oak and never look back? If not, could she bear to stay here and live the life that would be forced upon her? To live without Alexander?

"Come away with me, Josephine."

"I-I can't. It would hurt too many people if I just disappeared. My family has suffered enough, endured too much. I can't add to it."

"What if I found a way to ask for your hand?"

"That's impossible. They hate you."

"But what if I found a way to make peace with them, and I asked for your hand, and we left here with their blessing—would you marry me then?"

"Of course, but . . . it can't possibly happen. They'll never make peace with you, much less give us their blessing."

He leaned forward and kissed her again. "I'll find a way. Trust me, Josephine. And trust God."

He stood and reached for her hands, pulling her to her feet. Her legs felt stiff from their cramped position, her muscles tired from running. "Wait. Shouldn't we stay hidden a while longer? What if they're still searching for you?" He was leading her out of the sanctuary and back through the vestry. "Where are we going?"

"I'm going to make sure you get home safely."

"No, wait!" She stood in front of the door, barring it before he had a chance to open it. "I can get home by myself, but you can't risk being seen. It's still too dangerous."

"I won't leave you, Josephine. I need to make sure you're safe." He reached to stroke her hair, her cheek.

"God got me here safely tonight. You can trust Him to get me home again." Josephine knew then what she needed to do. She took his hand and kissed his fingers before letting it go. "Where's your horse?"

"In the livery stable."

"Ride to Richmond—as fast as you can. Don't come back unless you have a squad of soldiers with you. Armed soldiers. If you
return without protection, these men will kill you. They won't
fail the next time."

"But you—"

"I'm going to create a distraction." She stood on her tiptoes and
kissed him one last time, cutting off his protests. As she did, she
reached behind her and opened the door. "Good-bye, Alexander."

"No, wait—!"

But Josephine was already running before he could stop her,
racing to reach the alarm bell across the village square from the
church. Behind her, the night sky above the train station was lit up
by the orange glow of flames, the hot air filling with smoke. She
grabbed the bell rope and pulled as hard as she could, letting it ring
and ring to awaken the town. The fire was probably too far gone
to save the building, but Alexander could get to his horse during
the commotion and ride away.

She saw lights going on in several houses as she kept ringing the
bell. Dogs barked and howled. Men began to emerge from their
homes, struggling into their clothes, looking all around for the fire.
Josephine heard shouts, running feet, but continued to ring the bell.
None of the townspeople would care if the Freedmen's Bureau burned
to the ground, but they wouldn't let the nearby train station burn.

Her arm was growing tired, and she stopped ringing for a moment to rest. In the momentary quiet she heard a horse galloping
somewhere in the darkness and prayed it was Alexander making
his escape. But the sound of hoofbeats was coming closer, and as
she squinted in the gloom she saw a dark horse and a masked rider
racing straight toward her. She let go of the bell rope and turned to
run, sprinting in the opposite direction of the livery stable. Where
could she go? Where could she hide? Dr. Hunter's house was nearby.
She would run to him and beg for his help. But the horse easily
caught up with her before she could get there.

"Josephine! Josephine, stop!" She recognized Daniel's voice,
even muffled by the mask.

She kept running, desperate to reach safety. She glanced over her shoulder and saw that Daniel had dismounted and was running after her. Her bulky skirt slowed her down, and he quickly caught up to her, grabbing her. "Let me go!" she shouted. "Leave me alone!"

Daniel clamped his hand over her mouth. "Quiet! Stop fighting me!" He dragged her and his horse into the shadows alongside a carriage house. The townspeople were still waking up and running toward the fire. No one would hear her even if she could scream.

"You warned him, didn't you?" Daniel said, giving her a shake. He still gripped her tightly, but he slowly removed his hand from her mouth as if testing to see if she would cry out. "You shameless girl! You're helping our enemy. Don't you know what they do to people who aid the enemy? It's treason! You're a traitor!"

"You were going to murder him—I heard you. Even now, when you heard the bell, you thought Alexander was ringing it and you came to kill him."

"And how many of our people did the Yankees kill? What about Samuel and Father and the thousands of others? The Yankees murdered our family and took everything we had. They destroyed our lives. Can't you understand that? Why are you helping them?" A handkerchief covered her brother's face, and she could only see his eyes below the brim of his hat. But those eyes glittered with enough anger to kill an entire army of Yankees like Alexander.

"The war is over, Daniel. If you kill him now, it's murder."

"Grow up, Josephine. As long as their army is occupying Virginia, we're still at war. That bureau is a symbol of outside interference, telling us that we aren't free. Your Yankee friend represents a foreign government that's being forced on us. We have no choice but to protect ourselves from them."

"Haven't you had enough fighting and killing? When are you going to stop?"

"When the last Yankee and carpetbagger is gone. When they all go away and leave us alone and the land is ours again." Daniel glanced out into the street to see if the coast was clear, then turned to face her again. "Listen. We're going to get on my horse and go home. But I want you to understand that if your Yankee friend comes back with a pile of soldiers and punishes our community, it will be on your conscience, Josephine. You'll have to live with the consequences and the guilt for the rest of your life."

"How is it my fault? If you had succeeded in murdering him, don't you think there would have been retribution for that?"

"If you hadn't interfered, it would have been an unfortunate accident in a quiet town."

"I know the truth, Daniel. It won't stay hidden."

"And I know the truth about you and your Yankee, so we'd both be wise to keep our mouths shut, don't you think? I won't have to punish you if the people in this town find out. They'll be happy to get revenge on a traitor like you." He pushed her ahead of him, moving away from the square, away from the smoke and the chaos, staying in the shadows where no one would see them. When they reached the outskirts of town, Daniel lifted Josephine onto the horse and climbed on behind her to ride the rest of the way home.

They were nearly to White Oak when Josephine remembered the crate full of schoolbooks that Alexander had saved. Tomorrow, somehow, she would find a way to go back into town and retrieve them. Then she would make certain that Rufus and Jack and Roselle and every other Negro child who wanted to learn to read and write would get one of them.

And even if her family disowned her, even if she never saw Alexander Chandler again, Josephine was still glad she had saved his life.

30

When the rooster crowed in the morning, it seemed as if Lizzie had been having nightmares all night and had barely slept. Had Missy Jo really come in the middle of the night, waking her up with a terrible story about how Massa Daniel was going to kill Mr. Chandler? Lizzie rolled over, but Otis's side of the bed was empty. *Oh, Lord!* She sat up and looked around the dim cabin and saw him kneeling in front of a chair praying, his elbows propped on the seat. She lay back down and waited for her heart to slow down again.

Lizzie had been afraid to help Missy Jo, but Otis had said that they had to. Nearly half the night had slowly passed as she'd paced the floor and waited for him to return. By the time she finally saw Otis coming back, a dark shape against the darker sky, she had worried herself sick.

"What happened?" she'd asked. "Did Missy Jo get there all right? She make it there in time?"

"I could only go with her to the other side of the woods. Lord knows I sure hated to leave her on her own, that's for sure."

Lizzie had sunk down on their straw mattress, relieved to see him, worn out from worry, weary with sleeplessness. "Come back to bed, Otis. It'll be morning soon."

343

"No, I won't sleep. I think I'll sit here and pray, if you don't mind."

Now Lizzie couldn't help wondering about Missy Josephine. "Otis?" she whispered. He lifted his bowed head and looked over at her, then rose to his feet, stretching his arms and shoulders. "Did Missy Jo come back?" she asked him.

"I don't know. Guess we'll find out soon enough."

Lizzie stood and slipped into her dress and shoes. The July sun was already rising, fiery hot. Lizzie wished she was still asleep. Last night had seemed like a nightmare and she was afraid to wake up and see it had all come true.

Mornings were always hurried for Lizzie, trying to get the white folks fed, trying to get Otis and the other men fed so they could get out to the fields, trying to get the kids up and fed and off to school. The kitchen was the center of all this feeding and hurrying, and it was a busy place, most mornings. But as Lizzie stirred yesterday's coals and got the fire started in the hearth, she felt like somebody was holding a huge cast-iron pot over her head, filled with all kinds of bad things, and they were just waiting to drop it on her.

"Massa Daniel's horse is in the stall," Otis told her when he came in a few minutes later, "so he must be back."

"Well, we better keep the kids home today until we find out from Missy Jo what happened last night."

"What'll we tell Saul and Clara and the others?"

"The truth. They need to know what kind of man Massa Daniel is and what he was trying to do."

Otis nodded. "But don't tell the kids. I don't want them living in fear all the time."

"But shouldn't we warn them about him? They need to know."

"Let's just hold off and see what really happened last night first."

Lizzie didn't want to hold off. She wanted to gather her family together and run as far away from White Oak as she could and hide where it was safe. If only she knew where that safe place might be. She picked up the egg basket and went outside to let the hens out of the coop and collect the eggs. A few days ago she had been so content. Her kids were learning to read and write, Otis was growing his own crops with nobody bossing over him, and she had Clara to talk to all day and share the workload—washing and cooking and churning the cream from their new cow. Lizzie had been almost ready to believe the Bible was true and that every tear she had ever cried was going to bring a crop of joy. Not anymore.

Clara walked into the kitchen with a bucket of fresh milk just as Lizzie was putting biscuits in the oven. She knew by the fear in Clara's eyes that Otis had told her about last night. Clara set the bucket of milk on the table, but her shoulders still slumped like she was carrying a heavy load. "What are we gonna do, Lizzie?"

"I don't know. Otis says to wait and see."

Lizzie was on her way into the Big House with a platter of scrambled eggs in one hand and a basket of hot biscuits in the other when she happened to look down toward her cabin. A group of former slaves, maybe a dozen or so, were coming up the little hill from Slave Row. Were they coming for Massa Daniel the way he had come after Mr. Chandler last night? Would there be a war now, Negro against white? She shivered with fear and hurried into the dining room with the food, hoping to see Missy Jo sitting there just as nice as you please, hoping Missy would tell her it had all been a mistake, that nothing had happened last night after all. But Miz Eugenia and Missy Mary were the only ones seated at the table.

Lizzie's hands shook like an old woman's as she set the food on the table in front of them. "Anything else, ma'am?" she asked, slowly backing from the room.

"Where is the butter?"

"I'll bring it, ma'am. Sorry."

The strangers had gathered outside the kitchen door when she got back, talking with Otis and Saul and Willy and Robert. Roselle and Clara stood in the kitchen doorway, listening. Lizzie's stomach turned over when she saw how the men were all looking at each other, as if something terrible had just happened.

"Roselle, honey," she said, pushing her into the kitchen. "Fetch that dish of butter and bring it to the missus in the dining room."

"But I want to hear—"

"So do I. Go on now."

Roselle grabbed the butter and disappeared into the Big House, quick as a wink. Lizzie looked up at Otis, afraid to breathe. "Is Missy Josephine in there?" he asked. Lizzie shook her head. He closed his eyes for a long moment before opening them again. "It's gone, Lizzie. The Freedmen's Bureau burned to the ground last night. Ain't nothing left of it this time."

"Oh Lord, no." Her knees felt weak and she wanted to sit down, but there was no place to sit.

"Mr. Chandler's gone, too," one of the men said. "No one knows what happened to him, if he's dead or not, but from the looks of things . . . they'll have to dig through the bricks and ashes to find him."

"Oh, Lord." Lizzie covered her mouth to hold back her grief. Was Missy Josephine dead, too? Had something happened to her because they had left her all alone? This was all because of the school. That's why they had burned down the office. And Lizzie was the one who had talked Mr. Chandler into opening the school again.

"I guess there won't be no justice for the men who died in the woods," Willy said, shaking his head.

"And without that school," Clara added, "our kids will be slaves all their lives."

Otis drew a breath and exhaled. "Mr. Chandler was a God-fearing man, and if he's really gone I know he's in a better place. But Lord help him, all he was trying to do was help us out."

Everything was back to the way it was. Lizzie never should have hoped for something better. She was about to sink down on the back step and weep when Roselle came flying out of the door, her errand finished. "What happened? What's going on?" Otis put his arm around her.

"The school burned down, honey. I'm sorry."

"But . . . but we can sit on the grass and learn, can't we? We don't mind." When nobody answered her, she laid her head on Otis's shoulder and cried.

"We come to tell you we're moving on," one of the men said. "Mr. Chandler promised to move us out West somewhere and give us our own land and a mule. Guess that won't happen now, so there's no sense in staying around here. Thought we'd ask if you all want to come with us."

"We can't lose hope," Otis said. "The crops are still growing out there, ain't they? Why don't you all move back here and we can work the land together?"

"You think they're gonna let us keep that cotton and sell it ourselves? They take everything else away from us, why wouldn't they take that, too, when the time comes? Who's gonna stop them now that Mr. Chandler's gone?"

"We never should have trusted them," Lizzie said. "None of them. Our massa is probably one of the men who done this."

"We don't know that for sure, Lizzie."

"Let's go with them, Otis. They're right. There ain't no use in staying here." He didn't reply. He still had one arm around Roselle, and he rested his other hand on Lizzie's cheek, gently stroking it to calm her fears. As scared as she was and as much as she wanted to run, she knew her husband wouldn't leave now. Not after all the hard work he'd done. Besides, where would they go? How would they live? They would have to wait until after the harvest, at least, so they'd have food to eat on their journey.

"Well, I agree with all the others," Saul said quietly. "I wanted to help you, Otis, and I wanted my kids in that school. But now that it's gone and Mr. Chandler ain't watching out for us . . ."

Lizzie heard Otis sigh. He gazed out at his fields, his shoulders still straight and strong. "I need time to pray about what to do," he said. "God is my massa now, and I want to do what He says. If He says to stay here, then I can trust Him to watch over me. If He says to go, then I will. In the meantime, if you and Clara want to go with them, Saul, I won't have no hard feelings."

In the distance, Lizzie heard Miz Eugenia's bell ringing in the dining room. She groaned. She had forgotten all about the white folks and their breakfast. "I better see what they want," she said.

But her mind was miles and miles away as she made her way into the house and down the hallway to the dining room. Where could she and her family go to finally be free and live their lives without worry or fear? Was there any such place in the world?

"Lizzie!" Miz Eugenia said when she walked through the door. "What in the world is going on? Roselle practically threw the butter at me and ran off, and we've been waiting for our tea ever since."

"I'm sorry, ma'am. I'll . . . I'll . . ." She stopped. Missy Jo was sitting in her place at the table. Lizzie's entire body sagged with relief. She couldn't think what to say or do as tears filled her eyes. Missy looked as white as the tablecloth and had dark hollows like bruises under her eyes, but she was alive. Now if only Mr. Chandler was alive, too.

"Lizzie? What is wrong with you today?" Miz Eugenia asked.

"I-I'm sorry," she stammered.

"Tell us," Missy Jo said. "Please."

Lizzie looked at Missy Jo and saw her nod. She wanted her to tell the truth. "Well . . . we . . . we just got some bad news, ma'am. Our school burned all the way to the ground last night and . . ." She covered her mouth, unable to say the rest, remembering it was her fault.

"What about the Yankee who worked there?" Miz Eugenia asked. Lizzie looked at her, surprised that she would be the one to ask, surprised to see that Miz Eugenia had turned nearly as pale as her daughter. She was sitting perfectly still, her hands limp. For once, she didn't have her chin stuck way up in the air.

Lizzie swallowed a knot of grief. "They reckon they'll find him in the rubble, dead." She heard a loud scrape as Miz Eugenia slid her chair away from the table.

"Excuse me," she mumbled and hurried from the room. Lizzie stood frozen in place, unsure what to do next. How could anyone expect Lizzie to think clearly when Mr. Chandler was dead and it was all her fault? Missy Mary got up and hurried after her mother, leaving only Missy Jo at the table.

"Lizzie, come here," she said quietly. She obeyed, crossing the room to stand beside her. Lizzie had no idea what to expect, and her legs began to shake. "He isn't dead," Missy Jo whispered.

"W-what?"

"Mr. Chandler didn't die in the fire. I got there in time, thanks to you and Otis. He's safe, Lizzie."

"Oh, thank you, Lord." She swayed and nearly fell over. Missy Jo jumped up to take Lizzie's arm, steadying her.

"But please don't tell anyone else yet. Only Otis. My brother knows I was the one who warned Mr. Chandler and . . . and I don't know what's going to happen to any of us now."

Lizzie lifted her apron and covered her face, weeping into it. She couldn't help it. Relief and grief and fear and hope all battled inside her. She didn't know what was going to happen, either—there was no more school and the others all wanted to leave—but at least Missy Josephine and Mr. Chandler were alive. That was good enough news for one day.

31

Eugenia hurried from the dining room as a band of pain tightened around her chest. She couldn't breathe. The Freedmen's Bureau had burned to the ground. A man was dead! Why, oh why hadn't she confronted Daniel when she'd overheard him talking to Joseph Gray? Why hadn't she tried to stop him? Now her son had killed a man! Her son!

She tried to make her way upstairs to lie down so the girls wouldn't see that she was ill, but it was too far, the pain too intense. She stumbled into the parlor and collapsed onto the sofa. How could this have happened? What was she going to do? She closed her eyes, willing away the pain, telling herself the news she'd just heard couldn't be true.

"Mother? Are you all right?" Mary asked in her frightened, rabbit voice.

Eugenia opened her eyes. "I-I'll be fine . . ." she tried to say, but her words came out strangled, breathless.

She heard Mary running into the dining room, calling, "Josephine! Josephine, come quick!" Eugenia tried to call out to them, to say that she was fine, not to worry, but the pain had squeezed all the air from her lungs and she couldn't draw a breath. Before Eugenia could stop her, Mary thundered up the stairs to pound on Daniel's door. "Daniel, wake up! Wake up! Mother needs a doctor!"

Eugenia opened her eyes again and saw Josephine kneeling in front of her. "Mother? Mother, say something! Are you all right?"

She tried to nod, to reassure her. "I'll . . . be fine . . ."

"You're not fine! You're white as a sheet! What should we do? Do you want us to send for Dr. Hunter?"

"No . . . no, don't." She remembered what the doctor had told her just a few days ago. That she was strong enough to decide for herself what was best for White Oak and for her family. That she needed to teach Daniel that his attitude toward the Negroes was wrong. David had said that if she would accept change, then she could lead her children by her own example. She wished that David was here to help her, but she knew he was right about that, too: Daniel wouldn't listen to anything he said because he wasn't from their social class—and Eugenia had helped ingrain that attitude in her son.

Daniel rushed down the stairs and into the parlor, still buttoning his clothes. Mary was right behind him. Eugenia pulled herself up straight on the sofa, praying God would ease the pain and give her the strength she needed. Before Daniel had a chance to speak, she met his gaze. "Daniel . . . what have you done?"

"What do you mean?"

"Girls, kindly leave the room."

Neither of them moved. Eugenia didn't have the strength to insist. Maybe they should hear this, too. "The Freedmen's Bureau . . . burned to the ground last night," Eugenia said, struggling to speak against the pain. "The Yankee is dead. I know it was you . . . I heard you talking. Planning."

Daniel looked away for a moment as if ashamed. When he looked back at Eugenia, she saw his frustration. "I'm fighting for White Oak, our home," he said. "I'm trying to protect you and my sisters. That's all my friends and I are doing, don't you understand? We're acting in self-defense."

"I'm sure you believe that, but what you're doing and the way you're doing it are wrong. Violence is wrong. The war is over, Daniel. You can't run around at night killing people."

"I haven't killed anyone."

"Can you honestly tell me that you had nothing to do with the fire last night?"

Daniel paced a few steps in front of Eugenia, running his fingers through his hair, before sinking down in a chair opposite her. "Listen, Mother. I didn't want you to know what's been going on because I didn't want to upset you. I'm trying to protect you from such knowledge and to stop a potential disaster before it happens." He shot an angry glance at Josephine, who was still sitting at Eugenia's feet. "But here's the truth: Josephine has been carrying on with that Yankee from the Freedmen's Bureau, meeting him secretly."

"What . . . ?" Eugenia stared at him, then at her daughter. It couldn't be true. But the expression on Josephine's face, the tears in her eyes, told her it was.

"We haven't done anything wrong," she said. "He's not our enemy."

"She's lying," Daniel said. "Mary saw them meeting together in the woods. Alone. We found a pile of letters he had written to her. That's why I needed to run him off last night. If the truth got out, it would cause a scandal. Josephine's reputation would be ruined and so would ours. I had to defend our family's honor."

"You were going to kill him!" Josephine shot back. "I heard you. That's why I warned him. He would be dead right now if I hadn't gotten there first."

"So the Yankee is still alive?" Eugenia asked.

"Yes," Daniel said. "And now, thanks to Josephine, he'll be back and our town will soon be filled with Yankees, coming for revenge. She betrayed us, Mother."

"Oh, dear . . ." Eugenia murmured. How could either of her children have done these terrible things? How had everything spun so wildly out of control? The pain in her chest made it difficult to breathe, to speak. But as she listened to her children arguing, the pain in her heart was infinitely greater.

"You and your friends caused these problems, not me," Josephine said. "You attacked the Negroes' camp in the woods and beat them up. Two people died. And you tried to burn down the school the first time, too. You can't blame any of those things on me or say that you were defending our family's honor."

"If the slaves claim that we were responsible for the violence, they're lying."

"It was you! I know it was. You're the one who chased them out of the woods."

"That's private property, Josephine, and we had every right to kick them out. Do you want that gang of ruffians and vagabonds living so close to White Oak? We warned them and gave them a chance to leave the area peacefully, but they wouldn't listen."

"Two men died!"

"That wasn't our fault! The slaves went crazy out there and attacked us first! We were only acting in self-defense. We were outnumbered, and they had guns—"

"That's ridiculous. Where would they get guns?"

"The Yankees have been arming them—"

"Never!"

"I know you don't want to believe the truth about your little Yankee friend, but that's what has really been going on inside that bureau of his. I'm doing my best to protect you. That's all any of us are trying to do."

"You set the school on fire. Both times!"

"Only to scare all the vagrants away. They were hanging around because of the school and causing trouble. After they attacked us in the woods, we had to do something to stop them from getting their hands on more guns."

"I don't believe you. Willy wouldn't hurt a fly. How did he and Otis get beaten up so badly? And all the others?"

"It was chaos. You weren't there that night. These slaves are dangerous. It's bad enough we lost the war, but the way things are going, we're going to have another war with the Negroes, backed by the Yankees. We needed to scare all the vagrants off, show our strength."

Eugenia pressed her fist against her breastbone, pushing against the pain. Her world was falling apart for a second time. Though she had wanted to reclaim all she had lost, David had been right—the past was filled with hatred and violence. Returning to the past meant sticking her head in the sand, pretending everything was fine, letting Daniel take care of her. And he had made a huge mess of things.

"Who else knows about Josephine and that man?" Eugenia asked.

"No one," Daniel said. "Only our family."

Eugenia felt only mildly relieved. "What's going to happen now that you've burned down the Freedmen's Bureau?"

"I don't know." Daniel ran his hand through his hair again. "The Yankee knows who did it, thanks to Josephine. Why would you betray your family that way?" he asked, turning on her again. "How could you?"

"Because you were wrong, Daniel. I couldn't stand by and let you murder an innocent man. The Yankees would send all of you to the gallows."

"He isn't innocent. He's taking everyone's land and handing it over to the slaves. I'm sorry, Mother, but you don't know these Negroes the way I do. You gave them a foothold here at White Oak when you rented them a piece of our land, and you'll soon see it won't be enough for them. They'll want more land, and then our livestock, and eventually our home. The Yankees keep telling them they deserve everything. That's what they're teaching them in that school, insisting that Negroes are just the same as white people. That's why we had to close it. You know all too well what can happen once slaves learn to read and write, Mother. I know you do."

She couldn't reply. Daniel was only repeating what she and Philip had taught him. How could she ever convince him that they'd been wrong?

Daniel stood and paced in front of her again. "I'm sorry you had to hear all of this. I didn't want you to know about the terrible things that have been going on. You were so happy the night of your dance, and I knew this news would upset you—as it clearly has. From now on, when I decide not to tell you everything, you have to trust me."

"Never!" Josephine said. "I'll never trust you again!"

"Do you think any of us will ever trust *you*?" he shouted. "You're a traitor!" They glared at each other for a long moment, then Daniel turned back to Eugenia. "We had trouble with the slaves all the time when Father was alive, but he shielded you from it. That's all I've been trying to do. Please don't worry about it anymore, Mother. Everything is going to simmer down in a few days and this whole mess is going to go away, I promise."

"That can't possibly be true," Eugenia said. "What's going to happen when the Yankees come back? They'll want to punish whoever burned down their office."

"Nothing will happen. They won't be able to prosecute us because we're all going to stick together, the entire town. The fire was an accident—both times. Josephine won't dare to go against the entire community and betray us again."

"The Negroes know the truth, too," she mumbled.

"That's why we have to make sure they're afraid to open their mouths. I know it sounds cruel, but we have to."

"But when is all of this violence going to stop?" Eugenia asked. "It must come to an end, Daniel. Don't you see?"

"I know, I know! I'm trying to end it, I really am! Last night was supposed to be the last time. We could have ended the night patrols and everything else after the bureau was gone. But Josephine ruined everything."

"You can't end the cycle of violence with more violence," Eugenia said. "There must be a better way."

"Well, I wish I knew what it was, believe me."

Eugenia did believe him. She could see lines of weariness and desperation on his worried face. Her once-carefree son had yielded to bitterness, and now he didn't know how to stop.

"I know Father would hate this," he said, "and I've tried and tried to think of a better plan, but the Yankees want revenge—"

"Not all of them," Josephine said. "Mr. Chandler wanted to help us."

"You're a fool if you trust him," Daniel said. "And if Mother wants proof that you were carrying on with him, I can show her his letters."

Eugenia believed him. She didn't need to see them. But Daniel's violence was just as horrifying to her as Jo's betrayal. "Daniel, I want you and Mary to leave us, please," she said. "I want to talk to Josephine alone."

"Shall we send for Dr. Hunter?" Mary asked. "You still don't look well."

"That won't be necessary. I'm fine now. Please leave us and close the door." Once they were alone, Eugenia didn't know where to begin. She looked at her daughter, whose tears had been falling all this time, and she looked so pale and distraught that Eugenia pitied her, even if she had brought this misery on herself. "Tell me the truth," Eugenia said quietly. "Was Daniel really planning to kill that man?"

"Yes. I overheard them talking late last night. They were going to make it look like an accident."

Eugenia closed her eyes. How could her son do such a thing? She should be grateful to Josephine for preventing a murder, but at what cost? Betraying her own family to the enemy? She opened her eyes again and met Josephine's gaze. "Has that Yankee compromised your virtue?"

"No! Of course not! When Mary saw us in the woods, we were just talking. We're friends. He's an honorable man—"

"He isn't honorable or he wouldn't have met with you all alone. He wouldn't have exchanged letters with you behind my back and without your family's permission. How did he send those letters to you, by the way?"

Josephine stared down at her lap. "The children brought them to me after school."

"The slave children? After everything I've taught you about remembering your place? You just threw all of that out the window?

Isn't it bad enough you act like a slave half the time, doing their work for them?"

"Daniel is wrong about the slaves. They're not violent people, and they aren't going to hurt us. They just want to live in peace, the same as us."

Eugenia exhaled. She knew she had lost Josephine. She didn't know how or when, but her daughter was lost to her, and she didn't know how to get her back. "Are you in love with this Yankee? Look me in the eye, Josephine, and tell me the truth."

Josephine looked up, brushing away a tear. "Yes. And he loves me, too."

"Heaven help us . . ."

"You surely know how I feel, Mother. No one can help falling in love! But suppose you hadn't been able to marry Daddy or if you had been forced to marry someone else? What would you have done?"

"That isn't the question we're faced with, is it? It's no longer fair for me to arrange a marriage with any of your suitors under these circumstances. You'll have to reconcile yourself to spending the rest of your life alone."

Josephine didn't reply. Eugenia remembered the dreams she'd had for her family and for her own life before the war. All of those dreams had been destroyed, yet she had summoned the courage and the strength to start all over again. She had dared to dream of a happy future, a changed future, for herself and her children. Now even her new dreams were turning to ashes.

"Oh, Josephine," she murmured. "How could you? . . . How could you?"

Josephine rose and flung her arms around Eugenia, weeping against her shoulder. "I'm sorry, Mother . . . I'm so, so sorry."

32

Josephine sat beside her mother on the sofa, their arms around each other, wondering what to do next. It seemed as though the drama and sorrow would never end, a solution never to be found. After a nightmarish night of fear and joy, violence and tenderness, the morning had brought no end to the intensity of emotion. Josephine could think of little else but Alexander, remembering his kisses, the warmth and comfort of his arms surrounding her—and the emptiness of losing him.

Her mother brought her back to the present. "What are we going to do about Priscilla and Harrison?" she asked. "It will break Priscilla's heart, you know. She was so looking forward to having you for her daughter-in-law."

"I never wanted to marry Harrison. Or Henry Schreiber."

"Because you were in love with the Yankee?"

"Yes." She loved him, and her heart was breaking. If she had known how much it hurt to love someone, she never would have given away her heart. But it wasn't a question of giving as much as falling. Josephine had fallen—helplessly, unknowingly, unaware of the shift in footing until it was much too late.

"But we can't tell the Blakes you're in love with a Yankee," Mother said, pulling back to look at Josephine. "Daniel swears that no one outside our family knows the truth about your betrayal but—"

"I didn't betray anyone. I saved Alexander's life. And I saved Daniel from committing murder."

Mother was quiet for a moment. "The people in our community won't see it that way," she said. "You do know that, don't you?"

"If Alexander wasn't a Yankee, if you could take time to get to know him the way I have, you would see what an honest, considerate, God-fearing man he is. It was because of his Christian faith that he chose to come down here and try to help us rebuild, even though he knew that he would be hated."

"I don't want to hear anything more about that man, Josephine. He's gone. Now we need to figure out how to clean up this terrible mess."

Alexander had promised to come back for her. He'd said he would find a way. Did she dare to believe it, to hang on to hope? Josephine knew that Alexander might come back to arrest Daniel. And if he asked her again to run away with him, she still didn't think she could do it. That would be the ultimate betrayal of her mother, of her family.

She remembered Alexander's words, his promise to find a solution: "*What if I found a way to make peace with them, and I asked for your hand, and we left here with their blessing—would you marry me then?*" This morning it seemed impossible. He had said, "*I'll find a way. Trust me, Josephine. And trust God.*" But she was afraid to believe him, afraid to pray for God's help. This was one prayer that was impossible for God to answer.

"I don't know what to tell Priscilla," Mother said with a sigh. "I really don't. She has been through so much, and just when she has finally begun to hope . . ."

"Tell her the truth. Tell her I'm in love with someone else—never mind who he is. Tell her I don't love Harrison."

"She's my best friend, Josephine. She is going to want to know who the man is. I think she has a right to know."

"Then tell her about Alexander."

"We can't. Daniel doesn't want anyone to know about you and the Yankee, and he's right. The truth will bring shame on our family."

"What if I talk to Harrison alone? If I tell him the truth, he certainly won't want to marry me. Let him be the one to break the news to his mother. Let him say that he doesn't want to marry me. His mother will be disappointed, but she'll respect her son's choice."

"I don't know . . . can we trust Harrison not to expose this scandal? He made a huge sacrifice for the Confederacy, and he is likely to be as outraged as Daniel is by what you've done."

Mother was right. Harrison already hated her for saving his life, and he might jump at the chance to ruin her life. Or he might agree to marry her just for spite. No, she couldn't leave her future for Harrison to decide.

"Either way, Mother, we may not be able to protect our family from scandal much longer. The Yankees will surely want to punish the people who destroyed their office. Daniel's part in all of this is certain to be discovered."

"But in the eyes of this community, Daniel's actions are those of a hero. Our family's shame is that you were the one who exposed him."

Josephine covered her face for a moment, then asked, "Should I have looked the other way and allowed Daniel to commit murder? The war is over. We can't keep killing Yankees, no matter how everyone feels about them."

"This is such a mess. . . ." Mother murmured.

"I know, but must we solve it today? Can't we wait and see what happens before we tell Mrs. Blake that I can't marry Harrison? We don't have to say anything yet, do we?"

"It isn't fair to string her along. She has her hopes set on this marriage. Every day that we wait, she'll keep building it up in her mind, imagining her future with you and Harrison together. I can tell Mrs. Schreiber you're spoken for and she won't ask questions. But Priscilla has a right to know why."

"Can't it wait just a few more days?" Josephine was desperate for more time, to see if Alexander would really find a way out of this.

"Very well. I suppose we all need time to recover." Mother stirred in her seat, preparing to stand. "And now I need to attend to poor Mary. She is understandably upset."

Josephine stood with her, debating how much more to tell her. "Mother . . . there's something else I have to do, but I'll need Willy and the carriage to do it."

"Oh, Josephine. Please don't ask me to accept something more. I don't think I can bear to hear another thing."

"It's nothing bad, I promise. Trust me."

"I'm sorry, but you've forfeited my trust. Tell me what it is, and then I'll decide."

"Last night, when I warned Alexander to escape, he didn't want the children's schoolbooks to burn up again. He saved a box of them from the fire, and we hid them behind the train station. I would like to go into town and get them."

"Then what would you do with them?"

"They're for the Negro children. So they can learn to read—"

"No. Let it go, Josephine. That school has caused enough trouble already. It's quite clear that the people in our community don't want it here. I don't want you involved with it anymore."

Josephine didn't have the heart to argue with her. She had hurt her mother very deeply as it was. Mother looked as weary and grief-stricken as she had after Daddy died.

"Never mind, then," Josephine said with a sigh.

Teaching Lizzie's children had brought her so much happiness. Rufus, with his sharp mind, so eager to learn; Jack, with his innocent, trusting nature; and Roselle, so sweet and pretty and filled with hope for her future, wanting to be a teacher. The three new children had been delightful, too, but she wouldn't be able to teach any of them without causing another scandal.

What would Josephine do with the long, lonely days that stretched ahead of her? The dream of marrying a husband she loved, a man who loved her in return, was just that—a dream. Again she remembered Alexander's kisses, the feeling of his arms around her, and she wished—as fervently as her mother probably did—that she had never met him, never fallen in love with him.

Josephine wandered through White Oak's empty rooms, longing for someone to talk to, knowing her family wouldn't want to talk to her—and she thought of Lizzie and Otis. She had never thanked them properly for risking their lives to help her last night. Maybe they or one of the others could go into town and rescue the schoolbooks. She went outside through the back door and saw Otis working in his cotton field beyond the stables. The tops of Jack's and Rufus's heads were just visible above the cotton plants as they worked alongside him. She didn't see the other men, Saul and Robert and Willy. Josephine followed the wooden walkway to the kitchen and found Lizzie working all alone, shelling peas from their garden.

"Where is everyone, Lizzie? Where are Clara and the girls? Don't you have help today?"

"No, ma'am. It's just me from now on. The others are . . . they're packing up their things, fixing to leave."

"Packing . . . why?"

Lizzie looked all around as if afraid someone might overhear her. She seemed skittish and jumpy. "They're scared, Missy Jo. They know it was Massa Daniel and his friends who burned down our school and . . . and they don't want to stay here no more."

"Are you and Otis leaving, too?"

"I want to, Missy Jo. To tell you the truth, I'm just as scared as they are." She twisted her hands as if wringing laundry, her dark eyes filled with fear. "But it ain't fair to Otis if we leave now. He worked so hard planting that cotton and a garden of our own. And we got three kids to think about and another one on the way—" She stopped. Her hand flew to her mouth as if she had said something she hadn't wanted to say.

Josephine looked at her in surprise. A baby. Lizzie and Otis were expecting another baby. What future would they and their children have if Daniel and his friends continued to terrorize them? The Freedmen's Bureau was their only hope, and it had burned to the ground.

"Lizzie, do you think it would help if I talked to Clara and Willy and the others? I can tell them that Mr. Chandler isn't dead, that he'll be coming back. He promised he would. He can protect them."

She shook her head quickly, as if shivering. "They won't listen to you, Missy Jo, because . . ."

She didn't finish. She didn't need to. Josephine was Daniel's sister. And white. She thought of the schoolbooks again and knew she couldn't ask any of the Negroes to retrieve them. They would be accused of stealing them. No one wanted to see a Negro with a book.

"Never mind, Lizzie. I understand. But please believe me when I say that you can trust me. I'm not like my brother. I hate what he and the others are doing. Anytime you need my help, please ask."

She went back inside, feeling like a stranger in her own home. She wasn't like her brother or her mother or anyone else in this town. She didn't share their opinions and beliefs. But the servants didn't quite trust her, either. Where would she ever find a friend, a confidante? Would this terrible loneliness she felt be permanent? She had told Alexander that she couldn't leave her home or her family to go with him, but now she wondered if she could bear to stay.

33

JULY 24, 1865

More than a week had passed since the fire at the Freedmen's Bureau, and Eugenia waited in suspense for the Yankees to return and arrest her son, as they surely would. As each day passed, she lived with ever-growing tension, worried for her son, her daughter, not daring to leave the house, afraid to face anyone in case they had found out about Josephine and the Yankee. The steamy weather added to everyone's misery, making tempers prickly.

This afternoon seemed even hotter than all the ones before it, and in Eugenia's search for a cool place to sit down, she wandered into the drawing room, where she had held her dance. She propped open the doors to the terrace, and there did seem to be a hint of a breeze coming through them from the distant river. The terrace had looked so nice the night of her dance, but already she could see weeds sprouting between some of the stones, and there was no one to tend it. The slaves were all gone again except for Lizzie and Otis and their children. Eugenia remembered her shock a week ago—on top of everything else she had learned that terrible afternoon—when she had called for Willy to fetch her carriage and had learned that he was gone.

"What's going on?" she had asked Lizzie. "Where is everyone?"

"It's just me and Otis, ma'am. The others all left."

"Why? Where did they go?"

"They're scared, ma'am. After the trouble at the Freedmen's Bureau . . ."

Daniel's actions had chased off the help, and now Eugenia had to watch her home fall into disrepair again as Lizzie labored to do everything alone. Eugenia had been filled with so much hope on the night of her dance. Now this trouble with Daniel and Josephine had brought back all of Eugenia's other losses, making her grief fresh and sharp once again. She missed Philip desperately. And their son Samuel, who would have inherited White Oak. Daniel seemed as lost to Eugenia as her other two men were, destroyed by his anger and bitterness. Even if the Yankees didn't arrest him for what he'd done, she could never trust him to take care of her the way Philip had.

Josephine was lost to her, too. Jo had spent the week wandering around the house, pining for the Yankee, barely speaking to any of them. Eugenia had no idea what to say to her. Mary was the only child left to Eugenia, and the girl had her heart set on courting Joseph Gray, one of the men involved in the violence along with Daniel. Even if Joseph somehow escaped arrest, how could Eugenia allow her dear, sweet Mary to marry such a man?

Eugenia turned away from the doors and sat down at the small writing desk to do some work. It had occurred to her as she had tried in vain to sleep last night that if the Yankees imposed a fine for destroying their office, she could lose her plantation. But in the meantime, she had a home to run and people to feed and care for, even if the future of White Oak did seem precarious. She rang the bell to summon Lizzie, then had to ring a second and a third time before she finally came.

"Yes, ma'am?" She looked bone-weary, her dark skin glistening with sweat. If it was hot in this room, how must it feel in the kitchen? Before the war, Eugenia never would have given it a thought. Now she seemed to be seeing her slaves' needs for the first time. She cleared her throat.

"I thought I would give you a hand planning our meals now that Clara is gone. Are there some vegetables from the garden that are ripe? Would you like some ideas for—?" Eugenia stopped. Lizzie was supposed to be paying attention, but she was looking past her, gazing intently through the open doors. "What is so interesting out there that you—?"

Before Eugenia could look over her shoulder to follow Lizzie's gaze, the servant shot past her, running through the open doors, shouting, "No! Get your hands off her! Don't you dare touch her!"

Eugenia turned around. Daniel was holding Lizzie's daughter, Roselle, in his arms, waltzing around the terrace with her. What in the world was he doing?

"Let her go!" Lizzie screamed as she lunged at them, pushing them apart.

It took Daniel a moment to recover, then he raised his hand and slapped Lizzie across the face. "How dare you speak to me that way?"

"Mama! You hit my mama!" Roselle cried.

"Roselle, you get on out of here. Go home," Lizzie said. But the girl couldn't seem to move, and neither could Eugenia. "Didn't I warn you to stay away from him, Roselle? Get on out of here, now!" Lizzie gave her daughter a shove, and she stumbled away from her. As soon as Roselle regained her balance, she took off running, weeping as she ran.

"What in blazes do you think you're doing?" Daniel shouted. "I was teaching her how to dance." He stood with his hands bunched into fists, looking angry enough to strike Lizzie again. But Lizzie stood her ground, not backing down, looking just as angry.

"That ain't all you were doing. I see the way you keep looking at her, and I'm telling you to leave her alone. Stay away from her!"

"We were just—"

"You can't fool me. You hate us Negroes, and you always have. Why are you saying you want to dance with her? Why are you telling her she's pretty all the time? You're sweet-talking that little girl so you can do what you want with her."

"How dare you talk to me that way?" Daniel reached to slap her again, but Lizzie defended herself this time, grabbing his raised arm, struggling with him. Eugenia watched, frozen in horror. She had never seen anything like this in her life, and she couldn't seem to move.

"I know what you're trying to do because it happens all the time," Lizzie shouted. "White men are always sweet-talking until they get their own way. That's what you been doing with my Roselle, but you can't have her! That gal is a Weatherly the same as you!"

Lizzie's words struck Eugenia as if she was the one who had been slapped. How could Roselle be a Weatherly? What was Lizzie saying?

Daniel slapped Lizzie again, and she stumbled backward and fell.

"Daniel!" Eugenia tried to shout. "Daniel, stop it!" But he didn't seem to hear her. Eugenia's heart was pounding so hard she could barely walk to the door as Daniel and Lizzie continued to argue.

"You can slap me around all you want to," Lizzie said from where she'd landed on the ground, "but it ain't gonna change the fact that she's your kin. Ask that white doctor of yours, he knows the truth. Massa Philip told him the night Roselle was born."

Daniel lifted Lizzie by one arm and dragged her to her feet. "You ever speak that lie again or say it in front of my mother, I'll kill you!"

Lizzie looked back toward the house as she tried to free herself from his grip. She saw Eugenia in the doorway. Daniel followed her gaze and saw her, too.

"Mother! You . . . you . . . Don't listen to her lies!" He shoved Lizzie away.

"It ain't a lie, it's the truth," Lizzie said. "Roselle is a Weatherly just as surely as you are. That's why Massa Philip promised he'd always take care of me and Roselle, we'd always have a home here."

Eugenia didn't want to hear any more. She turned and staggered away from the door, the room spinning and whirling. She had barely recovered from the trauma of what Daniel and Josephine had done and now this? This couldn't possibly be true because it would surely kill her. Philip and Lizzie? No.

She had to stop partway across the room, feeling nauseous. She was going to be sick. It couldn't be true! It couldn't! The pain in her chest, in her heart, were the worst she had ever known.

"Mother! Mother, wait!" she heard Daniel calling behind her. She staggered forward again. She had to get away from him, to escape upstairs and find refuge in her room. But the dizziness was too great, the pain overwhelming.

Eugenia had heard stories of white masters fathering children with their slaves, but surely not Philip. Surely not! Yet Lizzie had been nothing but a field hand until Philip moved her up to the Big House. Had this been his reason? To have her close to him?

"Mother . . ." Daniel caught up with her and tried to take her arm. Eugenia shook him off.

"Leave me alone!"

Her world had shattered. Everything she'd ever believed about her husband had been a lie. Philip hadn't loved her—he couldn't have if he could do a thing like this. He had married her for show. She had been nothing but a prize in society's matchmaking game. Eugenia's life was falling apart just as it had during the war, only this time she would have nothing left, not even her memories. The pain grew and swelled as if her heart might burst. She didn't know what to do, where to turn. She wanted to die.

She was nearly to the drawing room door when her legs began to go numb. She couldn't feel them, couldn't walk. The margins of her vision darkened and shrank. *Philip and Lizzie*. Eugenia felt herself spinning, falling, as if she were tumbling down a deep, dark hole. Then the world went black.

When Eugenia awoke, she was lying on a chaise in the drawing room. Dr. Hunter held a vial of smelling salts beneath her nose and was gently slapping her cheeks.

"Eugenia . . . ? Eugenia, open your eyes. Wake up." She saw Daniel, Josephine, and Mary standing behind him, looking distraught. She closed her eyes again and turned her head away, trying to escape the smell. "No . . . No, take it away . . ." The pain in her chest was excruciating, her body on fire, and she longed to sink back into oblivion and never wake up. But David was insisting that she did.

"Don't close your eyes, Eugenia. Look at me."

At first, she couldn't remember what had happened to her, but then she did.

Philip and Lizzie.

Eugenia wanted to die. She wanted David to go away and let her die.

"Can you hear me, Eugenia?" he asked. "I'm going to help you sit up so you can swallow these laudanum tablets. They'll stop the pain and help you sleep."

"No . . . no . . . I don't want to sleep." Because when she woke up, nothing would have changed. Roselle would still be Philip's daughter, proof of his betrayal.

"You need to take them for the pain, Eugenia. They will calm you and make the spasms stop."

She shook her head. The pills would do no good. The pain in her heart would never go away until the day she died. And she wanted to die now.

"Mother, don't believe that filthy slave!" Daniel said. "She was lying! Nothing she said is true!"

"Eugenia, listen," David said. "You've suffered a shock. Would it help to talk about it?"

She shook her head. She didn't want anyone to know how Philip had humiliated her, shamed her. How he had come to her bed after sleeping with a field slave. But then she remembered what else Lizzie had said, that the doctor had been there the night Roselle was born. David already knew about Philip and Lizzie.

She would make him tell her the truth. If she heard it from him, maybe her heart would finally burst and she could die. "Make everyone leave but you," she mumbled.

She closed her eyes while David issued the orders. She heard scuffling footsteps as her children left the room. Then silence.

A vague memory began to stir in Eugenia's mind, a commotion

in the middle of the night when her daughter Mary had been young. One of the slaves had come into the room to awaken Philip, whispering about a baby and asking to send into town for the doctor. Eugenia had panicked, fearing that something had happened to Mary, her baby.

"What's going on, Philip? What's wrong?" she had asked him.

"Nothing. One of the slaves is having trouble giving birth. I'll take care of it. Go back to sleep." And so she had. She had believed Philip, trusted him.

Now David sat down beside her again. "They're gone, Eugenia. Talk to me."

"What did Daniel tell you?" she asked.

"He said one of your servants had told a terrible lie about Philip and that it caused your fainting spell."

"But was it really a lie? Lizzie said that you knew the truth."

"Me? Are you sure? How would I know . . . ?"

"I want the truth, David. I don't care if Philip was your friend, I want to know!" She struggled to sit up, but he held her still.

"Eugenia, stop. If it's something from the past, why not let it stay there? You need to calm down and give your heart a chance to recover."

"My heart is breaking, David. I want to know the truth. I won't let you leave until you tell me the truth."

"Fine . . . yes . . . just lie still. Try to relax . . . take a few deep breaths."

She did as he said, trying to calm herself, bracing for the truth. "Philip called for you late at night, not long after Mary was born, to deliver a slave's baby . . . do you remember?"

He stared down at his lap as if thinking. "So long ago? I think . . ." He looked up, and a glimmer of recognition shone in his eyes. "I remember that Philip had a slave who was very young. Only fourteen or fifteen. The Negro midwife usually delivered their babies, but this girl was so young that she was having difficulty giving birth."

"Was her name Lizzie?" Eugenia squeezed her hands into fists, trying to remain composed and not cry. The pain behind her breastbone was still intense.

"I don't know. I just remember being outraged to see a girl that young giving birth—just a child herself. I confronted Philip and told him he needed to get to the bottom of this and punish the slave who raped her, get rid of him. How could he allow such things to go on? I asked. Couldn't he or his foreman protect these young girls?

"Philip didn't say anything. When the baby was finally born, I saw why. She was very light-skinned. Lighter than the mother. It was obvious the baby's father had been white." Dr. Hunter paused a moment. "Then the mother started calling for Philip. I saw him holding her hand, comforting her, and I was outraged."

Eugenia could no longer hold back her tears. "Go away now, David. I want to be alone."

"Wait. That isn't the end of the story, Eugenia. When I confronted Philip, he said, 'It's not what you think. I'm not the father—not that it's any of your business. But I'm going to take care of the girl and her baby, and move her up to the house to work. And the child will be cared for, too.'

"I argued with him. I said, 'If that baby is your daughter, you can't in good conscience let her grow up to be a slave.'

"'It wasn't me,' he insisted.

"'Who was it, then? The man who did this needs to be stopped. Punished. She's just a child, for heaven's sake. Tell me you aren't going to allow this to continue?'

"Philip told me that he had taken care of it. I don't know what became of either the girl or her child, Eugenia. That's the last time either Philip or I ever mentioned it."

Eugenia felt no relief at all. "If he wasn't the father, then who was?"

"Philip wouldn't say. I thought maybe it was his white foreman."

"But my slave said that the baby was a Weatherly. Get her in here, David. I need to know the truth."

"Do you really want to do that? Who are you going to believe, her or Philip? How will you know who's lying?"

"Tell Josephine to go find Lizzie and bring her in here."

"Fine. I'll do that. But please take one of these laudanum tablets while you're waiting. Whatever this girl says, it's certain to upset you again and—"

"No. I don't want laudanum. Just let me lie here and wait." Eugenia knew that David was right—she would have no way of knowing who was telling the truth. She couldn't confront Philip face-to-face, but she could make Lizzie frightened enough to never speak that lie again.

A long time seemed to pass before Josephine returned with Lizzie. The servant was trembling from head to toe and clinging to Josephine's arm as if terrified to let go. She had a welt on her cheek from where Daniel had struck her. "Thank you, Josephine. Please leave us."

"I can't, Mother. Lizzie only agreed to come and talk to you if I stayed with her. She's terrified. She and Otis were packing to leave White Oak. I'm the only person she trusts."

Eugenia exhaled in frustration and asked David to help her sit up. She didn't want her daughter to hear this, but Eugenia had no choice. It was the only way she would ever learn the truth.

"You aren't in trouble, Lizzie. My son had no right to hit you. Now, I heard what you said about your daughter, Roselle. That she's a Weatherly. I want to hear the whole story from you. Don't think you need to spare my feelings. I want the truth. Nothing is going to happen to you, I promise. I want you to tell me who Roselle's father is."

Lizzie clung to Josephine's arm while she talked, never lifting her eyes from the floor. Tears ran down her dark face, and she kept brushing them away with her other hand. "It started the same way as Massa Daniel was doing with my Roselle. He kept taking me aside, telling me I was pretty. That's how I knew . . . That's why I had to stop Massa Daniel—!"

"Never mind what Daniel did, for now. I want to know your story."

Lizzie drew a shuddering breath. "Sometimes he would be there, watching me when we all went out to the fields in the morning or came back at night. When we stopped for lunch, he would tell me to come in out of the hot sun, that I was too pretty to do such hard work. He kept saying such nice things to me, and I believed him. The other slaves tried to warn me, telling me to watch out, but he was our massa, wasn't he? Ain't I supposed to obey him?"

Pain stabbed through Eugenia's heart at her words. David took her hand, holding it tightly as Lizzie continued.

"My mama said, 'Do it, girl. Make a better life for yourself. Ask him to get you a job in the Big House.' No one dreamed we would ever win our freedom. I didn't have to sleep with him to get a better life. But I was tired of the cotton fields, so I let him start kissing me and holding me. He gave me presents, a nice dress, and food from the Big House, things I never ate before. He made me feel so wonderful. I never felt loved before because my mama was always afraid to love me, afraid we'd be separated and sold to different places. She always told me to make sure I never fell in love, but I couldn't help it. I loved him, so I let him love me back."

Eugenia couldn't bear to hear the rest, but she had to. Would Philip really do all those things? Woo a young girl that way? Seduce her, lie to her? Or is it possible that Philip had loved Lizzie, too?

"He made a special place where we'd go," Lizzie continued. "A special bed he fixed with pretty blankets and things. Then one day when we went there, it wasn't just the two of us. Massa's friend was waiting there, too. I wanted the other man to go away and leave us alone, but Massa said he shared everything with his friend and so he was going to share me with him, too. I told him I didn't want to. I didn't love his friend, I loved him. But they laughed at me, both of them. And when I tried to leave . . ."

"Oh . . ." Eugenia moaned.

"Lizzie, stop," Dr. Hunter said. "You don't have to finish."

"Miz Eugenia wanted to know who Roselle's father is," Lizzie said, "but I can't tell her for sure because I don't know. It might be Massa Samuel, or it might be his friend, Massa Harrison."

Eugenia closed her eyes as her own tears began to fall. Her son

Samuel had done this terrible thing, not Philip. She was sorry she had ever doubted her husband, but she found no comfort at all in knowing that her son and his friend had raped a young slave girl and gotten her pregnant. And if Eugenia were honest with herself, she knew that Daniel had probably intended to do the same thing to Roselle.

And what about Harrison Blake? Eugenia had been furious at the thought of Josephine and the Yankee, yet she had nearly arranged a marriage between Josephine and a man who was capable of raping a young girl.

"Massa Philip took care of me," Lizzie finished. "He sent Massa Samuel away for a while, and he gave me a job up here in the Big House. And as bad as it all was, I had my Roselle, and Massa promised that nobody can ever take her away from me." Lizzie finally lifted her face, looking up at Eugenia for the first time. "Otis and me will be leaving White Oak now. I know Massa Daniel won't let us stay here anymore. Just give us some time to pack our things and—"

"No, Lizzie. I'm in charge of White Oak. You and Otis don't need to leave. Daniel is the one who will be leaving." As her eyes met Lizzie's, Eugenia saw her as a woman and a mother like herself, perhaps for the very first time. "I promised Otis that he could rent my cotton fields until the harvest, and I intend to keep my promise."

"Yes, ma'am. Thank you, ma'am."

Eugenia had never apologized to a slave in her life but she knew that she needed to. She met Lizzie's gaze again. "I'm sorry, Lizzie. I'm sorry about what happened, and I'm sorry for making you relive it."

"Thank you, ma'am."

As soon as Lizzie and Josephine were gone, she told David to send in Daniel. "Are you all right, Mother? We were so worried about you. I could kill that slave for upsetting you this way."

"I'm fine, Daniel. Lizzie told me the whole story—"

"You can't possibly believe her!"

"I do. Dr. Hunter was there the night Roselle was born. It was Samuel and Harrison Blake. They are the ones who . . ."

"What!"

She paused to swallow a knot of grief. "Listen, everyone's emotions are very high right now, and I think it would be best if you went to Richmond for a while. I'll write a note for you to take to Aunt Olivia—"

"Wait! You're sending *me* away? Why not send those Negroes away? They're the ones who—"

"Just for a while. Your father sent Samuel away when he found out about what he and Harrison had done."

"But that makes no sense." Daniel was growing angry, unable to stand still, yet Eugenia could tell that he was trying to restrain his temper so she wouldn't have another spell. "I can't leave you and the girls here all alone without protection. You can't trust those slaves."

"The girls and I managed when you were away at war, and we can manage now. You need to go to work for your uncle Charles in Richmond for a while. I don't think you're cut out for running the plantation. These so-called friends of yours have had a bad influence on you." Although Eugenia couldn't help wondering if Daniel, in fact, was the leader.

"I can't believe you're sending me away, taking their side."

"It's the right thing to do."

"What about White Oak? You're going to let that slave run your plantation? That's crazy!"

"He has been running it these past few months, and he has done very well—although he may not want to stay after everything that's happened. I wouldn't blame him. But he has a right to harvest what he has already planted."

"White Oak is my home, not his. I can't imagine what Father would say about this."

"I think he would agree that I'm doing the right thing. He took care of Lizzie and her baby after what Samuel did to her, and he brought her into our house to work for us. Your father never laid a hand on any of our slaves—and I just watched you slap Lizzie and knock her to the ground. You need time away from here, Daniel.

Let your temper cool. Then we'll decide how we're going to move forward. This is the best solution for everyone."

"You've changed, Mother." His voice was cold with barely controlled rage. "You're not the same woman you were before the war."

"I suppose I have changed. For the better, I hope." But she didn't think that Daniel heard her as he stalked from the room. She felt David squeeze her hand and realized he had been holding it all this time.

"You did the right thing, Eugenia," he told her. "Philip would be proud of you. He hated slavery, did you know that? We used to talk about it. But he couldn't see how he could run White Oak without slaves. It just wasn't economically feasible."

"I don't know where I went wrong with raising my children."

"Don't upset yourself again. You're not to blame. Our entire Southern culture had an influence on them, too. Now, listen to me, Eugenia. I am your physician, and I'm ordering you to take these two laudanum tablets. Then you need to go to bed and stay there for at least a week until your heart has a chance to recover. You won't survive many more of these spells, you know. And you're needed here. Your family needs you." He handed her a glass of water and the medicine.

"Thank you, David. You've been a dear friend to me. I don't know what I would do without you." She took his hand again and held it tightly before finally letting go.

34

Lizzie still clutched Missy Josephine's arm tightly as they left the drawing room. She was afraid to believe what Miz Eugenia had just told her. She and Otis didn't need to leave White Oak? Massa Daniel was leaving instead? Lizzie had told the truth about Roselle after all these years, yet Miz Eugenia hadn't sent them away.

"Everything will be all right now," Missy Jo told her. "My mother will treat you fairly, just like my father did."

"I done a terrible thing, fighting with Massa Daniel that way and saying what I did. I know that, Missy Jo. But I was just so scared for my Roselle."

"It's over now. You can go back to your cabin and tell Otis that everything will be fine."

But Lizzie was still worried. Massa Daniel was spitting mad, and she was afraid of what he might do. Her legs wouldn't stop trembling as she walked down to the cabin all alone and told Otis what had happened. "Can you ever forgive me for fighting with Massa Daniel and messing things up?" she asked him.

"Lizzie, nothing that happened today was your fault. I would have done the same thing if I had seen what you did."

She looked around the cabin. Their belongings were tied up in bundles, ready to go. Roselle, Rufus, and Jack were wide-eyed with fright as they watched and listened. Lizzie saw Roselle's tears and her heart went out to her. "Roselle, honey . . . I'm sorry."

"Me too, Mama," she said softly. "I should have listened to you." She threw her arms around Lizzie and held her. Lizzie knew she would have to talk to Roselle and explain about her father in a way that she would understand. But not now. Lizzie had relived that ordeal enough for one day.

"Miz Eugenia said we could stay," she told Otis, "but I still wish we could leave."

"Everything is packed, Lizzie-girl. We'll leave right now if you're afraid to stay."

"Where could we go? How would we live? There's no more Freedmen's Bureau to help us out. You went to all that work planting cotton and corn and vegetables for nothing?"

What had she done? Why had she made Massa Daniel mad that way? But Roselle was safe. Lizzie would do it all over again to keep her daughter safe.

"None of that matters, Lizzie. You and our kids are worth more to me than a field full of cotton. The good Lord will take care of us whatever we decide to do."

Missy Jo had said they could trust her. Miz Eugenia had been kind to her for the first time Lizzie could remember. There was only Massa Daniel to worry about, and he was going away. Lizzie looked at her family and felt the weight of her decision. Is this what freedom meant? Being able to decide, yet worrying that you might make the wrong choice?

"Miz Eugenia says she's sending Massa Daniel to Richmond," Lizzie finally said. "We'll wait and see if that's true. I guess we can breathe a little easier once he's gone. But as soon as the cotton is picked and sold, we're going. We'll take our money and the food from our garden, and we'll go far away from here."

"Are you sure, Lizzie?"

No, she wasn't sure at all. But what else could they do?

The next morning after breakfast, Missy Jo came out to the kitchen with good news. "My brother Daniel left early this morning.

He's going to stay with our relatives in Richmond for a while. Things will be better now, Lizzie. You'll see." But it took three more days before Lizzie could stop looking over her shoulder or jumping at every little sound she heard. Miz Eugenia was still staying in bed all day, with the two missies keeping her company. The house was so quiet it seemed empty. The doctor came every afternoon to check up on Miz Eugenia, and Lizzie would carry a tea tray upstairs to serve them. There were no more meals in the dining room for now, no more tablecloths and napkins to wash and iron. Lizzie kept busy in the garden or the kitchen with Roselle until suppertime, while Otis was out in the field with the boys, grubbing his plants.

On the fourth day, Lizzie agreed to let Roselle and the boys out of her sight, allowing them go down to the barn alone to take care of the animals and then out to the row of raspberry bushes to pick berries. They had been gone all afternoon and still hadn't returned when Otis came up to the kitchen for his supper.

"Will you call Roselle and the boys for me?" Lizzie asked him. "Tell them it'll be time to eat pretty soon, and they have chores to do."

"Sure, Lizzie-girl. Where are they?"

"Aren't they down by the shed, picking berries?"

"I didn't see them."

Lizzie went to the kitchen door and stood on the step, gazing all around. Her heart had started pounding hard, but she told herself not to worry. They couldn't have gone far. "I told them not to wander off. Are they working in the garden?"

"I don't see them. I'll go look down by the barn."

Lizzie watched him go, unable to shake the feeling that something wasn't right. She decided to go outside and search for them herself and ran down to their cabin, her heart a heavy stone in her chest. Maybe they were playing down on Slave Row. Roselle loved to play teacher with the boys, using the books Missy Jo had given them. Maybe they got so busy playing school that they forgot all about the raspberries and their chores, forgot it was even dinnertime. But Slave Row was deserted. Lizzie called their names over and over, but there was no reply. She could hear Otis calling to them, too, in the distance. She ran back up to the kitchen, her panic building.

Please, Lord . . . Please don't let anything happen to my children. Please, please bring them back to me. Please . . .

She checked the chicken yard again, knowing how much Roselle loved playing with her ducks—and saw the three tin pails she had given them, filled to the top with raspberries, just sitting there like they'd been forgotten. Otis came back a few minutes later, and she showed him the buckets.

"Don't worry, Lizzie. The kids have to be around here someplace. You go on and fix the white folks their dinner, and I'll keep looking." He was trying not to show it, but Lizzie could tell he was worried, too.

She finished making supper in a daze. Her hands shook like an old woman's as she carried the tray upstairs to Miz Eugenia's room. All the windows were open in the July heat, and she could hear Otis calling for Roselle and Rufus and Jack outside. *Please, Lord. Show him where to look,* she prayed. But when Lizzie returned to the kitchen, Otis still hadn't found them. He stood gazing around the yard with a hollow look in his eyes, his arms hanging limp at his sides. She grabbed the front of his shirt and shook him.

"Where are they, Otis, where are they? What are we going to do?"

"I-I don't know . . . I've looked everywhere. . . ." He called their names again, and as he listened in vain for an answer, Lizzie realized how quiet the kitchen yard was. Usually Roselle's ducks would start quacking and squawking at any little noise but there was no quacking at all.

"Otis, the ducks! Roselle's ducks are gone!"

"Do you think she took them down to the river to set them free? She's been talking about doing that."

Lizzie felt a sliver of hope and a surge of fear. "All that way? How would she know where to go? She's never been to the river, has she?"

"No, but the boys have. I take them fishing down there. I'll go look."

"Wait! I want to go with you."

"Don't you have to tend to Miz Eugenia and the girls?"

"I don't care about them, Otis! We have to find our kids!"

"Come on, then." He took her hand and led her down the rough, narrow path through the woods to the river. It seemed to take forever. Lizzie didn't dare to cry as she kept her eyes on the dirt track, watching out for stones and brambles and tree branches in her way. She prayed the whole way there and knew that Otis was praying, too.

She heard the rushing water before she saw it. Lizzie was panting from running so far in the heat. She held her breath, listening for children's voices and the sound of squawking ducks, but when they emerged from the woods onto the riverbank, there was no sign of life at all. Otis shouted their names. Listened. Shouted again. Lizzie began to moan, fighting hysteria. Otis pulled her into his arms, and she could feel his heart trying to pound out of his chest.

"Shh . . . shh . . ." he soothed. "Oh, Lord, help us! Show us what to do. . . ."

"I'm scared, Otis! I'm so scared! If anything happens to them . . ."

"I know, I know . . . Come on, we better go back."

They followed the path back to the plantation, running as fast as they could. Every time they paused for breath, Otis shouted the children's names, then listened. The woods were silent, terrifying. Lizzie wanted to scream.

The yard was still deserted when they returned. Lizzie could hear the cow down in the barn, lowing to be milked, and Miz Eugenia's bell ringing inside the house. "What are we going to do?" she cried.

"You better go on in and see to the white folks. Maybe ask Missy Jo if she seen them. I'll go look in the woods the other way, down by that old tree house."

Lizzie dried her tears and tried to compose herself before hurrying into the house. Her knees felt so weak she could hardly climb the stairs to Miz Eugenia's bedroom. The three women had finished their dinner a long time ago and the tray was sitting on the vanity, waiting to be taken away.

"Where in the world have you been?" Miz Eugenia asked. "When you didn't answer the bell, I was ready to send Josephine to look for you."

"I-I'm sorry, ma'am." Lizzie hadn't answered her question, but if she tried to say any more, she would burst into tears. Besides, Miz Eugenia didn't really want to hear about Lizzie's missing children. She still looked very weak and gray-faced, lying back against her pillows. There was nothing that she or the two missies could do to help.

"Well, kindly remove the tray, Lizzie. And stay where you can hear the bell the next time."

"Yes, ma'am."

Otis still wasn't back from searching when she returned to the kitchen. She should wash the dishes and clean the kitchen. The cow needed to be milked and the chickens fed. She and Otis still hadn't eaten their dinner. But Lizzie was too sick with worry to do any of those things. She stood in the doorway, watching the path, waiting for Otis to return.

When she finally saw him, he was alone.

Lizzie's knees gave way. She sank down on the step and wept.

Otis sat down beside her and pulled her into his arms. "I ran all the way into Fairmont," he said, still panting for breath. "I thought they might of gone to the school. I asked everyone I saw along the way, but . . ."

"What are we going to do, Otis? What are we going to do?" He didn't reply. She knew he was praying. Lizzie was too upset to think, let alone pray. He would have to talk to God for the both of them.

It seemed like a very long time passed as they sat huddled together on the ground. The sun had sunk below the treetops. It would be dark soon. Lizzie felt hollow and empty inside, like one of the discarded shells on the riverbank. At last, Otis struggled to his feet and pulled Lizzie up with him.

"I need to milk the cow," he said, his voice hoarse. His eyes were red, his face wet with tears.

"I'll come with you. I-I can't stay here all alone." He nodded and went into the kitchen to fetch the milk bucket. Lizzie gripped his hand as they walked down to the barn together. She stood in the barn doorway while he worked, watching him milk the cow one minute, watching the ever-darkening path the next. When she heard the faint cry coming from the woods, Lizzie thought she had imagined it at first. Then she heard it again.

"Otis, come here! Listen!"

It was the sound of a child crying and calling "Mama!"

She and Otis ran from the barn together, racing toward the woods, following the sound. And then—a miracle! Rufus was running toward them, calling to her. Lizzie reached him first and lifted him into her arms, squeezing him tightly, rocking him.

"Thank you, Lord . . . Thank you, Lord!" she breathed. "Oh, Rufus, baby! Are you all right?" He mumbled something in reply but he was crying so hard that Lizzie couldn't understand him. She set him on the ground and knelt in front of him. "Where are the others, baby? Where are Jack and Roselle?"

"The . . . the men st-still have them."

"The men . . . ?" Lizzie's joy and relief vanished in an instant.

Otis grabbed Rufus's shoulders. "Talk to us, son. Tell us what happened."

His story came out with agonizing slowness between tears and sobs. "We-we heard Roselle's ducks in the woods. . . . They got out of the fence. . . . And so, and so, she said for me and Jack to help her . . . to help her catch them. We kept following the sound, Papa. We kept going farther back in the woods. And then . . . and then the men grabbed us!"

"Oh God, no . . ." Lizzie moaned.

"What men, Rufus?"

"I don't know. They have their faces covered. They . . . they had the ducks, but it was just to trick us!"

"Where are the men now?" Otis asked. "Do they still have Jack and Roselle? How did you get free?"

"They . . . they let me go!" Rufus started to wail, and Otis took him into his arms, rocking him gently.

"Hush, son. It's all right now. It's all right. Tell me why they let you go."

"Because . . . because they want you and Mama to come. They said . . . they said they'll let Jack and Roselle come home if you and Mama come and talk to them."

"Oh, Lord!" Lizzie wept.

"Where are they, son? Did the men tell you where we should meet them?"

"Uh-huh . . . They said . . . where the slave camp was."

"We have to go, Otis. Come on. They have Roselle and Jack!"

Otis set Rufus down again and pulled Lizzie near. "It's a trap," he whispered. "They'll trap all of us."

"Then we'll get help. We'll find Saul and Robert and Willy and the others and get them to come help us."

"We don't know where they are. Besides, we can't put them in danger. If we come armed, the white men will say that we attacked them first. It'll be just like before."

"But . . . but what are we going to do?"

"I don't know, but let's go on back to the kitchen and get the boy something to eat, get him calmed down. While you're doing that, I'll pray. Maybe the Lord will show us what to do. Maybe He'll send someone to help us."

Lizzie did what Otis said, even though her every instinct screamed at her to run into the woods and save her children, her babies. She fixed Rufus a slice of bread and butter and held him on her lap, stroking his face, his hair while he ate. Otis sank onto his knees beside them, then fell forward on his face, silently praying. It seemed to Lizzie that hours and hours passed while she waited, sick with grief and fear.

"Lizzie . . . Lizzie . . . Lizzie . . ." Someone was calling her name. The voice sounded very far away, but when she looked up, Missy Josephine was standing in the kitchen doorway. "Oh, Lizzie, what's wrong!" she asked when she saw Lizzie's face. Otis had looked up, too, his face wet with tears. He slowly rose to his feet. "What happened?" Missy Jo asked again.

Lizzie hadn't meant to tell Missy Jo, but the words just came rushing out all at once. "They took my children! My babies! They have my Roselle and Jack in the woods, and they won't let them go!"

"Who does, Lizzie?"

She knew the answer. Massa Daniel. It had to be. No one else hated them that much. But she was afraid to say it out loud.

"We don't know who they are," Otis said. "But they have our kids, and they sent Rufus back here to tell us to come get them. They say they only want to talk and then they'll let them go, but—"

"Don't go," Missy Josephine said. "It's a trap."

"I know, I know . . . but we don't know what else to do. I've been praying for an answer and—"

"And then I came," Missy said. "Don't you see? God answered your prayer. You need to stay here while I go get help."

"But who, Missy Jo? Who's gonna help you? Everybody in this town hates us Negroes."

"I want my children back!" Lizzie said. "Please, Otis! Please don't make me wait anymore. I need to go to them. Before the men hurt them."

Missy Jo covered her mouth as if to hold back her own tears. She stared at Lizzie and Otis and Rufus for a long moment. "No, neither one of you can go. You have to trust me and stay right here. I'll go into town and ask Dr. Hunter for help. He must know some other people who would be willing to help us."

"How're you getting to town?" Otis asked. "Massa Daniel took the horse to Richmond."

"I'll take the path through the woods again, like I did the last time. You can lead me to it, can't you?"

"No, Missy Jo. No. That's where them men are, back in those woods. They'll hear us coming and neither one of us will ever get through."

"I'll take the road, then. It will take longer, but I'll get help, Otis, I swear I will. Promise me that you and Lizzie will stay right here and wait until I get back. Don't try to rescue Roselle and Jack yourself. Promise?"

Lizzie couldn't speak.

At last, Otis nodded. "Yes, ma'am. I promise. It'll be the hardest thing I ever done, but I'll wait. And I'll be praying for you."

35

Josephine ran out the kitchen door and around the house to the long, gravel driveway. Her bulky skirt hampered her movements, and her legs felt like stones were tied to her ankles as she raced up the lane and out to the main road. She didn't have time to think about the ever-darkening night or the dangers along the way as she sprinted toward Fairmont as fast as she could go. Josephine knew she should have told Mother or Mary where she was going, but she didn't want to add any more strain to her mother's heart. And she didn't trust Mary to keep quiet.

The summer night was as hot as White Oak's kitchen when the hearth was burning, and her garments quickly became drenched with sweat, plastering the fabric to her skin. If only she could run faster. If only she didn't have to stop so often to catch her breath and ease the stitch in her side. This was taking much too long. It would be more than an hour at this rate before she reached Dr. Hunter's house in town—and what if he wasn't even there? Then what? She prayed—really, truly prayed—that Otis and Lizzie would have the patience to wait and that the men wouldn't harm Jack and Roselle—and she kept on running.

Daniel was behind this kidnapping, Josephine knew it. If he could plot one murder, he was capable of this, too. Years of shooting

386

Yankees during the war had made him immune to killing. He would lure Lizzie and her family into the woods and make them disappear. Everyone would assume they had left White Oak on their own like all the other Negroes had. Otis had to die because he could testify to Daniel's guilt. The children were bait in the trap. Jo shuddered, knowing he would kill them, too. Lizzie would die because she had dared to tell the truth about Samuel. Daniel would kill her to keep her from ever telling anyone else what Samuel and Harrison Blake had done.

Josephine halted. Harrison Blake! She was almost to the Blakes' plantation. Maybe she could borrow their carriage to get to town. She didn't think she had the strength to run all that way. Jo turned up the lane to Harrison's house. Then she had another thought. What if she could convince Harrison to help her? He owed Lizzie an enormous debt for what he had done to her, so the least he could do was save her and her children. Daniel and the others would listen to Harrison, their former captain.

Josephine decided to go around to the rear door and get one of the servants to go inside and fetch him. She wouldn't let Priscilla know she was there. But Harrison was sitting in his wheelchair on the front porch as Jo jogged up his driveway, and he saw her before she saw him.

"Who's there?" he called out to her.

"It's me, Josephine," she panted. "I need your help."

"Josephine . . . ?"

"Yes." She halted, leaning against the hitching post to catch her breath. The front door was open and so were all the windows. She prayed he would come down to talk to her so that Priscilla wouldn't overhear them. It seemed like an eternity before Harrison stood and reached for his crutches, then hobbled down the steps.

"What are you doing here? You look a mess."

"I ran all the way here."

"Ran . . . ? Why?"

"Because I need your help, Harrison. Please listen to me—I'll do anything you want me to do in return, but please, please help me."

387

"Slow down and catch your breath. I can't understand you."

"I'll marry you, if that's what you want, and I'll be your loving wife. Anything, but I'm begging you to help me."

"What's wrong?"

"My brother Daniel and his friends are planning to do something terrible to our Negroes. They took Otis and Lizzie's children and—"

"Wait. If it's a problem with your slaves, you need to know I'll believe your brother's word before I'll ever believe a Negro's. Settle it with him yourself."

"No, listen to me, Harrison. It's a trap. Daniel is setting a trap. He's holding our servants' children captive. He's trying to lure Otis and Lizzie into the woods, and when he does, he'll probably kill them."

"I don't believe it. Why would he kill them?"

"Otis was a witness the night two Negroes were killed in the woods. He knows that Daniel was there. And Otis knows it was Daniel who burned down the Freedmen's Bureau. Lizzie knows the truth, too. Daniel is afraid that when the Yankees come back, Otis and Lizzie will testify to his guilt. He plans to kill them all! Please, Harrison. We have to save them."

"Why involve me?"

"Because . . . because I know the truth about what you did fifteen years ago. You told me you were going to hell for your sins and . . . and I know what you meant. You and my brother raped one of our slaves. She was just a young girl, and the two of you seduced and raped her."

Harrison teetered on his crutches and nearly lost his balance. Jo grabbed his arm to keep him from falling. The look on his face was one of shame and horror.

"I paid for that crime a thousand times over," he said, his voice quivering with emotion. "I've been to hell . . . and I'm still in hell for that crime. I'll have to live this way for the rest of my life. How is helping you supposed to atone for my past?"

"Because the slave you raped got pregnant. She had a daughter.

That's the girl who Daniel kidnapped tonight—your daughter. He's going to kill her."

"My daugh . . . ? Are you making this up?"

"No, I'm not. It's the truth, I swear it. Please, Harrison. Daniel will listen to you. He and the other men respect you. This is your chance to make up for what you did to Lizzie. You can save her and her family."

"Harrison?" Priscilla had come out onto the porch. "Who are you talking to? Who's here?"

"It's nothing, Mother. Go back inside." He and Josephine waited, neither one daring to speak. But Priscilla didn't move from the porch. "She doesn't know," Harrison whispered. "She never found out about what Sam and I did. It would have killed her."

"Then help me. Please," Jo whispered back.

"Josephine? What are you doing here?" Priscilla had come down the stairs. She stood staring at her, and Jo knew she must look a wreck, her hair falling loose, her clothes plastered with sweat. "What in the world is going on? Is something wrong?"

"I'm so sorry, Mrs. Blake. I promise to explain it to you later, but I need Harrison's help, and we have to hurry." She looked up at him, pleading silently. He hadn't agreed to help her, and she held her breath, waiting. If he refused, she would ask to borrow his carriage and go find Dr. Hunter by herself. But she was running out of time.

"Is something wrong at White Oak?" Priscilla asked. "Is your family all right?"

"Yes, my family is fine . . ." Jo gripped Harrison's wrist, the one he had slashed with his razor. "Please," she whispered.

At last he spoke. "I'll explain everything later, Mother. Jo needs help with one of her slaves."

"But . . . but where are you going?"

"It's nothing, Mother. I'll tell you all about it when I get back. Come on," he said to Josephine. "We'll need to take my horse."

His progress was painfully slow as he limped all the way across the yard to the stables on his crutches. Jo didn't know how he could maneuver over the rough ground in the dark. He was panting and sweating with exertion before they were even halfway there, and Josephine saw the enormous effort it cost him to go such a distance. She opened the stable door for him and couldn't see a thing inside. How would they ever find the horse, much less get it saddled?

"Henry!" Harrison called out. "Henry, are you in here?"

"Yes, sir," a voice called back.

"I need you to saddle my horse for me."

"Yes, sir. Just let me light this lantern first, sir."

Josephine sagged against the doorpost with relief. Thank heaven the Blakes had Negro servants to help them. Thank heaven for Alexander and the Freedmen's Bureau. A light flared a moment later, and she watched as the young Negro boy got Harrison's horse ready for him to ride, exchanging the halter for a bridle, putting on the blanket, then the saddle, cinching it tightly, adjusting the stirrups. Jo wanted to plead with him to hurry, but she knew it wouldn't help.

"Now help me up," Harrison said at last. The boy took Harrison's crutches, then held him upright as he leaned against the horse and pulled himself up into the saddle. Harrison was weary from their trek across the yard, and it took a great deal of effort for him to heave himself up. How humiliating it must be for him to need so much help. And Jo could tell by the grimace on Harrison's face that the maneuver had been painful, as well. He was sweating and pale by the time he was finally astride.

"Help me up, too, please," she told the servant.

"No, Josephine. You're staying here. Tell me where I should go."

"I want to come with you. I know how to ride. Tell him to help me up."

The horse snorted and stamped in place, waiting. "You don't trust me, do you?" Harrison said. "You don't think I'll really help your slaves."

"Harrison, please. I don't want to argue with you. I promised Lizzie and Otis that I would bring their children back. They will be terrified if I'm not there. I'm going with you."

"Why must you always be so stubborn?"

"I promise I'll never defy you again. I'll do whatever you ask of me for the rest of our lives, but please, please let me come with you."

He finally nodded to the servant, and the boy helped boost Josephine up to ride behind him. She wrapped her arms around him, clinging to him. Harrison flicked the reins, and the horse moved through the door and out into the night. "Where to?" he asked.

"They're hiding back in the woods between White Oak and town. Where the Negroes were camping out for a while. Do you know the place I mean?"

"I think so. If we go out to the main road, there's a path that will take us back there."

"Just hurry, Harrison. Please."

They went down the drive and out to the main road at a trot, and she felt an enormous relief to be traveling so quickly at last. But then it seemed to take forever to find the path in the dark, and when they did the horse made slow progress through the dense brush. The moon and stars weren't able to penetrate deep into the woods. It had become a night from hell with mosquitoes biting and insects buzzing in the steamy summer heat as Josephine raced against time, praying she wouldn't arrive too late.

She had begun to think they were lost, but then the trees and brush thinned out and Josephine saw a clearing ahead. She heard a horse whinny and the low murmur of voices for just a moment before the woods went deathly still. Harrison halted. She heard the slide and click of rifles on the other side of the clearing. Why hadn't she told Harrison to bring a gun?

"Can you slide down by yourself?" Harrison whispered.

"Yes . . . I think so." He held the horse steady as she turned and lowered herself to the ground, her stomach pressed against the horse's body. The ground was farther away than she had thought, her legs weak with fatigue, and she landed on the hard ground with a painful thud.

"Stay here." Harrison rode forward into the clearing. Was she a fool to trust him? Jo began to pray, as hard as she had on the night she'd saved Alexander, pleading and bargaining with God. It couldn't be His will that innocent children died, could it?

"Hello!" he called. "It's me, Harrison Blake."

The silence lengthened. Jo held her breath, waiting. Then a masked figure stepped into the clearing. "Captain Blake? What are you doing here?"

"I should ask you the same thing . . . Is that you, Joseph? Who else is with you?"

"Just some . . . friends. It's nothing you need to worry about, Captain." Two more men emerged from the shadows, rifles in hand. Jo was certain the man on the left was her brother, but none of them removed their masks. Another dark figure remained half hidden near the edge of the clearing, and Jo saw two small forms huddled on the ground at his feet. Roselle and Jack. She could hear them whimpering.

"Is that you, Daniel?" Harrison asked. "I understand you're having a problem with your slaves."

"Isn't everyone these days?" His voice was muffled, but Jo recognized it. "They're getting out of hand, Captain. Trying to take over and endangering our women. They have to be stopped."

"You mean the children you took? How are they a danger to you?"

There was a long pause before Daniel said, "With all due respect, Captain Blake, there's no need for you to get involved in this."

"Maybe not, but your sister asked me to."

"Josephine? I might have known. Don't believe a word she says, Captain. She's a traitor. She's been collaborating with that Yankee and—"

"Enough!" Harrison shouted. "Hasn't there been enough bloodshed? We lost the war! If you continue to fight, you'll lose all over again!"

"My slaves are going to betray us to the Yankees. They have to be silenced."

"There would be nothing for them to tell if you hadn't burned down the Freedmen's Bureau in the first place. Everyone knows it was you."

"We wanted that Yankee out of town, but he wouldn't take a hint so—"

"Stop it! Stop wasting your time with more hatred and killing and revenge. It'll never end. It's time to start all over again and rebuild our homes and our lives. Can't you see that? I didn't understand it either until Josephine made me see the truth. But she's right. We have to stop hating and start living."

Daniel moved into the clearing, closer to Harrison. "Listen, Captain. Thanks to my sister, we're all going to be turned over to her Yankee friend. Not only that, one of my slaves spewed a bunch of lies about you and Samuel, and it nearly killed my mother. They need to pay for it. Then none of the others will ever try to get out of line again."

"Your slave wasn't lying, Daniel. She was telling the truth. I was there. Sam and I raped her, just like she said. When your father found out, he said it was an affront to God and he sent Sam away. I was too young and cocky to understand. I thought it was my right to treat slaves any way I wanted to. But I've paid for it. Samuel paid an even greater price. Don't add guilt to your soul the way we did. End this right now. Let those children go home. And you go home, too."

"Since when are you on the slaves' side?"

"There are no more *sides*, don't you get it? The war blasted all of that away. None of us have anything left. All that's left is right and wrong, and this is wrong. It's wrong! Even if the Yankees let you go free, God won't. You'll pay for what you did one way or another. Believe me, I know."

He paused, waiting. Josephine couldn't breathe.

"Let them go, Daniel," he repeated. "Go home. Seeking revenge is just another way to commit suicide."

Daniel took another step closer. "And if I don't do what you say?"

For a long moment, no one spoke. Sweat trickled down Josephine's back. Harrison's horse fidgeted in place. "Then I guess you'll have to kill me, too," Harrison said quietly. "That Negro girl you have over there? She just might be my daughter."

Daniel stared up at Harrison for what seemed like a very long time. Finally he turned away and strode over to untie his own horse. Without another word, Daniel swung up into the saddle and rode away. After a long pause, the other men did the same, leaving Roselle and Jack behind. Josephine ran across the clearing and pulled them into her arms. They clung so tightly to her that her ribs ached.

"It's over now. You're safe," Josephine soothed. "Everything is going to be all right."

"I want to go home!" Jack wailed.

"Yes, Jack. Yes. Captain Blake is going to show us the way home."

Harrison found the path and led them through the woods. Jack and Roselle clutched Josephine's hands as they stumbled along behind him in the dark.

"What about the ducks?" Jack asked. "They took Roselle's ducks."

"They'll be all right. They're wild creatures, Jack. They'll be happier now that they're free."

Josephine's legs ached by the time they emerged from the woods near the tree house. They were almost home. Harrison halted, and the children let go of Josephine's hands to run toward the house. Lizzie and Otis stood outside the kitchen, watching, waiting. They saw them coming across the yard and ran to meet them.

"Oh, thank you, Lord! Thank you!" Otis cried. Lizzie couldn't seem to speak at all as she pulled her children into her arms. Josephine was so tired she wanted to sink down to the ground and cry with relief and weariness and joy. She looked behind her to thank Harrison and saw that he had turned the horse around to ride back into the woods.

"Harrison, wait!" When he didn't stop or slow down, she summoned her last reserve of strength and ran after him, grabbing the horse's bridle to stop him. "Wait! . . . Listen . . . how can I ever thank you for what you've done?"

He shook his head, gazing straight ahead into the woods. He wouldn't meet her gaze. "Is that girl really Lizzie's daughter?" he asked softly.

"Yes. Listen . . . I meant what I said about marrying you. I'll—"

"I'm going home now. I'm sure my mother will be worried." The horse moved forward.

"Harrison!" He glanced over his shoulder at her. "Stop punishing yourself. You've earned Lizzie's forgiveness. And God will forgive you, too, if you ask."

"Since when are you His spokesman?" he asked bitterly. He flicked the reins and the horse started forward again.

Josephine watched him go, feeling sorry for him. Whether or not she married Harrison, she knew she owed him something in return. She promised herself that she would spend more time with him. Maybe she could help him find God again the way Alexander had helped her.

She trudged back to the house, so weary that she could probably sleep for days. Lizzie and Otis wanted to show their gratitude, but she told them to take their children home to bed. "Thank God, not me," she said. As she watched them go, she wondered how they would ever feel safe again.

The war had ended—but it hadn't. The Yankees would be back. Daniel's bitterness would likely grow worse, and Mother would be forced to grieve another loss if the Yankees took him away. Would any of their lives ever be the same? Would the sorrow and fear ever stop? The war may have ended, but the effects of it seemed to go on and on. *"Nobody wins a war,"* Alexander once told her. *"We all lose in one way or another."* As she staggered up the stairs to bed, Josephine knew he was right.

36

Josephine was exhausted the next morning, but she rose at her usual time, afraid her mother would ask too many questions if she remained in bed. She dressed quickly and went outside to the kitchen to find Lizzie and Otis. She wouldn't have been at all surprised to find them too shaken and exhausted from their ordeal to do any work. Nor would she be surprised if they were packing up their family to leave White Oak for good. But the kitchen looked as it did every morning, with a fire on the hearth, Lizzie hard at work, and the aroma of fresh biscuits in the air. Roselle was churning butter, Rufus filling the woodbox, Jack pumping water—all the morning routines proceeding smoothly.

Jo looked around at the activity in amazement. "Are you all right? I wasn't sure you would even want to work after . . ."

Lizzie set down her bowl and spoon and hurried over. To Josephine's surprise, she took both of Jo's hands and gripped them in her own. "We owe you, Missy Jo. We owe you for saving our lives, and so we decided we'll stay here and help you out until the cotton is picked, or until you can find someone else to work for you here at White Oak."

"But . . . I thought you might be afraid to stay."

"Tell you the truth, I am scared to stay. But Otis says it's hard for us Negroes no matter where we go. And he says that the good Lord is looking out for us."

"Otis is right. The good Lord has been answering all our prayers, hasn't He?"

"Yes, ma'am. Tell your mama I'll have her breakfast up to her as soon as the biscuits are finished."

Jo returned to the house and went upstairs to her mother's bedroom. She and Mary had been eating their meals with their mother since the doctor had ordered complete bed rest. But this morning, Jo found her mother out of bed and getting dressed. "Help me finish, Josephine. I want to eat my breakfast downstairs."

"Are you sure? Shouldn't we wait for Dr. Hunter? I thought he wanted you to stay in bed for a week."

"Nonsense. I'm feeling much better and I'm tired of this room. A change of scene will do me good. Maybe I'll even let the doctor take me for a carriage ride when he comes."

Mary walked into the room a moment later and looked at their mother in surprise. "What's going on? Why are you out of bed? And why is Daniel back from Richmond?"

A jolt of fear rocked through Josephine. "Daniel's home? Are you sure?"

"Yes. I heard him rummaging around in his room just now. And when I was opening our bedroom curtains, I saw his horse."

"I don't know why he's back," Mother said, "but go down and tell Lizzie that we'll all eat in the dining room. I'll be down as soon as Josephine helps me with my hair."

The news about Daniel made Josephine uneasy. She feared for Lizzie and Otis's safety and worried that Mother would find out about last night. Jo couldn't risk having her suffer any more shocks. "Shall I go knock on Daniel's door and see why—?"

"No. Help me with my hair and we'll talk to him together." Mother sat down at her dressing table while Jo quickly pinned her hair in a loose chignon. They went down the hall and were about to knock on Daniel's door when it flew open and there he stood. Josephine could barely look at him, knowing what he had tried to do to Lizzie's family. Daniel smiled as though nothing had happened at all.

"Good morning, Mother. Are you feeling better?"

"Yes I am, in fact. But I'm wondering what you're doing home. You're supposed to be in Richmond."

He shot a glance at Josephine, and she shook her head to let him know that Mother hadn't learned about last night's events. "I didn't go to Richmond," he said. "I've been staying with Joseph Gray for the past few days, and it gave me time to do some thinking. First of all, it isn't right for me to take our only horse and leave you with no transportation. And . . . and second, I wanted to tell you how sorry I am for upsetting you . . . for that whole misunderstanding with the slaves."

"They aren't slaves," Mother said. "They're servants."

Tears sprang to Josephine's eyes at her words. Mother was trying to change, she truly was.

"Anyway," Daniel continued, "my friends and I also agreed that it wasn't a good idea for me to leave town right now. If the Yankees come looking for me, it would seem as though I had run away, that I was guilty."

Josephine couldn't help thinking that Daniel *was* guilty. She wondered if Mother was thinking the same thing.

"I see," Mother said.

"Finally, I still don't feel right about leaving you here all alone. So . . . may I please come home? Will you forgive me and give me another chance?"

Josephine eyed her brother with suspicion. Should they trust him—could they trust him? Would Mother welcome him back if she knew what he'd tried to do to Lizzie's family? The memory of it chilled Josephine, and she fought the urge to run down to the kitchen and warn Lizzie to take her family and run. They needed to go somewhere far away from here.

"Yes, of course I'll forgive you," Mother said. She pulled him close for a quick hug. "Now let's all go downstairs and eat our breakfast, shall we?"

But before they reached the top of the stairs, they heard Mary shouting up at them from the front foyer. "Daniel, come quick! It's . . . it's the Yankees! Dozens of them! And they're coming here!"

Mother's knees seemed to go weak, and she leaned against Josephine for support.

"Let me take you back to your room, Mother." Josephine wrapped her arm around Eugenia's waist. "The doctor said you can't risk getting upset. If . . . if it's Mr. Chandler, I'll speak with him."

"Stay here, all of you," Daniel said. "I know how to deal with Yankees."

"No!" Mother said sharply. "I'm sorry, Daniel, but we're going to deal with them my way, not yours. Help me down the stairs, Josephine. I want to hear what they have to say. I'll be more upset if I'm left up here to wonder what's going on."

Josephine held one of her mother's arms and Daniel took the other as they guided her down the stairs to the front door. When Mary opened it, a sea of blue uniforms was rapidly approaching down the long lane. "They have no right," Daniel murmured. "This is our property. . . ."

"Hush!" Mother said. She was clinging to his arm, keeping him from running forward. "Let's hear what they have to say."

The troop halted a hundred yards from the house, and a single rider in civilian clothes broke from the pack to ride out ahead of them.

Alexander.

Josephine could tell it was him by the set of his shoulders and the way he sat in the saddle, even before he drew close enough to see his face. Her heart began to pound so hard she thought it might burst. He had returned, just as he'd promised. But judging by the troop of soldiers with him, this wasn't going to be a friendly visit. Alexander was here to arrest Daniel. He hadn't found a way for the two of them to be together, after all. He couldn't possibly arrive with two dozen soldiers to arrest her brother and then expect her to ride away with him. How could she leave her mother under such circumstances?

Alexander stopped near the hitching post and dismounted. "Good morning," he said pleasantly. He looked up at them, standing in a row on the front porch. He must see that this was where Josephine had to be—with her family.

"Forgive me for bringing so many men," he said. "It wasn't my idea, I assure you. And I'm not armed." He lifted his arms and spread his hands, then let them drop to his sides again.

"What do you want?" Daniel asked.

"I simply want to talk. And I can say what I need to say right here. I understand how you might feel about having a Yankee in your home. But I'm glad to see that all of you are here. I would like your entire family to hear what I have to say."

"Leave my mother out of this. She hasn't been well."

"I'm very sorry to hear that. It isn't my intention to upset you, Mrs. Weatherly, believe me. And if you don't mind, I would like your two servants, Otis and Lizzie, to come and hear this, too."

Daniel started to protest, but Mother cut him off. "Mary, please ask Lizzie and Otis to come here." Mary nodded and hurried off to fetch them.

Josephine was relieved that Mother hadn't sent her on the errand. She had begun to tremble so violently that she didn't think she could take a step. She clung to her mother's arm, waiting, wondering what Alexander was up to. She searched his face for a clue, but he hadn't once met her gaze as he'd addressed her mother and brother. Why did he want Lizzie and Otis? Alexander couldn't possibly know about last night's events. If Lizzie told him now, it would create a terrible scene, and the doctor had said that Mother's heart couldn't bear the strain of more bad news.

"Let's go down below and talk," Mother said as they waited. She led the way down the porch steps, still clinging to Jo's arm. Daniel stayed right beside them. Jo stared at Alexander, but he still didn't meet her gaze. *"Trust me,"* he had said. Could he really find a way for them to be together with her family's blessing?

Mary finally returned with Otis and Lizzie, walking around from the rear of the house because Otis would never dare to go inside.

He was holding Lizzie's hand, and they both looked frightened half to death. "Good morning, Mr. Chandler," Otis said.

"Good morning, Otis. Thank you for coming to meet with us. I wanted you and Lizzie to hear what I came to say, since it involves both of you, as well. So, Mr. Weatherly." Alexander took a step closer to Daniel, looking him in the eyes. "I'm here to try to reach an agreement with you. I believe I have enough evidence to convict you of at least some of the charges the government might hold against you: the two fires at the bureau office, the destruction of the school. But as of this moment, the evidence lives or dies with me. I haven't filed any reports with my superiors in Richmond. Until I tell them otherwise, the fires may have been accidents, not part of a plot against my life. I'm willing to make sure those reports are never filed if I can have your word that the violence will end right now."

Mother seemed to sway. "Wait . . . You would drop *all* of the charges against my son?"

"Yes, ma'am. As long as Mr. Weatherly swears to me that he and his friends will make peace with the Negroes. That there will be no more night riders. That they'll allow the freedmen in your community to settle down here, be given jobs and homes here, be treated fairly. Will you agree to that, Mr. Weatherly?"

Daniel took a long time to reply. He was the larger and stronger of the two men and could probably overpower Alexander. But two dozen Yankee soldiers were watching from the end of the lane. "What game are you playing?" Daniel finally asked.

"I'm not playing any game. I'm offering you amnesty. I'm trying to reach a truce. Now, you may have noticed I didn't mention the violence in the woods or the two Negroes who were shot and killed. That's a separate issue, and it's why I asked Otis to hear what I have to say." Alexander turned to face him. "Otis, if you and the others want to come forward with evidence and press charges against the men who were responsible, then I'm honor-bound as a bureau agent to proceed with an indictment and see the guilty parties are punished. Is that what you'd like me to do?"

Jo held her breath. What would he say? Daniel had tried to kill his entire family last night, and if Otis wanted revenge, this was his chance to get it. Alexander couldn't possibly know what he was asking. Jo would be forced to testify against her brother—or watch him get away with another attempted murder.

"Well . . ." Otis said slowly. "I believe that sending people to jail is only going to make things worse. There will be more killing, more revenge, and it won't bring the two dead men back. No, sir. I would like to make sure the dead men's families get some help so they can get by without their husbands and fathers. But the Almighty says that vengeance belongs to Him, not us. He says He'll pay back the guilty on Judgment Day if they don't repent. If you can forgive them, Mr. Chandler, then I guess I'm satisfied to wait and let God do the punishing, too."

"So, Otis, if we can figure out a way to compensate the families, are you content to make peace?" Alexander asked.

"They have to let us have our school, too," Lizzie said.

"Yes, that's a good point. The school must be part of the arrangement." Alexander turned back to Daniel. "Can you agree to these terms, Mr. Weatherly? Otis and I will agree not to pursue any indictments if you agree to end the violence and live in peace."

"Why would you do that?" Mother asked. "I don't understand."

"It must be some sort of trick," Daniel said.

"It isn't a trick. It's called grace, and it's what Jesus came to offer all of us. He forgives us even though we're guilty. He lets us have a brand-new start. That's what I'm offering you. We can forget the past and start all over again, beginning right now. We can make different choices this time."

"I haven't asked you for mercy," Daniel said.

"That's true. But I'm offering it to you anyway. There's a beautiful passage in the book of Revelation, where Jesus talks about the end of time when God will wipe away all the tears from our eyes. He says there will be no more death or sorrow or pain—all those things will be gone. And He says, 'Behold, I make all things new.' We've experienced enough pain and sorrow for one lifetime, haven't we? I'm offering you a chance to make all things new. If I can forgive you for burning down my office and trying to kill me, maybe you can finally forgive me for being your enemy during the war. If Otis can forgive you and your friends for beating him and destroying the school, then maybe you can forgive them for wanting to live free lives. . . . But if you'd rather not accept grace, we can continue this war and all the suffering that comes with it. It's up to you, Mr. Weatherly."

Josephine could see that Alexander's words had moved Daniel. If only he would swallow his pride and make peace.

Mother had tears in her eyes, too. "Daniel, do it," she whispered. "You said you wanted to end the cycle of violence, that you wanted a way out. This is your chance."

"Why—?" Daniel had to pause to clear his throat. "Why would you show mercy? What's the catch?"

"When God offers us grace and mercy, the only stipulation is that we repent. That we turn around and move in a new direction, living by His laws from now on to show Him our gratitude."

"And then . . . everyone will just walk away as if none of this ever happened?"

"Yes, Mr. Weatherly. That's right. So . . . will you agree?" He extended his hand for Daniel to shake. A long moment passed as everyone seemed to hold their breath. Jo glanced at Otis and Lizzie and saw the fear and suspense on their faces, too. Finally, Daniel reached out and accepted Alexander's hand.

"I agree," he said softly. He looked as broken as he had on the day he arrived home from the war. "I-I still don't understand why you would do this, though. What's in it for you?"

Alexander smiled the shy grin that Josephine had grown to love. "I understand why you might be suspicious," he said. "And I admit that I do want something else in return along with an end to the violence. I believe that a person's actions reveal their character, and so I hope that my actions will show I'm not here to hurt any of you. That I'm a God-fearing man who would like to help you rebuild your lives. If you can bring yourself to trust me,

I'll be in a position to throw myself at *your* mercy and ask you for something in return."

"What?" Daniel asked.

"I'm in love with Josephine."

Her heart began to race. Alexander looked at her for the first time and the whole world could have seen his love for her shining in his eyes. "I would like to ask for her hand in marriage—if she will have me, that is."

"Yes!" she said, but it came out in a whisper, her heart too full of hope and joy to speak.

"Your marriage will never be accepted in this town," Daniel said. "You'll both be despised. Shunned."

"I know . . . I'm not coming back here to work. That's why I'm no longer in uniform. Another bureau agent will be in charge from now on. I have accepted a job up north, where I promise to make a good home for Josephine."

"You seem like a good man, Mr. Chandler," Mother said. "Josephine has already told me that she loves you, too. I think we should accept his proposal, Daniel."

"But it's not proper to just send her away with him."

"I don't expect you to, Mr. Weatherly. We owe it to Josephine to give her time to consider my marriage proposal and to think about what it will mean for her and for her future. I'm working in Richmond, for the time being, and I understand you have family there. If she were to stay with them for a while, we could spend time courting properly. Then if she's willing, the army chaplain will marry us."

Josephine didn't need time to think. She longed to run to Alexander and throw herself into his arms. But she could see the wisdom in waiting, for her family's sake.

"Daniel will take her to Richmond," Mother said. "My sister, Mrs. Charles Greeley, lives on Church Hill." Josephine squeezed her mother's arm, her heart brimming with joy. "And, Mr. Chandler," Mother added, "I suggest you leave the soldiers behind when you come to court my Josephine."

"Yes, ma'am," he said, grinning broadly. "Yes, ma'am, I will." He turned and mounted his horse. No one seemed able to move as they watched him ride away. Then they all looked around at each other—Mother and Daniel and Mary, Lizzie and Otis—and it seemed to Josephine that a miracle had just happened here today at White Oak.

37

AUGUST 14, 1865

Lizzie folded Missy Josephine's worn-out skirt and tucked it into a satchel. It was the skirt she always wore when she helped out in the garden, and the memory of all the things Missy had done for Lizzie and her family brought unexpected tears to her eyes. "I sure am going to miss you, Missy Josephine."

"I know. Me too." Missy Jo's eyes glistened with tears. "I'm not sure if I'll ever get back to White Oak again, Lizzie."

"This place won't be the same without you."

Missy exhaled as if pulling herself together. "Thank you for taking the time to help me pack."

"That's okay. It didn't take no time at all." Missy didn't have much in the way of belongings, but she looked all around the bedroom just to be sure. "You have everything?" Lizzie asked before closing the satchel.

"Yes, I think so." She turned to Lizzie and took her hands in her own for a moment. "Listen, Daniel will be staying with me in Richmond for several months, working with my uncle. You'll be safe."

"I know, Missy Jo."

Otis would drive them there and stay overnight, then drive the carriage back home alone tomorrow. Lizzie remembered the long months he had been away during the war and how much she had worried, wondering if she would ever see him again.

"It's been hard, Missy Jo, I won't say that it hasn't. Me and Otis have been through some bad times. But Otis always says we can trust the Almighty, and after everything that's happened . . . well, I'm learning that he's right."

"I understand your school will be reopening again. I hope Roselle has a chance to become a teacher. She'll make a good one."

"What about you and Mr. Chandler? Will you be getting married and moving up north, far from home?"

"I expect so." Missy smiled—a rare sight these days. If she loved Massa Chandler half as much as Lizzie loved Otis, she would be smiling a lot from now on.

"I don't suppose I'll ever see you again, Missy Jo . . ." Lizzie felt sure she was going to cry.

"In heaven, Lizzie. We'll meet again in heaven." Missy opened the drawer in the stand beside her bed and pulled out a book. "Listen, I'm so sorry for the way my family has treated you, and so I want you and Otis to have this. It's my Bible. Someday you'll be able to read it."

Lizzie's hands flew to her face. "I can't take your Bible!"

"Of course you can. Please, I insist." She pulled Lizzie's hands down and forced the book into them. Lizzie stared at it, her tears dropping onto the cover.

"This . . . this is the best present anybody ever gave me. I don't know what to say, Missy Jo . . . And I have nothing for you . . ."

"You've given me your friendship, and that's enough. Keep it, Lizzie, to remember me."

Lizzie wiped her eyes again, still gazing at the book. "I'll never forget you or all the things you did for us."

Missy exhaled again. "I've decided not to look back at the past from now on. I'm only going to look ahead. . . . Good-bye, Lizzie, and may God bless you." She picked up her satchel and hurried from the room.

Lizzie stayed behind, clutching the Bible, unable to bear the sight of Missy Josephine riding away forever. Suddenly Lizzie felt a tiny stirring as the baby moved inside her for the very first time. She rested her hand on her middle. There! She felt it again, a gentle flutter as if the baby had a feather duster in her hand and was waving it all around. Lizzie had felt the same excitement when this happened with her other three babies, when at last she felt the touch of this tiny person growing inside her. A brand-new baby.

She'd been upset when she first learned she was having this child because everything else in her life seemed so hard. Why bring another child into this world? It would be one more person for her to worry about, someone else she would end up loving and grieving over if anything happened. But as Lizzie looked out the window at the thick green rows of Otis's cotton plants, she knew that she and her family would be all right. There would be more hard times, to be sure. But praise God, this child dancing inside her would never know what it meant to be a slave.

Eugenia wandered through the empty rooms downstairs not knowing quite what to do with herself. After a hectic morning, Daniel and Josephine had finally left for Richmond. Mary had decided to go with them to spend time with her cousins. Eugenia was alone, and although she had insisted that she looked forward to a few days of solitude, she didn't know how she would spend the time now that she had it.

She was resting in her morning room when she heard the sound of a carriage arriving out front. Eugenia went to the door herself, knowing how busy Lizzie was. And there was Dr. Hunter.

"Come for a ride with me," he called as he climbed down from the driver's seat. "Doctor's orders."

"I'm not up to it today, I'm sorry."

He strode up the porch steps and took her hands in his. "I heard that your family was leaving for Richmond today. I thought it might be hard for you. A change of scene is just what you need. Please, Eugenia."

"Right now? But it's nearly—"

"Lunchtime. I know. I would like to treat you to lunch, if I may. My mother taught me to always repay my social obligations, and I realized I never returned the invitation to your dance. I'm sorry for the short notice, but everything is ready. Please?"

Eugenia was trying to come up with a tactful excuse, but his smile disarmed her. He linked his arm through hers and gestured to his carriage. "Our ride is waiting."

"Fine. You win, David. Let me get my hat and gloves. And I should tell Lizzie that I'm leaving."

A few minutes later, they were riding down the road together toward town. "I know you must be grieving yet another loss, Eugenia. It must have been difficult to let your children go."

"You're right. It was hard to say good-bye. Nearly as hard as when I sent my sons off to war. But perhaps Daniel and Josephine will be able to forgive each other after spending time together in Richmond." She swallowed a knot of emotion. "I doubt if I'll ever see Josephine again once she marries."

"But at least you'll know she's with a very fine young man. I have gotten to know Alexander Chandler and found him to be wise beyond his years. He'll take good care of her."

"Yes. I know he will." Eugenia still marveled at the way Mr. Chandler had brought an end to the vicious cycle of hatred and violence and given everyone a new start.

"And who knows," David said, "once the rail lines are running again, you may be able to travel to Pennsylvania to see her, or she may come to you."

"Yes. And she promised to write."

The carriage passed Priscilla Blake's plantation and continued toward town. Eugenia would have to talk to her friend soon. Priscilla would be disappointed to hear the news about Josephine, to be sure. But there was no shortage of young women in the community searching for a suitable husband, and the Blake plantation was one of the very few that was prospering again.

"Before Josephine left this morning, I told her that life was short—and that love was important. I said that if she had even a small measure of the love and happiness I had with Philip, then she would be blessed."

"That's very good advice."

"You know what she told me?" Eugenia asked, looking up at him. He shook his head. "She said, 'Don't remain alone, Mother. Daddy wouldn't want you to.'"

He gave her a warm smile. "That's very good advice, too."

The carriage arrived in Fairmont a short time later, and David pointed out the storefront where the Freedmen's Bureau and the Negro school were relocating. "Will you do me a favor, David? Will you come with me next week to talk to the new agent? I would like to see about hiring more servants. Otis is in charge of my plantation, but he and Lizzie can't do everything all alone."

"I would be happy to."

They turned onto the street where the doctor lived, and he drew the carriage to a halt in front of his house. David helped her climb down, and Eugenia walked through the door of his home for the first time. She was stunned to see how simple yet elegant it was, the rooms filled with beautiful antiques. "Why, it's lovely, David!"

"Thank you. But I can't take any of the credit. I have a housekeeper." He led her into the dining room, to a table that was set for two with a linen tablecloth and fine china. He pulled out a chair and helped her sit down.

"Oh, David . . . I had no idea . . ."

"That I lived this well?"

"I'm so sorry. I didn't mean to—"

"It's all right, Eugenia," he said, laughing. "I have greatly enjoyed surprising you. I inherited nearly everything you see from my mother's side of the family. The Blandfords did welcome us back in the end." He took the seat across from her and uncorked a small bottle. "I have a tiny bit of cherry cordial left—would you care for some?"

"Yes, thank you."

He poured a small amount into each of their glasses, then lifted his. "Shall we offer a toast, Eugenia?"

"Yes. To the future. I don't want to live in the past any longer. My life can never be the same as it was, and I was foolish to try to retrieve it. If I've learned anything during these past terrible years, it's that life is a treasured gift, not to be taken for granted. So, let's toast to the days ahead."

"To the future," David said, touching his glass to hers.

"Yes. To the future."

SEPTEMBER 15, 1865

Josephine stood by the bedroom window in her aunt's house, gazing at the leafy view of Richmond's treetops below her. It seemed as though years had passed since she'd stood here watching flames and smoke churn into the sky as the city burned—and she was surprised to realize it had been only five months. Such a short time, yet so many, many changes!

In a few minutes Alexander would arrive with the chaplain. They would pronounce their vows to each other in Aunt Olivia's parlor and begin a new life together. Josephine looked down at the ring he had given her and saw that her hands were trembling. She admitted she was scared—but not in the way she had been the last time she'd stood here. The world had seemed to be ending that terrible day, and she had feared what tomorrow would bring when the Yankees arrived. She never would have imagined it would bring Alexander Chandler—and joy.

In the street below, two men on horseback turned the corner and approached the house. One of them was Alexander. Jo turned from the window, ready to run down the stairs and throw open the door—then she stopped as she heard her mother's voice, speaking to her heart. *Tidy your hair, Josephine. And don't run. Young ladies must always walk with poise and grace.*

"Yes, Mother," she whispered, smiling. She took a moment to check her hair in the mirror, then descended the stairs to begin her new life. She didn't know what changes were in store for her, but she was certain of one thing: God would be with her and Alexander wherever they went.

Discussion Questions

1. At the beginning of the novel, what do Josephine, Eugenia, and Lizzie want most now that the war has ended? Did each of these women get what she'd hoped for?

2. In what ways did each woman change throughout the course of the book? What particular events brought about these changes? Which woman changed the most?

3. What does the novel say about the effects of war on people's lives? How did the war change Alexander Chandler, Daniel Weatherly, and Harrison Blake?

4. Which character in the book had the strongest faith? How did he/she develop that faith? How was it tested?

5. Why do you think Harrison helped Josephine to rescue Lizzie's children?

6. Do you think Daniel will keep the agreement he made with Alexander Chandler at the end of the story? Why or why not?

7. What were some of the ways the chaos and lawlessness of the Reconstruction era were shown in the novel?

8. If you could write a sequel to *All Things New*, what do you think will happen to Josephine and Alexander? To Lizzie and Otis and their children? To Eugenia and Dr. Hunter?

Lynn Austin is a seven-time Christy Award winner for her historical novels *Hidden Places, Candle in the Darkness, Fire by Night, A Proper Pursuit, Until We Reach Home, Though Waters Roar*, and *While We're Far Apart*. In addition to writing, Lynn is a popular speaker at conferences, retreats, and various church and school events. She and her husband have three children and make their home in Illinois.

More Historical Fiction by Lynn Austin

To learn more about Lynn and her books, visit lynnaustin.org.

Don't Miss Any of Lynn Austin's Award-Winning Novels

As three sisters flee unexpected sorrow and a tainted past, they find they have nothing to rely on except each other—and hope for a second chance.

Until We Reach Home

Venturing to the World's Fair in Chicago, Violet Hayes has one goal: to find her mother. But what she truly finds is something priceless—herself.

A Proper Pursuit

Experience the history, drama and promises of the Old Testament in this dramatic series of truth and loyalty. When invading armies, idol worship, and infidelity plague the life and legacy of King Hezekiah, can his faith survive the ultimate test?

CHRONICLES OF THE KINGS
Gods and Kings, Song of Redemption, The Strength of His Hand, Faith of My Fathers, Among the Gods